RENDER
UNTO
CAESAR

ALSO BY GILLIAN BRADSHAW

The Wolf Hunt

The Sand-Reckoner

Island of Ghosts

Cleopatra's Heir

Gillian Bradshaw

RENDER UNTO CEASAR

A TOM DOHERTY ASSOCIATES BOOK
New York

RENDER UNTO CAESAR

Edited by Claire Eddy

A Forge Book
Published by Tom Doherty Associates, LLC
175 Fifth Avenue
New York, NY 10010

www.tor.com

Forge® is a registered trademark of Tom Doherty Associates, LLC.

Library of Congress Cataloging-in-Publication Data

Bradshaw, Gillian, 1956–
Render unto Caesar / Gillian Bradshaw.—1st ed.
    p. cm.
"A Tom Doherty Associates book."
ISBN 0-765-30654-9
EAN 978-0765-30654-8
1. Rome—History—Augustus, 30 B.C.–14 A.D.—Fiction.
2. Alexandria (Egypt)—Fiction. 3. Greeks—Rome—Fiction. I. Title.
PS3552.R235R46 2003
813'.54—dc21   2002045487

First Edition: August 2003
First Paperback Edition: August 2004

Printed in the United States of America

0 9 8 7 6 5 4 3 2

RENDER
UNTO
CAESAR

H ERMOGENES WAS ALMOST ASLEEP BY THE time the carriage stopped.

He'd hired the vehicle that morning in Ostia: a four-wheeled cart with a canvas awning, drawn by a team of four mules and driven by a villainous-looking muleteer with a knife scar on one cheek. It had a bench seat along each side: Hermogenes sat on one side, the slaves sat on the other, and the luggage went in the middle. They traveled for nearly four hours, rattling slowly through the town of Ostia and then on along the main road. At first Hermogenes had stared eagerly at everything—the streets and houses of Ostia; the market gardens and vineyards of the Tiber plain; the cypress trees, the blue hills in the distance—but it was a hot day, and the mules plodded steadily along a good road. The rumbling sway of the carriage was soporific, and he hadn't slept well for months. Gradually he slipped into a daze.

When the movement stopped, though, he sat up abruptly and looked around. They'd pulled into a large stableyard, and the driver was just tying the reins to a post. There seemed to be buildings around them again, but he was pretty certain that they hadn't gone through any city gates, and he was absolutely certain that this wasn't the place to which the driver had been paid to take them.

He leaned forward. "Why do we stop?" he demanded sharply—then wondered if he'd got the Latin quite right. Would "Why are we stopping?" have been better?

The driver grinned back at him, showing stubby brown teeth, and jumped down from the cart. He waved an arm expansively at a pair of stone towers just up the road. "That's the Ostian Gate." He said it loudly: he didn't seem to believe that a Greek really might be able to understand Latin unless he shouted. "We're here. Rome. This is where we stop."

Hermogenes glanced at the towers. They did look like a city gate, but if there had ever been a wall to go along with them, the city had swallowed it up. Shoddy houses of mud brick, and even shoddier tenement blocks, cramped and darkened the road. The livery stables where they had pulled in was the most substantial building around. He looked back at the mule driver with a frown. "This is the Via Tusculana?" He very much doubted it.

The muleteer shook his head. "No. This is as far as I can take the raeda. Understand? No carts are allowed into the city during the day." He said the last slowly as though he were speaking to a child. "No carts"—he slapped his vehicle—"in the city"—he pointed up the road—"during the day." He indicated the bright June sun, which stood just past noon.

Hermogenes gave him a flat stare. "You agreed that you would take myself, my slaves, and my luggage, as far as the Via Tusculana."

"No, no!" the mule driver protested with another stump-toothed grin. "I agreed to take you to Rome, and here we are. I can't take the raeda into the city. No wheeled traffic is allowed into the city during the day, understand?"

"How much further is it to the Via Tusculana?"

The man shrugged.

Some distance, then. Hermogenes looked at the road which led onward into Rome. Narrow, and ankle-deep in dung and dirt. There were no carts or carriages to be seen on it, so probably the man was telling the truth about wheeled traffic; most big cities had traffic regulations. He was still annoyed. The driver hadn't seen fit to mention this detail back in Ostia: instead he'd said that yes, he knew the Via Tusculana, and yes, he could take them there. That was why Hermogenes had hired him rather than one of his fellows.

He sighed. Menestor and Phormion, the slaves, were both watching him anxiously: neither of them spoke any Latin. "He says he can't go any further," Hermogenes informed them in the Greek native to all three of them. "He says that carts aren't allowed into Rome during the day. He probably has an arrangement for porterage at this livery stables." He turned back to the driver, reminding himself that this might, still, be an honest misunderstanding. "How do we reach the Via Tusculana?" he asked politely.

"You can hire porters and a sedan chair here." The muleteer waved negligently toward the livery stables. "They'll bring you right to your friend's door. I can arrange it for you."

"Ah. And their charge is included in the fare we agreed to pay you?"

The driver pretended surprise at the very idea. His knife scar suddenly became more prominent. "No, no, you pay them separately—*after* you've paid me."

It couldn't be pushed too hard, Hermogenes told himself. The driver would have friends around—the stable workers, and any fellow muleteers in the vicinity as well. It would be lunacy to risk life and luggage in a brawl over a porter's fee. On the other hand, Hermogenes had no intention of allowing himself to be cheated any more than he absolutely had to—and he'd been careful to refuse the muleteer's demand for full payment in advance.

"Very well," he told the driver mildly. "Will you go and find me two porters?"

The muleteer's grin returned, and he swaggered off toward the stable. Hermogenes snapped his fingers. Menestor and Phormion obligingly took hold of the big chest and dragged it out of the carriage. Hermogenes hopped down after them, then turned to take out the two baskets. Now at least the driver couldn't drive off with the luggage still on board.

Phormion flexed a hand he'd banged hauling the trunk out of the cart. "We don't want to carry this far," he said, eyeing the heavy wood-and-leather chest with dislike.

Hermogenes nodded. Phormion and Menestor were

capable of carrying the chest if they had to, but the local neighborhood didn't look the safest, and he would prefer them to have their hands free to deter any would-be robbers. The chest contained vital business documents and most of his funds for the journey: he could not afford to lose it.

"Take it on to the stables," he ordered. "I'll hire porters."

A couple of men lounging in front of the stables eyed them hopefully as they came up. The muleteer, however, had gone into the building, and was speaking to somebody just inside the door—not a porter, by the look of that fine red tunic, possibly the head groom. Of course: the stable had an arrangement with drivers to take passengers out of the city, and with porters to take them into it. Hermogenes cast an assessing eye over the hopeful casuals: they looked strong and reasonably presentable. "I need porters," he told them.

The muleteer glanced round in surprise, then hurried from the stable with the other man in his wake. Hermogenes smiled at them politely. The head groom, if that was what he was, gave an oily smile back. "Sir," he began, ignoring the casual laborers, "Gallio says you need porters and a sedan chair . . ."

Hermogenes raised his eyebrows. "No. I did not ask for a sedan chair. Only for porters to carry these things here to the house of Fiducius Crispus on the Via Tusculana."

The groom smirked again. "Sir, it's a long walk, a couple of miles, and a gentleman such as yourself . . ."

". . . has spent too much time sitting already today," said Hermogenes, with another false smile. "How much for two porters to the Via Tusculana?"

The groom grimaced reproachfully. "Two sestertii."

He was undoubtedly expecting to get a cut of that very handsome fee. "Too much," Hermogenes said calmly. "My slaves will carry the luggage. Gallio, here is the remainder of our fare." He opened his purse, took out two small bronze coins, handed them to the mule driver, then turned away, snapping his fingers for Menestor and Phormion to pick up the chest again.

"Sir," the groom began, but Gallio interrupted with an indignant cry of "This is only two sestertii!"

Hermogenes turned back to him. "Your charge was two denarii. I paid one in Ostia, and agreed to pay the second when we reached our destination. The cost of carrying the luggage to that destination is another two sestertii, it seems, so I have subtracted that from your fee."

The muleteer's face darkened and the scar stood out again. "Don't cheat me, Greekling!" he said loudly.

Hermogenes was aware of Phormion and Menestor setting down the chest again, and saw the groom's eyes flick to them uneasily. Menestor was nothing to worry him—seventeen years old, a valet and clerk—but Phormion was another matter. Big and dark, with a broken nose and cauliflower ear, he looked like the bodyguard he was. This was not going to end in blows, however: Hermogenes was determined on that.

He pretended surprise. "Cheat you?" he repeated. "No! At home if a mule driver agreed to take me from Canopus to my house near the harbor, he would not expect full fare if he set me down at the Canopic Gate. I would be entitled to subtract not merely the porters' fee, but something for the inconvenience as well. You do things differently in Rome, do you?"

The two casual laborers had been watching with close attention; at this one of them laughed. The muleteer's face darkened further.

The head groom intervened. "You must have misunderstood something, sir. If you agreed a price with Gallio, you must pay it. In Rome we pay the price agreed."

"Even when you do not deliver the service agreed?" Hermogenes asked him. "Ah, well. I am a Roman citizen myself, as it happens: I will remember that." He waited just a moment to let his citizenship register, saw the looks of uncertainty, then dug another coin out of his purse. "I will split our difference with you," he offered. "Here is another sestertius."

He'd judged it right: cheating a Roman citizen—particularly one with a dangerous-looking bodyguard—was more trouble than one sestertius was worth. The muleteer snatched his coin, spat emphatically, and strode off to see to his team. Hermogenes nodded politely to the groom and signaled for Menestor and Phormion to pick up the chest.

One of the casual laborers stepped forward. "Sir," he said eagerly, "Quintus 'n me'd carry your things to Tusculana f'ra sestertius." At least, that was what Hermogenes *thought* he said. The accent was so thick that he had trouble following it.

"You don't want to hire men off the street!" exclaimed the groom, glaring at them.

"It is true, I hired Gallio that way," said Hermogenes, smiling slightly. "And he promised to take me to my destination, then set me down two miles short of it. However, I hope these men will be more honest."

"Sir, sir, *sir*! Gallio wasn't cheating you! You're a foreigner—"

"Yes. A 'Greekling,' as he put it."

"—you probably you don't know how things are in Rome. Gallio couldn't take you to the Via Tusculana: carriages aren't allowed into the city during the day."

"It is true, I did not know that. All the more reason Gallio should have explained it when I hired him."

"You must have misunderstood—"

"I assure you, I did not misunderstand. I have been doing business with Romans since I finished school, and I cannot afford to misunderstand. Tell Gallio that he has lost custom by this. I might have hired him again, had he been honest. Good health." He turned to the porters. "I accept your offer. I will pay you when we reach our destination."

The porters grinned. The groom swore, then shrugged and went off back to his work. Menestor and Phormion stepped away from the heavy chest with expressions of relief.

The pair of porters turned out, in fact, to be sedan-chair bearers. Their chair was propped up against the stable wall, a simple wooden seat slung between two stout poles: presumably they'd carried a passenger out to the livery stables, and had been hoping for someone to pay them to make the journey back. They now turned the chair upside down, heaved the traveling chest onto it, and secured it with a piece of rope. When the burden had been lifted and securely balanced on their shoulders, each man picked up one of the additional baskets. The leader looked expectantly at Hermogenes.

"The Via Tusculana," Hermogenes ordered, and they set off.

In spite of his tiredness and the lingering sourness from the confrontation with the muleteer, Hermogenes felt his heart speed up as he followed. He was treading the streets of Rome! He had been hearing about this city all his life.

All the years that he was growing up, his native Alexandria had been full of Roman troops—Roman *allies,* they'd been then, supporters of the queen. That hadn't made them respectful toward the citizens, of course: the city had been perpetually full of angry whispers about what one soldier or another had done, though the queen had been happy enough. Then had come that strange, hot summer when Hermogenes was eighteen, and Roman "enemies" completed the conquest of his homeland and its Roman "allies." The final stages of the war had been played out amid the familiar landmarks of Alexandria. He had stood on the city wall with his father, and listened as an old veteran pointed out the standards of the different legions encamped around the hippodrome, naming the campaigns each had fought in before. Iberia, Gaul, Africa, Armenia . . . it had seemed as though all the world belonged to Rome, apart from the doomed stones beneath their feet.

Alexandria joined the rest of the world only a few days later. For a little while no one had known whether or not the city would be given over to pillage. He remembered a dreadful day of waiting in the stifling dining room where the household had gathered, listening to the drone of the flies and the crying of the cook's baby. The older slaves of the household had all been silent, sick with fear. If the city was handed over to the victorious legions, everyone would suffer, but slaves would suffer more, and their masters would be unable to protect them. He had never felt so helpless, or so angry.

Caesar had spared Alexandria, thank the gods. "Why shouldn't he?" Hermogenes' father had asked in relief. "He's just acquired the right to tax our trade: if he let his soldiers ruin that, he'd lose money."

Even taxed, Alexandrian trade had flourished in the new Roman peace, and the household had flourished with it. Five years after the conquest, Hermogenes' father had been able to afford the investment that brought the Roman citizenship to himself and his son. That had been satisfying, though also oddly unsettling. Hermogenes remembered how uncomfortable he had felt when he first saw the diploma with his new Roman names written on it: *Marcus Aelius* Hermogenes. It was as though he had suddenly acquired a ghostly Roman as a twin. He had wondered how you could be a citizen of a city you had never seen, a faraway place you knew as bullying ally, conquering enemy, and powerful ruler, but never as a friend. Still, he had been proud and glad of his new citizenship. It had meant that he was an equal of the conquerors, entitled to the same rights and privileges.

He had wondered, though, if he would ever come to Rome. And now, ten years later, here he was. Walking along a street in the city that ruled the world, finally seeing with his own eyes the place where the ghostly "Marcus Aelius" was a citizen.

It wasn't much to look at—at least, not here. The streets were quiet, as was normal in most cities in the early afternoon, and the few people around were lounging in the shade. The buildings were tall but shoddily constructed, and the road was full of dung, rotting refuse, and flies. Fortunately they did not actually have to walk in the filth: a narrow pavement ran on either side of the thoroughfare, and at every corner stepping-stones allowed a pedestrian to cross without dirtying his feet. Hermogenes noted horse and ox dung amid the rest and wondered if Gallio and the groom had been lying to him—but no, they'd both insisted that carriages couldn't go into the city *during the day,* which implied that the rule was relaxed at night. Presumably carts trundled through the streets all night to deliver goods to the markets. He glanced round at the flimsy apartment blocks and wondered how well their inhabitants slept.

"Tall, eh, sir?" the lead porter remarked proudly. "Mos' foreigners, they jus' can' b'lieve their eyes, how tall the insulae are here in Rome. There's one near the forum seven stories high!"

Hermogenes shook his head. Seven stories high on how wide a base? These buildings looked as though they would fall down at the passage of a particularly heavy cart: the gods help those caught in one during an earthquake!

The porter took the head shake for an expression of amazement, and was encouraged to continue. "Mos' foreigners, they jus' can't b'lieve how big this city is, neither," he declared. "Your home city, now, sir, with respec'—how big is she across, eh?"

Hermogenes shrugged. "Three, four miles?"

The man blinked, surprised. "Oh. Tha's . . . tha's near as big." He looked sideways at Hermogenes. "That'd be Alexandria?"

Hermogenes nodded.

"They say she's a great city, too," the porter conceded.

It was pleasing that even this ignorant man knew of Alexandria's greatness, knew that she rivaled Rome. Hermogenes smiled. "I am glad to behold the city that rules her." *Even if it isn't as beautiful,* he added privately. "What is your name, fellow?"

"Gaius Rubrius Libo, sir," the porter said promptly. "This here's my brother, Quintus." His partner grinned.

Taken aback, Hermogenes ran the names through his mind again: three names, all solidly Latin. Could that mean . . . ? "Are you citizens?" he asked in amazement.

Gaius Rubrius grinned. "Yessir. Sons of a Roman, born and bred in Rome."

It should not have been so disconcerting, Hermogenes told himself. Obviously at Rome itself there would be *ordinary* Roman citizens, men of no particular wealth and importance. It shocked him, nonetheless, to discover that he'd just hired two Roman citizens to carry his luggage. In Alexandria the Roman citizenship was a thing only wealth and power could aspire to gain. He felt obscurely ashamed of the way he'd just flaunted his own citizenship.

"No' many like us, these days," Gaius Rubrius admitted. "Most'a the other fellows you find carrying things these days, they're freedmen or freedmen's sons if they're not slaves outright. Sons of Gauls or, gods hate 'em, Syrians like tha' bastard Helops." He spat, noticed Hermogenes' blank expression, and explained, "The fellow in the red tunic, head groom a' tha' livery stable. Has all the drivers send their fares to him, and charges the porters and chair bearers before he'll send 'em on. Makes trouble about a fellow waitin' in his courtyard to see if anyone wants a ride. Real bastard."

"You tripped him up, sir," Quintus Rubrius put in slyly, and laughed.

Hermogenes shrugged, embarrassed. He could see nothing particularly reprehensible in a livery stable groom arranging porters and sedan chairs for customers, even if he did take a cut. At least the customers would have somewhere to turn if the porters made off with their possessions. He would have been willing to pay a little more for that reassurance himself, if he hadn't been so dissatisfied with the service he'd received from the driver. He glanced back, and was reassured to find Phormion and Menestor close behind, alert, unencumbered and ready to deal with any trouble that arose. Not that he expected any: it was just better to be ready. "My quarrel was with the driver," he remarked, returning his attention to the porters.

"Gallio's a bugger, too," Gaius Rubrius assured him.

They walked on for a few minutes in silence. They had passed through the Ostian Gate now, and the tenements rose up hills to each side, one above another, quiet in the afternoon sun. In their thick shade the street seemed narrower and darker. Some of the ground-floor apartments seemed to have been given over to shops or cookhouses, but at this time of day they were shut, their fronts sealed with heavy wooden shutters, giving the street a blank, walled-in feeling. In dirt-paved alleys which twisted from the main road women stood talking in low voices while children played amid the rubbish. Dogs barked and babies cried. The air smelled of sewage.

A gang of boys at the entrance to one of the apartment blocks watched them go past with sullen dark eyes. One of them shouted something, the words unclear but the jeering tone unmistakable. A man at the window of another building spat, the gobbet of phlegm falling on the dirty pavement by Hermogenes' feet. It reminded him uneasily of parts of Alexandria's Rhakotis quarter. He wished he had not put on his best cloak that morning, and that he'd used a copper pin for his tunic. He'd wanted to impress the Romans as a man of substance, but he would never have walked through the Rhakotis quarter wearing Scythopolitan linen, expensively doubled-dyed gold-russet, and a tunic fastened with a gold pin. It was as good as a proclamation: "Rich man! Worth robbing!"—and here the cut of the cloak proclaimed him not merely "Rich man!" but "Rich foreigner!" which was even worse. He glanced uneasily back at Menestor and Phormion again. Even their plain tunics—clean, of good quality linen, and decorated in Menestor's case with patterned edges—would have been ill-advised in the Rhakotis quarter. And they did look foreign here, there was no denying it. Phormion was too dark, and Menestor's seventeen-year-old honey-colored grace too exotic.

"Is this a bad part of the city?" he asked at last.

"Not so bad, no," Gaius Rubrius said judiciously. "Nowhere in Rome's really *safe,* unnerstan', but there's worse than this. Transtibertina, f'r starters: never go there after dark. Subura's bad, too, and around the Via Appia beyond the Capena Gate. Via Appia itself isn' too bad in town—main roads, see, they're better than alleyways."

"It is the same in Alexandria." He had been taking some comfort from the fact that this was a main road.

"Via Tusculana, now—most of that's a good area. The top of it's up by the Sacra Via, right near the Palatine. The bottom by the Caelimontana Gate, tha's not so good, but not too bad neither. 'Bout like this. Which end is it you want, sir?"

Hermogenes hesitated. "Probably the better end, but I am not certain," he admitted. "I have never before been to Rome. I will ask for the house."

"It's a house? Not an insula?"

An island? Hermogenes thought, then remembered that the apartment blocks were called insulae; Rubrius had even used the term to him before. "I believe it is a house," he said cautiously. "Crispus is a businessman, like myself." He used the term Crispus had always employed for himself: *negotiator.*

"Sacra Via end, then," the porter said confidently. "I'd'a looked there first anyway, seein' as how you're a gentleman."

Well, the cloak had impressed *someone,* anyway. He hoped the porters had him down as a man who could reward helpfulness generously, and perhaps provide more custom in future—that they would work to please him.

"Is y'r friend expectin' you?" Rubrius asked.

"Yes," Hermogenes said at once, although he wasn't certain that was true. He had sent Crispus a letter before setting out from Alexandria, but there was no way to know whether Crispus had actually received it—and of course, even if Crispus was expecting him, the vagaries of ships and winds meant he couldn't know *when* his guest might arrive. A foreigner adrift in a strange city, however, was a foreigner who could be robbed with impunity, and he wouldn't appear any more vulnerable than he had to—particularly not with those valuables in his trunk.

"Sacra Via end f'r sure," Rubrius repeated.

They came out from between the hills, and to Hermogenes' relief, the neighborhood improved. The wood-and-brick bleachers of what Rubrius said was the Circus Maximus—Rome's main racecourse—towered above them to their left. To their right, the tenements gave way to more substantial apartment blocks faced with plaster painted to resemble marble, punctuated by the occasional private house. The roadway curved about the end of the Circus Maximus, then ended in a small public square. Ahead of them rose another hill, this one covered with large houses set amid fine gardens. Marble gleamed white against the green of leaves.

"Tha's the Palatine," said Gaius Rubrius, nodding at it. "Where the emperor an' his friends live, when they're in the city. The Sacra Via goes past it on the other side. This is the end of the Via Ostiensis, but we'll jus' nip across by the lanes. No' too much further now."

"Jus' as well," muttered his brother, Quintus. "This thing's heavy."

24

"Isn't the emperor in the city now?" Hermogenes asked with interest, gazing up at the Palatine.

"Na," Gaius said with resignation. "He's off in the West, and his friend Agrippa's off in the East. Nothin' happenin' this summer. There haven' been no games since the beginnin' of the month, and the circus has been empty even longer. It'll kill me with boredom; I love the games. You'd think Taurus would put on some games—he's prefect of the city right now, Statilius Taurus the general, and he loves the games himself; built the big amphitheater for 'em over in the Campus Martius. But everythin's been dead."

They crossed the square at the entrance to that deserted circus, and followed another street right, then left about the foot of the Palatine. The neighborhood became richer still. Now the apartment blocks were faced with real, rather than imitation, marble, and their entranceways were decorated with mosaic titles, while the wooden shutters of the closed shops were painted in bright colors. They joined another road which Rubrius said was the beginning of the Via Appia: here there were no apartments at all, only private houses, large ones with facades of polished stone, doors of carved oak, and torches set in ornamental iron brackets along the road front. The occasional portico of shops or small temple made columned gaps in a sweep of plasterwork and marble. The pavements had been swept, and even the street was cleaner. The scent of sewage was replaced by that of cook fires, herbs, and stone pavement in sunlight.

On the other side of the Palatine, as Rubrius had promised, they reached a crossroads with another major thoroughfare.

"Tha's the Sacra Via," said Gaius Rubrius, gesturing left down a wide, marble-lined avenue. "It goes to the forum. An' tha's the Via Tusculana." He jerked the basket of luggage right. "Y'can start askin' fer yer friend's house, sir."

The first man Hermogenes asked—a water vendor on the corner—had never heard of Fiducius Crispus. They had to go another six blocks along the Via Tusculana, to a point where the houses were far less grand and had been joined by insulae again, before they found someone who knew his house.

"Crispus the moneylender," said the old woman, grimacing. "On the right, three blocks north. A big place with a door all studded with iron and dolphin torch brackets. But if you're thinkin' to borrow money, think again. It's always better to sell than to borrow."

Hermogenes thanked her and started on. Gaius Rubrius followed more slowly, frowning. "A moneylender, sir?" he asked hesitantly. The word, *faenerator,* was far less respectable than the *negotiator* Hermogenes had used.

Hermogenes shrugged, slowing his own steps to keep beside the porter. "He lends money at interest. So do I. Large sums, mostly, at moderate interest, and only to those who can repay me. Not small sums to poor men, at extortionate rates which are extracted with violence."

"Oh," said Rubrius. His expression, however, said he was not convinced. Moneylenders were cruel and disreputable men.

Hermogenes sighed, wondering whether to say more or just leave it. Say more, he decided. Gaius and Quintus

Rubrius seemed reasonably honest and helpful, and they appeared to know the city well: he might want to hire them again, and if he did he would want their goodwill. "It isn't always better to sell than to borrow," he said quietly. "What would you do if your sedan chair broke, and you didn't have enough saved to buy a new one?"

"Gods avert the omen!" exclaimed Rubrius.

"Would you just carry things on your back until you had enough for a new chair?" Hermogenes went on.

"You'd have a hard job tryin' to buy a new chair tha' way," Quintus Rubrius put in contemptuously. "You don' make half as much carryin' sacks as you do wi' a sedan chair."

"Well, then, would you sell your wife's jewelry, or your winter cloaks, to pay for one?"

Rubrius shook his head. "Wouldn' be worth the grief from my wife, and if I sold the cloak I'd have to buy a new one or shiver all winter. New cloaks cost a lot more'n I'd get for the old one. Y'r right, sir, to think that me 'n Quintus'd borrow the money."

"And so the man who lent you that money would be providing you with a service that benefited you. If he was a dishonest man who made loans to those who could not repay him, and who sent in bailiffs to seize their goods or their children when they were overcome by debt, you would be right to despise him—but if he was an honest man who never did those things, why should you think ill of him? Carrying luggage is also a useful service. Some porters steal from their customers, or damage or lose their goods. Should I despise you because of them?"

There was a silence, and then Quintus Rubrius laughed. "Greeks c'n prove that black is white!"

"All I am saying is that moneylending is an honest trade, even if some who practice it are dishonest."

Gaius Rubrius looked at him sideways. "But you don' give loans for sedan chairs, do you, sir?"

Hermogenes smiled. "On the whole, no. Most of my money—like most of the money of my friend Titus Fiducius Crispus—is in shipping. The building and equipping of ships for trade is costly, and the risks they meet on the seas are great. It's customary to defray both by spreading them among syndicates of investors, who may make a great profit on a successful voyage, or lose money on an unsuccessful one: trade benefits either way. I—and Titus Fiducius—also have money invested in buildings, and in some loans to private individuals. But neither of us can rightly be termed a moneylender. If a man handles large sums, he terms himself a businessman. I agree, though, that the principle is the same. We charge for the use of our money as you do for the use of your chair."

Gaius Rubrius looked down. He shifted the poles of the sedan chair on his shoulder, then smiled. Hermogenes, assessing that smile, decided that the porter was not convinced that moneylending might be an honest trade, but that he was flattered that a rich Greek thought him worth conciliating. Hermogenes sighed: he should have kept his mouth shut. He never could seem to manage to look after his dignity as he should.

Not that Romans, from all he had ever seen, allowed

much dignity to Greeks in the best of circumstances. Dignity, as far as he could make out, was supposed to be a purely Roman attribute: Greeks were supposed to be clever. It was odd, the way they always exclaimed over Greek cleverness while treating it as somehow inherently dishonest: *Greeks can prove that black is white!* If you actually asked them about their own tradesmen, merchants, or politicians, they had no hesitation in telling you that some were thieves and liars; likewise, they'd readily agree that such-and-such a Greek banker or ship captain was an honest man—but somehow or other this never dented their assurance that Romans were honest and Greeks weren't.

He'd met the attitude often enough in Roman merchants. He supposed he shouldn't be surprised to see that it went right to the bottom of Roman society.

"Is that y'r friend's house?" asked Quintus Rubrius.

It was, unmistakably: the only house in a block of insulae. It was a large, fine house, with a wrought-iron torch bracket in the shape of a dolphin on either side of the iron-studded double door. Gaius and Quintus Rubrius set down the sedan chair with the luggage in front of that door, and Gaius knocked. Menestor abruptly hurried forward from his place at the back of the procession and edged the porter aside. Dealing with the slaves of his master's associates was his job, and he was always very protective of his position. He rapped smartly on the iron-studded oak.

There was a long silence, but at last a window in the lodge swung open, and a hideous face looked out—a shiny white mask of scar tissue from which two red eyes blinked suspiciously. It was hairless, and the ears were no more than stumps. A fire, Hermogenes thought, wrestling with his shock: the poor fellow was burned in a fire.

"What d'you want?" growled the doorkeeper suspiciously.

Menestor hesitated, then asked hopefully, "Do you speak Greek?"

The doorkeeper merely blinked at him. Hermogenes sighed and stepped forward: it was undignified to negotiate with Crispus's slaves himself, but it seemed he had to do it. "Is this the house of Titus Fiducius Crispus?" he asked politely.

The doorkeeper blinked again. "Yes," he admitted. "But the master isn't in. Try again tomorrow morning."

"He has invited me to be his guest. He should be expecting me. I am Marcus Aelius Hermogenes, of Alexandria."

"He never said he was expecting nobody," the doorkeeper objected.

Hermogenes firmly squashed his rising anger and embarrassment. Letters could easily miscarry, or instructions from a master could fail to reach the person responsible for carrying them out—neither of which was a doorkeeper's fault. "Your master has invited me," he repeated calmly, "and I believe he is expecting me. If he is out, will you check whether he's left any instructions about me?"

The doorkeeper blinked at him some more. "Marcus Aelius Hermokrates of Alexandria, you said?"

"Hermo*genes*!"

The doorkeeper grunted and disappeared, closing his window behind him.

There was a silence, then a snigger from Quintus Rubrius.

Young Menestor turned a dusky red and glared at the porter. Then he gave his master a look of angry apology. "I'm sorry, sir," he said. "You shouldn't have had to deal with a freak like that. He was rude, wasn't he?"

"No," Hermogenes told the boy soothingly, "merely abrupt in his manner. He said that his master is out, and that no one had told him to expect us. I should have sent a letter from Ostia yesterday." It had been dusk by the time they'd disembarked from the ship the previous day; he hadn't wanted to search the streets and taverns for someone willing to carry a letter through the dark, and most likely wouldn't have found anyone if he had—but still, he should have *tried* to send a letter.

"*I* should have learned Latin," said Menestor unhappily.

"We've been busy," Hermogenes comforted him. He looked at Gaius Rubrius, who was watching with an expression of amusement. "As you see, there is some confusion," he told the man, in Latin. "If my friend has forgotten to leave instructions for my reception, do you know of an inn nearby where we could—"

"My *dear* Hermogenes!"

Hermogenes turned back to the door, and found the sweating, pink-cheeked face of Fiducius Crispus himself beaming from the lodge window.

"Titus Fiducius," Hermogenes said formally, "greetings!"

"And to you, dear fellow!" replied Crispus. He turned from the window and snapped "Dog! What are you standing there for? Let him in!"

A bolt squealed on the inside of the door, and then the iron-studded oak swung open. The scarred doorkeeper pushed open its mate, then stood aside. Crispus pushed past him—a fat man in his late forties, rumpled in an unbelted tunic and no cloak, barefoot as though he'd been asleep. He reached for Hermogenes' outstretched hand with both his own and clasped it in two moist meaty palms.

"What a pleasure to see you here in Rome!" he exclaimed, still beaming. "Come in, come in; welcome to my house!"

"I thank you," Hermogenes said, smiling. He extricated his hand and went on, "I must first pay the porters—"

"Let me!" Crispus interrupted.

Hermogenes shook his head and turned to the Rubrius brothers, who had just finished removing the chest from the sedan chair. He took two sestertii from his purse and handed one to each man. The porters' looks of surprise gave way to wide grins.

"Thank you for your assistance," Hermogenes told them. "You seem to know the city well. If I wish to hire you again, where should I look for you?"

"Thank *you*, sir," said Gaius Rubrius at once, still grinning. "You can send word to us at the Cattlemarket, at the foot of the Aemilian Bridge. We could come by here for you whenever you want, if we're not on another job. We charge a denarius n' a half the day, sir, if you want the chair for longer. Half a denarius after noon."

"I may send for you, then, once I know more about how I should conduct my business here in Rome. Good health to you both."

"Good health to you, sir!" chorused the Rubrii, and set off down the street, their empty chair dangling from one pole between them.

Crispus tut-tutted. "You shouldn't be so polite to rabble like that," he informed his guest. "It makes them greedy—and you paid those fellows too much, too."

"I know," said Hermogenes, turning back to his host. "In a strange city, I try to acquire every potential asset I meet." *Besides,* he thought to himself, *it was worth a bit extra, to have a pair of Roman citizens carrying my luggage.*

Crispus laughed. "Asset? A ragamuffin pair of sedan-chair bearers? If you need a chair, my friend, you are welcome to borrow mine. But come in, come in! Are these men yours?"

"My slaves," Hermogenes agreed. "Young Menestor here is my valet and secretary." He snapped his fingers for them to pick up the luggage.

"Dog!" snapped Crispus to the scarred doorkeeper. "Do I have to tell you everything? Help them!"

The doorkeeper went silently to the traveling chest and took one end of it. Hermogenes realized that Crispus had called the man "dog" in Greek, even though the rest of the conversation was in Latin. "Does your doorkeeper speak Greek?" he asked in confusion. The man had not appeared to understand Menestor.

Crispus giggled and shook his head. "Not a word of it. But I give all my slaves Greek names; it's the fashion. His is

Kyon." He giggled again. "Good name for a doorkeeper, don't you think?"

Hermogenes tried to keep his feelings from his face. The idea of renaming slaves to fit a current fashion was repulsive, and the thought of obliging one to answer to Dog made him queasy. He didn't like the idea of a fashion for giving slaves *Greek* names, either.

His attempt at concealing his emotions obviously hadn't succeeded, because Crispus cried, "Oh, dear! You're offended. I assure you, this fashion for Greek names is only because we admire Greek culture so much, not because . . . *obviously* we don't think of Greeks as naturally servile!"

Hermogenes forced himself to smile understandingly. Inwardly he wondered if staying with Crispus was really such a good idea. It had seemed the obvious thing to do: Crispus was an old business associate of his father, after all, and had been a guest in Alexandria on several occasions. He had always declared himself eager to return the favor. It was very much the done thing to stay with guest-friends if you had any, much more respectable than a public inn . . . but now that he was here, he was remembering that he'd never actually *liked* Fiducius Crispus much.

Too late to do anything about it now. Besides, he needed advice, and Crispus could give it to him. He followed his host into the house.

The street door opened onto a wide entrance corridor decorated with a mosaic picture of a barking dog; the doorkeeper's lodge was a tiny cell to the right of it. Through the entranceway was a vaulted atrium, with a pond in the center to catch the rainfall from the open circle of the impluvium in the ceiling. An archway beyond revealed a small courtyard with a garden.

An anxious-looking man of about Hermogenes' own age hurried in through the archway. He wore a tunic of plain bleached linen and a heavy leather belt through which was pushed a short leather whip. He bowed to Crispus and cast Hermogenes a worried look from mild blue eyes. "They're getting the Nile rooms ready, master," he informed Crispus in a hoarse whisper. His voice was so strained that Hermogenes wondered if there was something wrong with it. "And I've had wine sent to the dining room."

Crispus nodded. "That's something, then." He smiled at Hermogenes. "I told my slaves to get a room ready for you as soon as I received your letter—but, of course, the lazy things did nothing about it, and the place is perfectly squalid. Come and have something to drink while they do what should have been done days ago. Stentor, see my friend's slaves and his luggage to his room."

Stentor, thought Hermogenes, looking at the hoarse-voiced man incredulously. Named after the brazen-voiced herald in Homer.

Stentor gestured for Menestor and Phormion to pick up the trunk again; both at once looked to Hermogenes. Menestor's expression held a touch of panic. Hermogenes couldn't blame him: the prospect of being led off into a strange household by a man with a whip would frighten any slave, and the young man couldn't even understand what that croaking voice said to him. Hermogenes touched his arm lightly. "They are getting my rooms ready," he explained in Greek. "This man will show you where to put the luggage. I will ask if—"

"Ah, yes!" exclaimed Crispus. "I should have said, shouldn't I? Stentor here is my steward. If you want anything during your stay, ask him."

The worried blue eyes of the steward blinked. Hermogenes smiled at him in what he hoped was a reassuring fashion. "Stentor," he said, "these are my valued attendants, Menestor and Phormion. They are tired and thirsty from our journey, and I would be grateful if you could ensure that they are looked after. Unfortunately, neither of them speaks Latin."

"I speak some Greek, sir," the steward volunteered. There *was* something wrong with his voice. "And so do some of the others in the household. Our master is a man of culture—but I'm sure you know that." He turned to Menestor and said in accented, hoarse, but acceptable Greek, "Put the things in your master's room, and then I will give you to drink."

"*Moderation,*" Hermogenes reminded Phormion. The big bodyguard, who was fond of drink, rolled his eyes and nodded.

The slaves followed Stentor through the archway and to the left. Hermogenes allowed Crispus to escort him through and to the right, into a large room facing into the courtyard. It was decorated with garish red panels, augmented by rondels depicting exotic animals—elephants, tigers, and giraffes. A girl and a boy were busy with cups and mixing bowls at the sideboard, but they turned and bowed as the two men entered. Crispus flopped onto the nearest of the three couches and put his feet up on the red leather upholstery. Hermogenes sat warily on the next one. He glanced at his sandals: they were dirty. The girl hurried over, unfastened the guest's sandals, and wiped his feet with a damp towel. The boy followed with a pitcher and two red Arretine-ware cups, but Crispus stopped him with a gesture before he could pour.

"What's the wine?" he demanded.

"The Sabine, master," quavered the boy. "Mixed half and half with water, Stentor said."

"Ah!" Crispus nodded approvingly. "Good, good! One of our local Italian vintages, Hermogenes; I hope you like it. Go on, Hyakinthos, pour it for him!"

"Please, I do not want it so strong," Hermogenes said hurriedly. "I have just walked from the Ostian Gate, and I would like more of water."

The boy filled the guest's cup halfway before turning to pour wine for his master. The girl hurried back to the sideboard, dropped the towel, and came over with a second pitcher, this one containing cold water. She topped up the guest's cup.

"Your health!" Hermogenes said, raising his cup, and Crispus returned the toast.

The wine was a harsh, rather sour red, but deliciously wet after the hot carriage and the walk across the city. Hermogenes drained his cup, and the boy instantly refilled it. Hermogenes wondered how the lad felt about being called Hyakinthos. The myth of the beautiful boy loved by the god Apollo was routinely invoked by pederastic poets, and it seemed very likely that other boys would greet the name with knowing sniggers. Then he remembered that Crispus liked boys: during one visit there'd been some trouble over one he'd picked up in the marketplace. Hyakinthos was probably well aware of the implications of his name.

"You *walked* from the Ostian Gate?" Crispus asked genially. "You didn't even use that sedan chair you paid so much for?"

"That was for the luggage. In truth, I had not intended to walk, Crispus. I had intended to come all the way by carriage, but . . ." He shrugged, gave a deprecating smile. "I did not know that carriages are not allowed into Rome."

"Call me Titus," offered Crispus. "That's right, this *is* your first visit, isn't it? I'm pleased that I can finally offer you some hospitality in exchange for all the kindness you and your father have shown to me." There was a pause, and then he added solemnly, "I was very sorry to hear of your father's fate. I pray the earth is light upon him."

Hermogenes bowed his head. The first time anyone had prayed that the earth was light on his father's grave, he had shouted furiously, "How could it be? He *drowned* at sea!" The grief then had been raw, savage, and unwieldy. It had seemed impossible that the father who had shaped his own life so entirely, could so suddenly and absolutely vanish from it. Sometimes he had woken up convinced that it had been a mistake, that his father's ship had not sunk but merely been driven off course, and his father would soon be home. It had been more than half a year now, though, and he knew that Philemon was never going to return from the deep salt water. He had learned to hide his pain, to wear a polite mask over his smoldering rage. He had even learned to accept condolences gracefully.

"And you are his sole heir?" Crispus continued. "It must have been some comfort to him to know that he left his affairs in capable hands."

Hermogenes took another sip of wine and murmured that it was kind of Crispus to say so.

"Oh, I don't say it from kindness!" the Roman protested. "It would be a comfort to *me,* I promise you, if I had an able son instead of a worthless nephew to inherit all my hard work." He took a swallow of wine and went on, "Of course, these days a man's made to feel like a traitor to the state if he's a bachelor. We've all been told that it's our duty to marry and breed Romans. You've heard about the Julian laws?"

Hermogenes had indeed heard of the new laws to encourage marriage and punish adultery. "You're thinking of getting married because of them?" he asked, amused. He remembered, vividly, how Crispus had once told him that marriage was a trap to enslave men, and that any man of spirit should thank the gods if he escaped it. The speech had been intended to comfort him for the death in childbirth of his own wife, and it hadn't seemed funny at the time.

Crispus sighed deeply and gazed into his wine. "I think about it. Then I think again. How could I live without boys—or with the grief a wife would give me over keeping them? What about you? Have you remarried yet?"

Hermogenes suppressed the grimace of disgust. He heard far more than he wanted on the subject of remarriage from all his father's associates. At least Crispus didn't have a daughter. "Not yet," he said mildly.

"You ought to. Get yourself a son and heir. Your first wife didn't give you any children, did she?"

"She gave me a daughter."

Crispus dismissed female offspring with a negligent wave, then straightened with a look of mock alarm. "Gods and goddesses, I'd forgotten that! Shouldn't have mentioned that I was thinking of marriage myself, should I? Any man with a daughter is looking to buy her a rich husband."

Hermogenes thought of his daughter, who had informed him that she intended to be an acrobat when she grew up ("With a costume all made out of red leather with gold on!"), who was always in trouble at school for dirtying her clothes, whose luminous grin could persuade her respectable father to such feats as climbing the garden wall and sneaking into a neighbor's shed to see a nest of young kittens. He looked at the fat man sweating on his red-upholstered couch and thought *I'd see you dead first*. He smiled, and said, "She is only ten years old, Cris—Titus. I am not looking yet. Besides, I am sure you can find yourself a wife here in Rome, if you decide you want one. How is business?"

Crispus told him, at length, about his interest in a new shipping syndicate and some building work in Rome. Hermogenes listened attentively, occasionally making a mental note of something that might be useful. At last his host exhausted the subject and looked at his wine cup. It was empty, and he snapped his fingers to fetch the cupbearer.

"What about you?" he asked, as Hyakinthos refilled it.

"In your letter you said that you had some important business in Rome, but you didn't say what it was."

Hermogenes refused a top-up of his own cup. *Important business.* He was uncomfortably aware that the powerful impulses which had driven him to leave his home and family and come to Rome had little to do with business. Oh, there was money at stake as well, but it wasn't what mattered to him. He did not want to admit to Titus Fiducius that what he was really hoping to find in Rome was that elusive and impractical thing: *justice.* Any businessman would find that suspect and disturbing. Justice could well end up being far more expensive than even the worst-judged commercial transaction.

"I am here like a bailiff, to collect a debt which is overdue," he declared, smiling as though it didn't matter to him. "I would welcome any advice you have to give me on how I should go about it."

Crispus laughed. "Whose furniture are you looking to seize?"

"I will not 'seize' anything. The debtor is a wealthy and powerful man. What I want advice on is how to approach him tactfully."

"Who is it?"

"Lucius Tarius Rufus." In Alexandria he had once written that name out on a wax tablet, then scored it over with the stylus so deeply that he had taken all the wax off and gouged the wood beneath. He was pleased that he could utter it now with such casual calm.

Crispus sat up straight and stared in amazement. "The general? Jupiter! He's *consul!*"

"Is he?" Hermogenes asked in surprise. "Surely, the consuls this year are"—he recalled the date on his most recent Roman business contract. *It was agreed during the consulship of*—"Domitius Ahenobarbus and Cornelius Scipio?"

"Tarius Rufus replaced Scipio at the beginning of the month," Crispus told him. "It happens a lot these days. The nobles expect the consulship by right of birth; the new men think they've earned it, and they end up having to share. Scipio's blue blood undoubtedly boiled at having to step down for a farmboy from Picenum, but step down he did. Rufus is a friend of the emperor, and Augustus trusted him to command the army of the Danube. You don't argue with a man like that." He got to his feet, carried his cup to the sideboard, then turned around still clutching it. "I can see why you're eager to be tactful. He owes you money? I never knew he had any business in Egypt."

Hermogenes swirled the wine round his half-empty cup. "He doesn't, as far as I am aware. However, twelve years ago he was proconsul of Cyprus—an island which, as you know, has always had the closest ties with Egypt, since it used to belong to the kings. My father's sister married a prominent businessman there, a man by the name of Nikomachos—he of the shipping syndicate, yes! Rufus borrowed half a million sestertii from him at five percent per annum."

"He signed a contract?"

Hermogenes nodded. "Signed, sealed, and witnessed. In fact, during the first five years after he borrowed it he did make regular repayments—all the annual interest, and a hundred thousand of the principal. Then, however, the payments ceased. Rufus was in Illyria at the time, with the army of the Danube, and at first Nikomachos thought that he had simply failed to authorize his man of business in Rome to release the money. However, when he pursued the matter, he was unable to obtain anything more than another forty thousand of the interest. The default began to place a strain on his own affairs, and he pursued it more urgently, but received only threats from Rufus's secretary and no reply at all from the man himself, even after he left the Danube and went back to Rome. Last autumn Nikomachos died, leaving his estate heavily in debt. The heir to the estate—and the debt—was my father."

Hermogenes took a sip of wine and swilled it round his mouth. "Nikomachos's creditors were threatening to seize his house and turn his widow, my father's sister, out into the street, so my father decided to go to Cyprus himself to set things right, even though it was late in the year."

He made himself have another swallow of wine, and was able to continue in a more-or-less normal voice, "He never arrived there. There was a storm, and his ship went down. In the spring I went to Cyprus myself, liquidated the estate, paid off the most pressing creditors, and persuaded my aunt to come back to Alexandria with me. Now I am, as you have mentioned, sole heir to my father's estate, and that includes the debt he inherited from Nikomachos. Lucius Tarius Rufus owes me five hundred and twenty thousand sestertii." *And the lives of my father and my uncle.* He met Crispus's eyes. "I presume he does have the money."

Crispus shrugged. "I'm sure he does, my friend, I'm sure he does. As you said, he's a very wealthy and powerful man. But he may well be a bit short of cash in hand. The consulship is an expensive proposition. You are not going to be a welcome visitor."

Hermogenes shrugged. "He borrowed the money." He paused, considering, then went on, "It could be lucky for me that he *is* consul right now. He will not want the embarrassment of a summons for debt while he actually holds the supreme magistracy of Rome."

Crispus stared at him, aghast. "Oh, Jupiter!" He began to laugh. "You're not going to tell him you'll do *that*?"

"I hope to settle the matter quietly. I do, however, hold a valid and binding contract—and, unlike Nikomachos, I am a citizen and entitled to use the Roman courts."

Crispus laughed again. "Oh, gods and goddesses! Imagine it! A *Roman consul* summoned for debt by an *Egyptian moneylender*! He'd be the laughingstock of the city for the rest of his life!"

Hermogenes looked up in surprise and indignation. "I am not an Egyptian!"

Crispus flapped a hand in concession. "I know, I know—but in Rome, nobody cares whether you're an Alexandrian Greek or an Egyptian Greek or a plain ordinary Egyptian Egyptian. You come from Egypt: you're Egyptian."

"I am a Roman citizen."

"Hermogenes, you're an Alexandrian to your fingernails! Your father lent money to Aelius Gallus when he was governor of Egypt, and accepted the citizenship in lieu of payment. That isn't the same as being a *real* Roman."

"I am Roman enough to take Rufus to court."

Crispus stopped laughing. "You're *serious*? No, my

friend, don't do it. Don't even threaten it. A man like that, sitting there in the curial chair—do you *know* what the consulship *means*?"

"Probably not," Hermogenes admitted. "I thought the consuls had very little real power, these days."

Crispus looked uncomfortable. Of course: the emperor boasted that he had restored the republic, which ought to mean that the consuls were once again the supreme governors of the Roman state. To admit that they were merely figureheads was to disagree with the emperor, and that was not wise. "It's not a question of *power*," Crispus declared, skirting the issue. "It's the *honor*. I'm equestrian class, as you know; I'm not a noble, I don't run after magistracies—in fact, I think they're a waste of time and money!—but even I feel awe when I look at the consulship. You can go into the forum and read the names of every man who's held the office, two of them every year, all the way back to the founding of the city—all the most famous names in history. Once a man has sat down in the curial chair he's a noble, whatever he was before, and what's more, all his sons after him are noble. The consulship is the summit of any man's achievements. Tarius Rufus . . . he's a nobody by birth, he's scrambled his way up through the army to get where he is now, but he's there, he's made it. If you came in, at his hour of triumph, and threatened to make him a *joke* . . . he'd kill you! And who could stop him? He's a general and a friend of the emperor."

Hermogenes met his eyes and saw the boundaries of the other man's hospitality. Crispus would not keep in his house a man who threatened a Roman consul with disgrace—not because he supported the consul but because he feared the consequences for himself.

Hermogenes wondered, not for the first time, how bad those consequences could be. Crispus had implied they might even include death. It would be a terrible thing to die far from home, for nothing, leaving a household headless and a daughter orphaned. Nothing he could gain here was worth that.

Was that extreme consequence very likely, though? Tarius Rufus was a powerful man, yes, but he was not an emperor: he was still subject to the ordinary laws of Rome. Surely even a Roman consul would find it difficult to murder a Roman citizen just because he was a creditor? Rufus was undoubtedly able to pay his debt if he wanted to. Confronted with a creditor who was a citizen, able to summon him in a Roman court, surely he would find it easier to give in and pay up?

Rufus had chosen not to pay his debt before, and Hermogenes' uncle and father had died because of it. To abandon the struggle before it was even begun would be a betrayal of their memory. No: Crispus was merely being timid in the face of consular authority. Hermogenes would press his claim—but he would try to involve his host as little as possible.

He bowed his head. "Titus, I already told you that I want your advice on how to approach him tactfully. I do not want to offend him in any way. I want to settle this as quietly and peacefully as I possibly can." It was all true, as far as it went. "Thank you for your warning."

"Good," replied Crispus, relaxing. He noticed that his

cup was empty again and held it out to the boy. When it was full he sat down on his couch again and gulped some. "I don't see why he wouldn't agree to pay you," he said after a minute, wiping his mouth. "He might not give you all the money at once, but it isn't as though he can't afford it, after all. It may well be that he never even saw your uncle's letters, and has forgotten all about the debt. Maybe he even thinks it was all paid off long ago. It's entirely possible that his secretary has been taking the payments from his master's estate and putting them in his own purse." He frowned. "It might be better if you didn't mention your uncle's name when you make an appointment with the consul. That way the secretary, if he has been thieving, won't try to stop you seeing him. And it would definitely be a good idea to take your contract, and any papers relating to the debt, and get them stored and registered at the public records office, so that nobody can interfere with them."

"As you say," Hermogenes said meekly. "How does one make an appointment to see a consul?"

FOR MONTHS HERMOGENES HAD BEEN sleeping badly. Since the first news of his uncle's death, he'd woken two or three times a night and lain awake, staring into the darkness, or—unable to endure his midnight thoughts—got up and gone through accounts by lamplight. The first night in Crispus's house, however, he slept deeply and dreamlessly, and woke to find bright daylight lancing through the cracks of the window shutters.

He rolled over onto his back and stared up at the ceiling. It was plain white plaster, decorated in the corners with a motif of wreaths and garlands in light relief. Voices were talking not too far away, and from the street outside his window came the cries of a vendor, *Fresh, fresh, fresh!* He wondered what was fresh. Bread? Fruit? Shellfish?

There was no time to lie in bed thinking about street cries: he had things to do. He sighed, swung his feet over the side of the couch, and wandered, barefoot and in his tunic, out from the sleeping cubicle into the adjacent day-room.

Crispus had called this suite the Nile Rooms, and the river certainly figured prominently in its decoration. There was a large painting of the river god on one wall, crowned with papyrus and surrounded by gamboling crocodiles and hippopotami. A statuette of the same subject stood in one corner, with two more paintings—the harbor of Alexandria and a Nile scene—hanging above it. The legs of the writing table were carved to look like Egyptian gods—Anubis, Isis, Thoth-Hermes, and Serapis—the chair had finials shaped like papyrus flowers, the lampstand was shaped like Alexandria's Pharos lighthouse, the lamps were little bronze crocodiles, and the lamp trimmer was a striking asp. Hermogenes could remember Crispus buying most of the things—or remember him coming back to the house in Alexandria with them, at least, and unwrapping each absurd purchase to display it proudly to his bemused and embarrassed hosts. Here was where many of those souvenirs had ended up. He wondered if the businessman's other guests found them as silly as he did.

Perhaps not. Crispus had always assured his hosts that Egyptian themes were very popular in Rome, very fashionable—like Greek names for your slaves. He grimaced and looked about for Menestor, who as valet had been given a sleeping mat in his master's dayroom while Phormion went to the slaves' quarters. The mat was rolled up in the corner, and the young man was nowhere to be seen. It was late, then. Hermogenes yawned and scrubbed at his face.

His chin was bristly. He would have to find a barber. Was there time for that? Crispus had said that all the public offices would be shut during the afternoon, and he needed to deposit his documents. What time was it, anyway?

He opened the door that led into the courtyard. A pair of slaves who'd been sweeping the colonnade—a threadbare woman in her thirties, and a girl of about six—stopped their work. The woman stood warily to attention, and the little girl ducked behind her and peered round at the visitor.

The child's big dark eyes reminded Hermogenes of his own daughter, and he smiled at the pair. "Greetings. I appear to have overslept. Do you know what is the time?" Something about that sentence was not quite right—but then, he'd only just got up.

"It's the third hour, sir," said the woman nervously. "Leastways, it was when I started sweeping. I hope we didn't wake you up, sir."

"You did not," he told her, "though if you had, I would thank you for it. I do not usually sleep so late." The third hour, and he was normally out of the house by the end of the second! Oh, well, he felt better for the rest, and there were still three long midsummer hours until noon. He smiled at the little girl. "You were working hard while I was lazy in bed, were you, little one?"

The child hid her face in the woman's skirts. The woman gave the visitor a timid smile. Her front teeth were missing.

"Your daughter?" Hermogenes asked, returning the smile.

The woman nodded, her smile widening. "Yes, sir. Erotion, the master calls her. He says it means 'Little Love.'"

"It seems a good name for her."

She blushed. "I like it, sir, I do."

"I'm Mama's little love," said the child in a muffled voice, her face still pressed against the skirts.

"I am sure you are," Hermogenes told her, with grave courtesy. To the woman he added, "I suppose you have a Greek name as well?"

"Me? Oh, no, sir!" She laughed. "He only renames important slaves, sir, and favorites. My name is Tertia, sir."

"Tertia. I am Hermogenes. I hope you will find me no trouble as a guest in your master's house. Can you tell me where I might find my valet?"

"I think he's with Stentor, sir. Erotion could fetch him if you want."

Erotion took her face out of her mother's skirts and nodded.

"Clever girl! Listen, then. Menestor does not speak Latin. You will have to ask Stentor to explain to him why you want him."

"What does he speak?" asked the child, with interest.

"Greek."

"He must be clever, then. You have to be clever to learn Greek, my brother says."

"Ah, but you do not have to *learn* it, if you are born a Greek baby: you grow up speaking it. My daughter would think *you* must be very clever to speak such good Latin."

Erotion's eyes widened at this extraordinary notion.

"Don't keep the gentleman waiting, darling!" her mother scolded gently. "Go fetch his slave."

"Yes, Mama," said Erotion, and skipped off.

"She is a good girl, sir," Tertia told him, "but easily distracted."

"My daughter is the same."

They nodded at one another in parental sympathy, and then Hermogenes returned to his room. The sound of the broom began again behind him, and he felt an instant's guilt about that sympathetic exchange. A freeborn citizen should not stand about discussing the trials of parenthood with a domestic slave, as though the two of them could possibly be equals. *You're reducing yourself to their level,* his father would've told him. *Be kind and gracious, by all means, but never forget that you are their superior.* He had offended against his dignity once again, and what was more, he wasn't sure why he'd done it. The first time he'd been friendly to another man's slaves it had been because he was genuinely interested, but he'd since discovered that it could be very useful, and now he was never sure himself when his friendliness was genuine and when it was calculated.

No, this time it had been genuine. The little girl had reminded him of his daughter. He remembered how Myrrhine had clung to him when he set out from the house in Alexandria, sobbing and begging him to take her with him, and how she'd stood in the doorway with her nurse, waving and waving until he was out of sight. She was terrified that her father's ship would go the way of her grandfather's.

He went to one of the luggage baskets, looking for the writing supplies. It was the wrong basket, and he looked in the other one. There, under the copies of the debt documents: pen case, seal boxes, sheaves of papyrus, and a jar of dried ink. He took them all out, sharpened a pen, and sat down at the ornate table to write a letter.

MARCUS AELIUS HERMOGENES GREETS HIS DAUGHTER, AELIA MYRRHINE: I HOPE YOU ARE IN GOOD HEALTH.

My sweet life, I have arrived in Rome safely after an untroubled voyage, which I know is the thing you most want to hear. I am staying with my guest-friend Titus Fiducius Crispus, who has a fine big house and a great many slaves to look after it for him. One of them is a little girl called Erotion: she is younger than you, and she thinks you must be very clever to speak Greek. I told her you would think she must be clever, to speak Latin.

Rome is as big a city as Alexandria, and has many very tall buildings, but it is not as beautiful—at least, not on the outskirts. It doesn't even have a proper wall with gates! And, of course, it has no harbor and no lighthouse. Our ship came into the nearest port, which is called Ostia, and we had to take a carriage to the outskirts of Rome, and then walk. The laws don't allow carriages in during the day, so everyone either walks or uses a sedan chair. I hired porters to carry the luggage and discovered that they were Roman citizens. Tell your aunt Eukleia that: she'll like it.

I may see some prettier parts of the city today,

because today I go into the forum to start my business. I will tell you about it if I see anything interesting.

The door opened abruptly, and Menestor came in with little Erotion.

"I fetched him," said the little girl proudly.

"Sir?" asked the young man. "You wanted me?"

Hermogenes waved his pen and got ink on his hand. He sighed and looked for a blotter to wipe it off. "Yes. We need to be about our business. Do you know if I need to greet our host before we set out?"

"I think he's gone out, sir," said Menestor. "In the sedan chair, while you were still asleep. But I know that there's a dinner party for you this evening. Stentor was asking me what you like."

Hermogenes nodded: he'd been invited to the dinner party. "We'll be back in plenty of time for that. Very well, then, tell Stentor we're going out and will be back this afternoon, and go fetch Phormion. Oh, and if you can, ask Stentor how I can send a letter home."

"Yes, sir." Menestor left again.

Erotion lingered, curious. Hermogenes smiled at her. "I am writing a letter to my daughter," he informed her. "I told her how well you speak Latin."

The girl beamed. "What's your little girl's name?"

"Myrrhine."

"Mur-ree-nee. That's pretty. Did you tell her my name?"

"I did."

"Oh!" Erotion was surprised and delighted with the idea that a little girl in a faraway city would know her name. "Tell her I wish her health!" she ordered eagerly.

Hermogenes nodded and wrote,

> Little Erotion asks me to say that she wishes you good health, as do I. Greet Aunt Eukleia for me, and Nurse, and all the household. Remember you must be kind to Aunt Eukleia, even if she does tell you not to practice your acrobatics, because she is very sad after losing her husband and her own house. I miss you very much, and I hope I can finish my business soon and come home to my own darling daughter.

He blew on the ink to dry it.

"Will your daughter be able to read that?" Erotion asked him.

Reading must seem a marvelous accomplishment to Erotion. No one bothered to educate female slave children. "Yes, she can read."

The child nodded wisely. "I thought so. I knew she'd be a lady."

He thought of Myrrhine practicing cartwheels in the garden, skinny legs in the air and tunic around her waist. "She *will be* a lady," he said cautiously. "Now she is just a little girl."

"Will she write back?"

"She may, but I think there will not be time for me to receive her answer. It is a long, long way to Alexandria. By the time she receives this, I will probably already be on my way home."

"Oh." Erotion picked her nose. "I have to go help my mother now."

"You are a good girl to do that. Good health to you."

He rolled up the letter, inscribed the address on the back, and tied and sealed it. Then he took out a second sheet and wrote carefully,

MARCUS AELIUS HERMOGENES OF ALEXANDRIA, TO LUCIUS TARIUS RUFUS, CONSUL OF THE ROMANS, VERY MANY GREETINGS.

My lord, you do not know me, but you have had dealings with an uncle of mine. He has recently deceased, and I am his heir. He has bequeathed me some business which involves yourself, and since I am eager to resolve all his commitments and set his estate in order, I have come to Rome to see you. I hope that you will grant me an appointment to discuss this business with you at your convenience. I am staying in the house of Titus Fiducius Crispus on the Via Tusculana.

I pray that the gods grant you health.

He read the letter over, then gave a nod of satisfaction. He had written in Greek, since his Latin spelling tended to the erratic, but that should present no difficulty. Rufus undoubtedly spoke Greek, and would certainly have a secretary to deal with his Greek correspondence. And the tone was right. Rufus would probably think the "business" involved a legacy of some kind, and grant an early audience. He rolled and sealed this letter as well, then went back to the sleeping cubicle to put on his belt, cloak, and sandals.

When he came back to the dayroom, Menestor and Phormion had arrived. With them was Crispus's cupbearer, Hyakinthos.

"Stentor says you need pilot," said the boy in clumsy Greek. "In order that you not lost. I speak Greek."

Hermogenes regarded him a moment. The boy was about thirteen, tall and slender, with long black hair and dark eyes. He wore a fine orange tunic, short enough to show more of his thighs than was really respectable. He shifted uneasily under the scrutiny.

"I hope it is no trouble to you," Hermogenes told him.

"No," replied the boy, relaxing a little. "I like to go to the forum."

"We do need a guide," said Menestor approvingly. "Sir, Stentor says that if you want to leave your letter on the table, he'll have someone collect it later. Titus Fiducius shares a courier service with some other men of business, and he sends letters out every day."

Hermogenes nodded and left the letters on the table. He turned to the big trunk, which had been set against the wall next to the lampstand, fished out the key on its chain around his neck, unlocked the chest, and took out the box of documents relating to the debt—the original documents, of which the ones in the basket were copies. He handed it to Menestor; after a moment's thought he added the papers that proved his own citizenship, and the party set out.

The center of Rome was, indeed, very much grander than its outskirts. It was also, plainly, grander than it had been a generation before, and in another generation would be grander still: everywhere there was building work. Old brick temples along the Sacra Via were being renovated in marble; new porticoes, new basilicas, and new monuments sprouted like mushrooms. Hyakinthos pointed them out in his rudimentary Greek: "That *up*, on the Palatine—that the Temple of Apollo," "That the Parthian Arch. Two year old," "That the Temple of Caesar the God."

The morning streets were crowded, quite different from their shadowed emptiness the previous afternoon. Slaves in plain tunics, carrying baskets of shopping, rubbed elbows with citizen-women in their long fringed stoles. Occasionally there was a male citizen draped in a snowy toga, hurrying about on business. Water sellers and pastry vendors competed to cry their wares; sedan chairs lurched along the road, usually with a togaed gentleman swaying high above the sweating bearers. The occasional covered litter sailed past like a merchant ship among the small craft, carried smoothly upon the shoulders of eight bearers, its occupant invisible behind fine curtains.

Foreigners were common. Hermogenes spotted a couple of northern barbarians before they'd even reached the Sacra Via—Germans or perhaps Celts, fair-haired men with beards, dressed in breeches. There were probably many other northerners who were wearing Roman dress, for there were far more blond and red heads among the crowd than he had ever seen in Alexandria. A pair of women from one of the caravan cities of the East stood together at a cloth merchant's, dressed in long dark cloaks from head to foot, their necks and veils hung about with gold; a Phrygian eunuch priest sat begging in a public square, chanting the praises of the Great Mother in a reedy voice and occasionally striking a tambourine; a stout man in the stitched shirt and trousers of a Parthian, his beard dyed blue, pushed frowning through the crowd. The commonest sort of foreigner, however, was certainly the Greeks. The himation—the rectilinear cloak of the Greek East—was almost as common on the street as the curved Roman toga, and on every other corner he heard the accents of Athens or Antioch, Ephesus or his own Alexandria.

Down the Via Tusculana they went, and down the Sacra Via, past the temple of the Deified Julius and into the Roman forum. The crowds were even thicker here, and there were far more togas. Hermogenes commented on it, and Hyakinthos hesitated.

"You can say in Latin," Hermogenes told him gently.

"Oh," said the boy, blushing. "Yes. Well, Romans are supposed to wear the toga if they have business in the forum. Otherwise they mostly don't bother."

Hermogenes was taken aback. "Should I wear a toga, then?" He had no idea how one *did* wear the garment: the drape did not look easy.

"You're not a *real* Roman," Hyakinthos told him immediately. "I don't think anyone will mind. As a matter of fact, they'd—" He stopped.

"What?"

When the boy said nothing, Hermogenes asked in amusement, "The officials I must approach would sneer at a Greek in a badly draped toga?"

Hyakinthos seemed surprised that he had guessed this. "Yes, sir, they would!" He looked at Hermogenes appreciatively and added, "That's a very nice cloak. They'll be more impressed by that than by a toga. You have to be rich to have a cloak like that, but every citizen has a toga."

"Then let us proceed to the record office—but I would like to visit a barber's first, if I can."

There were no barbershops in the forum. They walked the length of it, past the temples, the law courts, the statues, the towering-columned public buildings, right to the far end, where a particularly tall and plain building frowned down upon the marketplace. Hyakinthos led them up a stairway into an arcade of shops. "This is the Tabularium," he explained. "The record office you want. The front faces the other way, though, into the Campus Martius. We have to go through—but there may be a barber's in here."

There was. Hermogenes sent Menestor and the boy off to buy something to eat for breakfast while he himself submitted to the razor. They returned just as the barber was finishing, Menestor with a double-handful of fried sesame cakes wrapped in vine leaves, Hyakinthos with both hands and his mouth full.

"Menestor said you wouldn't mind if I had some too, sir," he said in a muffled voice.

"Nor do I," agreed Hermogenes, "but leave some for me!"

They walked into the Tabularium eating sesame cakes. Undignified, Hermogenes thought resignedly, but they were good cakes, and he was hungry.

Depositing the documents proved to be quicker and easier than he'd anticipated. While the archives had been built for official papers, the public slaves who ran it had established a profitable sideline in providing safe storage for private papers, for a fee. The face of the young clerk in the entrance hall sharpened with interest at the sight of Hermogenes's cloak, and he smiled with satisfaction when he heard what was wanted. He took the box of documents, then fished out a bronze coin, placed it across a small iron balance weight, and hit it with a mallet. The coin broke jaggedly in half, and he gave one half to Hermogenes. "You know how these work?" he asked.

Hermogenes nodded and slipped the half coin in his purse. When he came to reclaim the documents, he would have to produce his half of the coin, which the clerk would match with its mate before handing over the box. "Will you keep your half of the token with the documents?" he inquired.

The clerk shook his head. "No. I'll tag your documents and put them upstairs in the archives. We keep the tokens down here. Here, I'll show you."

He took string, beeswax, and two small papyrus tags from a box on his desk; he tied the string round the box and secured one tag to it, then attached the other to the coin with the wax. On each tag he wrote a string of letters—FIIIXLII—then glanced up. "The letters mean your documents go up to the corridor on the third floor on the forum side of the building," he explained, "and that they're the forty-second lot stored there."

He opened another large box at the side of his desk; it contained three separate compartments, each already containing numbers of other tagged half coins. He set the token in the compartment labeled FIII. "When you come back, tell whoever's on duty that it's in forum three," he ordered. "I'll put the documents there now: they'll be perfectly safe until you come back to claim them. If you lose the token, we can probably give you the documents if you tell us they're lot forty-two in forum three and describe them accurately—but *try* not to lose it, because it makes it hard."

"Thank you," said Hermogenes, and paid him. As he closed his purse again he decided he would have to find somewhere else to keep his token. Leaving it in his purse meant he risked losing it every time he spent some money.

They went back out into the forum, and Hermogenes stretched, feeling a sense of accomplishment. He had sent Rufus a letter asking for an appointment, and he had done all he could to ensure the safety of his vital documents. Now there was nothing to do but wait for the consul's response.

"Hyakinthos," he said, and smiled at the boy. "What should a visitor do in Rome?"

It turned into a pleasant day. Hyakinthos took them back through the forum, this time pointing out everything of interest (Hermogenes made a mental note to tell his daughter about the gilded milestone labeled with the distance to Alexandria, among other cities). They visited a couple of temples, which, as was common, contained many fine works of art. The Temple of Caesar the God, Hermogenes discovered with amazement and awe, contained Apelles' *Aphrodite Rising from the Waves,* a towering masterpiece of Greek painting: it lived up to its reputation. There were other famous Greek masterpieces as well— sculptures by Praxiteles and Phidias; paintings by Polygnotos and Apelles. In fact, Hermogenes thought sourly, the temples of Rome did not seem to contain anything made by an Italian.

When the glories of Art and Architecture began to pall, they did some shopping. They turned right down the narrow Vicus Tuscus, which was lined with shops. Hermogenes bought a small leather bag to keep his token in, and a jar of good wine as a present for his host. Phormion greatly admired a lamp decorated with molded chariots, but could not quite bring himself to part with any of his savings to buy it.

By this time it was after noon, and the shops were closing. Hyakinthos recommended a bathhouse. It was a big place near the bank of the Tiber, with a swimming pool and an exercise yard as well as the usual hot and cold plunge baths. The three slaves took turns guarding the party's clothes and the shopping so that everyone could have a wash and a swim. Afterward they bought some cheese pastries and sweet wine cakes from a vendor in the colonnade which flanked the exercise yard, and sat in the shade to eat them. Hermogenes bought two extra cakes and set them aside.

Hyakinthos, who'd relaxed into noisy thirteen-year-old boisterousness during his swim, challenged Menestor to a ball game. Balls could be hired in the yard, so Hermogenes paid the tiny charge for one, and watched the two slaves running energetically up and down their end of the yard, trying to toss the ball into the corners designated as goals. The thirteen-year-old was no match for a seventeen-year-old, and after Menestor's third goal, Phormion got up and went to join Hyakinthos. Menestor, laughing, protested that that made it two against one, so Hermogenes got up and joined him.

They played until they were all red-faced from exertion and drenched with sweat. Hyakinthos and Phormion were declared the winners—as Hermogenes had known they would be, since Phormion was by far the fastest, strongest, and toughest member of the party. Everyone had a drink of water and another swim. They dressed again, feeling pleasantly tired and relaxed, and set out for the house of Fiducius Crispus.

Hyakinthos eyed the two extra cakes, which Hermogenes carried himself. "I could eat one of those, sir, if you're not hungry," he said hopefully.

Boys that age were always hungry, Hermogenes thought with amusement. "These are for a couple of your fellows," he said mildly.

The slave looked surprised. "For *my* fellows?"

Hermogenes waved a hand negligently. "For a little girl called Erotion, and for her mother Tertia. I was talking to them this morning."

Hyakinthos frowned. "But they're slaves of my master. Why buy them cakes?"

"The child—because she's charming, and reminds me of my own daughter. The woman—because she seems gentle and kind, and I think she'd appreciate a cake even more than the child. I suspect that little Erotion may be a household pet. Is that so?"

The boy made a sound expressive of deep disgust. "She *is. Everybody* thinks she's just so *cute,* she can get away with *anything.* But—"

Hermogenes laughed. *You have to be clever to learn Greek, my brother says.* "She's your sister, is she?"

"Yes," said the boy, startled. "But . . ." He stopped, looking worried.

A moment's consideration showed Hermogenes the reason for the worry. "I have no amorous intentions toward your mother," he said gently. "The cake is only because she has to clean up after me, and I thought she deserved thanks."

The boy went a deep red and bit his lip. "I'm sorry, sir," he mumbled, staring at the road. "I didn't . . . I know it's not . . . I mean, if you *did,* you wouldn't even have to give her cakes . . . it's just that she's my mother."

"What is the matter?" asked Menestor, in Greek. Hyakinthos had been speaking in Latin.

"The cleaning woman I bought one of the cakes for is the boy's mother," Hermogenes told him matter-of-factly, "and he feared the fact that I bought her a cake means I intend to take her to my bed,"

"Oh, no!" Menestor said, amused. "He's always buying cakes."

"Not always!" Hermogenes protested.

"Everytime you go to the market." Menestor insisted. "One for Myrrhine, and one for Myrrhine's nurse. And every big cleaning day, one each for the cleaners, 'because they've been working so hard, and the house looks splendid.' And sometimes you buy them because one of your ships has come in, and you want everyone to celebrate. And sometimes for no reason, just you saw something that looked good, and you thought your household would enjoy it."

"Very well, very well!" his master said, embarrassed now. "I'm always buying cakes."

"We're not complaining, sir," said Phormion in his growling voice.

"My master never buying cakes for slaves," Hyakinthos stated in Greek, with more than a touch of bitterness.

"I bet he gives cake to *you,* though," said Menestor lightly.

Hyakinthos turned red again and stopped in the street. "What you mean?"

"Well—you're his catamite, aren't you?"

Hyakinthos looked as though he might hit him. "I never *want!*" he shouted. "What I do, heh, what? He is the master—I say *no?*"

"I didn't mean—" Menestor began, taken aback.

"I *hate* it!" screamed Hyakinthos.

"Calm down!" Hermogenes ordered him, in Latin. "Calm down. Menestor was not blaming you for anything, boy. Calm down."

"I *hate* it!" Hyakinthos repeated, in Latin this time. He glared at Hermogenes through tears. "Getting away today— that was so good, just getting out in the forum and then swimming and playing ball, I had so much fun—and now I've got to go back there and let him fuck me, and I *hate* it."

Hermogenes had no idea what to say. Menestor took the boy's arm and pulled him over to the side of the road. "Of course you must obey your master," he said in Greek. "I never said otherwise. Calm down."

Hyakinthos took several deep breaths and rubbed his streaming eyes. "I hate it," he said again.

"Does he hit you?" Menestor asked seriously. "Hurt you?"

The boy shuddered. "No," he said in a low voice. "I . . . I just never want." He wiped his eyes again. "He is a good master, everyone say. He . . ." His Greek ran out, and he went on in Latin, "He keeps his slaves in the household even when they're damaged. I mean, my father, after the fire lots of people said he should be sold to the mines or at least sent out to the country where people wouldn't have to look at him, and that would have killed him. The fire hurt his lungs, and he isn't strong. But the master paid all the doctors' fees, and then made him doorkeeper so he wouldn't have to do any heavy work. That was kind. He *is* kind, even if he never does buy cakes for anyone. And he keeps Stentor, who can't hardly talk, and he hardly ever has anyone beaten, and then only when they really deserve it. Everyone knows he's a good master. I do, too, even if . . . I just don't like it when he touches me. It makes me feel sick."

"What's he saying?" Menestor asked anxiously.

Hermogenes shook his head. "That his master is kind, but he still hates his bed."

"I'm sorry, sir," said Hyakinthos. He wiped his eyes again and took another deep breath. "I shouldn't have said anything in front of you." He gave Hermogenes a frightened look. "Oh, I shouldn't have! Sir, you won't tell him I said . . . anything?"

"Not if you don't want me to."

"I don't!" the boy said fervently. "I don't!" He drew another deep, shuddering breath. "Mama says I'll get used to it—she says probably I'll even be unhappy when he gets tired of me and finds somebody else. She says it's something that just happens if you're young and pretty, and there's no use hating it. She says I ought to think of all the advantages I'm getting because of it." He shook himself, and began walking on along the street again. "But I hate it," he muttered, almost inaudibly. "I hate it!"

"What's he saying?" Menestor asked again.

"That he hates it, but his mother tells him he must endure it until his master grows tired of him. And that he doesn't want anyone to tell his master what he said."

"No," agreed Menestor soberly. "That would be stupid." He hurried after Hyakinthos and patted the boy on the shoulder.

Hyakinthos shrugged the pat off, and the party walked on in uncomfortable silence.

When they arrived back at the house on the Via Tusculana, the others went on into the house, but Hermogenes paused in the entranceway looking at the doorkeeper. Now that he knew to look, he could see that the face under the scars had once been handsome, and the reddened eyes were still large and dark.

"Sir?" asked the doorkeeper uneasily.

"Nothing much," said Hermogenes. "Your son was our guide to Rome today. He did his task well."

The doorkeeper blinked, pleased. "He's a good boy."

"Does he have another name than Hyakinthos? And must I call you Dog?"

"Those are the names our master gave us," Kyon replied severely. "It wouldn't be right for us to use different ones, particularly after all his kindness to us."

"Your loyalty does you credit. Good health, then."

"Good health, sir."

He was aware of the doorkeeper staring after him as he continued into the house.

It was the end of the eighth hour, the middle of the afternoon, and Crispus's dinner party was to start at the ninth. Hermogenes went to his room to wash his face and comb his hair. Menestor was there, unpacking the baskets. Hyakinthos was with him, probably because he wanted to put off the hour he saw his master. The letters had gone from the table.

Hermogenes held out the two wine cakes in their leaf wrappings. "Hyakinthos, will you take these to your mother and your sister? Or would the temptation to eat them yourself be too great?"

The boy smiled weakly. "I'll take them, sir. And . . . thank you for buying the one for my mother. It's true, nobody ever buys her cakes, and she'll be very pleased."

He set off on the errand. Hermogenes picked up the jar of wine he'd bought for his host, then set it down again, troubled by the boy's unhappiness. He wondered if his own slaves ever found their servitude that bitter.

Menestor was smiling as he arranged things on the desk, relaxed and contented after an enjoyable day. Or was that an illusion? Did the young man ever lie awake, longing for a freedom he had never known?

Hermogenes thought of Menestor's parents and the rest of the household in Alexandria, then found himself blinking at an unexpected wave of homesickness. He imagined his daughter receiving the letter he had written that morning, running an ink-stained finger along the words that he had penned for her, smiling, sitting down to produce some badly spelled reply. He wished he could pick her up and hold her, feeling her thin strong arms around his neck and smelling the sweet scent of her hair.

His wife's hair had always smelled sweet, too.

He sighed: Myrrhine and Alexandria were over a thousand miles away, and his wife further, much further still. He had business in Rome. He picked up the jar of wine again and went off to find the dinner party.

It was a big dinner. Crispus had invited seven of his friends to meet his Alexandrian guest, and had provided a meal of three courses, each consisting of six separate dishes. There were eggs in fennel, olives stuffed with cheese, shellfish in dill sauce, sausages, Parthian-style chicken, ham boiled with figs, pepper-stuffed dates, and so on and on over several hours. The quantities of wine consumed were even greater than the quantities of food. Hyakinthos and his girl partner were kept hard at work fill-ing the cups. Kept busy in other ways, too: by the end of the night Crispus was openly fondling the boy, though he rebuked a guest who let his own hand wander in that direction. The girl was pawed freely without comment from the master of the house. She tolerated it with a glittering false smile, but Hyakinthos had a rictus grin under glazed eyes.

All the other guests were also in business or shipping, and the conversation circled around from interest rates to the dealings of shipping syndicates to the likely harvest in Egypt to the price of land in Italy and then back to interest rates again. About halfway through the evening Hermogenes found himself looking around at the drink-flushed faces and despising them, and he reprimanded himself severely. He had no cause to be self-righteous. These men were in the same trade as himself—though, from all he could tell, mostly not as good at it.

The guests had been told the reason for his visit to Rome, and the discussion of land prices provided some information about the consul Tarius Rufus.

"Rufus has bought up half Picenum, from what I hear," declared a fox-faced banker. "A hundred million sestertii worth of it, anyway."

The head of a shipping syndicate guffawed. "I would've thought that for a hundred million you could buy *all* of Picenum!"

"Good farmland," retorted an investor judiciously. "Not cheap. Where did he get the hundred million?"

The banker rolled his eyes and sketched a crown around his own head with a significant forefinger.

A financier shook his head gloomily. "He won't get a good return on his money. Everyone always *says* land is safe, but one bad harvest and where are you? And if you take farming seriously, you have to invest. Wine presses, olive presses, oxen, plows, wells, irrigation—a farm can ruin you as fast as a ship, if you don't manage your investments right. He should have put some of those millions out into buildings. That's where the wise money is these days."

"Rufus is from some little hole in Picenum, though, isn't he?" said the banker. "He didn't buy land there because he wanted a good return; he bought it because he wanted to go back there as the biggest man in Picenum."

"Biggest cocksucker in Picenum," murmured the head of the shipping syndicate, and laughed.

"How much was it you said he owed you?" asked the banker.

Everyone looked at Hermogenes, who smiled, shrugged dismissively, and replied, "Half a million, including the interest." The banker whistled.

"Well, good luck getting it out of him!" said the head of the shipping syndicate. "I hope you want a farm in Picenum."

About an hour after the late June nightfall, the party ended, and the other guests were collected by their slaves and escorted stumbling off toward their own houses. Crispus said good night and set off for his own bed, towing Hyakinthos.

Hermogenes went back to his rooms, tired, unhappy, and more than a little drunk. Menestor was already lying on his pallet in the dayroom, but he stirred when the door opened. "Sir?" he said sleepily.

"Nothing," said Hermogenes. "The party's over, that's all. Go back to sleep."

He went into his cubicle and took off his cloak, belt, and sandals. He suddenly saw again Hyakinthos's face as he cried "I *hate* it!" and his glazed expression as his master towed him off to bed.

He sat down on the bed, remembering his own first love. She had been a slave, too; most men did seem to begin that way. Thaïs had belonged to a neighbor, though, not to his father. He had seen her fetching water from the public fountain and followed her home, and she had stopped in her doorway, looked back at him, and smiled. That had been enough: he'd hung about that house for days, on and off, hoping to see her again, and when he finally did he had hurried to talk to her. She'd laughed at him, called him "young lord," and asked him what he wanted with a mischievous look that said she knew very well. He had been sixteen; she, a year older. There had been snatched meetings and stolen kisses; he had ignored work his father had set him, stayed out from home at odd hours, skipped school all day once, to meet her for ten minutes. His father had finally confronted him over his derelictions, and he had confessed all. His father had sighed in exasperation, gone off to talk to Thaïs's master, and come back with the girl, a new and expensive present. "I sell her if you don't keep your mind on your work!" his father had warned him.

Thaïs had stayed in the house for four years. Then his

father had decided that it was time for his son and heir to marry a respectable girl of his own class. He'd given Thaïs her freedom and found her work making perfume, and they had wept in each other's arms as they said good-bye. They still saw each other sometimes in the marketplace, and smiled and waved, but she seemed to have married—at least, she generally had a child with her—so they did not speak.

He believed, still, that she had loved him—but she had never had any choice about sleeping with him, once his father had paid over the sum her owner demanded. *Of course you must obey your master,* Menestor had said. Hermogenes had always believed that, too. If a master wanted to sleep with a slave, and if he wasn't married and offending his wife by it, and if he didn't mistreat the slave, then he wasn't doing anything wrong. It might cause problems to have a favorite in the household, but those could be sorted out. He had never slept with any slave in his own household since Thaïs, but that had been because he loved his wife, and, after her death, because he hadn't wanted to upset his daughter. He had always accepted other men's right to indulge themselves—but now Hyakinthos's expression of hopeless desperation would not leave his mind.

He went back to the door of the dayroom and said, "Menestor?"

"Sir?" said the young man's voice out of the darkness, thick with sleep.

Hermogenes hesitated. Menestor had never, so far as he knew, slept with anyone—and if the boy had somehow managed to lose his virginity without his master's knowledge, it had been by his own choice. Perhaps he wasn't a good person to consult. He was awake now, though, so he asked "Will Hyakinthos be all right?"

There was a silence, as though the question was a surprise. "He should do well," Menestor replied at last. "His master dotes on him. He's getting a good education out of it and all sorts of privileges. He should even be able to get his freedom. He's lucky with his looks, and he ought to do very well."

"But he hates his master's bed."

"Now," said Menestor dismissively. "But it's not as though Titus Fiducius is hurting him. He will get used to it, sir. Sir, please do as he asked you, and don't mention what he said. You'd upset his master and it could ruin his chances completely."

"'His chances,'" said Hermogenes flatly. "Menestor, would *you* sleep with a man like Crispus for *your* freedom?"

There was another silence. "Titus Fiducius isn't my master, sir," Menestor said in an uncertain tone. "You are."

"I don't want to sleep with you!" Hermogenes told him in exasperation. He hesitated again, wondering what he wanted to hear, why he was bothering a slave who only wanted to get back to sleep. "Do you hate being a slave so much?" he asked at last.

"No," Menestor replied slowly. "But I'd like it if . . . if . . . if you . . . if you freed me. Sir." His voice was full of longing. "Not that I don't like working for you, sir, it's just that . . . well, anybody'd rather be free than slave."

"Very true," Hermogenes said quietly. "Very true."

He thought of all the slaves in his house—people he'd grown up among, people familiar and loved. Did they *all* want so badly to be free? He hoped they didn't: he couldn't free all of them. There was a tax on manumissions of slaves; there were laws limiting how many could be manumitted in a will. Free people needed wages to buy food, too, and money to pay rent: unless they were paid well, they'd be worse off than slaves, who had food and accommodation free. He thought of his uncle's debt—that ulcer which was eating its way steadily into his own affairs, for all his efforts to block and baffle it. He tapped the doorframe. "I will free you one day, Menestor," he promised. He could make no promises for the others.

"I . . . thank you, sir. Thank you very much."

"Thank me when I do it." He went back to bed.

He woke next morning with a sore head and a queasy stomach to find Menestor opening the shutters. He groaned.

"I'm sorry, sir," said the slave soothingly, "but there's a letter for you from the consul, and I thought you'd want to see it at once."

He groaned again, but got up and stumbled into the day-room. The letter lay on the table, a neat scroll of papyrus, inscribed in bold black lettering with the address: *Hermogenes of Alexandria, at the house of T. Fiducius Crispus*. He felt a stab of irritation that the writer had treated his name as purely Greek while giving Crispus his full Latin nomenclature. He grimaced at the letter, and went to the water pitcher to get himself a drink of water and splash his face before he sat down to open it.

L. TARIUS RUFUS, CONSUL, TO HERMOGENES OF
ALEXANDRIA: GREETINGS.

You may visit my house on the Esquiline today
at the fifth hour.

That was all, but Hermogenes felt his heart speed up.
Today.

He set the letter down carefully and glanced round at
Menestor, who was waiting in the door to the sleeping
cubicle.

"Today," he informed the young man, "at the fifth hour.
What time is it now?"

"The beginning of the third hour, sir."

"*Again?* Never mind. I need a clean tunic and a shave.
Zeus! The Esquiline, he says. I'll have to find out where
that is."

Fiducius Crispus was still in bed. Stentor informed him
that the Esquiline was one of the seven hills of Rome, and
that it was less than a mile to the north of the house. Hermogenes considered that, then decided that he did,
nonetheless, want to travel by sedan chair. Given that either
the consul or his secretary had ignored his status as a
Roman citizen, it seemed desirable to do as much as he
could to show that he was a man of substance.

"May I ask you to send someone to fetch me a sedan
chair?" he asked Stentor. "I would send one of my own
slaves, but they do not have the Latin. I would prefer Gaius
and Quintus Rubrius, who said they might be summoned
by an inquiry in the Cattlemarket, at the foot of the Aemil-

ian Bridge, but if they are not available, then a chair with other bearers."

"The master said you could use his chair," the steward whispered hoarsely.

"I do not want to impose on him. I do not know how long I will be, and he might want it himself."

Stentor seemed pleased at this consideration. "I'll send someone at once, sir."

"Also, can you tell me where is the nearest barber?"

The steward smiled. "In front of you, sir. That was my work in the household for many years, until the master made me steward. I still shave him myself."

"Oh! Then could you—"

"My pleasure, sir."

Stentor did send someone for the chair at once, but even so it was nearly an hour before the Rubrius brothers arrived at the house. Hermogenes was waiting in the atrium by that time, walking up and down, stopping occasionally to check his reflection in the pond of the impluvium. The pond always showed him the same thing: a short, muscular, dark-haired man, impeccably dressed in a long cloak of linen dyed an expensive shade of dark red-gold, neatly draped, worn over a fresh white tunic pinned on the right shoulder with a gold fibula—the picture of confident wealth, if it hadn't been for the expression of worry. Menestor and Phormion sat quietly on the atrium bench, both in their best clothes, Menestor holding the copies of the debt documents in a leather satchel.

At last the chair arrived, and Kyon the doorkeeper announced it. Hermogenes strangled his impulse to bolt out into the street: he thanked the doorkeeper, proceeded out onto the Via Tusculana in a stately fashion, and smiled at the sedan-chair bearers.

The Rubrii grinned back and set the chair down for him. "I wish to go to the house of the consul Tarius Rufus, on the Esquiline," he told them, and was pleased at his own matter-of-fact tone.

"Right, sir!" agreed Gaius Rubrius. "Should be easy to find. Climb in."

He climbed in and held the shafts tightly to keep his balance as the bearers picked it up and set it on their shoulders. He glanced round to check that Menestor and Phormion were ready, then tried to sit back and relax as the party set off.

Gaius Rubrius talked quite a bit at first: "You're seein' the consul, sir? On business? He gave some good games to celebrate his consulship. You like the games, sir?" Hermogenes answered pleasantly but noncommittally: yes, it was on business; no, he did not like gladiatorial games—had never cared for bloodshed. Then they reached the slopes of the Esquiline, and Gaius stopped talking and used all his breath for climbing.

The towering insulae had climbed in a gray tide from the Via Tusculana and up the Esquiline's southern slope, but when the sedan chair neared the top of the hill, it came into a region of luxurious villas, set back from the road behind high walls. The one belonging to Rufus was, indeed, easy to find: the first person Gaius Rubrius asked for directions—a slave woman off with a shopping basket—gave them at once. No one who could afford a villa on the Esquiline was obscure.

Rufus's villa was enclosed, like its neighbors, and access was through a gatehouse. The gate was kept not by a single slave but by four armed guards. It was a shock to see them there—tall, fair-haired men in mail shirts and red-crested helmets, out of place in a city which forbade the carrying of arms. They eyed the sedan chair suspiciously. Hermogenes gave his name to their leader and produced the letter making the appointment. The guardsman merely glanced at the Greek writing, but studied the seal carefully. He gave the visitor a long, cold stare. "What time is your appointment?" he demanded. His Latin had a strong accent which Hermogenes could not recognize—German, perhaps, or that of some other tribe of northern barbarian.

"The fifth hour," Hermogenes informed him.

Another hard stare. "You're early. The fourth hour is only half finished."

"I am a stranger to the city, and I did not wish to insult the consul by being late," Hermogenes replied.

At this the guard grunted and jerked his head for his fellows to open the gate. "Go round the back of the house," he ordered.

The sedan chair proceeded through into a formal garden, enclosed between the wings of a tiled two-story house. There were cypress trees, and small hedges of box and rosemary clipped in complicated forms. The morning sun glittered on a fountain, and shone on the paths of immaculate white sand.

"Never been in a place like this b'fore," said Gaius Rubrius in a subdued voice. "Pretty."

They went round the back of the house, as they had been ordered. There was a stable there, with a number of horses inside it, another thing Hermogenes had not expected to find in a city outside a palace. A groom ordered them to wait in the stableyard while he fetched another slave from the house. The second slave, a middle-aged man, looked at the seal on the letter in a supercilious fashion, then instructed the bearers to take their chair into the stable and wait there. With a disapproving air he gestured Hermogenes himself toward the house.

Menestor and Phormion followed, but the house slave stopped them. "You wait there," he ordered, gesturing toward the stable and speaking in the loud, simple Latin used to address foreigners.

The two looked anxiously at Hermogenes. They understood the slave's meaning, but knew that a gentleman shouldn't go to a meeting with no attendants at all.

"The young man is my secretary," Hermogenes told Rufus's man calmly. "He is carrying documents relating to the business I have come here to discuss."

The man grimaced. "Very well. He can come with you. The other fellow stays. The master doesn't like his house cluttered with people who have no business there."

"Phormion, wait with the chair," Hermogenes ordered. The big bodyguard hesitated, then went obediently back to join the Rubrii. Menestor followed Hermogenes into the house.

The house of Tarius Rufus was even finer than his gardens. Everywhere there were mosaic floors, painted ceilings, luxurious hangings of red and green, frescoed walls. The slave showed them to a bench in a marble atrium, told them, "You're early. You'll have to wait," and departed.

They waited. Hermogenes passed the time by trying to estimate the value of the house and that part of its contents he'd seen. Houses in Rome were very expensive, he knew—that topic, too, had surfaced at the previous night's dinner—and a place like this, right in the middle of the city, must have cost well over a million even without the furnishings.

He thought of his uncle's letters to the man he was about to meet, copies of which lay in the satchel over Menestor's shoulder. Nikomachos, struggling against a mounting tide of debt, had pleaded for "at least the interest on the money!" for years, and received only insults and threats. The man who had refused to pay that money had been living in this house, and buying a hundred million sestertii worth of land in Picenum, wherever that was.

He shifted, suddenly sick with anger, then closed his eyes and forced himself to breathe slowly. *O you gods of Olympus,* he prayed silently, *and you, Isis, Lady of the Waves—don't let me lose my temper.*

He had plenty of time to grow calm again; indeed, he had time to grow bored. At last, however, the slave returned, announced, "The consul will see you now," and ushered him out of the atrium, through a courtyard, and into a lavish reception room.

The floor was a mosaic in red, black, and white; the walls were frescoed with country scenes, and there were a couple of very fine marble portrait busts sitting on ebony tables. The consul Lucius Tarius Rufus was sitting in a chair of ebony and ivory, with another two men standing behind him. Rufus was a thick-set, heavy-featured man in his late forties. His hair was dark, peppered with gray, and his mouth was thick lipped and seemed naturally inclined to a sneer, though he was smiling when his visitor came in. He was wearing the purple cloak of a consul, and Hermogenes estimated that his rings alone were worth over four thousand sestertii. There was a jug and a single cup on the table beside him. Hermogenes realized that he was thirsty, and ran his tongue over dry lips.

"Well," said the consul, giving his visitor a genial glance up and down. "You're Hermogenes, and you've come to see me about a legacy left me by your uncle." He spoke in Greek, fluently and confidently.

Hermogenes inclined his head. "A legacy? I am sorry, Lord Consul, no. I should have made it clearer in my letter. I have come to see you, my lord, about a *debt* I inherited from my uncle."

"Your uncle owed me money?" Rufus was surprised and confused.

"No, Lord Consul. The other way round, I fear. You owed him money. Twelve years ago—"

The consul's face folded into a thunderous frown. "Get out! How dare you come into my house demanding money?"

"My uncle was Nikomachos, son of Lysander, of Cyprus," Hermogenes said levelly. "I am his heir. I have copies of the contract you signed."

There was a crash of silence. Hermogenes saw at once that Rufus knew all about the outstanding debt: no secretary had deceived him. He had feared that it might be the case—there had been three different secretaries writing to his uncle, and it had seemed unlikely that they were *all* dishonest—but he had hoped that at least there had been forgetfulness and negligence.

"I told you to get *out*, Greekling!" said Rufus in a low voice.

One of the men behind the consul took a step forward, and Hermogenes heard the slave who had admitted him stir at his back. "Lord Consul," he said, in a very calm, level, and reasonable voice, "I have not come here as your enemy. You are much mistaken if you believe that." That created enough of a pause that he was able to continue. "If I were your enemy, Lord Consul, I would not have come here to you. I would have taken my documents to your predecessor in office, Cornelius Scipio, and asked him to protect me while I sued you for recovery of the debt."

Sharp, sharp silence. The consul stared at him, nostrils rimmed with white, eyes wide, the irises looking pale about the contracted pupil.

"I have no wish at all that a Roman consul should be subjected to the disgrace of being summoned by an Egyptian moneylender," Hermogenes went on deliberately. "That, my lord, is why I have come to you, and not to your enemies."

Rufus erupted from the chair, took three running strides across the floor, and hit him.

It was like being kicked by a horse. The whole world went white for a moment, then red. Hermogenes found himself lying on the floor, one hand pressed against a throbbing face, with Menestor kneeling over him and giving little gasps of shock and horror. The consul towered over his head, glaring down from a face red and swollen with rage. "That was for threatening me in my own house," he said harshly. "Very well, Egyptian. You shall have your money."

Hermogenes pushed himself up off the floor, hand still clasped against his face. His cheek was wet and his eye hurt. "When?" he asked.

"I told you, you shall have it!" snarled the consul. "Do you doubt my word?"

"Nikomachos accepted your word," Hermogenes replied. "He died bankrupt, his house was seized by his creditors, and his widow was turned out into the street."

He thought the consul would hit him again. He remained where he was, half sitting, half lying, looking up unflinchingly into the other man's eyes.

When nothing happened, Hermogenes went on, "I have heard that the consulship is a great expense. I do not insist on receiving the entire sum at once. I would accept a down payment and a schedule for repayment of the rest."

Rufus spat on him. The gobbet of spittle splashed against his forehead and dribbled down onto the hot throbbing under his fingers. "You Egyptian scum!" the consul said, with deep loathing. "I commanded the left wing at Actium. My flagship gave chase to your whoring queen, and sent her flying back to her filthy nest on the Nile. I conquered your whole degenerate nation, and helped raise Rome to the rule the world. And it's come to this: an Egyptian thief will 'accept' a down payment, and refuse my sworn word!" He spat again.

"I am a *Roman* citizen, Lord Consul," Hermogenes pointed out. "A resident of a *Roman* province subject to the emperor and to the Senate and People of Rome. The Senate and People have passed laws regarding debts and their repayment. I ask that the supreme magistrate of the Roman state see to it that those laws are enforced. What grounds is there in that for calling me a thief?"

Rufus turned away angrily and stamped back to his chair. He sat down heavily and glared at his creditor. One of his attendants came over and whispered in his ear.

Hermogenes sat up the rest of the way, nursing his face. Blood was oozing out from under his palm and trickling down the side of his neck. One of those expensive rings had split his cheek.

"I suppose you can prove your title to the debt?" the consul at last demanded bitingly.

"My secretary has copies of all the relevant documents," Hermogenes replied at once. "Menestor!"

The boy was still kneeling, shocked and frightened. He fumbled open the satchel with clumsy fingers, then took out the wad of documents. He got to his feet and looked around uncertainly. His face was white.

The attendant who had been whispering came over and took the papers. He glanced through them, then looked up at his master. "These are unsealed," he remarked.

"Yes," agreed Hermogenes. "I said they were copies."

"Where are the originals?" demanded the attendant, looking him in the eye.

"In a safe place. I assure you, I could produce them in

court. But, as I told the lord consul, I am not his enemy, and I do not wish to take him to court and disgrace him at the summit of his achievements. I am sure those copies will serve your purpose."

The consul glanced round at his other attendant, a tall, thin man with a hollow-cheeked expressionless face. The man stepped closer and whispered in his master's other ear. The consul gritted his teeth, then asked harshly, "How much do you want?"

"All that is owed," Hermogenes replied steadily. "The debt stands at four hundred thousand sestertii, as you probably recall, Lord Consul, plus six years' unpaid interest, amounting to another hundred and twenty thousand sestertii. I would accept a down payment of ten percent—that is, forty thousand—plus half the outstanding interest, with the balance to be paid in quarterly installments over the next two years. Interest would continue to accrue on the outstanding balance, of course, until the entire sum is repaid, and would be at the rate fixed by the contract—that is, at five percent. Given that the debt is in default, however, I am bound to insist upon a fresh contract, with penalties for nonpayment."

Rufus hit the arm of his chair so hard that the ivory cracked away from the black wood. "You are *bound to insist,* Greekling?" he screamed.

"While you were ruining my uncle," Hermogenes said evenly, "you invested a hundred million sestertii in land. Forgive me, Lord Consul, if I take the view that you are unlikely to pay this time unless there is some severe penalty attached to the default." It felt extraordinarily good to say that. It was even worth having been hit.

The consul went puce again. "Get out!" he ordered. "My secretary will look over your documents, and if he is convinced that they are genuine, he will arrange for you to receive the down payment."

Hermogenes climbed slowly to his feet; Menestor hurried over and helped him. "How long will your secretary need to convince himself?" he asked politely.

The consul set his teeth. The hollow-cheeked man whispered to him again. "Three days," he said at last, almost choking on the words.

Hermogenes bowed slightly, even though the movement hurt his face. "Then I expect to have word from you by the evening three days from now, Lord Consul, or by the morning of the following day at the latest. I will have a fresh contract drawn up for your consideration. Good health to you."

He walked unsteadily from the reception room into the courtyard of the house. The noon sun shone brightly from a clear sky, and the air was full of the scent of the jasmine that shaded the colonnade. He stopped, looking up at the sky, and drew in a deep breath.

Menestor hurried up. "Sir?" the boy whispered. "Sir, are you all right?"

He wanted to laugh, but his face hurt too much. Triumph beat through him in waves far fiercer than the pain. He had *won*. He had taken on the man who led the left wing at Actium and broken the power of Egypt, and he had *won*. Rufus had struck him, spat on him, and insulted him, but Rufus had to pay. He had to, or he handed his blue-blooded predecessor a weapon that would turn him into the laughingstock of Rome for the rest of his life.

"Yes," he told Menestor joyfully. "I am well."

HERMOGENES WAS GLAD HE HAD THE sedan chair. By the time he had walked back to the stables he was shaking, and he felt a desperate desire to have a long cold drink and lie down. It was a relief to collapse into the chair and rest his throbbing face against his knees.

The two Rubrii were dumbfounded at the state in which he'd returned from a meeting with a Roman consul; Phormion was furious. He gave them no explanations, only ordered them to set off at once. When the gate guards permitted the chair back into the free streets of the city without comment, he heaved a sigh of relief.

They plodded in silence back down the hill and past the blocks of insulae to the Via Tusculana. The Rubrii set their chair down by the gate of Crispus's house, and Hermogenes climbed out rather stiffly and paid Gaius a denarius. The man took it without smiling, then looked up and met his passenger's eyes with a resolute expression. "Sir," he said, "can I ask what this is about?"

Hermogenes had to consider his reply, and before he could find one, the other man went on, "See, you overpaid us again, even more this time, and . . . well, sir, wha' I mean is, I don' . . . we're loyal Romans, me'n Quintus, and we don' wan' ta get mixed up in a foreigner's quarrel with a consul."

Hermogenes gave a snort of mingled amusement and disgust. "Lucius Tarius Rufus owes me money," he said flatly. "He got very angry when I asked him politely to pay, but he has now agreed to do so. That is what this is about. Shall I hire someone else next time?"

"Oh!" exclaimed Gaius, staring in amazement. "He borrowed money from *you*? But he's richer'n what you are, isn' he?"

"Very much so. I believe the sum he borrowed was merely to spend while he was in Cyprus."

"Oh. And he flew into a rage when you asked him to pay it back?" Gaius Rubrius looked at his brother, who shrugged.

"You c'n hire us again, sir," Quintus Rubrius volunteered. "We were jus' worried it was somethin', you know, political."

Hermogenes had no energy to reply. He nodded to them and went through the door, which Kyon was holding open for him. Now that the first flush of triumph had worn off, he was feeling shaken and sick. His head ached, too.

Back in his room, he discovered that the blood from his split cheek had run down his neck and left a great blotch on the breast of his clean white tunic; it had also, to his dismay, caught the edge of his best cloak. He took both off, ordered Menestor to get them into cold water at once, and went into his sleeping cubicle to lie down on the bed while his slaves went to find washing water, ointments, and bandages.

When the door first opened, however, it was to admit Crispus, looking alarmed. He stopped in the entrance to the cubicle and looked down at his guest in dismay. "Jupiter! I couldn't believe it when Kyon told me you'd come in all covered in blood. Hermogenes, my dear fellow, what happened? Were you robbed?"

"No," Hermogenes said wearily. He wished he could have put this conversation off for a few more hours, at least until after he'd had a chance to wash and put something on his cut. Still, Crispus was his host, and he owed the man the courtesy of an explanation. "No, you were right to say that Rufus would not find me a welcome visitor. He considers it disgraceful that a victor of Actium should be asked to pay a debt to an Egyptian." He spoke in Greek: his head was aching so much that it would require an effort to speak Latin, and Crispus spoke Greek fluently.

"He *hit* you?" asked Crispus in horror.

"Hit me, spat on me, called me Egyptian scum. He has, however, agreed to pay what he owes." Something of the heat of that triumph warmed him again.

Menestor and Phormion came into the dayroom carrying jugs and a basin; they hesitated at the sight of Crispus. The businessman moved aside, and Menestor slipped past him and set the basin down on the floor beside the bed. Phormion passed in the jugs, and Crispus watched Menestor pour hot water into the basin, then top it with cold.

"Stentor put vinegar in this, sir," Menestor said in a low voice, "and some salt. It may sting. Can you sit up?"

Hermogenes sat up, and Menestor began to clean the cut with a sponge. It did sting. He became uncomfortably aware of Crispus's eyes on his body, and pulled the sheet across his lap.

"What did you do to offend him?" Crispus resumed in a strained voice.

Hermogenes sighed. "My great offense was to ask him to pay his debt. But he's afraid that if he doesn't pay, I'll go to his enemies, and that they will help me in order to embarrass him. I implied that that might happen. Titus, I understand that you don't want any trouble to touch your household. If you like, I'll leave here and find an inn."

"You're blackmailing him?" Crispus's voice was shrill. "You're going to his enemies? He's a *friend of the emperor!*"

"I said that he was afraid I would, not that I would do it," Hermogenes told him soothingly. "I don't want to involve myself with Roman factions—though, as to that, you're probably mistaken if you think Rufus's enemies aren't also friends of the emperor. Still, I don't want to get caught in Roman politics, and won't, unless my life depends upon it. I would certainly leave this house before I did. But this is beside the point. He has agreed to pay."

"You said you were going to ask quietly and peacefully!"

"I said, as quietly and peacefully *as I could.* That was how I wanted to do it and that was how I tried to do it. I think now, though, that the only way Rufus would have *received* me quietly and peacefully would have been if I'd agreed to write off the debt—and I'm sorry, Titus, but that is something I will not do."

"My master was very polite, sir," Menestor put in tentatively. "Even after the Roman hit him." He squeezed out the sponge and applied it again, tenderly mopping the half-dried blood off his master's shoulder.

"Hermogenes . . ." Crispus said uneasily. "You said you inherited all your uncle's debts. Are you facing ruin if you don't recover this money?"

Hermogenes laughed, then winced at the effect on his face. "No," he said. "No, I wouldn't be ruined. Nikomachos was very imprudent, though, and dug himself into a deep hole in his attempts to save himself, and even the sale of his estate didn't cover his debts. To meet his obligations in full, I'd have to call in some of my money, and that would cause problems for those who borrowed from me or accepted my investments. Why should I cause hardship to people who have behaved honestly and honorably in all their dealings with me, when there is Lucius Tarius Rufus—who ruined my uncle and occasioned my father's death—sitting in a palace on the Esquiline? He can pay, and he will." He acknowledged, with another thrill of triumph, that he wouldn't have dared admit that burning desire to claim his rights if it hadn't been for the fact that Rufus had agreed to pay.

Crispus stood staring at him with an expression of deep misgiving.

"I think this needs stitches, sir," Menestor commented, studying the cut.

Crispus took a couple of steps forward and bent over to have a look for himself, bracing himself with a hand on Menestor's shoulder.

"He was wearing rings," Hermogenes explained, turning his face to be inspected. "Titus, as I said, if you are concerned that this may harm your business or your household, I will take myself off to an inn. I do believe, though, that it is essentially over. He has agreed to pay. He asked for three days for his secretary to study the documents—the copies, that is; obviously I didn't give him the originals—and he agreed that if his secretary was satisfied, he would pay. I'm sure he hopes to find some kind of defect in either the contract itself or in my title to it, but there isn't one. I am going to accept ten percent now, give him a contract scheduling repayment of the rest, and go home to Alexandria."

"I don't think Tarius Rufus was really as angry as he pretended to be," Menestor volunteered suddenly, looking up sideways at Crispus. "Not at first, anyway. That is, he *was* angry, but he also thought that if he flew into a rage, my master would be so frightened by it that he'd back off. When he saw that my master *wasn't* frightened, he didn't know what to do."

Hermogenes looked at him curiously.

"That other man who was with him," Menestor explained. "Not the secretary who took the papers, the other one. The thin one in the red tunic. When Rufus jumped up and hit you, he smiled and nodded, like he was saying, yes, that's the way. Then when you'd been knocked down and you *still* asked Rufus when he was going to pay you, he looked . . . he looked like something had gone very wrong. Rufus didn't know what to make of it, either. The way he was angry was different, after that. At first it was like a master—like *some* masters, I mean—shouting at a slave to scare him, but after that it was quieter and more real. And the other man was angry, too, after that, even though he hadn't been before."

Hermogenes realized, with chagrin, that he hadn't really noticed anybody in that room except the consul.

"You're an observant boy," Crispus commented appreciatively, and squeezed Menestor's shoulder. He straightened with a grunt, gazed down at his guest for another moment, then said resolutely, "I can't possibly turn you out of my house, not after all the times you and your father received me in Alexandria, and that time I . . . well, you remember. Besides, I've been telling my friends about Alexandria for *years,* and now I've introduced some of them to you. What would they think of me if I admitted that you'd left my house for an *inn?*"

Hermogenes was both touched and surprised. "I don't want to bring trouble down on your house, Titus."

"You said you thought it was essentially over," Crispus said, with growing confidence. "No, no, my friend. You stay here. I think your lad's right, and that cut needs stitching. I'll send for my doctor." He smiled broadly and went off.

The doctor came, stitched the cut, and provided a dose of hellebore for the headache, which had not diminished.

He advised rest and a low and cooling diet. Hermogenes spent the rest of the day in bed.

He woke in the small hours of the morning. The headache was better, but had left in its place a black shadow of acute anxiety. He remembered the scene with the consul in tiny, crystalline detail, from the first genial smile to the final furious dismissal. He remembered, too, the way the consul's attendants had whispered in his ear. He was filled with a panicky certainty that Rufus was going to have him murdered.

He sat up, then leaned his hot cheek against the cool wall and tried to reason with himself. If Rufus was going to have him killed, he would have done it then and there. It would have been easier than sending men to break into Crispus's house and slaughter him in his bed. To be sure, there were plenty of people who had known that Hermogenes was at the consul's house—but who would bring charges against a consul, a friend of the emperor? Crispus certainly wouldn't. Rufus could have had him killed, but Rufus hadn't, so therefore Rufus wasn't willing to go that far over a debt which he could easily afford to pay.

It didn't satisfy him. Rufus might have delayed only because he wanted to investigate the situation first. He might want to get his hands on the documents that proved his debt and his default before he took action.

Hermogenes got up and went through to the dayroom, silent on bare feet. He fumbled around on the lampstand until he found the lighter, then struck it repeatedly, the spark brilliant in the dark room.

Menestor's sleepy voice from behind him said "Sir?"

"Go back to sleep," Hermogenes told him. "I just want to write a letter." The tinder caught, and he lit one of the little crocodile lamps and moved it over to the writing table. The gold light showed him Menestor sitting up on his pallet, his eyes wide and black in the dimness.

"Just go back to sleep," Hermogenes told him.

The boy lay down again, but remained awake, watching as his master took out the writing things and sat down.

MARCUS AELIUS HERMOGENES TO
PUBLIUS CORNELIUS SCIPIO: GREETINGS.

My lord, you do not know me, but your reputation for nobility makes me bold to approach you. L. Tarius Rufus, who supplanted you in the consulship, owes me a debt of over four hundred thousand sestertii, and I fear that he may have me murdered rather than repay it. If you receive this, it is because I am dead.

If you wish to bring Rufus to the disgrace he deserves, take the enclosed token to the Tabularium. The documents deposited there in FIII will prove that Rufus borrowed the money from my uncle and defaulted, and that I inherited the debt, an offense for which I have paid dearly.

If this information is useful to you, my lord, I beg you to ensure that my daughter receives the money for which I died.

He read it over, then pulled out the little leather bag with the token, which now hung about his neck next to the trunk key. He folded the sheet of papyrus, rolled it up, and stuffed it into the bag with the token. He drew the drawstrings tight, then melted some wax onto them and marked it with his seal.

"What are you doing?" asked Menestor, not sleepy now at all.

Hermogenes took another sheet of papyrus and wrote on it, *To be delivered to the consular, P. Cornelius Scipio, on the first of July, unless it is first reclaimed by me, M. Aelius Hermogenes.* "I want to ensure that Rufus sees no advantage in killing me," he said in a low voice. "If he knows that this will go to his enemies unless I reclaim it, he has nothing to gain from my death." He frowned. "The question is, who to leave it with?"

"You think he might kill us?"

"Yes. No. I don't know. It seems to me that paying would be by far the most reasonable thing for him to do. He can afford it, and murdering a Roman citizen must be a risky undertaking, even for a man as powerful as he is. Even if no one charged him, the rumor of it could hurt his reputation, and he seems to care for that. He seemed very indignant, though, at the prospect of paying, and he also seemed very arrogant, accustomed to thinking himself above the law. He might do it. This should ensure that he doesn't—if I can find someone to leave it with."

"So why . . ." began Menestor, who then paused and licked his lips.

"So why?"

"So why are you doing this?" Menestor burst out. "I was so scared when he hit you. I thought he was going to kill you, and then . . . I don't know, kill me and Phormion, or cut out our tongues and send us to the mines or something. You said that even at the worst this wouldn't ruin you, and I bet you could fix it so that it didn't ruin anybody else, either. So why are you setting yourself up against a consul of Rome?"

Hermogenes looked at him for a long moment, then turned away and began to attach the direction to the drawstring of the little leather bag. "When Rufus was commanding the left wing at Actium," he said slowly, "I was your age. I grew up under the queen, Menestor. I know my family never supported Cleopatra—she was a cruel, incompetent tyrant!—but at least she was *Greek*. I grew up in an independent nation." He dribbled some more wax onto the tag, and pressed his seal into it again. "She was the last Greek to rule a kingdom, the last of the heirs of world-conquering Alexander. After she died, sovereignty abandoned the Greeks altogether, and passed entirely to Rome."

He looked Menestor in the eye. "Rufus called me 'Greekling' and 'Egyptian' and spat on me. He thinks that the fact that he defeated us in war gives him the right to take what he wants from us, even now, after fourteen years of peace. My citizenship he regards as a fraud. While he was only a proconsul he felt bound to make payments on his debt, but as soon as he grew powerful enough, he thought it beneath him. To him, no Greek is any better than a slave.

"You said last night that anyone would prefer freedom

to slavery. You are a slave, and you would be willing to prostitute your body to obtain your freedom. Well, I am a free man, and I would be willing to *die* rather than submit to the iniquity of Tarius Rufus. He borrowed the money, and he *will* repay it."

"What about Myrrhine?" asked Menestor.

It was the most potent argument he could have found. Hermogenes had to look away, down at the sealed bag between his hands. He remembered again how his daughter had clung to him before he set out. "I hope I will not die," he said at last. "I am doing everything I can to ensure that I don't." He touched the little bag. "He has agreed to pay. I must find someone to leave this with—as a precaution."

The boy was silent for a moment. "You don't think Titus Fiducius . . ."

"No," Hermogenes said firmly. "If I were dead and he were threatened, he would give it to Rufus immediately. He is a well-meaning man, but he is not strong." He frowned again. "Not the record office again: I doubt I could persuade them to send it on. Perhaps a temple. I will ask in the morning." He glanced back at the young man, ironically now. "Go to sleep, Menestor, and I will try to do the same."

In the morning his face had swollen and it was impossible to open his left eye. When he borrowed a mirror it showed him the stitched gash sitting like a red caterpillar on a livid black-and-purple bruise. He sighed and resolved to spend as much of the day as he could resting quietly in the house. First, however, he had to find someone to take charge of the bag with the token. In the light of day the possibility that he would be murdered appeared far less real, but the precaution still seemed worth taking. He could not, however, ask his host's advice on where to leave the token. Crispus would undoubtedly offer to take charge of it himself, and a refusal would insult him.

Crispus came in to check on his health while he was considering the matter. He took one look and exclaimed "Hercules! You look even worse than you did yesterday." "I'll tell the slaves to make up a poultice for you. One of the women is good at that."

The woman who was good at poultices turned out to be Tertia. She came into the room a little while later, carrying a steaming herb-scented cloth on a plate and smiling nervously. Erotion was at her heels.

"You look terrible," the little girl said, eyeing him with something amounting to admiration.

"I know," he admitted. "But I expect your mother's poultice will help it."

Erotion nodded and Tertia smiled.

"Thank you for my cake," Erotion continued primly, and looked at her mother for approval.

"And thank you very much for *my* cake," her mother added warmly. "It was delicious."

Hermogenes smiled lopsidedly and waved a dismissive hand. "I have been grateful for the kindness with which my friend's household has received me, when I know I have given you extra work."

"You're very kind, sir," the woman said. "Here, let me give you your poultice."

She folded the cloth, arranged it against his cheek and

the corner of his eye, and secured it around his head and across his nose with strips of linen. "There you are, sir," she said. "I'll come back with a fresh one in a couple of hours."

"Thank you. Tertia, don't go yet. There's another thing I would like your advice on."

"*My* advice, sir?" she replied, very taken aback.

"As well yours as anyone's. You're a sensible woman. I have a package containing some valuables which I wish to leave with some honest and reliable person who will keep it safe for me until I come to collect it—or, if I don't come, send it to the person I have designated. I do not want to impose on your master, and—"

"Why can't you just leave it here, sir?" she asked innocently. "If you're worried that one of us might steal your things, you can lock it in your trunk."

"It's to do with my business," he said truthfully; and, less truthfully: "I want it available from the forum. I was thinking that the best place to leave it might be in a temple. Do you know if there's a temple to the Lady Isis near the forum?"

The slave woman's eyes opened wide. "To *Isis,* sir? No. The Egyptian cult is banned in Rome. Didn't you know that?"

He had not known it, and he was stunned. Isis was a divinity adored by men and women of all classes and nations, worshipped throughout the Greek world and honored even in the cities of the West. He had never been a religious man—his education had always ridiculed the superstitions of the masses—but he'd always respected Isis more than any of the Olympian gods. She was the Lady of the Waves, protectress of trade and of civilization; the goddess of a thousand names, of whom all other goddesses were mere reflections. And she was good and just, a wife and mother and lover, not a jealous and vindictive tyrant like so many other divinities. "Why?" he asked in bewilderment.

Tertia shrugged. "They first banned it years and years ago, sir, I suppose because it isn't Roman. I heard they were going to change their minds, and there was even going to be a big official temple, but then came the war. The queen of Egypt used to say she was Isis incarnate, so the emperor banned the goddess from Rome all over again. Since then people have kept on building temples and setting up shrines, but every now and then the order goes out, and the praetorians come round and tear them down." She paused, then added, "It's only in the city itself, sir, and the suburbs for about two miles. There's a temple in Ostia, but that's too far."

"Oh," Hermogenes said weakly.

Tertia took a step toward him, watching him closely, and with her left middle finger sketched over her breast the Isiac knot—the sign of the initiate into the mysteries of Isis.

Hermogenes had been initiated into the mysteries when he was sixteen—Thaïs had been an enthusiast of the goddess—and he returned the gesture. Tertia broke into a wide smile.

"There are private chapels, sir," she informed him. "Nobody ever bothers those. I go to one myself. I could take you there now, if you could get permission from my master for me to leave my work during the morning."

For a moment he debated whether to accept the offer or

whether to opt for some more approved divinity. Then he decided that the secrecy of a banned cult, and the bond created by his own involvement in it, made it ideal. "Yes," he agreed. "Thank you."

The rest was easy. Crispus appeared to be well aware that his slave woman was a devotee of Isis; he was a little surprised when Hermogenes declared an interest in worshiping the goddess that morning, but accepted it as an not-unnatural consequence of being struck by a consul, and quickly gave his permission for the visit.

The "private chapel" turned out to be a converted basement in a temple of Mercury about six blocks away, a place whose luridly Egyptianizing wall paintings made Crispus's Nile Rooms look positively tasteful. A young priest of Mercury had conceived a devotion to Thoth, the Egyptian form of his god, and had wanted to worship the queen whom Thoth honored and advised. He welcomed Tertia, and was pleased to meet an Alexandrian worshiper of the goddess, particularly one named after his own favorite god—Hermes, of course, being the Greek god identified with Thoth or Mercury.

It wasn't possible, however, simply to leave the token without an explanation. Hermogenes found himself compelled to give a version of the truth, emphasizing his growing belief that his fears were groundless, and telling Tertia that he was ashamed even to mention them to his host, but saying that it would set his mind to rest to know that the token was safe. At this the young priest readily accepted the little leather bag and set it behind the pedestal of the statue of Isis, in the curtained-off alcove at the far end of the shrine. They all joined in a prayer to the goddess—Hermogenes found it very odd, saying the familiar phrases in Latin—and anointed themselves with the sacred water of the Nile, of which the priest had a supply in an urn.

As they walked back to the house again afterward, Hermogenes was half-amused and half-dismayed by the way the touch of that water had comforted him. He found himself thinking longingly of the Nile—the waters that flowed to Alexandria through the Canopic canal; the blueness of Lake Mareotis in the sun, even though the water was brown when you looked down at it; the seasonal rise and fall of the life-giving stream; the taste and the rhythms and the scents of home.

Would he ever see home again? He tried to tell himself that of course he would, that it was merely a question of remaining firm and refusing to be intimidated for a few more days. Now that the token had been hidden, the consul had nothing to gain by killing him. The shadow of his midnight fears, however, refused to be shaken off entirely. He kept remembering the brutal rage in which the consul had erupted from his chair. There had been nothing there that he could reason with.

He thought of Myrrhine waiting for him to come home. Again he imagined her writing him a letter, but this time his mind threw up the image of her scribbling in happy ignorance while he lay dead in some Roman cemetary.

He shook his head. Rufus had agreed to pay. It made *sense* for Rufus to pay. It made no sense at all for Hermogenes to weaken now, when he had almost won. That would be sheer cowardice, and, even worse, stupidity.

When he got back to the house, Crispus invited him to share a light meal, and the two of them reclined side by side in the dining room eating bread and cheese and olives. Hermogenes expressed his amazement at finding water from the Nile in Rome.

"I think ships from Egypt sell off the surplus of their water supply when they come into port in Italy," Crispus told him. "There are a lot of Italians who worship the goddess. Even here in Rome."

"I had not realized that the cult was banned."

Crispus made a condemning sound. "It's a piece of idiocy that it should be! Cybele has a great temple right in the middle of the Palatine, her festivals have a place on the calendar, and her eunuch priests are everywhere. Why should Isis be banned? She's far more civilized than a goddess who requires her priests to cut their balls off!" He pulled himself up. "You know what I think it is, Hermogenes? It's that we Romans know that the Phrygians are barbarians, so we aren't afraid of their gods—but you Greeks, especially you Alexandrians, are another matter. Rome can call Phrygia her handmaid, but Alexandria was her rival."

"You are kind to say so," Hermogenes murmured.

"No, I mean it! Everyone knows that if Antonius and the queen had won the war, they would have moved the capital to Alexandria. People still hate your city because of it." Crispus helped himself to another olive, then added ruefully. "Of course, I'm Philhellenic to a fault. All my friends laugh at me for going on about how much I love Alexandria."

Hermogenes didn't know how to reply to this. He had a drink of watered wine instead.

"That valet of yours . . ." Crispus began, changing the subject.

"Menestor?"

"Yes. He's a lovely boy. Have you had him long? I don't remember seeing him in your house before."

Oh, no, Hermogenes thought in alarm. "We've had him since he was born," he said firmly. "And both his parents before him. Probably you didn't notice him before because the last two times you came he was out of the house much of the time, being educated. I started to employ him as a secretary about a year ago. He's only my valet for this trip. Normally I employ his father for that, but I didn't want to take Chairemon onto a ship. He gets seasick."

"He seems a bright, observant boy."

"He is. I value him highly." He hoped that would make it clear that Menestor was not small game, to be preyed upon at leisure.

It seemed to. Crispus looked morose and ate another olive. "I don't think the boy I have now likes me," he said in a low voice.

Hermogenes floundered in acute discomfort. "He has a great regard for you," he managed at last. "He was telling me how kind you were to his father." He still didn't feel that it was kind to call a man Dog, but Kyon himself seemed to feel differently.

"He was telling you? . . . Oh, yes, he went to the forum

with you as a guide, didn't he. Well, perhaps you're right, and he has a 'regard' for me." He looked even more morose. "The trouble is, I *adore* him, and he seems to hate it when I touch him. He cries sometimes."

Hermogenes had no idea what to say. It seemed to him that if you adored someone, you wouldn't force yourself on them and make them cry, but he could not say that.

"I keep telling myself he'll get used to it and start to enjoy it, but it's been months since I first took him to my bed, and he doesn't seem to like it any better now than he did the first time." Crispus sighed and tossed his olive stone back into the dish. "Love is nothing but heartbreak." He looked at his guest, then frowned. "Is your face hurting?"

"It is," Hermogenes agreed, glad of the excuse. "I'm sorry. If you don't mind, I think I will go ask Tertia for another poultice."

Back in his room, he found Menestor sitting at the desk reading. The young man set the scroll down and stood up when his master came in.

"Where did you get the book?" Hermogenes asked in surprise.

"Titus Fiducius lent it to me," Menestor replied at once. "He has a lot of Greek books. It's poetry."

"Titus Fiducius is a cultured man." Hermogenes hesitated, then continued resolutely, "Menestor, just now he was telling me what a lovely boy you are. I want you to know that you are not obliged to sleep with him just because he is our host. If he harasses you, come to me."

Menestor gazed at him with an unreadable expression.

"He's noticed that Hyakinthos can't stand him, has he?" he said at last. He shook his head. "The stupid boy was making it obvious. That's *stupid,* to throw away all your chances like that!" He sounded both exasperated at the stupidity, and concerned at the loss to Hyakinthos.

Startled, Hermogenes said, "If he really can't endure it, how's he supposed to hide it?"

Menestor looked puzzled. "I don't know, sir." He made a face, and said, "He should have had a master like you."

Nothing about the conversation had gone the way Hermogenes expected. "What do you mean by that?" he demanded irritably.

Menestor winced at the tone. "Nothing, sir. Only that you're never interested in boys, even if . . . even if they're pretty."

Hermogenes almost replied, "Even if I *were* interested in boys, I hope I wouldn't take one against his will!" An uncomfortable fair-mindedness prevented him: how much had Titus *known* that he was taking a boy against his will? There was no suggestion that Hyakinthos had ever tried to resist, and he'd begged the guests not to tell his master how much he hated what was required of him. The household expected him to be a good and obedient slave, and he was trying to be just that, even though his whole nature rebelled at it.

Could any master ever be certain that a slave was willing? Could the slave himself be certain of it, if the act wasn't actually repugnant? Without the freedom to refuse, what difference was there between love and mere obedience?

He shook his head, confused by his own thoughts. Menestor was still looking at him expectantly.

"Whatever happens to Hyakinthos," Hermogenes told him, trying to push the conversation back in the direction he'd intended for it, "I want you to be clear that you are not obliged to sleep with Titus Fiducius."

Menestor bit his lip. "Sir, Titus Fiducius told me I could keep this." He lifted the book slightly. "Do you want me to give it back?"

Hermogenes stared. Menestor was certainly sophisticated enough to know what Crispus would think if he *kept* a gift, especially a book of *poetry*. The young man had always seemed honest and well-behaved. Would he really be willing to prostitute himself—not just for his freedom but for a few books or items of clothing?

Perhaps, he thought incredulously, Menestor *wanted* to go to bed with Crispus. Perhaps his natural inclination was toward men, and an affair with a rich and cultured Roman, however fat, seemed exciting.

"If you *want* to go to bed with Titus Fiducius, that's your business!" he said in disgust. "All I was saying was that you don't have to."

Menestor looked deeply hurt, so much so that Hermogenes feared he was about to burst into tears, but he said nothing. Hermogenes gave up and went to look for Tertia and a fresh poultice.

The rest of that day and the next passed quietly. If Crispus did offer presents to Menestor, they did not appear in the Nile Rooms. Hermogenes' bruise faded from black and purple to purple and red, with green about the edges, but the swelling went down enough that he felt it might soon be possible to appear in public again. In the meantime, he read Crispus's books, wrote some letters, and cultivated Crispus's slaves.

The slaves confirmed his growing impression that his host was a kind master, but not a particularly good one. The nervousness he'd sensed in them from the first sprang not from fear but from uncertainty. The master frequently failed to give orders about what he wanted done, and then shouted in annoyance to find that it hadn't been done, or had been done wrongly. He combined acts of humanity, like retaining his scarred doorkeeper, with acts of crass insensitivity, like naming the man Kyon. He provided a generous allowance for the household, ensuring that everyone was well fed and adequately clothed, but he neither noticed nor rewarded anyone who put in extra effort. In consequence, the household worked much harder to please Stentor, who was competent, and who *did* notice, than they did to please the master. Fortunately for Crispus, Stentor was loyal, deeply grateful to his master for promoting him despite the childhood fever which had cost him his voice, but Hermogenes suspected that Crispus was still aware of his household's lack of devotion, and obscurely hurt by it. He wondered if he could give Crispus a few hints, but knew that he would do no such thing. Such interference in another man's household would be deeply offensive—and it wasn't as though the household didn't work.

On the morning of the third day after he first went to meet the consul, the anxiously awaited letter arrived.

L. TARIUS RUFUS, CONSUL, TO HERMOGENES OF
ALEXANDRIA.

Your documents appear to be in order. Come to my
house this evening at the tenth hour, and I will sign
your contract.

He showed the letter to Crispus, and the fat man
beamed at him. "Excellent news!" he said happily, and
slapped his guest on the back.

Then he frowned, and said, "I don't like the thought of
you going to his house again, though."

Hermogenes didn't much like it, either. He would have
far preferred to send Rufus the contract by a courier, and
receive his down payment the same way. However, given
that the consul was caving in, it seemed unwise to insult
him by refusing even to enter his house. Besides, the token
was safe.

"It will be all right," he reassured Crispus. "Since he has
agreed, there should be no reason for him to lose his temper
again, and I intend to be extremely polite."

"That's what you said before."

Hermogenes smiled and shrugged helplessly. "*I* was
polite. Maybe this time he will confine himself to merely
being rude."

Crispus yet again offered his own sedan chair. Hermogenes again declined. He did not want to strain the other
man's resolutely maintained hospitality by taking Crispus's
own bearers to the consul's house and towing his host fur-

ther into the conflict. He sent another messenger to the Aemilian Bridge for the Rubrii, and Crispus seemed relieved.

The tenth hour was early evening, but there was still a long interval of daylight left when the chair arrived after dinner. Crispus himself came out to see his guest off this time. When Hermogenes had taken his seat in the chair and arranged his freshly laundered cloak, the Roman suddenly hurried forward and caught his hand in both meaty palms. "Do be careful, my friend!" he said urgently.

"I will be," Hermogenes promised, surprising himself by a sense of real affection for the fat man.

"Good luck, then!"

"Thank you."

They set off along the route they had taken before. Gaius Rubrius did not talk this time; in fact, he seemed subdued and ill at ease. Evidently he'd found the previous visit disturbing. Hermogenes kept himself from worrying by reflecting on whether to hire the pair again. They seemed reliable and reasonably honest, but probably he would not have sought them out if he hadn't been so charmed by the idea of being carried about by Roman citizens, and probably they'd prefer a more conventional hire. Maybe next time he needed a chair he *would* use Crispus's.

The shadows were long on top of the Esquiline, and the cypress trees in Rufus's garden streaked the enclosing wall with darkness. The guards at the gate once again admitted the party after cold scrutiny, and the chair once again wound its way along to the stable at the back. This time Phormion didn't even attempt to follow his master into the house, but settled resignedly to wait beside the Rubrii in the stables.

Hermogenes had taken care not to be early again, but he and Menestor were still left sitting on the stone bench in the atrium for nearly an hour. This time, however, instead of the slave arriving to tell them that the consul would see them, one of Rufus's attendants showed up—the hollow-cheeked man who had worn a plain red tunic, and who had, Menestor said, nodded approval at the consul's assault. He was still wearing red, but this time the tunic had been joined by a short cloak—a military cloak, Hermogenes decided, without surprise. The man had never struck him as being a slave, and it stood to reason that a general would have retained some of his military staff.

"Hermogenes of Alexandria," said the man in red, studying him coldly. "Come with me." He spoke in the Greek they had all been using last time.

Hermogenes obediently got to his feet and followed him, Menestor trailing nervously behind him.

They did not go back to the reception hall where the consul had met them on the previous occasion; instead, the man in red led them around a colonnade and into a small office or study. It was empty, apart from a table with a single chair and a small iron chest with a large lock.

The military man turned the chair away from the table and sat down. "Shut the door," he ordered.

Menestor glanced nervously at his master, then shut the door. Hermogenes stood where he was, trying to keep his face showing mild inquiry and not panic. "I was told that the lord consul was going to sign the contract this evening," he said.

"In due course," said the other man. "There are a few matters to clear up first."

"As you wish. Excuse me, but I do not know who you are, sir."

The man snorted. "Tarius Macedo. A freedman of the general. I speak with his authority."

Hermogenes blinked. A freedman? He was certain now that this man was military. He supposed, however, that there was nothing to stop an important Roman from taking his freedmen into the army with him. Important Romans always relied heavily on their freed slaves. The use of the former master's family name expressed the strength of the bond.

"Very well," he said neutrally. "What do you wish to ask me, sir?"

"Have you approached Scipio?"

It was a blunt, flat question, and Hermogenes answered it just as bluntly. "No. I do, however, have a letter deposited with someone who will send it to him on the first of July, unless I collect it first. It would give him access to the originals of the documents I left here last time. My host, Titus Fiducius, knows nothing about it."

Macedo seemed more offended than surprised. He snorted angrily, then leaned back in his seat. "Suspicious, aren't you, Greekling?"

"Sir," said Hermogenes, politely, "I regret it if the precautions I have taken offend you."

"Do you," said Macedo, with a hardening of his eyes. "Your whole attitude is *extremely* offensive, Egyptian."

"All I am asking is the repayment of a debt which I am fully entitled to claim, and which your patron can easily afford."

"Well, we're suspicious, too," Macedo told him. "We want the documents. The originals, and this letter of yours. We want them before we sign."

Hermogenes stared at him. Despite the sunny evening outside, the room seemed to turn dark and cold. "Sir," he said slowly, "if your patron pays the debt, the fact that he incurred it is no disgrace, and the documents are no threat to him. If you insist upon having the documents, then I must conclude that he does not mean to pay."

"Who are you to dictate terms to a Roman consul?" Macedo bellowed, suddenly as angry as the consul had been when he jumped from his chair.

Hermogenes stepped back hurriedly. "A *Roman citizen!*" he replied passionately.

"You're a *Greek,*" Macedo spat at him. "Worse than that, an *Egyptian!* Aelius Gallus, that incompetent idiot, borrowed fifty thousand from your father to help fund his attempt to conquer Arabia—and when he botched it, and couldn't repay, he sold the citizenship to an Egyptian moneylender for remission of the debt. He was a pimp, and he made his country a whore."

"At least he did something to repay it," Hermogenes retorted. Inwardly, the sense of coldness grew. The consul must have ordered an investigation of him, to have that figure of fifty thousand so exactly. "Sir, I was brought here by a letter saying that your patron would sign an agreement to pay what he owes me. I ask you plainly, was that a lie?"

Macedo glared. "Forget the debt, Greekling. I warn you, forget about it. Write it off, and send those documents to us, and you can go home to Alexandria alive and whole. If you persist in these demands, things won't go so well with you."

"Sir," Hermogenes told him coolly, "I am a Roman citizen who holds a valid contract entitling me to collect a debt from your patron. I have no wish to shame your patron by dragging him out of the curial chair and into the courts, but I will do so if I must. If I am murdered, however, your patron will face not just ridicule but infamy and execution, should his enemies choose to prosecute him. You know better than I whether that is a course they would pursue."

He saw that Macedo considered it a course they would pursue eagerly. The man's eyes blazed, but his pale face was strained and baffled. He seemed to know that he had given himself away, because he swore suddenly in Latin, and spat.

Hermogenes drew in his breath sharply in indignation and disgust. "I do not see why repaying a debt is so disgraceful a thing that it needs *this*!" he cried. "Doesn't he have the money?"

"I advise you one more time, Greekling," Macedo said in a low voice, "write off the debt."

Hermogenes glanced behind himself. "Menestor," he said deliberately, "the contract."

The boy had backed shivering into the angle of the door, but he obediently brought out the document Hermogenes had drawn up that morning. Hermogenes took it, walked over to Macedo, and set it down before him on the table. "If your patron is willing to sign that," he said evenly, "let him do so, and send it back to me by tomorrow morning. If he is not willing to pay, he must accept the consequences. If he kills me, he must likewise accept the consequences. I swear by Isis and all the immortal gods and goddesses that I will sooner die than write off the debt which he has incurred to me."

He expected the man to leap at him as he went to the door, but Macedo remained where he was, glaring bleakly. He expected someone to come after him as he hurried back along the colonnade, but there was only calm—a gardener watering some rosebushes in the cool of the evening, a cook coming to pick thyme. He expected to be stopped in the stables, but no one interfered when he collapsed into the sedan chair and ordered the Rubrii to take him back to his friend's house. He expected, finally, that the guards at the gate would not permit him to leave—but they let him pass without comment.

He sat back in the sedan chair, shaking, and touched the stitched gash on his face. "Sweet Lady Isis," he whispered at random.

Menestor was beginning to cry. "Oh, sir!" he wailed. "Oh, sir, he'll kill us!"

"Be quiet," Hermogenes told him, though without harshness. "I need to think."

"Sir," said Phormion urgently, "sir, we're going the wrong way!"

He looked up and saw that it was true: they had turned left out of the gate instead of right, and were progressing down a wide avenue he had never seen before.

"Where are you going?" he asked Gaius Rubrius sharply, in Latin.

"Down to the main road, sir," Gaius Rubrius replied. He sounded anxious. "The way we come before, up through the back streets—tha's good for the day, but now it's evening, and you don' wan'ta go that way in the dark. We'll go down the Via Collatina to the Julian Forum, an' then across to the Sacra Via an' up to your friend's house. It's a lot longer, sir, but it's safe."

"Yes," he agreed, letting out his breath with a shudder. "A good idea." Getting caught in the back streets after dark by some of Rufus's men was a very bad idea indeed. If his body were to be found mutilated in an alley behind some insula, who was going to accept that a consul had been responsible? He told Phormion what Gaius Rubrius had said.

"I don't trust those buggers," Phormion muttered, but he relaxed. Hermogenes hunched over in the chair, trying to think.

I do not see why repaying a debt is so disgraceful a thing that it needs this! he had said to Macedo. *Doesn't he have the money?*

It was true: Rufus's response to his demand was, and always had been, excessive. However arrogant the consul was, however much he resented being forced to pay by a mere Egyptian, he risked so much now by *not* paying that it simply wasn't worth it. He clearly *did* have enemies who would be glad of a chance to disgrace him—and it stood to reason that he would, since he was, as Crispus had said, a "nobody by birth" who had achieved the supreme honor over the heads of a proud and jealous aristocracy. So why was he still refusing to pay—unless he *didn't* have the money?

How *could* he not have the money? Crispus's guests had agreed that he had acquired a hundred million through his military services to the emperor, and that he had invested it all in real property—in land.

Hermogenes shivered, remembering what the financier had said at the banquet: *Everyone always says land is safe, but one bad harvest, and where are you? A farm can ruin you as fast as a ship, if you don't manage your investments right.*

Say that Rufus had *not* managed his investments right. Say that, in his new wealth and his eagerness to become the biggest landowner in Picenum, he had bought run-down farms at inflated prices, and that he had spent everything he had on the land itself, without keeping anything back to invest in it. Say that he had then discovered a whole raft of improvements he needed to make to get a profit from his land, and borrowed to pay for them, using the land as security for the loan—borrowed not from a man like Nikomachos, whose demands he could ignore, but from a member of his own circle. Interest rates had been low since Rome acquired the wealth of Egypt, but the standard rate for a business loan would still have been 5 or 6 percent. Profit on land was usually only 2 or 3 percent of the land's value per annum. If the land had been replanted with olives or vineyards, which needed time to grow, then there would be no return on it at all for years.

Say that Rufus was, in fact, deeply in debt, unable to pay off the loans he had taken out without selling land, and at risk of losing much of that land if his creditor decided to press him. Say that he had carefully concealed this from the world, because he was afraid his powerful creditor *might* press him. Say that that Esquiline mansion was perched on top of a cliff of debt, and that the base of the cliff was crumbling.

Say that then an Alexandrian businessman turned up trying to recover his uncle's money . . . an amount too great for Rufus simply to pay out of his ordinary expenses.

Rufus would be bound to sell one of those properties he had mortgaged, and that would inevitably alert his other creditor to the true state of his finances. His total assets were still far in excess of his liabilities, but if he tried to realize them, they would collapse like a mud bank undermined by a flooding river. One or two farms in Picenum might fetch a good price, but half Picenum coming onto the market at once would see good land selling for a song.

The normal course for an important man in such a strait would be to turn to his rich friends—but the emperor was absent from Rome, and so was his second-in-command, Marcus Agrippa. Rufus had no one to turn to and no way to pay Hermogenes without exposing himself—and Hermogenes had just pointed out to him that the consequences of not paying were even worse. If Rufus were summoned for debt he would not only be exposed to his creditors but he would also become a laughingstock.

Hermogenes gripped the shafts of the sedan chair hard, biting his lip. Was this analysis correct? He had no evidence for it, except Rufus's extraordinary reluctance to pay. Crispus's friends in business had heard no rumor of any insecurity in the consular finances.

That meant nothing. Crispus's friends would *not* know such a thing. Rufus wouldn't have borrowed from merchant bankers and middle-class financiers but from his own circle, the fabulously wealthy intimates of the emperor Augustus. Men like Maecenas or Vedius Pollio, who cultivated the wealth of kingdoms, had very little to say to men like Fiducius Crispus.

If the analysis was correct, what was the best course for Tarius Rufus to take?

That question had suddenly become the most urgent question in the world, because Rufus might well answer it, "Get the Alexandrian's papers and kill him before he can expose me"—and if Hermogenes was to survive, he needed to provide an alternative.

Hermogenes picked his head up and stared out at the city, seeking some distraction from the rising tide of panic. They had descended from the Esquiline while he wrestled with the problem, and now they were moving briskly along a main road into a small public square, where an aqueduct ended in a lavish public fountain. The long June dusk was finally beginning, and street and square both were shadowy and deserted. The last of the sunset turned the water of the fountain red as blood. The only human figure in sight was a woman who sat on the edge of the fountain. She was dressed simply, in the gray-brown tunic of a slave, but the long hair tied behind her head was the color of fire. Something about the way the red light caught her, and the way she sat staring into the depths of the bloody water, made her seem frightening and unearthly, like some creature from the Underworld waiting for the hour of an appointed death. Hermogenes shivered and looked away from her. He told himself that she was only a slave fetching water—or, perhaps, given the hour and her solitude, a whore waiting for custom. There was no reason to feel this superstitious horror of her.

The sedan chair moved on across the square, the bearers walking very quickly now, as if they too found something disturbing in that solitary women. The main road resumed beyond the square, and Hermogenes could see another open space a few blocks distant, the columns of public buildings pale in the dusk—the Julian Forum, undoubtedly, where they would turn left to find the Sacra Via.

The sedan chair turned right as it left the square.

Hermogenes sat bolt upright. The Rubrii were now hurrying into a narrow alley, black in the gathering dark and stinking of dung. "What are you doing?" he demanded.

Their only answer was to quicken their pace. The chair jolted as they broke into a jogging run.

Several things seemed to jump into a sharp pattern, like a landscape revealed by lightning: Gaius Rubrius's silence on the way up the hill; his distrust of foreign moneylenders and loyalty to Roman consuls; Phormion, who'd been left in Rufus's stable with the chair bearers saying, "I don't trust the buggers." Hermogenes yelled "Phormion! Help!" grabbed the left shaft of the sedan chair, and swung himself out.

The chair tipped and swung over even as he jumped:

the Rubrii had felt him move and thrown it off. Unbalanced, he landed heavily, twisting his right ankle, and sprawled into the filth of the alleyway. The chair fell bruisingly on top of him. Behind him there was the sound of blows, but he had no attention to spare for it: Gaius Rubrius was rushing at him out of the dimness, shouting loudly.

Hermogenes grabbed the sedan chair with both hands and swung it at the bearer with all his strength. There was a crack and an impact that jarred his arms to the shoulders. He struggled to get to his feet, striking again, blindly. His right ankle flared with pain when his weight came on it and he staggered. He was aware of shouts coming from further down the alley—the men Gaius had been calling to, the ones to whom he had intended to deliver his passenger.

He dropped the chair and began to stagger toward the entrance to the alley. Phormion caught his arm and helped him, which had to mean that Quintus Rubrius was the heap on the ground; he had no idea whether he himself had downed Gaius or whether the man had simply given up the attack because reinforcements were about to arrive. Menestor caught his other arm, and between them he managed to hobble out into the square.

It was still empty, apart from the solitary woman. All the shops were closed and shuttered for the night. Hermogenes blinked at tears of pain, looking frantically around for some way out. He could not run, he was unarmed, and from behind him came the sound of men running—several of them. He pulled his arm from Menestor's.

"Run!" he ordered the boy, shoving him. "Get help!"

"I won't leave you!" wailed Menestor, and tried to take his arm again.

"Run!" he shouted furiously. It was almost too late: already the pursuers were almost upon them. He glanced round again, saw the woman watching, apparently unafraid.

"Help!" he shouted at her. "Robbery! Murder!" There was no response, and he checked himself and shouted again, forcing himself to use Latin this time. "Help! I beg you, fetch help! Tell them I will pay a hundred denarii to anyone who comes to help me now!"

Phormion let go of him and turned to face their pursuers. Hermogenes staggered, then turned as well, dropping to one knee and casting desperately around for a branch, a loose cobblestone, anything to use as a weapon.

There were four of the men, all plainly dressed, all carrying knives. They had seen that he couldn't run, and slowed to a walk, wary of Phormion, who faced them in a boxer's stance, his knees flexed and his hands high.

"Get out of the way," one of the men warned him. "It's your master we want."

Even if Phormion had understood the Latin words, he would not have moved away: he had always been a fighter. He roared an obscenity in back-street Greek and shifted his feet eagerly, waiting for his attack.

Hermogenes found no weapon but a handful of dung. He threw it in the face of the first man who rushed forward.

Blinded, the man missed his thrust, and the knife that had been aimed at the bodyguard's chest slid helplessly past it. Phormion's fist connected with his jaw with a resounding crack and the attacker flew backward onto the cobbles. It was only a momentary triumph, however: the second attacker was only fractionally behind, and his knife caught Phormion in the side. The slave screamed, lashing wildly at his assailant; the knife came out and went in again, and Phormion collapsed onto the cobblestones.

Hermogenes shoved Menestor again. "Run!" he ordered despairingly; but the lead attacker was shouting, "Get the boy alive, too!" He had, Hermogenes saw with dread, sheathed his knife. They didn't mean to kill their victim until they had tortured him into telling them where to find the documents—and if he didn't tell them, Menestor would.

Menestor didn't even try to run; he threw dung, as his master had, then launched himself shrieking at the leader as the man rushed forward. The attacker brushed him aside almost casually; Hermogenes tried to dodge the onslaught, but his ankle gave way, and he found himself back on the cobblestones with the other man on top of him. A blow against his ear half stunned him, and then a powerful hand seized his wrist and twisted his arm behind his back. He tried to struggle, then screamed as his arm was jerked savagely upward. More blows thudded against his ribs.

"What are you doing?" asked a woman's voice.

Hermogenes twisted his neck and saw that the red-haired woman had not run for help, as he'd begged and hoped: she had come over, and now stood calmly looking at the scene. In despair, he'd realized that he'd begged help of the local lunatic.

"Stay out of it, bitch!" one of the attackers told her. He was holding a knife to Menestor's throat; the third man was seeing to the fourth, the man Phormion had hit, who was lying on his back on the cobbles groaning.

The woman looked directly at Hermogenes. "A hundred denarii," she said—and strolled over to kick the third attacker as he crouched over his injured companion.

There was nothing rational or restrained about the kick: the woman pivoted on one heel and brought the whole weight of her body and all her strength onto the opposite toe, angling it in and upward and smashing it directly between the man's legs, which were slightly splayed as he squatted over his friend. The force of it lifted him a foot into the air and flung him head over heels screaming onto the cobbles. There was never any question that he was going to get up and hit back: he was blind with agony and probably maimed for life. Casually, almost leisurely, the woman bent and picked up the fourth man's knife from the pavement. With the same casual air she strode toward the man who held Menestor.

The man hesitated, uncertain whether to let go of the boy to face this unheard-of monster. The woman did not hesitate in the slightest: she shoved her knife smoothly into the man's side, twisted it, and pulled it out again. He was already falling as she turned to face the fourth attacker.

The fourth man thrust Hermogenes facedown onto the pavement and leaped to his feet. There was a scuffle, a rasp of metal, and then silence.

Hermogenes picked his head up, shook it. The woman

was wiping her knife on the fourth attacker's cloak. The man she'd kicked was lying curled up around his groin uttering awful, thin sobs; the man Phormion had downed was still groaning and only semiconscious.

"You owe me a hundred denarii," the woman told Hermogenes.

"She's a goddess," whispered Menestor in awe. "She's Pallas Athena."

Hermogenes did not believe in goddesses who kicked men in the balls and wanted a hundred denarii. He struggled to his feet and hobbled over to Phormion. It was growing too dark to see the slave's face clearly, but his fingers found no trace of breath, no pulse. He bowed his head.

"What happened to the chair bearers, rich man?" asked the woman, coming over to have a look herself. She spoke Latin with a strong accent he could not identify. "Or weren't they part of it?"

"They were," he replied numbly. "I don't know. Phormion knocked one of them down, the other . . . I don't know." He tried to pull his wits together. "They were trying to take me down there." He waved toward the black mouth of the alley. "I think they meant to question me. There may be more of them somewhere. We've got to get away." He got to his feet again, wincing, "Menestor!"

The young man stumbled over and caught hold of him like a frightened child. Hermogenes shook him loose. "We've got to get away," he told him, in Greek.

"I *said* he would kill us!" quavered Menestor. "Oh, Isis, they've killed Phormion!"

"We will send someone to fetch Phormion's body in the morning!" Hermogenes snapped. "Now we must go." He caught the boy's shoulder to keep his balance, then looked back at the woman.

She was standing watching him, the knife now thrust through her belt. She was, he thought, possibly the most frightening individual he had ever encountered—but she had saved him.

"I owe you a hundred denarii," he told her. "I will pay you at the house of my friend Titus Fiducius, on the Via Tusculana, and add another fifty denarii if you take me there now."

She grunted. "Agreed. It's quickest that way." She pointed down a narrow side street on the left of the square.

It was black as the alley where the Rubrii had been taking him. He shuddered. "Is it safe?"

She grinned, her teeth white in the dimness. "It is if you're with me."

THE WALK BACK TO CRISPUS'S HOUSE
seemed endless. Hermogenes stumbled through it
doggedly, one arm over Menestor's shoulders, leaning on
the boy heavily and gritting his teeth every time his weight
came down on his right ankle. The narrow back streets
were uneven, often unpaved, full of potholes and littered
with rubbish, so that he stumbled often. He kept listening
for the sound of footsteps behind them, but the only ones
he heard belonged to the woman, and she walked quietly,
with a steady tread.

"Who were they?" she asked abruptly, after the first
crossroads. "They weren't robbers."

He gave a sobbing laugh. "They were from a man who
owes me money."

"Huh. So why do they want to question you?"

He didn't answer at once, and she persisted, "You said they wanted to question you. I saw how they wanted you alive. I want to know who I killed, rich man."

"My name is Hermogenes."

"What is that? Greek?"

"Yes. Those men . . . I have some documents which prove my right to collect a debt. They wanted to know where I put them. Once they knew, they would have killed me."

"So you're a moneylender?" She sounded disappointed. "It's all a money matter?"

"Yes. My uncle was foolish enough to lend more than he could afford." He hadn't said that before, but suddenly the rage at Nikomachos was overpowering. "He was stupid enough to give that barbarian almost the sum of all his assets, the sum! I would *never* have done that, no matter what he threatened me with!"

"What barbarian?" the woman asked suspiciously.

His foot slipped just then on a patch of something slimy and stinking, and his weight crashed down on his right foot. He gasped and stood clutching Menestor while the pain burned white hot. The young man's flesh was warm, damp with sweat, and he could feel tremors going through it, but whether they came from Menestor or from himself, he couldn't tell.

"What's wrong with your foot?" demanded the woman.

"I twisted my ankle when I jumped from the chair," he told her, and began to limp grimly on.

"Huh," said the woman, following. "Far to your friend's house?"

He gave another sobbing laugh. "I thought *you* knew the way!"

In fact, after another crossroads, they emerged onto the Via Tusculana only a couple of blocks from Crispus's house: when he looked up the road trying to get his bearings, he saw torches blazing in the iron dolphin holders, the only lights in the stretch of gray insulae which lined the road with dark and shuttered faces. He began hobbling eagerly toward those beacons.

"That your house?" asked the woman appreciatively. "That big one?"

"My friend's house," he corrected her. "I am his guest."

"You lend him money, too?"

"No!" he said distractedly. "He is a businessman. We have investments in some of the same shipping syndicates. We're guest-friends."

This didn't seem to impress her. "Huh!" she said again.

He limped at last to the door and beat on it as though the attackers were running up the street after him.

The window in the lodge opened instantly, and Kyon's scarred face looked out. It creased, its expression rendered unintelligible by the burns, and then the door flew open. "Oh, sir!" cried Kyon, in what sounded almost like reproach, "Oh, sir, look at you! The master will be horrified!"

Hermogenes could think of no answer to that. He stumbled into the house, wanting only to get in out of the night. Kyon let him through, then moved to bar the passage of the woman following.

The woman drew herself up and declared fiercely, "Your guest owes me a hundred and fifty denarii!"

"I owe her my *life*," Hermogenes told the doorkeeper. "Please. Let her in."

Kyon stood aside to let her in, then closed and bolted the door behind her.

Titus Fiducius Crispus came running in through the atrium, alerted by the noise. He gave a cry of dismay. "My dear friend! Oh, gods and goddesses! What has he done to you?"

"Let me sit down," Hermogenes begged him.

"Of course, of course. Stentor! Some wine. Oh, Jupiter, look at you!"

Hermogenes found himself escorted through into the dining room and deposited on a red-upholstered couch. His ankle was swollen, he noticed as he sat down, and there was blood over his leg from a scraped knee he had not even felt. He was filthy and bruised all over; his shoulder ached savagely where the attacker had wrenched it, and there was blood down his front. He touched his face and discovered that the stitches in his cheek had torn and that he had a nosebleed. Various members of the household crowded around, exclaiming in horror. He was aware of the red-haired woman standing silently at the side of the room, watching him as though she suspected he meant to slip away without paying her. In the bright lamplight he could see that she was about thirty, with a crooked nose, what looked like a sword-scar across one side of her face, and cold blue eyes. Her forearms were crisscrossed with knife cuts, and she was thin to the point of being gaunt. Her tunic was dirty, threadbare, and patched, and her heavy leather sandals had been repeatedly mended. She no longer had any resemblance to a goddess or a creature from the Underworld.

Hyakinthos hurried over and set a large cup of wine in his hands.

"Some for Menestor, too, please," he said. "And for . . . for this woman here, whose name I do not know, but who saved my life."

"Where's Phormion?" asked Hyakinthos anxiously.

At that name, Menestor burst into tears. Hyakinthos at once looked as though he might do the same. Hermogenes remembered Phormion playing ball with the boy only a few days before—remembered the bodyguard's evil grin as he made yet another goal, and the strength and vigor with which he ran and dodged. It seemed incredible that he was dead. He would still have been alive if it hadn't been for his master.

"Dead," Hermogenes admitted painfully. "He tried to protect me, and they killed him."

"Rufus tried to *kill* you?" exclaimed Titus. "In his own house?"

"It was on the way back," Hermogenes informed him. He took a gulp of the wine. "I think his people told some lie to the bearers that persuaded them to betray me. I don't think it was just money. They tried to take me down into an alley where he had men waiting. It would have looked like robbers. Titus, I don't think he has the money. I think he spent it all on land, and then borrowed from somebody important to improve the land, and if he tries to pay me, his other creditor will guess how things stand with him and he's afraid of that. He means to kill me before I can expose him. I'm sorry." He finished the cup of wine.

"He didn't sign?" Titus said in bewilderment.

"No. The real point of the meeting was the ambush on the way back. I am sorry, Titus. I never intended to involve you in something like this." He rubbed a filthy hand over his hair distractedly. "I think my best option is to find his other creditor and arrange to consolidate the debt, then get out. I . . . I will go to an inn, of course, while I do that." It cost him some effort to say that: the thought of leaving this haven of light and friendliness and going out into the dark and dirty streets was almost unbearable. He had known all along, though, that Titus would not back him against a consul. He could even see that he should not: Titus lived in Rome, and would have to go on living there when Hermogenes went back to distant Alexandria.

"How can you suggest such a thing?" Titus asked reproachfully. "Look at you! You can barely walk: how could I *possibly* turn you out of my house? A *Roman consul*, and he does such a thing to a respectable citizen! A debtor, and he does it to his creditor!"

"You said the man who owed you money was a barbarian!" interrupted the woman.

Titus cast her a glance that wondered who she was and what she was doing in his house.

"Figuratively speaking," Hermogenes said unhappily. "Factually speaking, however, he is a consul. General Lucius Tarius Rufus." He could afford to say it, here: on the streets he had been too afraid.

Strangely enough, the woman seemed pleased rather than alarmed. She grinned, showing uneven white teeth. "A fine enemy you have, Greek!"

"Not by my choice. I told you that my name is Hermogenes, not Greek. Yours I do not know."

Her smile disappeared. "Cantabra."

There had been a small war, or series of wars, with a tribe of barbarians who lived in the wild mountains of Iberia . . . yes, they were called Cantabrians, and they were supposed to be savage and warlike in the extreme, which certainly fit. "That is a nationality, not a name," he told the woman mildly. "Like Greek."

"Maybe I like it," replied the Cantabrian woman. "You owe me a hundred and fifty denarii."

"And I will pay it gladly. Titus, this woman, Cantabra, came to help me when I was attacked. If it had not been for her, I would have died." *If it had not been for her,* he admitted silently, *I would be at the back of that alley now—and not dead, not for some time.* They had wanted to know where he had put the documents, and they wouldn't have killed him until he told them. They probably could not have broken him quickly or easily, but probably they could have done it.

Titus looked at the woman very dubiously, but said, "Then you are very welcome to my house."

For the first time the barbarian seemed a bit unsure of herself. She looked down, straightened her ragged tunic, and adjusted the knife. Then she looked up again. "May I have some food, then?" she asked, her voice all at once hoarse and hesitant. "And a bed for the night? It's late to find a place to sleep."

"You are welcome to both," Titus told her stiffly. "Stentor! See that this . . . this *person* . . . has what she needs."

"My money first!" Cantabra insisted immediately, with a wary glance at Hermogenes.

She clearly expected him to try to cheat her. "By all means," Hermogenes told her. "I will take it out of my strongbox now. Menestor, help me up."

Menestor came over and helped him to his feet, and with the boy's support he hobbled slowly out of the dining room and along the colonnade to the Nile Rooms, closely followed by Titus and the barbarian woman, who were followed in turn by most of the household.

He knelt beside the trunk, with everyone watching him, pulled out his key, unlocked it, dug in the trunk for the strongbox, unlocked that, and counted out a hundred and fifty denarii. It was most of his supply of coin, but he did not grudge it in the least. "Have you anything to put this in?" he asked the woman.

She seemed completely speechless at being given what he had promised and she had earned. She fumbled at a small leather strip twisted around her belt, the sort that could be used to hold a few small coins at most. Hermogenes shook his head. He rummaged in the trunk, found a spare pen case, and tipped the pens out. He scooped the coins into it and handed it to the barbarian. "Take this, then, and thank you," he told her formally: some things ought to be said. "Your courage and resolution saved me from a wretched and shameful death. I am deeply grateful, and I pray that the gods favor you."

She blushed, the color showing very clearly in her pale

skin, and bobbed her head. Muttering something incomprehensible, she backed out of the room. Stentor gestured to her and led her off into the house.

Hermogenes remained where he was, kneeling on the floor by the trunk. It seemed too much effort to move.

"My dear fellow!" said Titus gently, coming over to clasp his shoulder. "Shall I call my doctor again?"

Hermogenes shook his head weakly. "Don't send anyone out into the dark tonight. Tomorrow will be fine. Titus, I meant what I said about the inn. Tonight, I confess, I would be very glad to stay here, and I doubt very much that he'll do anything more until day comes, but tomorrow—"

"Please don't speak of it!" Titus told him in distress. "I'll have the slaves bring you water here so you can wash, shall I?" He turned to Menestor, who was leaning shivering against the wall. "And for you as well, dear boy! Dear lad, you stayed faithfully by your master's side through all of that horror, did you?"

Menestor wiped his eyes angrily with the back of his hand. "My master told me to run for help," he whispered, "but I couldn't. I was too scared. I would've been lost all on my own, and I don't even speak Latin. I just couldn't."

"You're a brave young man," Titus said admiringly.

"No, I'm not," whispered Menestor. "I was so scared. They killed Phormion. One of them put a knife at my throat, and I was afraid to move. They had my master down on the ground, and they were hitting him and twisting his arms, and he was screaming, but I didn't dare move. I was sure we were going to die." He started to cry again. "I pissed myself, I was so scared. Herakles! I'm a *coward*!"

"Dear boy!" protested Titus helplessly.

"You did very well," Hermogenes told him, feeling equally helpless. "Calm down. You are not a coward. You tried to fight them. You stayed with me, and I leaned on you all the way back. You were brave and loyal, Menestor, and I am grateful."

"I'll tell them to fetch the water," Titus muttered, and slipped out.

It was indescribably wonderful to be clean, to lie down on a bed in a bedroom in a quiet, peaceful house, with the savagery of the streets locked outside. Hermogenes fell asleep almost at once, and slept deeply.

He woke in darkness, his ankle throbbing and his face sore, certain that somebody was creeping into the room with a knife. He sat bolt upright in bed and listened.

There was no sound but the wind against the shutters, the muffled rumble of a cart on the road outside, and Menestor's even breathing from the dayroom. Hermogenes lay down again and stared up into the darkness.

There were things which would have to be done when day came, and decisions which would have to be made. He would have to report the attack to a magistrate; he would have to claim Phormion's body, and arrange for his funeral. He knew, suddenly, that he wanted the priest of Mercury and Isis to assist with the rite. He wanted Phormion to be washed with the water of the Nile, and sent to the gods with the touch and scent of home.

There was a more important decision to make first, though: what to do about the consul and his debt?

It seemed to him that he had three options. First, he could capitulate: send the consul the documents with a letter saying that he was writing off the debt and going home, and hope that that was enough to persuade the man to leave him alone. It might be the most reasonable course; it was undoubtedly the one his poor wretched slave wanted him to take. If he'd followed it before, Phormion would be alive, and he himself would be safely on his way back to his family—but it was no use considering it, because he knew already that he would not do it. Less so than ever, with Phormion dead and himself nearly murdered in the street. Rufus was going to pay every last sestertius of his debt.

Second, then, he could do what he'd threatened, and try to use Rufus's political enemies. He could write to Scipio and get his protection while he summoned the consul to court. True, he had told Titus that he would do that only to defend his own life, but it now seemed it had indeed come to that.

He still felt, however, that it was a course fraught with incalculable risks. He did not understand Roman politics, but he knew that they were both secretive and violent. There was no reason to believe Scipio would respect him any more than did Rufus: he suspected, in fact, that a Roman aristocrat would regard an Alexandrian moneylender as a contemptible tool, to be used and then thrown away. There was, too, that looming absence from the Palatine. Rufus was a *friend* of the emperor; Scipio, though wealthy and assured of privilege, was a mere acquaintance. Trying to use Scipio to extract the money from Rufus might well be an incredibly stupid thing to do.

That left the third option—the one which, he found, he had already chosen: find Rufus's other creditor or creditors, if they existed, and arrange for one of them to buy the debt. He could endure selling it on if that meant it *was* collected and he received at least a part of it—particularly if it meant financial ruin for Lucius Tarius Rufus. Once the debt had been transferred Rufus would have no motive to kill Hermogenes—apart from vengeance, which, though real, was probably not going to be as high a priority for the consul as keeping his own head above the waters of financial ruin.

The biggest difficulty with the third option was that the consul wanted to kill him. Somehow he would have to stay alive long enough to find another creditor and persuade him that he wanted to buy another piece of Lucius Tarius Rufus.

He opened the shutters as soon as the first gray light of dawn showed against them, then inspected his ankle. It was still swollen, but he could swivel it round in every direction, if at the cost of some pain, so he supposed that it was sprained rather than broken. He was not sure he wanted to see what his face looked like, but at least bruises wouldn't impede him.

He got up, then stood on his left foot and gazed unhappily at the long distance of eight or nine paces out the door of the sleeping cubicle and over to the desk in the dayroom. He found that he definitely did not want to put his right foot onto the ground.

He dropped to hands and knees and crawled into the

dayroom. He had gone to bed naked from his bath, and he had a sudden ridiculous image of what he must look like—the respectable Alexandrian financier Marcus Aelius Hermogenes, as battered and bruised as a boxer, crawling across that absurdly decorated Nile Room stark naked. He had to pause and stifle a laugh.

Menestor was still asleep. Trying not to wake him, he pulled himself up and sat down in the chair. A letter to Tarius Rufus, that was what he needed—one that would persuade the consul to leave him alone for perhaps ten days.

Pretend that the attack had terrified him so much he was going to write off the debt and go home? Would they believe that, after all his oaths and his defiance?

They might. They might say to themselves, "I knew that the Egyptian would give in once we squeezed him! All Egyptians are cowards at heart." They would still want those vital documents, though—and he didn't *want* to play the role of the coward.

He took out a sheet of papyrus, considered a moment longer, then picked up the pen and wrote:

M. AELIUS HERMOGENES TO L. TARIUS RUFUS, CONSUL, AND TO HIS FREEDMAN TARIUS MACEDO.

Probably you are already aware what happened last night near the Julian Forum, and aware that it failed. I have considered going directly to Scipio, but the desperate nature of that attempt has convinced me that you are unable to pay your debt. I suspect that your lands are so encumbered that if you attempted to sell, you would risk financial catastrophe. Should such occur, I would find myself denied in favor of your Roman creditors, and would likely obtain nothing.

Seeing that this is the case, it seems to me that I must agree to write off the debt and go home empty-handed. I am certain, however, that you will not accept this course from me unless I also hand over to you the documents which prove your obligation. This is difficult, since your conduct toward me hitherto has made me fear that if those documents are in your hands, you will instantly order my death.

I therefore suggest the following compromise: I will send you the documents when I have secured my own departure from Rome. You will then be able to destroy them at your leisure, and your enemies will know nothing about the whole affair. If you make any move against me before then, however, I will turn to Scipio and his friends. I remind you, too, that there is a letter I have left to be sent to Scipio in the event of my death—and, I repeat, it is not at my friend's house, nor does my friend know anything about it, so you will not find it by threatening him. I will reclaim it before I leave Rome, if I am able to do so safely, and send it to you with the documents you so desire. I intend to leave when I am sufficiently recovered from the events of last night. My ankle was broken, and I am currently unable to endure the

stresses of travel, but I hope to be able to depart in
about ten days.

I hope that this suggestion proves acceptable to
you. As a token of good faith, I am reporting the
events of last night as an attempted robbery, with
no blame attaching to you at all and no mention of
your debt.

I pray that the gods grant you all you deserve.

He read it through again, trying to be critical. Was that
final line perhaps too heavy-handed?

Probably—but it was satisfying. All in all, he thought
the letter would serve. There was enough of the truth in it
that it ought to sound convincing, and with luck Rufus and
his man would believe that they were going to get what
they wanted—that he would spend the next ten days holed
up in his friend's house nursing his broken ankle, and that
they would have the documents when he left Rome. They
would not want to risk sending him to Scipio by making
another attempt on him—not unless they were completely
insane with arrogance, and he did not think they were insane.

They would, however, probably have the house watched,
to make *sure* he wasn't going to Scipio or another of Rufus's
enemies. He would have to think of some way around that.

He rolled and sealed the letter, then hopped over to the
trunk, unlocked it, and got out clean clothing. Menestor
was still asleep, so he dressed very quietly, then crawled
silently to the door, resolving that another thing he would
do that morning would be to get some kind of crutch.

It was still very early, and nobody had yet come to sweep the colonnade, but a male slave whose name he thought was Gallus was watering the plants in the garden. He greeted the startled man and asked for Stentor. The slave shot off. By the time he returned, with the steward, Hermogenes had been able to crawl unobserved over to the fountain in the center of the courtyard, and was soaking his swollen ankle in the cool water.

"Sir!" whispered Stentor doubtfully. "Shouldn't you be in bed?"

"I have a letter which needs to be delivered urgently." Hermogenes told him. "I hope that it will prevent further trouble, Stentor. I very much want to avoid having any of my troubles touch this house, so I hope you can spare someone to carry it at once."

Stentor looked embarrassed. "That's . . . I am glad of that, sir. I will send someone with your letter immediately."

Hermogenes handed him the letter and advised him to tell the messenger to deliver it to the guards at the consul's gate with the information that it was urgent and should be given directly to the consul or his freedman. The steward nodded and went off to arrange it, and Hermogenes remained where he was, soaking his ankle. The carp in the pond came over to nibble agreeably at his toes. The sunlit peace of the morning seemed both artificial and ineffably sweet.

Gradually the house woke up. There was a smell of burning charcoal as the morning fires heated water and baked bread, and a sound of voices as the slaves set to work on the daily war against dirt. Eventually Hyakinthos appeared, sent by Titus to check the guest's health. Hermogenes assured the boy that he would be fine.

"Tell your master that I have already sent a letter to Rufus which I hope will prevent more trouble," he said.

To his surprise, the boy looked acutely disappointed. "You're giving in, sir?" he cried indignantly.

Hermogenes wondered how much the household actually knew of what was going on. Probably most of it: he and Titus had discussed things freely in front of Hyakinthos at least, and slaves did talk among themselves. They would undoubtedly have discussed why their master's Alexandrian guest had twice come back to the house covered in blood.

"You think I should not?" he asked mildly.

Hyakinthos scowled. "It's not up to me to say, sir."

But that was clearly what he did think. Well, he'd liked Phormion. "I am not giving in," Hermogenes told him in a low voice, "but I want Rufus to think I am." He paused, evaluating again, then added, "I think he will probably have this house watched, and he may send people to try to pick up gossip about me, so I would prefer it if he heard that I am prostrate and depressed with a broken ankle."

The boy's face lit up. "Yes, sir!" He grinned. "I didn't think you'd give up. I'll tell the others to spread the news in the neighborhood that you're . . . what does 'prostrate' mean, sir?"

"Lying down."

Hyakinthos laughed. "Lying down in bed with a broken ankle!" He looked anxious. "It *isn't* broken, is it, sir?"

"I don't think so." He lifted the ankle out of the pond

and swiveled it cautiously. "I will need a crutch for a few days, though. Could you mention that to Stentor, please?"

"Yes, sir. Sir, how is Menestor?"

Hermogenes glanced back at the door to his room. "Still asleep. He was very badly shaken, poor fellow."

"My master said they put a knife at his throat."

"They did. He was very brave, though he thinks he was not. He tried to fight them. I leaned on him all the way back."

Hyakinthos nodded, but something more seemed to be preying on him. He hovered, fidgeting, then finally looked Hermogenes in the eye and said, "Sir—could I ask you something?"

"Ask away."

"Are you . . . is Menestor your boy? Like me, I mean, to my master."

Hermogenes looked back at the nervous young face for a long moment, trying to puzzle out what was transpiring behind it. "No," he said at last. "Menestor is my secretary and my valet. He was born in my house and I have considerable affection for him, but I have never had the least desire to sleep with another male; in fact, the idea is repugnant to me. I suspect that in that I am like you."

Hyakinthos reddened. "I'm sorry, sir, if I was insolent."

"I did not find your question insolent," Hermogenes told him. Slowly he went on. "I think that you have been wondering why you find your position so bitter, when your master is kind and your family and fellow slaves urge you to take advantage of your good fortune. I understand that you were curious about Menestor, who urges the same thing. Let me say only that I do not think you are either foolish or ungrateful because you hate to sleep with your master. It is simply that you are not by nature a lover of men, and that is something you cannot help. Eros is a god, and will neither come nor go at our command. I think you have a hard lot, child, and I wish I could help, but there is nothing I can see to do."

Hyakinthos went even redder. "I wish *you* were my master," he blurted out.

"But I am not," Hermogenes replied gently. "Nor, I think, would Titus be willing to sell you. I am sorry."

The boy nodded, then took a deep breath. "Thank you anyway, sir." He forced a smile and walked off down the colonnade to report to his master. Hermogenes watched him go, wondering how much courage that took, and whether perhaps Titus would really be so unwilling to sell the boy. It would be extremely useful to have a slave who spoke Latin . . . but no, of course Titus wouldn't sell a boy he was in love with.

He might be willing to swap him for Menestor, but that would be an abominable trick to play on Menestor, especially after promising him his freedom. Hermogenes was slightly shocked that he could even bring himself to contemplate it.

He realized that he could contemplate it because he was, obscurely, *angry* at Menestor. The young man had fallen in his estimation because of that tacit admission that he would be willing to prostitute himself for freedom, and perhaps for lesser benefits. He had been no use at all in the attack, refusing to run for help when he was ordered to. Worst of all, he thought his master should give up this disastrous insistence on collecting the debt, and go home before the consul destroyed them. Hyakinthos's approving admiration had been soothing balm.

Hermogenes sighed and stirred the pond with his sore foot. He himself had forced Menestor to make that degrading admission—and when a slave was brought up knowing that a master had a right to his body if he chose to take it, how was it fair to blame the slave for being willing to make use of that fact? He had no right to be angry because of it, still less because the young man had stayed with him rather than run away: looked at fairly, that had been brave, loyal, and admirable. The crux of the matter was that he himself had taken two members of his household into a situation where one had been killed and the other nearly so, and he knew at heart that he was at fault. He was the master: they had relied on him to make wise decisions, and he had failed them. That, he supposed, was the real reason he was angry with Menestor, and if he could not help the way he felt, he should at least admit that it was cruelly unfair, and try to give no hint of it to the boy.

Hyakinthos came back, this time with Titus Fiducius. "My dear Hermogenes!" the fat man trilled. "I couldn't *believe* it when Hyakinthos told me you were already up and sending off letters! Are you sure you're all right?"

"I think I probably look worse than I feel," Hermogenes told him ruefully. He pulled his foot out of the pond again and wobbled reluctantly upright: he owed his host a full account of what he had guessed and what he intended.

"I've already sent for the doctor," Titus informed him, coming over and offering his arm. "I think he should have a look at that ankle. I presume you'll want to send someone to the magistrates, too, to report the attack and ask about the body of your poor slave?"

"I will, thank you." An arm wasn't going to be enough support. Hermogenes hesitated, then put his arm around Titus's shoulders. "Titus, what I said in the letter I sent—"

"Let's discuss it over breakfast," suggested Titus, smiling as he helped him away from the pond and along the colonnade.

Over a breakfast of bread and honey he told his host most of what he'd said in the letter. Titus sent a messenger to the aediles of the fourth region—the magistrates responsible for the area where the attack had occurred—reporting an attempted robbery and asking about Phormion's body. The doctor arrived while the messenger was setting off. Hermogenes lay back on the breakfast couch to have his ankle prodded and his face examined.

To his relief, the doctor decided that the ankle was indeed sprained and not broken. He bound it up, recommended bed rest and a light diet, and replaced two of the stitches on his patient's cheek. He departed, shaking his head unhappily because his patient had refused a dose of hellebore on the grounds that it would dull his wits.

Hermogenes went back to explaining to Titus everything he'd guessed about the consul's financial problems.

Titus frowned and shook his head repeatedly, but raised no objections.

"I think you must be right," was his final, reluctant comment on the consular finances.

"Who do you think he borrowed from?"

The Roman grimaced and shrugged. "In *that* circle? Gaius Maecenas or Publius Vedius Pollio are the obvious possibilities; they're both in the business of lending at interest. But it could have been a personal loan. It could be the emperor himself."

Hermogenes considered it. "No," he said at last, firmly. "If it was a personal loan, it would have been interest free and with no fixed date for repayment—particularly if it came from the emperor. This has to be something that put pressure on Rufus, that he's afraid will bring him to collapse. That means a commercial loan. Would Maecenas or Pollio be willing to put so much pressure on a member of their circle?"

Titus shrugged. "They're both rich as kings from business, so you can be sure they know all about commercial loans." With a touch of nervousness, he went on, "Pollio, by all accounts, is a dreadful person—utterly inhuman. Maecenas is supposed to be a gentleman, but . . . he's no longer the friend of Augustus that he once was, so perhaps Rufus has fallen out with him as well."

Hermogenes nodded. He had heard of the falling-out between the emperor Augustus and the onetime chief of his finances and head of his diplomatic service. The reasons for it, and its extent, were unclear: Maecenas had backed the emperor's nephew Marcellus against Marcus Agrippa for the succession, and chosen the wrong horse; Augustus had been sleeping with Maecenas's wife, and was resented; or, most simply, Maecenas was tired of politics and wanted to spend more time cultivating his business affairs and his outstanding collection of poets. There had been no open breach, so no explanation could be expected.

"Augustus quarreled with Pollio as well," Titus went on, in a nervous whisper. "Just last year. Did you hear about that?"

Hermogenes shook his head, his interest sharpening. There had been a lot of talk about Publius Vedius Pollio in eastern financial circles at one time, but it had been dying down, and he'd heard no gossip about him at all for a couple of years. The man was a freedman's son and military contractor—a military profiteer, most said, though only in whispers. The emperor had made use of his services to raise money during the war, and to order the tax system in the eastern provinces afterward. Pollio had become richer than any of the kings who had once ruled there.

"Pollio has a mansion on the Esquiline," Titus told him. "An *enormous* place, with huge gardens—and fishponds. He likes fish, particularly lampreys." He shuddered. "If any of his slaves misbehave, he feeds them to his lampreys— alive. Last year, he had invited the emperor over to dinner, and one of the slaves waiting on the table accidentally broke a cup of very valuable crystal. Pollio ordered him fed to the lampreys, and the poor wretch appealed to Augustus— begged him to persuade his master to have him put to death any other way then through the mouths of those unspeakable fish. The emperor urged Pollio to spare the man, and

Pollio replied that he could do what he liked with one of his own slaves."

Titus beamed suddenly. "So the emperor asked to see the rest of that set of crystal cups, as though he wanted to admire them, and he picked them up one by one, and dropped them. A hundred thousand sestertii, lying in shards on the floor! They say that Pollio just sat there, not daring to say anything. He couldn't execute the slave for doing what the emperor had done, but they say he was very angry."

"Good for the emperor!" Hermogenes exclaimed, surprised to be uttering the sentiment with sincerity.

"That's what I thought." Titus smiled.

Hermogenes had a drink of water and mulled over what his host had told him. "I think it's probably Pollio," he said at last.

Titus's face fell. "I don't see—" he began.

"Rufus is *afraid* of having his financial problems exposed," Hermogenes explained. "Unless I am wrong about the whole business, I have to believe that he sees real danger there. That doesn't fit with it being Maecenas. Presumably when he borrowed the money, he felt he was borrowing from a friend—a member of the imperial circle, and his own neighbor. But Pollio is a cruel and ruthless man, and now that he's has fallen out with the emperor, Rufus would have real reason to feel worried about being indebted to him. Pollio might want to use him to get back into the emperor's favor—or he might feel that if he ruined Rufus, it would repay the emperor for destroying his property. No, I think it's Pollio—or possibly Pollio *and* Maecenas, but it is Pollio who worries him."

"Unless it's a commercial loan from some completely different source," Titus pointed out.

"Would he have borrowed outside his circle if he could borrow inside it?"

Titus shrugged. "He borrowed from your uncle."

"When he was in Cyprus, for money to spend in Cyprus. This would have been in Rome—or, I suppose, Picenum. Where *is* Picenum, anyway?"

Titus looked surprised. "Oh . . . other side of Italy from here, east and a bit north. I've never been there myself. It's supposed to be an absolute backwater."

"So there'd be nobody there to borrow from—except people a consul could dismiss as easily as he dismissed Nikomachos?"

"You have a point." Titus sighed. He blinked anxiously. "Hermogenes, my dear, I don't like this. That man is as dangerous as Tarius Rufus, and a great deal less straightforward."

"I don't like it either," Hermogenes admitted. "But the alternative is to write off the debt, and I will not do it. Let me see if I can persuade the lamprey to kill the shark."

Titus looked at him unhappily. There was a knock on the door, and Stentor came in, carrying a crutch, unpadded and far too long. Behind him was the barbarian woman Cantabra.

She had washed, and someone had found her a clean tunic, worn and somewhat too short, but far better than the one she had had before. She was carrying the pen case with the money in it thrust through her belt, and if she still had the dagger, she'd hidden it. She nodded to the two gentlemen.

"The woman asked to see you, sir," Stentor whispered to Hermogenes. "Sir, first could you just check this crutch? We need to know how high to make it."

Hermogenes tried out the crutch, and Stentor marked the wood at what appeared to be the right height. He took it off to be finished, giving the woman a wide berth on his way past her.

"Har-mo-genes," said the woman carefully, inclining her head again in what he thought was probably intended as respect, though it looked very haughty. "I have been thinking. The man the enemy killed last night was your bodyguard, yes?"

Hermogenes warily admitted that this was so.

"Then you need a new bodyguard!" Cantabra told him triumphantly. "You could hire me. I am good: you've seen that. I was a gladiator. Two years in the arena. I—"

"A *gladiator?*" Hermogenes repeated incredulously. He knew that there were such things as female gladiators— some people liked to watch women butcher each other— but they weren't very common.

Cantabra nodded curtly. "I was enslaved when the Romans destroyed my people. They sold me to the arenas. I fought thirty times, won nineteen fights, lost two, was dismissed standing in the rest. I fought as a secutor and also as a dimachaeri. I am good. In January I was given the wooden sword and discharged—honorably, with my freedom, because I fought well. I would be a good bodyguard. People do not suspect a woman, they would not watch me the way they would a man. I would serve you faithfully and honestly for two denarii a day."

Hermogenes stared at her for a long moment, completely taken aback by the idea. He was not sure he wanted this frightening creature anywhere near him.

Titus was even more aghast. "My dear friend!" he exclaimed. "You mustn't even consider it!" He gave the woman a nervous glance, then leaned forward and continued in Greek, "I understand that this creature saved your life, and I bless her for it, but you've rewarded her generously and now you should send her off. She's a total savage. Hardened *legionaries* were afraid to face the Cantabrians in the last war, and this . . . well, look at the creature!"

Hermogenes looked. The woman was standing with her arms crossed, watching them anxiously. In the harsh light of day, she looked even thinner than she had the night before. He remembered her hesitant request for food and a bed. He suddenly guessed that since being discharged she had wandered the streets, sleeping in alleys and subsisting on whatever she could get—prostitution, perhaps, or scraps and odd jobs. Who, after all, would want to employ a barbarian ex-gladiatrix? Last night she had come in out of the black violence of the streets, and eaten and washed and slept in peace, and she wanted that gentler life to last. A hundred fifty denarii would keep her half a year at most, and it would be dangerous to carry that amount about, or to leave it in a cheap tenement. She had every reason to snatch at the opportunity of a real job.

"She has a point, Titus," he said impulsively. "I *do* need a bodyguard—and a bodyguard who doesn't look like a bodyguard would be an advantage. Rufus always made poor Phormion wait for me in the stables; a woman might be allowed into a house, and I confess, I would like to have help I can call upon if I have to visit Pollio. I agree, she's frightening, but that's what one wants in a bodyguard, isn't it?"

Titus grimaced. "I don't think you should trust her. She helped you for money: who's to say she wouldn't kill you for it?"

Hermogenes considered that, then turned back to Cantabra and addressed her directly in Latin. "I already know that you are a good fighter, Cantabra. What I do not know is how honest you are. I have seen you kill two men because I offered you money for your help, and you knew nothing whatever about me at the time. I am not saying that you would betray me, but how am I to know that you wouldn't, if someone should offer you money to take my life?"

"I did know things about you," she said, meeting his eyes. "I knew you were not Roman, and I knew your enemies were. Also, I knew that they were attacking you, not you them, and that they had laid a trap for you, and that what they were doing was not lawful. Carrying a knife isn't allowed in the city, and the law doesn't ambush men in dark alleys. I wouldn't have helped you otherwise, even for the money. Since then you have treated me fairly and honorably, and everyone in this house speaks well of you. If you hired me I would *not* betray you. I swear it by the gods of my people. I would serve you faithfully and set your life before mine."

She had, he thought, a logical mind, to set it out like that, and he thought she was honest. She was so strange and so utterly foreign that it was hard to be sure, but he *thought* she was honest. She had, moreover, saved him from something his mind still shuddered away from contemplating, and, whatever Titus might think, he himself was certain that a hundred and fifty denarii didn't repay *that* debt.

He looked at Titus. "I would like to hire her," he said in Greek. "Can you bear to have her in your house?"

Titus flung up his hands in disgust. "If you *want* her, my friend! But please, I beg you, place no reliance on her. The woman is plainly the worst sort of savage."

"You are a host whose generosity the gods themselves would honor," Hermogenes told him warmly. "Cantabra, I will hire you. I warn you that it will not be for very long, because I intend to go back to Alexandria next month, but if you serve me well I will try to find you another place before I go."

She was pleased about it, there was no doubt of that. She saluted him—a sweeping gesture with an outflung arm, which might have been Cantabrian or might have been something she learned in the arena—and grinned. "You will not regret it, I promise you," she declared. "You will be glad of this decision."

"I hope that is true," he replied.

Stentor returned with the crutch. The freshly trimmed end of the implement had been shod with a piece of shoe leather, and the fork at the top had been carefully padded with leather wrapped about wool. The steward smiled widely as he offered it.

"This is wonderful!" Hermogenes exclaimed, taking it. "And so quickly done! Thank you, Stentor, and thank—who made it?"

"Gallus, sir. The gardener," Stentor replied, still smiling with satisfaction.

"Thank Gallus from me, then. Here, give him this." He took a sestertius from his purse. He noticed Titus looking taken aback, and to his friend added, "You don't mind, Titus? I am not trying to corrupt and seduce your household, I assure you. It's only that your people have been very good to me."

"I don't *mind*," Titus told him. "And I'm pleased if they have been. But you don't *need* to pay them, my friend. They're only doing what they're supposed to do."

"I *like* to reward good work," Hermogenes told him. He tucked the crutch under his arm, got up, and essayed a few steps with it. He was clumsy, but the sense of being able to move about on his own again was a profound relief. He turned back to Titus. "If you don't mind, I need to write some letters. My friend, let me just add that I am very grateful for your continued hospitality and help. I would be utterly dismayed if you suffered any ill consequences as a result of your kindness. Please let me know at once if you see anything that causes you alarm, and I will remove myself and my people from your house immediately."

Titus burst out laughing. "Oh, gods! You think I haven't been seeing and hearing things that alarm me ever since you arrived? In Alexandria you always seemed such a quiet man—Philemon's faultless son, who respected his father and always managed his business wisely and never got into any trouble. Bring you to Rome, and suddenly you're Achilles, breathing defiance against mighty Agamemnon. It makes *me* feel like a brave young Patroclus instead of a fat old businessman. Please stop talking about going to an inn, or I'll conclude you don't like it here."

Hermogenes had no response to that, so he merely smiled feebly and limped out of the room.

The woman Cantabra followed him, and he was aware of her close behind him as he proceeded along the colonnade to his room. He stopped in front of the door and looked back at her inquiringly. He was glad of a pause: already the crutch was hurting his armpit, despite the padding.

The barbarian crossed her arms. "Lord," she said—hesitatingly, as though she weren't sure either of the title or his right to it—"Lord, now that you have hired me, you must tell me what to do to guard you." Her cold eyes glinted as she added, "Do you expect your enemy to send men against this house?"

She sounded almost eager for it, "No," he told her sharply. "In fact, I have written him a letter which I hope will convince him that I have given up, and that he will soon obtain what he wants from me."

She scowled, as Hyakinthos had. Perhaps, he thought, Menestor's unwarlike nature was not so deplorable, after all.

"I have *not* given up," he said impatiently, "but I want him to believe I have." He hesitated, studying her. She was taller than he was, probably stronger as well, and she would undoubtedly beat him in any fight. He told himself that he had taken all of that for granted in Phormion, so he should not find it so alarming in a woman. Wisely or not, he had decided to employ her, and if he was to do so, he had to trust her at least enough to let her know where the dangers lay. "Come in, and I will explain," he told her.

She frowned, glanced at the door, then said, with sudden ferocity, "One thing I should have said before, and I will say now. I am not a whore. If you think I will fuck you as well as guard you, I will go now, and you can keep your hire."

He was utterly flabbergasted. He remembered the man she'd disabled curled up sobbing on the cobblestones. Sleep with this child of the Furies? He'd prefer to take a leopard into bed!

"I do not expect it," he said shortly. "It is not something I normally require of my bodyguards."

She was abashed, but nodded, and he opened the door to the room.

Menestor was up, sitting at the writing table and staring at a sheet of papyrus with some lines written on it. He started when he saw his master, though he must have heard their voices outside the door, and snatched up the paper with a hurried, guilty air. Perhaps he simply hadn't attended to anything said in Latin. He looked tired and distraught, with dark circles under his eyes.

"What is that?" Hermogenes asked, holding out his hand for the paper.

Menestor bit his lip and gave it to him.

MENESTOR TO HIS FATHER CHAIREMON: GREETINGS.

I hope you are in good health. Please kiss my
mother for me, and greet all the household. I love
you all very much, I do not know whether I will ever
see you again. My master has sworn to die rather
than write off the debt, and last night the consul
sent men to kill us. Phormion is dead, and my master was hurt so he can't walk, but he still won't agree
to go home. I am very frightened.

He lowered the letter and looked at the boy unhappily.
"What is it you want me to do?" he asked slowly.

"Give it up, sir, please!" Menestor cried at once. "Tell
him he can have the documents if he'll leave us alone! It's
only money, and you can make more of that, you're good at
it, everyone knows. It's just a bad debt! You don't need to
make it such a . . . such a *feud*. *He* wasn't responsible for
the storm that killed the old master!"

"That's enough!" Hermogenes shouted, and surprised
himself by hitting the desk. He *wanted* to hit the slave.
Menestor flinched and bit his lip again.

"I will not give it up," Hermogenes told the young man,
leaning forward to deliver the words, harsh and low, directly
into his frightened face. "Do not ask it again, Menestor."

"No, sir," quavered Menestor.

Hermogenes leaned back on his crutch. He started to
crumple up the letter, then found his eyes snagged by some
of the phrases; . . . *I am very frightened . . . I love you all very*

much, I do not know whether I will ever see you again . . ."
He thought of Chairemon, his usual valet—a cheerful man, fussy and timid but good-natured—hearing that his only son was dead; he thought of Menestor's mother, and the rest of his household at home. He thought of Myrrhine learning that her father had died in Rome, that the family was without its head, that the steady flow of money which had supported everything unnoticed since before she was born was suddenly trickling away in all directions, lost: that her young life was irretrievably shattered.

He smoothed out the letter, set it down. He started to scrub at his face, but caught the bruises and stopped at once.

He thought of Tarius Rufus in his mansion on the Esquiline, smirking with satisfaction because the cowardly Egyptian had given up and gone home. The wave of rage that swept him made him feel physically sick.

"I *cannot* give it up," he said, more quietly. "Menestor. I have promised to free you one day; this is probably a good time. You deserve some reward for your faithful service last night. You can get out of this, and I will pay your fare back to Alexandria."

He had expected relief and gratitude, but Menestor looked at him in hurt and confusion. "You're sending me away because I'm a coward?" he asked.

"Isn't that what you want?" Hermogenes shouted, losing his temper again. "You *begged* me just now to get you out of this!"

"No, sir, I didn't!" Menestor shouted back. "I begged *you* to get out of it. But I won't, not again." He picked his letter up angrily and folded it in half, snapping the brittle papyrus.

Hermogenes glared at him helplessly, wondering if the boy had always been so senseless and contradictory, or whether it was an effect of adolescence. "You may send a letter," he said in a cold voice. "Though I ask that you show it to me first, and that you tell your father to keep it to himself until we have returned safely: I do not want you frightening Myrrhine and the household for nothing. I will also take steps to free you, even if you do choose not to be pleased about it. When you are your own man you can decide for yourself whether to stay with me or not. Now, get out. Get yourself something to eat."

Menestor got up sullen and resentful, and started for the door. He paused, as though for the first time noticing the barbarian woman standing there. Hermogenes realized that Cantabra would have understood nothing of the scene just played out in front of her; they had spoken entirely in Greek.

"I have hired Cantabra as a bodyguard," he informed Menestor, remembering that the boy knew nothing that had happened that morning. "And I have sent Rufus a letter which I hope will keep him from our throats for the next ten days, while I take other measures. I do not intend to die. Get yourself some breakfast."

Menestor flushed, edged past Cantabra, and went off. Hermogenes sat down heavily and ran his hands through his hair.

The barbarian woman slipped into the room and shut the door. She looked around at the decor curiously, then turned her attention back to her employer. "You said you would explain," she reminded him.

"Yes," he agreed; then exclaimed angrily, "That boy seems to have become incapable of reason!"

"Huh!" snorted Cantabra. "Young men are never capable of reason. Lord, explain to me first who that one is. When I first saw you, he was walking behind your chair like a slave, but he kept to your side like a kinsman, and you speak to him like a commander to one of his trusted men."

"I do?" he asked, startled.

The woman's blue eyes met his own levelly. "You spoke just now like a commander to a follower who had lost heart and was urging him to surrender."

He laughed bitterly. "You understood that? Do you understand some Greek after all, then?"

She shook her head. "I understood only the voices, not the words. It's clear, though, that that one is frightened, and you are preparing to fight. Is this young man Menestor your follower or your kinsman?"

"Neither. Your first guess was correct: he is my slave— though I have just decided to give him his freedom."

She looked at him steadily a moment. "You are a strange man."

That from a female gladiator! He laughed again, more naturally this time. "A fit employer, then, for a *very* strange woman. Let me explain our situation to you."

He ended up telling her nearly all of it: the loan, Nikomachos's bankruptcy, his father's drowning; his own threats to the consul to persuade him to pay; his suspicions about Rufus's finances; the letter he had written that morning. She listened attentively, occasionally asking a question. It was clear that she knew nothing whatsoever about contracts, debts, and finance, but she understood Roman power very well.

When he'd finished she asked at once, "So you wish to ruin your enemy to get revenge upon him?"

He shrugged. "I will be pleased if he is ruined. But what I *want* is for him to pay his debt." He glanced over the table and picked up a sheet of papyrus.

Cantabra blinked, then stood silently frowning while he collected ink and a pen. "I do not understand," she said suddenly as he was just about to begin to write.

He set the pen down and looked at her impatiently. She bobbed her head. "Forgive me, lord, but if I do not understand what it is you want to do, it is hard to know what to do to serve you. Last night when you said you were attacked because of a debt, I thought it was all a matter of money. Then I learned more, and I thought no, it is a *fight* between a Roman and a Greek, and money is only the thing the fight is about. Just now it sounded to me as though what you really wanted was revenge. But when I said so, you said no, all you want is the money."

"That was not what I said at all! I said I want him to *pay*."

"Isn't that the same thing?"

"Not at all! He thinks that he has no need to pay his debts to a Greek. He was furious at the idea that a victor of Actium could be summoned for debt by an Egyptian moneylender—as though that victory had given him the right to take whatever he wanted from me! If I make him pay, I show him that Actium counts for nothing. He may have conquered, and he may be a Roman and a consul, but he is still bound by the same law that binds me, and he cannot treat me as a slave. Yes, very well, you are right, and it *is* a fight. The way I win is if he is forced to *pay,* despite all his arrogance! Whether or not he is ruined is merely incidental."

"The Romans treat all other nations as slaves," said Cantabra in a low voice. "My people found that. We were conquered and oppressed. We rose against them, and were defeated again, and oppressed more savagely. The third war was the last. My husband swore that he would never accept slavery, and he went into the mountains with the rest of the men to continue the war to the end. When there was no way out, they killed themselves rather than surrender. And what happened? His children were murdered, and his wife became a slave."

He looked at her in shock. "You had children?" He could not imagine her as a mother.

"Two. They were killed," she replied bleakly. They were both silent, looking at each other, and then she said, "Maybe the Greeks are different. The Romans learn your language, they imitate you. I've seen that. They would laugh at the idea of copying anything from *us*. They never considered us to be any better than wild animals. Maybe you can force this Roman to yield. I would like to see that." She tossed her head suddenly, her face fierce. "Yes, I would like to see you humble him! What will you do?"

"The first thing is to find his other creditor," he told her. Inwardly, he was shaken, still trying to take in what she had said. Did she really mean that *all* the men in the last Cantabrian uprising had committed suicide rather than surrender? He realized that he had assumed all his life that Greeks were superior to any sort of barbarian, but he had never really considered how lucky he was that the Romans thought so, too. He had never really spoken to a barbarian before.

"You said that you think you know who it is," Cantabra said hopefully.

He shook his head, trying to clear it. "I have a good guess. I will write to him: that is the next thing. Then I must get someone to deliver the letter—which may be complicated. I suspect that the consul will have this house watched, and if he discovers that I'm trying to contact his other creditor, he'll probably try to kill me at once, even if he has to have his men break down the door to do it."

"Let me deliver your letter," Cantabra told him eagerly. "I know how to go unseen. Give it to me, and the consul will suspect nothing, until you ruin him."

Hermogenes hesitated, regarding her uncertainly. He had only just hired her: he might *think* she was honest, but how could he be sure? Suppose she took the letter to Rufus instead of to Pollio? The consul would probably pay her well for it.

On the other hand, who else could he send on such a delicate errand? He did not want to involve Titus's people any more than he had to, and sending Menestor would have been out of the question even if the boy spoke Latin.

He recognized, grimly, how absurd it was to try to humble a Roman consul when all the resources he could draw upon were one fat timid businessman, one frightened slave, and one untried barbarian hireling. Undoubtedly it would be wiser to do what Menestor wanted him to do, and go home. It wasn't as though the money, if he ever got it, would restore his father—or Phormion.

If he gave up, Rufus would win. Theft, robbery, and murder: Rufus would have subjected him to them all, and emerged triumphant and unscathed, the victor of Actium celebrating another Egyptian defeat. No. His own resources might be slight, but Pollio's were undoubtedly more substantial, if he could enlist them. He *thought* the barbarian was honest. She certainly had reason to hate the Romans, and she seemed eager to help. He would trust her.

"Very well," he told her. "I will write the letter now."

MARCUS AELIUS HERMOGENES RESPECTFULLY
GREETS PUBLIUS VEDIUS POLLIO.

Sir, you do not know me, but I am emboldened to
write to you because I believe we may have a business interest in common. I have inherited the right
to claim an outstanding debt from the consul L. Tarius Rufus, and I have come to believe that the same
man may also have borrowed from you. If that is the
case, may I apply for an appointment with you at
your convenience to discuss matters of mutual
interest?

    If I am mistaken, please accept my apologies for

troubling a gentleman of your distinction unnecessarily. I pray that the gods grant you health.

"What does it say?" Cantabra asked, leaning over his shoulder to frown at the letter.

He told her, tying and sealing it as he did so.

"You give away nothing," she commented, frowning.

"Indeed," Hermogenes agreed. "If he is not the man I want, I do not want to attract his interest, and perhaps have him interfere. If he is the man I want, I do not want him to know how hard I am being pressed, or he will expect me to sell him the debt for nothing."

She nodded understanding. "He may ask to question the messenger who brings this. What should I say if he does? He should at least be warned not to send a messenger back to you openly."

He hadn't thought of that. Titus and Stentor had come in while he was writing the letter to inform him that there were men watching the house. Titus had been dismayed and Stentor, grim. He hoped he'd managed to convince them that it was a sign that Rufus had believed his letter and decided to watch and wait—a *good* sign!—but he understood their unhappiness. In this residential area it would have been hard for Rufus to have set up his watch discreetly, but it seemed as though he hadn't even tried: he had four blond barbarians leaning against the wall of the insula opposite watching the house door. The blatant nature of the move was probably intended to intimidate, but it still seemed to Hermogenes very stupid. People would notice, and wonder why someone who could employ barbarian guardsmen was watching the house of a respectable middle-class businessman. It could even come to the attention of Rufus's enemies, and cause the catastrophe the consul was trying to avoid. A part of his mind was still worrying at that, wondering whether Rufus really was that arrogant and short-sighted, or whether there was some aspect of the move which he had not grasped.

"If he questions you," he said slowly, "tell him that you do not know what is in the letter, and that I only hired you after my own bodyguard was killed in a robbery. Say you think I have some disagreement with the consul, but try not to make too much of it. I agree, you must warn him not to send a messenger openly—but try to make it sound as though you might have got something wrong, so that he only takes the precaution *in case*. Offer to carry the reply yourself."

She nodded again, then grinned. "I will be a stupid barbarian who thinks mostly about what to put in her stomach, who can be trusted to deliver a letter, but nothing more. I will give away no more than you do."

He smiled back, pleased at this ready, rapid connivance, and handed her the letter. She stuffed it down the front of her tunic and tightened her belt. "The men watching will see that I leave the house with nothing in my hands or at my belt," she explained. She hesitated, then pulled the pen case with the money he'd given her out of her belt and set it down on the table. "I will leave this here," she told him, meeting his eyes.

"I will keep it safe," he promised her immediately. "Here." He maneuvered himself over to his trunk, unlocked it, and set the pen case inside. "That's so that the household slaves will not be tempted by it," he told her. "All hundred and fifty denarii will sit there to await your return."

"It is a hundred and forty-five now," she corrected him unsmilingly. "I have five here." She touched the strip of leather at her belt, then started off with a long, confident stride.

He limped after her along the colonnade to the atrium. In the entranceway, she glanced at him, and said, "You should move away from the door, lord, in case they see you. You are supposed to be in bed with a broken ankle."

He grinned. She was quick. "How do *you* intend to escape the attention of our friends across the road?"

"I do not. I will let them see me go down the road towards the forum, where I will buy some small things. I think probably that will satisfy them, but if they still follow me, it will be easy to lose them at a shop. Then I will go to the house of Pollio on the Esquiline, and wait to see if he wishes to send you a reply. Yes?"

"Perfect. Be careful."

"I am a careful woman, lord. Move back from the door."

When she had gone, he limped back into the atrium and sat down on the bench with his leg up, leaning against the crutch. He felt as drained and exhausted as if he'd been working without a pause for days—and it was still nearly an hour until noon.

The prolonged day was not over, however. Cantabra

had scarcely departed when there was another knock on the door. A moment later, Kyon summoned Titus: a young man from the office of the aediles of the fourth region, to whom they'd reported the attack, had arrived to inquire about the robbery. With him came two public slaves, carrying a litter on which lay a shapeless bundle wrapped in a torn sheet.

Titus stared at it as it was carried into the atrium, and began to wring his hands. The young aedile—a self-important pimply youth no older than nineteen—informed the master of the house that he'd come about the reported robbery, and asked if *this* was his murdered slave?

"No, no!" protested Titus. "My guest's!" He waved his arm toward Hermogenes, who was still sitting in the atrium. "Oh, Hercules, what a dreadful thing!"

The aedile stared at Hermogenes' battered face and bandaged foot a moment, then asked intelligently, "I suppose it was you who was robbed, then? Is this your slave?"

Hermogenes agreed that he had been the one attacked, and asked if they could uncover the body.

It was, indeed, Phormion. He looked smaller in death. His familiar features were set in an expression of savagery and rage, and his shrunken eyes seemed to stare in mute accusation.

Hermogenes discovered that he could not bear that gaze. He hauled himself off the bench, struggled over to the body with the aid of the crutch, and knelt down to close the staring eyes.

They would not shut. The eyes had dried overnight, and

the lids were glued open. Hermogenes found his hand shaking, and he drew it back. Some swollen dark emotion rose and pressed itself against his throat, and he found that he could not speak. He pressed the back of his hand against his mouth, trying to swallow the sobs rising in his gorge like sickness.

Titus exclaimed. He hurried over and pressed his guest's shoulder. "Oh, my poor friend!" he said; and, to the aedile, "Cover it quickly! You've upset him."

The public slaves covered Phormion again, and Titus helped his guest back to the bench and sat him down. Hermogenes bent over double, trembling, remembering with a horrifying vividness how the attacker's knife had gone into Phormion, and how he had screamed—remembering how he himself had been forced to the cobblestones, his arm twisted behind his back and the blows thudding into his ribs. All the self-possession he had clung to at the time seemed to have been ripped away, and he felt like a frightened child.

The aedile was talking officiously, describing how the body had been found in the square by the public fountain that morning. For a time the words simply washed over him without making sense—but suddenly he found himself alert again, realizing that Phormion's was the *only* body that had been found in the square that morning. The corpses of the two attackers must have been removed.

He was relieved, even through the tide of memory. He had been reasonably confident that nobody could convict him or his new bodyguard of *murdering* those two—but trouble over it had certainly been a possibility. Presumably one of the two injured attackers had recovered sufficiently to report to his patron, who had sent men to remove the bodies before any authority could trace them back to the man who'd sent them.

The aedile took out a set of wax tablets and asked him to describe what had happened. Hermogenes uttered a mixture of truth and falsehood: he had been on his way back from a business meeting on the Esquiline when he was attacked by robbers. (He described them honestly, as well as he could: it was easier than making it up, and probably just as little use to anyone who wanted to find the men.) The hired chair bearers had thrown down the chair and fled; no, he couldn't remember their names, they were simply men he'd hired that afternoon. The fall had broken his ankle. (It seemed as well to be consistent about that.) Phormion had tried to defend him, and had struck one of the attackers, knocking him out; he and his other slave had thrown things and struggled with the others. When a woman of the neighborhood had come to help them, the attackers had fled.

"Well, I'm afraid that's a common story," said the aedile, shaking his head. "The Subura's not safe after dark, and dusk is actually worse than later on at night. Later on you get the carts coming through, but at dusk there's nobody to call on for help. You were lucky to find anyone in the neighborhood willing to answer you: mostly they're wonderfully good at ignoring things. We find bodies four or five times a month—and who knows how many we *don't* find, because they've been thrown into a sewer or taken to the Tiber and tipped in?"

"I was in the Subura?" he asked in surprise, remembering Gaius Rubrius listing it as one of the worst parts of Rome.

"Oh, yes!" replied the young man cheerfully. "I suppose a foreigner like you *wouldn't* have known that. Your chair bearers certainly would have, though. I wonder if they were in league with the robbers? It's a pity you don't remember their names." He closed his wax tablets. He did not seem to have made many notes. Obviously a robbery in the Subura didn't merit much attention, not when the only person killed was a slave. It would have been the same in Alexandria.

"I'm sorry about your slave," he added. "He was obviously a good man, and loyal to his master: there are plenty who would've just run away. You'll look after the body?"

"Yes," Hermogenes agreed guiltily.

"Good," said the aedile, satisfied to have disposed of it.

He was just taking his leave when he frowned and turned back to Titus Fiducius. "There are some men outside watching your house," he said. "Do you know why?"

"That's to do with me," Hermogenes said at once. "With the business that brought me to the Esquiline."

"Oh!" exclaimed the aedile, startled. He stared at Hermogenes with sudden respect, obviously concluding that he must be richer and more important than he looked, to have business with a man who had now sent guards to protect him. "Pity they weren't with you last night, then, eh? But better late than never, I suppose."

He departed. Titus came over and looked at his guest with a mixture of admiration and reproach. "I never realized you were such a skilled liar," he remarked. "You had no idea who the chair bearers were'!"

"I told Tarius Rufus that I would keep his name out of it," Hermogenes replied. "I didn't dare give the bearers to the magistrates."

"And I suppose you were acting your distress over the body? Jupiter, you had *me* fooled!"

"That wasn't acting." He gazed soberly at the shrouded shape of Phormion. "Titus, he was in my household for more than *ten years*. He was always trustworthy and reliable when he was working, even if he did get into fights sometimes when he was drunk. He was a brave and honest man who trusted me. He deserved better of me than this." He was glad that the staring eyes were hidden. He looked away and added heavily, "I must arrange a funeral."

He wrote a letter to the priest of Mercury and Isis, explaining his need and sending it off with Tertia, then lay down on the bed in his cubicle to await a reply.

He woke when someone came into the room, and lay still for a moment, staring wide-eyed at the wall, trying to slow the pounding of his heart. Then he sat up.

Menestor was standing over him, with someone else in the dayroom behind him. The slave scowled when he saw that his master was awake. "I tried to tell her they should let you sleep," he announced angrily. "But she doesn't understand."

Hermogenes ran a hand through his hair, feeling groggy and unspeakably depressed. By the light coming through the window it was late in the afternoon: he had slept for hours. He noticed that behind Menestor were Cantabra, looking angry and impatient, and Tertia, looking timid and apologetic. Menestor's "she-they" resolved itself: they both wanted to see him, but only Cantabra had insisted on waking him up.

"You were right to wake me," he told Menestor. "Cantabra, I am pleased to see you back safely. Tertia, is it about the funeral? Is it urgent?"

The slave woman bobbed her head, then shook it. "No, sir. Just the priest says he can do it, and he'll come this evening to help wash and lay out the body. He wants to know how you want it done, but"—she cast a wary look at the impatient barbarian—"it can wait, sir, until he arrives."

"Thank you. Would you mind leaving me for now, then? Thank you."

She went out, with another very distrustful glance at the barbarian. Cantabra pushed past Menestor and dropped to a relaxed squat against the wall. Menestor made a face and went resentfully back into the dayroom. The barbarian reached down the front of her tunic and pulled out a letter.

He took it. It had been written not on papyrus but on a very small pair of wax tablets with the edges sealed together; the seal was of a female figure holding a horn of plenty.

"He gave it to me himself," said Cantabra. "But the mission did not go as smoothly as we wished, lord. I am sorry."

He looked back at her sharply. "What happened?"

She shrugged guiltily. "First Pollio recognized me. He'd seen me fight, and he asked me, wasn't I Cantabra the gladiatrix. I had to say I was. I acted the stupid barbarian, but I think he suspected at once that things were hotter than

your letter made them seem. He sent me to wait in the barracks of his own bodyguards, he *said* 'while he wrote a
reply,' but he took a long time about it, and I think he was trying to find out more about the situation. While I was waiting
in the barracks I met a man I knew." She grimaced. "Another
gladiator, discharged the same time as me. He got smart with
his mouth, and I told him to shut it. Then he thought he
would show his friends what a big man he was by waving his
cock at me, so I shoved it into his balls. Not enough to hurt
him badly, just enough to stop him. His friends got angry, and
there was nearly a fight, but the chief bodyguard stopped it.
When Pollio finally summoned me again, the chief bodyguard
came along and complained about me."

"I'm sorry," Hermogenes told her, shocked.

She shrugged again. "I don't think Pollio took much
notice. He just said 'Ajax should have known better.' What
does the letter say?"

He broke the seal and looked at it. It was in Greek,
written with very small, very scratchy cursive letters. He
tilted it at angles to the light until he found one where he
could make the letters out, then glanced back at Cantabra.
"It's in Greek," he warned her. "Let me read it first; I'll
translate when I've finished." He turned his attention back
to the letter.

P. VEDIUS POLLIO GREETS M. AELIUS
HERMOGENES OF ALEXANDRIA.

It is a pleasure to receive a letter from a businessman of your spotless reputation. I believe I have had

some investments in common with your father in the past—the syndicate of Philokrates of Rhodes, for one, and that of Nikomachos of Cyprus, who I believe was your kinsman, and whose penurious death last autumn you must greatly mourn.

I have indeed made a substantial loan to L. Tarius Rufus, and I would be very interested to hear of your concerns about him. I will expect you at my house on the Esquiline tomorrow at the fifth hour. I am aware that the house of your friend the excellent T. Fiducius is being watched, but I imagine that a gentleman of your resources will be able to elude the consul's notice.

I pray that the gods grant you a speedy recovery from your injuries.

He stared at the letter in deep disquiet, wondering if he wouldn't have done better to go to Scipio after all.

"So?" asked Cantabra impatiently.

He translated.

"He knows a lot about you," she observed, instantly latching onto the thing that had disturbed him.

He closed the letter slowly. "Probably he simply checked his own records," he said. "Most of his business has been in the East for years, and anyone who operates on the scale he does would have an archive full of notes on everyone else working in the same area." He began to feel more confident. "All he needed to do was tell his secretary to check the archive. He would find my name linked to my father's, and my father's referenced to the syndicates of Philokrates and Nikomachos, where Pollio had money of his own. Do you notice that he calls Nikomachos my kinsman, not my uncle? Whoever made the note on the syndicate would have mentioned that my father was related to its head, but probably not bothered to find out exactly how. Nikomachos was important enough that someone would have sent Pollio a note about his death, and as soon as he looked at that in the context of my letter, he would know exactly what this was about. Then he probably sent someone down the hill to see why I didn't want a messenger sent to the house. He isn't quite as omniscient as he pretends to be."

Cantabra looked at him with narrowed eyes. "What's 'omniscient'?"

" 'Knowing everything'."

"Huh! Nikomachus was your uncle, but who is this Pilokres? Does it mean anything that he mentioned him?"

"The only reason I can think of for mentioning Philo*krates* is to sound more knowing. There was never anything disreputable or peculiar about the shipping syndicate. No. I think Pollio was trying to frighten me, to drive down the price of the debt."

"Drive down the price of the debt," she repeated, and shook her head. "That still seems a strange idea, that you can sell a thing you don't have."

"Not so strange!" he objected. "If money you owe is a debt, then money owed to you has to be an asset. It is no stranger to sell it than to sell a share in a building you partly own, or a ship you have never even seen."

"And you sell those things, too, you Greeks?"

"Greeks and Romans and Syrians all sell those things. I have, often. Selling a debt, especially one this big, I have not done before, but I think it is my best option."

"How should it work?"

He shrugged. "I will see Pollio, establish my right to claim Rufus's money, and tell him I am willing to transfer it to him for a fraction of the total. I will ask for three quarters, I may have to accept two thirds, I won't go below half. When we have agreed, we will draw up a contract in duplicate. We both sign, and then he should give me the money, while I give him the documents, made over to him. Pollio will make a profit when he recovers the debt; I will recover enough to keep my own business affairs in good order—and Rufus will have to pay everything he owes."

Cantabra gazed at him evenly, then asked, "What if Pollio *doesn't* make Rufus pay? After all, he has not made the man repay what he loaned himself."

He frowned. It was not a pleasant possibility. If Pollio were to buy the debt and the documents and then do nothing with them, Rufus would probably believe that Hermogenes still had them—and there'd be nothing he could use to buy protection from the consul's enemies. He began to feel very tired again.

"I will speak to Pollio," he said wearily. "It ought to be possible to work out what he intends."

"Have you thought how you will get to the meeting?"

"I have an idea," he told her. "I need to work on the details."

The priest arrived just after dinner, a couple of hours

before nightfall, accompanied by a slave with a jar of Nile water. Titus welcomed him solemnly at the door, then left Hermogenes to escort him to the slaves' quarters at the back of the house, where the household had arranged Phormion's body.

Hermogenes made himself watch while the body was washed, dressed in a clean tunic, and laid out neatly on a litter. The women slaves sent up a clamor of lament—not heartfelt, the way it would have been if Phormion had died at home among his friends, but enough to signal to the gods that here lay the body of a man who would be missed. The priest prayed to Mercury, and then to Isis, and Hermogenes joined in the responses.

Afterward the priest drew Hermogenes aside to ask him how he wanted to manage the funeral the following morning. Was he willing to pay for a cremation, or would a cheap burial be sufficient? There were pits in the cemeteries outside the city wall where the bodies of slaves were often thrown one on top of another, but . . .

"I will pay for the cremation," Hermogenes replied at once. "He was a good man, and he died on my behalf. Would it be possible to arrange a covered litter for me to attend in? I wish to pay my respects to the dead, but my ankle is broken, and I am ashamed to appear in public looking the way I do."

The priest did not try to tell him he didn't need to be ashamed, which probably meant he looked even worse than he'd thought. Instead he agreed to arrange a litter, and they fixed a price for the cremation, arranged when and where to hold it, and wished each other good health.

Menestor hovered at his elbow for most of this, asking

plaintive questions about what was being said, until the priest had pity on him and began to speak Greek. When Hermogenes went back to his rooms, the boy pressed on his heels. "A covered litter!" he exclaimed, as soon as he'd closed the door behind them. "What do *you* want a covered litter for? *You're* not ashamed of the way you look."

Hermogenes sighed. "I am not planning to skip Phormion's funeral, Menestor. I'll only slip away afterward. Vedius Pollio wants me to meet him at his house at the fifth hour. I'm selling the debt to him."

Menestor scowled furiously. "You'll send the litter back to the house empty, is that it?"

"No. I thought you could ride in it. In my cloak."

The young man was shocked and outraged. "You're planning to go see Pollio on your own?"

"I'll have Cantabra with me."

"That's even worse!"

"You thought her a goddess last night."

"I was out of my mind last night!—sir. I don't trust her at all today."

"I think," Hermogenes told him irritably, "that she is intelligent and honest, that she has suffered terribly, and that she views me as her best chance of a better life. I think she will work very hard to satisfy me, and that I'm lucky to have found her."

"You thought that of the men who carried the chair!"

"Not in the least! I liked having Roman citizens wait on me, and I let that blind me. It was a serious error. They were stupid, and they were easily misled. Is this insolent accusatory tone—which, incidentally, is highly inappropriate toward your master!—because I promised to free you? I do mean to do it, Menestor; I would have spoken to the magistrate, or to the priest, but whenever I look at poor Phormion's body I find it hard to think of anything else."

Menestor went very red. "Sir," he said, with a sudden change of that tone from accusatory to pleading, "take me with you tomorrow!"

"To what end?" Hermogenes replied coldly. "There is nothing you could do that would help, and I find your belief that I am certainly going to die if I don't surrender a definite hindrance."

"Sir," said Menestor, with ragged dignity, "don't you understand that I'm *afraid* for you? You could be *killed!*"

"Yes, you've made that expectation quite clear," he replied shortly. "And it is hardly flattering. I will try to make certain that you're free before it happens. Will you fetch Cantabra, and ask Titus if he can spare a moment? I want to discuss the plans for tomorrow."

Looking hurt and furious in equal measure, Menestor stalked out. Hermogenes sat down at the desk. He swiveled his aching ankle and took several deep breaths, trying to compose himself and arrange his plans for the morning.

The priest had agreed to return to the house before the beginning of the third hour. Hermogenes had left orders that he was to be woken before the beginning of the second, but in fact he was awake before dawn. His face and ankle hurt worse than ever, and dread of the day ahead throbbed like a headache. He made himself rest quietly in bed until it was light, then got up and hobbled out into the dayroom to put on a clean tunic and have a drink of cold water. Menestor woke up, and he sent the boy to see if Tertia was up and able to provide another poultice.

She was, and presently came in with the steaming cloths and basins. Erotion was not with her, and he was secretly relieved: he would have felt compelled to put on a cheerful face for the little girl, and he didn't know that he could. Tertia shook her head over the old cut on his face and said she thought it was infected, and that he ought to spend the day resting quietly in bed.

"I can't," he told her simply. "Can you clean it for me? And perhaps splint the ankle? It may need more protection than just binding."

She cleaned the cut, and had him send Menestor to fetch an ointment of myrrh to combat the swelling, together with some laundry beaters to use as splints. He submitted to the anointing with myrhh, then lay down on the bed to have the foot splinted. Tertia knelt beside him, frowning as she arranged the flat splints on each side of the swollen ankle. "Sir," she said timidly, "is it just the funeral you mean to go to? Or . . . are you planning to do other things as well?"

"I do have other things to do today, yes," he admitted, "though I would prefer it if our friends across the road believe that I have simply attended my slave's funeral and come back. You know that I have fallen into a dangerous situation. I am trying to set it right."

"I am sure you are, sir," she replied, biting her lip. "Sir, are you taking that barbarian woman with you?"

"Yes."

"Oh." She looked more worried than ever.

"You have some reason to suspect Cantabra?" he asked in concern.

"Oh—no—only . . . it's just that she's a *terrible* woman, sir! and I don't like to think of you going off with her when you can't even walk. She frightens me. She stares at my Erotion, sir, with this look on her face like . . . like she's *hungry*. I think her sort of barbarian must *eat* children!"

He shook his head, moved by a stab of understanding and pity. "Tertia, she had two children of her own who were murdered by soldiers. What do you think she *feels* when she sees you embracing a lovely little girl?"

"*She* had children?" the slave woman asked, as astonished by the thought as he had been.

"Children and a husband," he replied. "They were killed in the war her people fought against Rome, and she lost her freedom and was sent to the arenas. She never chose to be what she is. I know you are a good and kind woman, Tertia. Please, be kind to Cantabra. She has suffered terribly."

"Oh!" Tertia was wide-eyed and red cheeked. "Of course. Oh, I didn't know! The poor creature!" She shook her head. "Oh, her poor little babies! I'm glad you told me, sir."

Cantabra, however, was not glad. A little while later, as he was eating a light breakfast with Titus in the dining room, the bodyguard appeared with a furious scowl on her face, saluted, then stood with her hands on her hips, glaring.

"Yes?" he asked politely.

"Lord," she said, "you told the slaves about my children!"

"Yes," he agreed, surprised. "Should I not have done?"

"No! What is my life worth, if I am pitied by *slaves?*"

"You prefer to be feared and hated by them?" he asked, becoming annoyed. "Tertia was afraid you wanted to *eat* her daughter. Should I have let her go on believing that? She is a gentle and decent woman who is readily moved to pity: why should that offend you? *I* pity you for your children: does that offend you, too?"

This seemed to throw her completely. She went red and stared at him speechlessly.

"I have a daughter myself," he told her. "I know how I would feel if she were killed."

"*You* have a daughter?" she asked, as though this were as extraordinary a notion to her as her role as a mother had been to him.

Titus, who had watched all this in astonishment, began to laugh.

"At home in Alexandria," Hermogenes explained with an irritated glance at his friend. "Woman, I know you are both freeborn and inexperienced, so I am making allowances, but this is not the way to speak to an employer. Most men would dismiss you for this outburst."

Cantabra looked as though she were about to choke. Still red in the face, she bobbed her head and backed stiffly out of the room.

"Did that creature really have children?" Titus asked in surprise and amusement.

"Apparently, yes," he replied. Hermogenes set down his piece of bread, feeling greatly dissatisfied with both the world and with himself.

"Hard to believe." Titus gave him a sly look. "She seemed quite astonished to think of *you* having children, too. Perhaps it made her jealous. I think she may be in love with you."

He shook his head. "I am quite certain that she is not. She made it very plain that it was not included in the hire."

"Did she? The insolent bitch!"

"Titus, she's a barbarian ex-gladiator! Where would she have learned how to express that sort of thing gracefully? I think just now she was angry because she felt I'd betrayed a confidence. It was a mark of trust that she confronted me about it." The memory of the furious look in her eyes came back to him—a *hurt* look, Hermogenes realized belatedly. "I should not have acted so superior," he admitted, suddenly ashamed.

Titus was now watching him with a different sort of look, puzzled and sober. "You really do work at it with *everyone*, don't you?" he asked.

"Work at what?"

"At . . . at trying to understand people, to reason them out. I remember your father telling me once that that was why you were so good at business—that you put yourself in the place of whoever you were dealing with and tried to work out what he really wanted. I watched you after that, and saw that he was right, that was what you did and you were very good at it. But it isn't just business partners, is it? It's *everyone*. That barbarian, your slaves . . . and my slaves, too." He met his guest's eyes. "You said you weren't trying to corrupt and seduce them, but you have. You've been here only a few days, and already they want to please you more than they've ever wanted to please me."

Caught and exposed. The cut on his cheek throbbed as the blood rushed into it. "That's not true," he said hurriedly. "They know you're a kind master and they do want to please you. They just don't know how."

"What do you mean?" The obscure hurt he'd sensed in his host was suddenly sharp and open. "Surely it's *obvious* how—"

"It *isn't*," Hermogenes insisted. "Look, Titus—when I first arrived here you were angry with them because they hadn't got the rooms ready for me. In fact, they hadn't been sure *which* rooms to get ready, and what you wanted done! You shout at them when they don't do things properly, but you never say anything when they do—so they're never certain whether or not they've done something right, and are frightened of doing anything, in case it's wrong. They do want to please you. You just have to let them know how to do it."

Titus stared at him with an expression he couldn't interpret. Kyon came to the door and announced that the priest had arrived with the litter for the funeral procession.

"I'm sorry," Hermogenes said vaguely, picking up his crutch. "Titus, I must go. Please, if anything should happen to me, look after Menestor. I want to give him his freedom; see if you can arrange that."

Titus paled. "You expect to be *killed*?" he asked shrilly.

"No! No, I don't. I expect to come back and arrange Menestor's freedom myself. I only ask you as a precaution. Good health!" He hobbled quickly out to the door.

The funeral procession was still assembling. Menestor was there, looking sullen. Cantabra stood a little apart, also looking sullen, wearing a good plain cloak over her slave's tunic—borrowed, but suitable for paying respects to the dead, though he found himself wishing that she had draped it properly instead of putting it on like a shawl. Hyakinthos hurried from the back of the house, together with his mother and his little sister. The priest wore the black robes of Isis, rather than the white ones of Mercury, though he had an attendant with him leading a lamb for a Roman-style funeral sacrifice. When Hermogenes came out, the priest came over to help him to the covered litter which stood waiting. Kyon followed with a borrowed black cloak suitable for use at a funeral.

The litter was a small one, with four slaves to carry it instead of the eight normal to more elaborate conveyances. The curtains were plain brown wool, and smelled musty. Hermogenes allowed Kyon to drape him with the cloak, and the priest helped him into the litter. When he was seated, his foot propped up on a cushion, he pulled back the opposite curtain to look across the street.

The four barbarians were there, two sitting on the curb over an interrupted dice game, the other two standing, all watching him intently. They weren't all blond, after all— one of them had brown hair—but they were all obviously foreign, with heavy, bearded faces and long hair. They were big men, dressed in red tunics and plain cloaks, and if they hadn't actually brought spears along, they were openly carrying knives. For a long moment he stared at them and they stared back. He beckoned one of them over.

The man stepped back hurriedly. Hermogenes glanced round and caught the eye of one of the bearers who would carry the litter. "Please, would you go across the road, and tell those gentlemen what we are doing?" he asked. "They will be concerned to know."

Looking distinctly nervous, the bearer went across the road and spoke to the guardsmen. Hermogenes watched as the four men scowled in embarrassment, looking from the messenger to him. The bearer came back. "I told them," he announced. He seemed relieved: his errand, and its tacit acceptance, made the guardsmen somehow official and nothing to worry about.

"Thank you," Hermogenes murmured. He drew the curtains of the litter.

A minute later two of Titus's slaves brought Phormion's body out of the house, and the procession set off.

Rome was encircled by small cemeteries, all—by legal requirement—outside the old and long-defunct city wall. The nearest lay straight out the Via Tusculana, past the Caelimontana Gate. Hermogenes remembered the Rubrius brothers saying that it was the bad part of the thoroughfare, but he saw little of it from behind his curtains. It was not a long walk—the procession turned right into the cemetery less than a mile from the house, and Hermogenes opened the curtains to watch as Phormion's body was carried onto the prepared pyre.

The priest prayed that the earth would be light upon the body of the departed, that Mercury would guide his soul safely to the Underworld, and that Lord Serapis, consort of Isis, would receive him kindly. He poured out a libation of wine and oil and sprinkled the assembled mourners with water from the Nile. The lamb brought for the purpose was led up and slaughtered. A cemetery attendant thrust a torch into the heart of the heap of firewood.

"Farewell, Phormion!" Menestor's voice cried, in Greek, and a ragged chorus of other voices repeated it in Latin, "Farewell!"

Hermogenes sat quietly in the litter until the fire was burning fiercely. Eventually Cantabra came, drew back the curtains on the side facing the pyre, and helped him out. "Two of them followed," she informed him in a low voice. "But they are both at the entrance to the cemetery, watching from there."

He nodded. He had been certain that the guardsmen would not actually attend the funeral of a man their comrades had killed. He beckoned Menestor over. The young man came reluctantly, and stood motionless while his master took off the borrowed cloak and draped it round him. The curtains of the litter hid them from the observers at the cemetery gate.

Hermogenes adjusted a fold of the cloak to cover Menestor's head. "Just get into the litter and let them take you back," he ordered. "Keep the curtains closed. When you get to the house, keep the cloak well over your head, and let them help you to the door. Remember to limp on the *right* ankle."

Menestor scowled, but said only, "Yes, sir."

The litter bearers were by this time looking worried and bewildered, and the priest came over frowning with concern. "Is something the matter?" he asked.

Hermogenes had resolved not to involve the religious man in his plans any more than he had to. The priest knew that the guardsmen had been sent by Rufus, but not why. Hermogenes had managed to imply that it was just an attempt to intimidate him about the debt. Now he put on a look of embarrassment. "Last night I checked my strongbox and found that I did not have enough coin to pay for all of this," he said. This was true, though he did not add that he'd already given Titus a bank draft for the cost.

The priest was horrified, and he went on quickly, "There is no need to be worried! My friend Titus Fiducius will pay you, but I must get some money to repay him. I am a businessman, and I can draw on an account with a bank in the city. I confess, though, I am somewhat concerned about what those guardsmen would do if they knew I was collecting a large amount of money, so I don't want them to know." He made a point of catching the eyes of the litter bearers as well as he said this. They nodded understanding: they were even less clear about why the guards were there, but they did agree that it wouldn't be good to let barbarians know he was carrying money. "I am sending my slave back in the litter in my place," he went on. "He is very distressed at the loss of his fellow anyway, poor young man, and he is not needed for this errand. My bodyguard will fetch a sedan chair to take me to the bank. I hope this is no problem?"

It wasn't. The bearers moved the litter to keep the watchers' eyes baffled while the priest helped Hermogenes over to sit down on the pedestal of a funerary monument, hidden from view. He sat waiting, crutch across his lap, while the procession reassembled itself and left. The others would return to the house, where the sacrificed lamb would be roasted to provide the funeral feast, and the assembled mourners would drink to the memory of Phormion. Cantabra would slip away quietly en route.

The fire still blazed, and the air was thick with the scent of burning flesh. Ashes, gray and crimson, drifted from an overcast sky. The cemetery attendant cast him a few curious glances as he raked up stray embers, but said nothing. He would keep the pyre burning through the day, and the following morning collect the charred bones for burial.

He waited for what seemed a long time. His mind darted nervously about at first, worrying about the neighborhood, the unseen guards, the meeting ahead of him. Then he made himself think of Phormion instead. He remembered when his father had first bought the bodyguard, picking the man out in the slave market to replace an attendant who had grown too old for the work, and leading him back to the house. Phormion had been about twenty then, a big, dark, silent young man, obedient but sullen: his previous owner had considered him stupid and beaten him frequently. As he became accustomed to a more tolerant household he had grown lively, and with it, bad-tempered. He had got into fights, at home and in the market, and he had stolen wine from the household stores and been beaten for it. Then he had found a girl in a neighbor's house. For about a year he had become all smiles—and then he'd broken with her and caused havoc. Eventually, though, he had settled down, seemed to resign himself to his place in life, and become the man his master now mourned: quiet, reliable, largely good-natured, though with an occasional outburst of drinking and violence.

"Farewell, Phormion," Hermogenes whispered to the fire. "I am sorry I was not wise enough to preserve your life. May the gods receive you kindly."

At last there came footsteps behind him, and he twisted round and saw Cantabra arriving with the sedan chair.

The bearers were strangers, hired at the livery stable up the road. It was unlikely they even knew Gaius and Quintus Rubrius: this was the other side of the city from the Aemilian Bridge. Cantabra had been instructed to tell them that he needed to go directly from a funeral to a business meeting, and they greeted him politely, with no trace of suspicion—though he did notice the shocked looks cast at his bandaged face and splinted ankle.

"I was robbed in the Subura," he explained, unasked; and the looks changed to sympathy.

"Happens all the time, sir," one of the bearers told him. "You want us for the day, then? Or just for the trip to your meeting?"

"For the day, please. I should pay you half your fee now, half this evening?"

He paid them a denarius as the advance, which pleased them, then got up. Cantabra pulled the cloak he had loaned her from her shoulders and handed it to him silently: a gentleman did not go a business meeting wearing just a tunic. He propped himself up with the crutch, draped the garment as well as he could, then allowed the bearers to help him into the chair. He was painfully aware that he was a travesty of his normal business self.

"I have the misfortune to have a meeting at the house of Vedius Pollio on the Esquiline," he informed the chair bearers, when he was seated. "At the fifth hour. Do you happen to know what time it is now?"

It was partway through the fourth hour, the men thought. There should be no problem. They would follow the road up along the old wall to the Esquiline Gate, then go left into the city; the house was not far from there. Yes, they knew where it was.

They began to walk steadily through yet another area of tenements. To their left the old wall appeared at intervals like a black outcrop in a gray sea of unwashed humanity. Cantabra walked silently beside the litter, her red hair brilliant in the sun. Her face was still sullen.

"Cantabra," Hermogenes said, after a long silence. He knew he was about to sacrifice some more dignity to her, and, worse, do it in front of the chair bearers, but he was not comfortable about the scene in the dining room, and he did not want to go into the meeting with Pollio feeling uncomfortable about his bodyguard.

The woman looked up at him quickly, her eyes hard.

"I am sorry I spoke to you that way, as though I were your master," he said quietly. "I understood afterward that you felt I had betrayed a confidence. I did not mean to do so, and I regret causing you offense."

The blue eyes regarded him for another long moment in silence. "I hadn't asked you to keep quiet about what I told you," she said abruptly. "You were not at fault." She looked away, then kicked viciously at a loose stone on the road and sent it spinning into the side of a building. "You were even right. That woman Tertia, she isn't going to be like they were in the school. She wouldn't laugh at me if I cried."

"People laughed at you if you mourned for your dead?" he asked, appalled.

The eyes came up again, angry this time. "You think gladiators are supposed to cry? When you arrive in the school they tell you that you are there to be burned, to be chained, to be beaten, and to be killed with iron. The free men who enlist swear an oath to endure it. The rest of us just endure it."

"This was a gladiatorial school?"

She nodded shortly. "Taurus's school. In the Campus Martius."

"You was a gladiatrix?" one of the bearers asked her, in surprise.

She nodded again, scowling.

"Huh! You was, yah! but I didn't recognize you without the armor! I like the games. Cantabra. You fought Bellona at the consular games in January, didn't you?"

"Yes," she said, still scowling. "I won my freedom."

"Well, good luck to you! That was a good fight."

Cantabra kicked another stone, scowling so forbiddingly that the bearer fell silent.

They trudged on through the narrow streets. There was another cemetery on the right, fenced off and planted with trees. A pack of scrawny dogs clustered around something under one of them, tearing at it and snapping at each other.

Cheap slave burials, Hermogenes thought with a shudder. He wondered if it would really have made any difference to Phormion if he'd been interred that way. He knew it made a difference to himself.

"Lord," Cantabra said suddenly, "does your wife know that you are doing this?"

He looked at her in surprise. "Doing what? And my wife's dead."

"Fighting," she said flatly. "But if she is dead it was a pointless question."

"She died of a childbed fever five years ago. You believe I should simply accept being robbed?"

She gazed at him thoughtfully, then shrugged. He remembered her earlier enthusiasm for an attempt to humble a Roman consul, and felt resentment at the way she'd changed her mind. Strange woman! Why should she be so concerned about what his *wife* thought of what he was doing?

Then he realized that he knew exactly why: because her own husband had fought Rome, and lost not merely his life but her freedom and the lives of their children as well. Of course she would remember that now, marching beside him into another conflict. In a way, the only surprising thing was that she *was* still beside him, that she hadn't just excused herself and left.

Perhaps she trusted him to win. The thought warmed him, and he realized, with a stab of shame, just how frightened and desperate he must be, if the fact that a barbarian bodyguard had faith in him made such a difference. He cast another glance at her stern profile under the fiery hair and felt comforted, but he said nothing. The chair bearers turned left smoothly to pass through the Esquiline Gate.

I T WAS NOT SURPRISING THAT THE SEDAN-
chair bearers had known the location of the house of
Vedius Pollio. The place was undeniably a palace, and
would have been a landmark in any city. They walked along
the enclosing wall for a long time before they came to the
gatehouse, a substantial building with two separate gates—
a small one for foot traffic, and a larger one for carriages.

There were four men on duty at the gatehouse. They
were not barbarians, like Tarius Rufus's men; they had
more the appearance of Roman toughs in red livery. Their
swords looked military enough, though. When the sedan
chair approached the gate, one of them stiffened and whispered to the others, and they all stared at Cantabra.

"This your rich Greek?" one asked her, as the chair

stopped. "Not in good shape, is he? What happened? He try to bed you?"

Cantabra stiffened. So did her employer. "My name is Marcus Aelius Hermogenes," he snapped. "I have an appointment with Publius Vedius Pollio."

The man who'd spoken looked startled, then embarrassed. Hermogenes saw that they hadn't expected him to understand that much Latin. He sat very straight in the chair, glaring haughtily down at the guard.

"Yes, sir," the man said, more humbly. "He instructed us. You may pass."

Pollio's formal gardens were larger and grander than Rufus's, and merged on the left with informal groves of tall pines, planted gracefully down a terraced hillside. There was a multitude of ponds and fountains. Hermogenes eyed them unhappily, wondering which of them contained the infamous lampreys.

The house itself was huge and ostentatious, faced with white marble columns whose tops were gilded and shone blindingly in the sunshine; the porch they enclosed was entirely paved with yellow Numidian marble. A slave doorman posted before the domed front entrance hall came out to greet them. Hermogenes produced the letter with Pollio's seal, and the doorman, smiling widely, welcomed him, and asked the bearers to set down the chair.

"Are they your own people, sir?" he asked. To Hermogenes' surprise, he spoke in Greek, with the accent of an Asiatic.

"No," Hermogenes admitted, "but I've hired them for the day."

"Then they may wait in the stables."

Hermogenes let the bearers help him from the chair, and propped himself on the crutch while the doorman spoke to them in Greek-accented Latin. He was dismayed at the way his heart sank to see men and chair trudge off. He told himself that it made very little difference: if his host didn't want him to leave, it wouldn't help him to have bearers.

The doorman looked doubtfully at Cantabra. "What is she?" he asked.

"My hired attendant," Hermogenes replied. "Please. Last time she came to this house, as my messenger, there was some trouble between her and Lord Vedius Pollio's bodyguards. This time I think it would be better to keep her with me."

"I will ask about it," said the doorman. "This way, sir."

The doorman handed him over to another, more senior Greek slave, who once again queried Cantabra's presence. Hermogenes repeated the story about the trouble with the bodyguards, and the slave seemed to remember it. He agreed that it would be better if she stayed with her employer.

They were led through an atrium and left down a corridor overlooking a garden, then left again. The house was a maze of marble floors and frescoed walls, rich carpets and priceless artworks. Hermogenes limped after the slave slowly, hop-thump on his crutch, aware of Cantabra following at his heels. He found himself inexpressibly glad of those soft footfalls at his back.

At last their attendant knocked on a door of polished

maple. A voice replied, and the slave went through and bowed deeply. "The Alexandrian businessman Hermogenes, sir," he said.

Hermogenes went through into the room. It was a study, a comparatively small room overlooking the terraced hillside, with a bookcase along one wall and a massive desk of carved ebony along the other. The man sitting at the desk turned in his chair to face the visitor, and the slave immediately hurried forward to turn the chair itself so that he could do so more comfortably. The master of the house was old, though the marks of sickness on him probably made him seem older than he was. He had the wrinkled, sagging skin of a man who has once been fat but has lost weight; his face was pale and puffy with ill health and his fingers were swollen like sausages; his lower eyelids drooped, showing rheumy redness. He wore no cloak, only a loose tunic of fine Indian cotton, dyed yellow with saffron and embroidered with gold. He inspected his visitor with an expression of growing amusement.

"Herakles!" he exclaimed, in Greek. "Did Lucius Rufus do that?"

Hermogenes made himself smile. "I was robbed in the Subura. I understand it happens all the time. Do I have the honor of speaking to Publius Vedius Pollio?"

Pollio smiled. "You do indeed. Socrates! A chair for my guest."

The attendant bowed, shot off, and returned a moment later with a folding chair of carved cherrywood. Hermogenes sat down warily, holding his crutch in front of him. The seat was low, and he found that he now had to look up at Pollio, whose own chair was tall and thronelike. Again he was glad of Cantabra standing silently behind him.

"I believe you speak fluent Latin," Pollio told him. "An unusual accomplishment for a Greek. Which language would you prefer for our business?"

Hermogenes spread his hands. "I defer entirely to you, lord."

"Let's speak Latin, then," said Pollio, switching to that language. "It will be a novelty to conduct business with a Greek in my own language. Does the arrogance of that never strike you? That your people expect even their conquerers to learn Greek?"

"If our conquerers choose to learn our language, lord, would it not be arrogant to reject their efforts?"

"Oh, very smooth. And the report was right: you *are* fluent. What is it you want of me, *Marcus?*—if I may presume to use your first name?"

Hermogenes found himself off-balance and embarrassed. He had barely even thought of that Marcus as a name: it had been a title, an indication of the status and power of his Roman citizenship. Pollio was watching him with amusement, well aware of it. He felt at once that it would be a mistake to ignore that thrust.

"I am deftly rebuked, lord," he said. "Tarius Rufus called me Greekling and Egyptian, yet never made me feel I had as little right to my Roman name as you do simply by using it. It is a name which I claim a right to, however, so if you wish to use it, how can I object?

"My lord, to answer your question: I am here to see whether you wish to buy a debt which I am owed by Tarius

Rufus. I inherited it with the estate of my kinsman Niko-machos of Cyprus, but it has proved difficult to collect, and, since you are his major creditor, it seemed best to offer you the chance to consolidate the loan before I tried anyone else."

"*Difficult* to collect?" replied Pollio, and leaned back in his throne smiling. "*Impossible,* I should think."

"I think not," said Hermogenes evenly. "Rufus has ene-mies who would be willing to protect me in order to see him disgraced by a summons for debt. Or perhaps Gaius Mae-cenas would buy the debt from me, if you have no interest in it."

Pollio did not betray much, but there was a momentary freezing of the smile and a contraction of the pupils of the eye that said that Hermogenes had hit a target. He'd thought it worth trying: it stood to reason that Pollio dis-liked Maecenas—both financiers, both intimates of the emperor, but the one a gentleman praised for his cultured generosity, and the other a freedman's son despised for his greed.

"That would be ill-advised." Pollio said softly. "I think that before he allowed you to do either of those things, my dear friend Lucius would . . . arrange for you to meet some robbers in the Subura. Your gladiatrix is a fierce fighter, no doubt, but I see only one of her."

Hermogenes inspected the handle of his crutch. "The consul knows he would not benefit from my death."

There was a silence, and then Pollio laughed. "Oh, Jupiter, dear Lucius *has* had bad luck, hasn't he? Who has the incriminating documents?"

Hermogenes looked back at him with an expression of polite bafflement. Inwardly he was beginning to feel a new chill. Whatever bound this man to the consul, it wasn't the simple commercial transaction he had thought. The tone and the language were wrong. There was something more complicated here, something political. He began to suspect that he had been extremely unwise to come.

Pollio laughed again, as though he'd seen that realization. "You're out of your depth, Alexandrian," he said, almost gently. "You're swimming well, but you're out of your depth. Tell me, how did you know I was Lucius's major creditor? I have not publicized the fact."

"He had every reason to pay if he could," Hermogenes replied. "That he didn't, had to mean he couldn't. If he had borrowed in Rome, it would have been from a member of his own circle, and that meant you or Maecenas."

"And he and Gaius Maecenas always loathed each other," Pollio finished, as though it were common knowledge. "Simple enough. How much does Lucius owe you?"

"Four hundred thousand of the principal," he answered at once, aware of his heart slowing in relief. Perhaps the political aspect was completely irrelevant to his own concerns, and he could still sell the debt and get out. "Plus a hundred and twenty thousand of interest. Given the difficulties I face in trying to collect—and my innocence of political matters, lord, in which, I do acknowledge it! I am indeed out of my depth—I would sell to you for two-thirds of the total." He would not press for more, not now. "My great wish is to be quit of this and go home. I have only one condition."

"Oh, conditions!" exclaimed Pollio. "I never fail to be astonished at the way you Greeks believe you can impose *conditions*. Winged Death could appear before you with his sword, and you would try to dictate to him the conditions under which he could claim your life. Tell me your 'condition,' then!"

His heart sped up again. He was not going to escape so easily. He made himself respond calmly despite his growing apprehension. "Whatever you do with the debt, Rufus must know that I no longer hold the title to it."

"And you believe that would save you now?" Pollio smiled, then snapped his fingers. "Socrates. Some wine for my guest. Make it the Caecuban. He amuses me."

The slave bowed and hurried out.

"I presume you have documents to prove title," Pollio went on, leaning back in his chair and resting his swollen hands on his stomach.

"In a safe place."

"Of course. Give them to me, and we will talk about payment and 'conditions.'"

Hermogenes put the end of the crutch on the floor and levered himself upright. "I am sorry to have disturbed you," he said, as calmly as he could. "I regret that we cannot do business."

"Sit down!" snapped Pollio, with the first hint of real annoyance. "I've just sent for wine."

Hermogenes remained standing. "All I want," he said evenly, "is to recover money that is owed to me. I have offered you the opportunity to purchase the debt. And—forgive me!—but what is business but a setting of conditions? If you reject the need for them, what is there left to negotiate about? If you are Death with his sword, and conditions mean nothing to you, then kill me. You should be aware, though, that I have left a letter which will go to one of the consul's enemies if I do not reclaim it."

He saw, with dismay, that Pollio wanted that event no more than did Rufus. "Sit down," the Roman said again. "Sit down or I may become angry with you! I do not reject your conditions. We will negotiate."

Hermogenes sat down. The slave Socrates hurried in, accompanied by a young male slave carrying a silver tray on which stood wine, water, and two cups, all made of a delicate Alexandrian glass. The young man bowed to his master, set the tray down on the corner of the desk, and poured wine, mixing it with only a third of water. He bowed to his master again and handed him a cup, then gave one to the guest. Hermogenes noticed that the young man's hands were trembling. Presumably he would be thrown to the lampreys if he dropped the glass. He accepted the wine with a murmur of thanks.

Pollio sniffed the wine appreciatively, then took a slow sip, rolled the drink around his mouth, and swallowed. "Superb!" he announced. "I find that Caecuban is one of the few things in life which never lose their savor. Try it."

Hermogenes sipped the wine cautiously. It was rich, very heavy, sweet and vinegary at the same time, with a complexity of flavor that instantly proclaimed a formidable expense.

"As you say," he agreed. "Superb."

Pollio laughed again, setting down his cup. "Oh, you do

have talent, don't you? Lucius should curse the day he decided he could ignore that debt. Being Lucius, of course, he will merely curse *you*. He's never liked Greeks. He has, more than most of us, that sense that you are sneering at us as uncouth barbarians behind our backs." He smiled, showing the points of his teeth. "Myself, I am very philhellenic. Most of my domestic staff are Greek, as perhaps you've noticed."

More fashionable even than ordinary slaves with Greek names, no doubt. And no doubt the lampreys liked them just as much.

"You said we would negotiate," Hermogenes reminded him.

"Yes. As it happens, I am not certain whether I want to buy Lucius's debt from you or whether I would prefer to help you collect it yourself. If I decide to buy it, I will give you the interest and the two-thirds of the principal you ask for, and you may be certain that Lucius will know that I have done so. If I help you to collect it, I will provide plenty of men to ensure your safety while you sue, and you may keep everything you get. I need a couple of days to decide which course to take. While I am making up my mind, I would like you to remain here in my house as my guest."

Hermogenes sat very still, gripping the crutch. "My friend Titus Fiducius will be very concerned for me."

"Ah, yes. Your friend. Does Lucius *know* that you have left your friend's house?"

"He should believe that I attended my slave's funeral,

then returned," Hermogenes admitted reluctantly. "Lord, I told my friend I would be back this evening."

"It is possible to send him a note, if we arrange for it to be delivered discreetly. You presumably had some idea of how to smuggle *yourself* back in, broken ankle and all, so I think I could manage a letter. You must stay here. I insist." Pollio's voice hardened on the last two words.

Hermogenes met the rheumy eyes. There was no menace there, only a ruthless satisfaction. Pollio had found a tool that he wanted; Pollio would use it. The tool had no choice in the matter.

"I have no interest in what your plans involve, lord," Hermogenes said deliberately. "As I have said, all I want is to get my money, and if you are willing to assist me in that, I am content. However, I am also concerned for the safety of people to whom I have obligations. If I were forced to sue for recovery, I would not want my friend or his household brought into any danger."

"Still making conditions? Very well. Agreed. Your friend will be protected. And for now, you will stay here. Socrates, have the White Rooms made ready for my guest. For his bodyguard . . . do you want to keep her with you?"

"Yes," Hermogenes replied, without hesitation. "I gather there was some trouble with one of your men last time she was here."

Pollio's eyes slid to Cantabra with a look of amusement, but he nodded. He heaved himself to his feet and hobbled over to his guest, walking with the straddled gait of a man whose feet pain him. Hermogenes pulled himself out of the low chair again and stood balanced on his left foot, holding the handle of the crutch with both hands.

Pollio reached out and touched his guest's cheek just under the bandage. The white eyebrows lifted slightly. "I thought I smelled myrrh," he remarked. "Infected, is it? I will have someone bring you something for it." He stroked the hot flesh with his swollen fingers, then dropped his hand to Hermogenes' shoulder and squeezed lightly. "I will take very good care of you, Alexandrian. You are exactly what I need."

⚜

The slave called Socrates led them back out to the long corridor, then along it. When they reached the atrium, Hermogenes stopped. The crutch was hurting his armpit, and he felt hot, weak, and sick. "Let me rest a moment," he said, when Socrates turned back toward him with a look of concern.

"I'll have a chair fetched," Socrates offered at once, in Greek.

Hermogenes shook his head. "I have a chair, and some bearers I hired for the day. They should be waiting . . ."

"I will see to it that they are paid and sent off," Socrates said immediately.

The quickness of that response confirmed it: he would not be *allowed* to slip off. "They expect a denarius," he murmured, as though he had noticed nothing.

Socrates nodded, clapped his hands to summon the doorkeeper and another passing slave, and gave orders. Someone went off to pay and dismiss the sedan chair;

someone else went off into the house, and came back presently with an ordinary chair and two young men to carry it. Hermogenes rode the rest of the way to the White Rooms.

The name obviously came from the stone used to pave and decorate them: Parian marble, pure and glittering as snow. There was a sleeping cubicle, a study, and a dressing room, separated by white curtains and provided with furniture of pale woods and white or gold upholstery. Two women slaves were already there, preparing the bed and topping up the oil in the lamps. The two young men set down the chair in the dressing room, and Hermogenes sat there, hugging his crutch, while the women finished arranging things. Socrates asked him if there was anything else he'd like.

"A drink of water, thank you," Hermogenes told him. "Is your name really Socrates?"

"Lord Pollio has five stewards," the man answered obliquely. "The others are called Plato, Aristotle, Zeno, and Epicurus. I am senior, and the oldest."

He'd suspected something of the sort. "Why philosophers?"

"Being a steward certainly teaches a man to be philosophical," Socrates said dryly. "I will see that you have the water, and I will bring someone to see to your injuries, as my master instructed."

Pollio's slaves went out. Cantabra prowled about the three rooms scowling, then came over and sat down on the floor by her employer's chair.

"I'm sorry," he said helplessly.

She looked up at him quickly. "You are getting what you want, aren't you?"

He threw the crutch furiously across the room and swore in Greek. Cantabra watched him impassively until he finished and put his hands over his face.

"So," she said then. "There *is* something wrong. I smelled it. Does he mean to kill you?"

"Isn't it *obvious*?" he shouted, taking his hands away from his face again. "No, he doesn't mean to kill me; he means to use me to blackmail Rufus. Oh, Zeus, oh Isis, I've been stupid!"

She continued simply to look at him. "You know I do not understand these dealings over money. How would this blackmail work?"

He drew in his breath raggedly. "I think," he said in a harsh voice, "that he will let Rufus know that he has me, and that Rufus will then have to decide whether he does what Pollio wants, and has the debt paid for him, or whether he refuses, and is forced to pay it himself.

"Pollio was never in doubt about any detail of Rufus's finances. Rufus was able to withstand his pressure, however, until now. His liquid resources aren't enough to let him pay me *and* keep Pollio off, and if I take him to court, not only does he suffer the disgrace of the summons itself but he'll have to sell property. That will bring his indebtedness out into the open, and the value of everything he owns will crash. Those farms in Picenum will go from being worth a hundred million to being worth nothing. Oh, I exaggerate: compared to someone like me he would still be a wealthy man—but compared to what he was, and what he believes he should be, he'd be nothing."

"But he is your enemy," Cantabra pointed out. "Why should you mind?"

"I don't mind what happens to *him*. What I don't know is what Pollio is blackmailing him *for*. I don't—" He brushed angrily at his face where the Roman had touched him. "I don't like being *used*, particularly when I don't even know what I am being used for!"

"He is an evil man," Cantabra said seriously. "He cannot be trusted to keep his side of any bargain he makes with you, but he will not permit you to reject his offer."

Hermogenes shuddered. *You are exactly what I need.* "I know that."

"So what do you wish to do?"

He drew in another deep breath. "I need to think. It may be that this is still my best option. It may be that it isn't."

"He believes that your ankle is broken," Cantabra said, very, very quietly.

"Hush." He glanced around the room, belatedly remembering that there might be eavesdroppers. Probably they would not have heard that, though, even if they had caught his own outburst. Perhaps it wouldn't help him— there were all the slaves in the household between him and the streets of Rome, to say nothing of the wall and the guards—but being able to run when they thought he couldn't might be the only trick he had left.

She nodded. "You must ask them to bring a mattress,"

she said, more loudly. "I do not share your bed. I will sleep here, by the door."

He nodded ruefully. She was managing better than he was. "I will ask them."

Then he hesitated, steeled himself, and added, "He has no interest in you. If you want to leave, I will write you a letter of recommendation, and another letter asking Titus to help you find other work. There is no reason for you to suffer this." Her life, he thought, had had more than its share of suffering already. He sacrificed some more dignity, and admitted, "This is my fault, not yours."

"I swore by the gods of my people that I would serve you faithfully and set your life before mine," she replied at once. "Besides, your friend would not help me if he knew I had abandoned you. He didn't want you to hire me at all."

"Then, thank you," he said. He fought his dignity again, and admitted, "I would hate to be here alone."

He decided later that afternoon that there had been no eavesdroppers on that conversation: at that point his keepers were still being organized. When Socrates returned, he brought with him a pair of slaves—an older man called Nestor, and a younger one called Pyrrhus—whom he introduced as "your attendants for the duration of your stay." An attempt to say that he needed no attendants was politely but firmly dismissed. The two were appointed to sleep in the dressing room, between him and the door. Cantabra's mattress, when it arrived, was put in the study.

Not that guards were needed. Socrates also brought along Pollio's personal doctor—another Greek slave—who declared that he needed to purge the vicious humors that had infected the cut on the patient's face. He let blood from the vein in Hermogenes's elbow and gave him a powerful concoction of drugs "to scour the poisons from your system." Then he cleaned the cut. He examined the ankle as well, but—fortunately—decided that to remove the splints at this early stage would be detrimental to the knitting of the bone, and contented himself with loosening the bindings and applying hot compresses. The compresses did not stay on long: he'd scarcely left when his purgative began to work, and Hermogenes spent the rest of the day getting up to use the chamber pot under his bed, and then lying down again groaning. He was only vaguely aware of it when Cantabra went out, though he was relieved when she came back safely.

He did pen the required letter to Titus—a very guarded missive, saying only that Pollio had invited him to remain at the house while they settled their business together. He gave it to Socrates, but had no further knowledge of what happened to it. By that stage he didn't really care, either.

The doctor returned at dawn next morning, and pronounced, with satisfaction, that the inflammation was much reduced. He cleaned the cut again, anointed it with more myrrh, and prescribed rest and a low and cooling diet. Hermogenes was so glad to escape another dose of purgative that he didn't argue. He drank the barley broth his two guardians brought him for breakfast, then looked at his keepers speculatively. He had said little to them before, apart from apologetic requests that they empty the chamber pot. Now he felt well enough to wonder how they would respond to cultivation.

Very badly, as it turned out. It was not that Nestor and
Pyrrhus were unfriendly, still less that they were rude: it
was more as though they had become perfect servitors, and
to that end had locked away every trace of normal human
feeling. They were, he thought, both Asiatic Greeks, but he
could not persuade them to discuss where they had come
from, what they had been before they arrived in Pollio's
house, or how they had come there. All his questions were
answered with requests to know if he wanted a hot com-
press, or more broth, or some other small service. If they
had feelings or desires of their own, they would not admit to
them. He found it very disquieting.

Cantabra went out again, which annoyed him: he felt
she might at least have advised him what she was doing. He
spent the morning in bed, recovering from the purgative,
considering his situation, and wishing that his bodyguard
would come back so that he would have someone to talk to.
As the hours wore on he began to wonder anxiously if she'd
got into a fight—or whether Pollio had hired her. By her
own account, the man had recognized her, and he had certainly seemed to find her amusing. From her point of view,
working for Pollio would be a great deal safer and more
secure than working for a man who would at best leave
Rome in a score of days, and, at worst, meet an inglorious
death.

Early in the afternoon the steward Socrates turned up,
with another strong young male slave. "My master believed
you might want a bath," he informed Hermogenes. "Xanthos and Pyrrhus can carry you to the bathhouse."

The thought of a long hot bath was actually very

appealing, but the reference to Socrates' master wanting him to have one put him instantly on guard. "Perhaps later," he said, smiling. "I was just about to have a nap."

There was a momentary silence. The new slave, Xanthos, shifted his feet uncomfortably and glanced anxiously at Socrates.

"The master wants the bathhouse for some other guests later," Socrates told him smoothly. "Please come now, sir. The doctor recommended bathing as good for your injuries, and now is the time that would be convenient for the staff."

He met the steward's eyes, and had no more doubts: Pollio had given orders that he be delivered to the bathhouse. A meeting? Very likely. With whom, though, and why?

"Very well," he said, trying to hide his queasy apprehension. "I do not wish to inconvenience any of the staff, after you have all been so . . . attentive. Do you happen to know where my bodyguard is?"

The steward showed a hint of what Hermogenes suspected was real amusement. "You want the gladiatrix to attend you in the bath?"

"No!" he snapped, more sharply than he'd intended. "I don't want her to come back here and think that I've been kidnapped. She is new to the work, and trying very hard to prove her worth. She might do something stupid."

"Nestor will stay here to tell her where you are," Socrates conceded. He snapped his fingers, and Xanthos and Pyrrhus helped the guest to the chair which had been used the day before, and carried him from the room.

Pollio's private bathhouse occupied a whole wing, descending the slope of the Esquiline in steps. It was, as

Hermogenes expected, enormous and sumptuous—hot plunge room, cold plunge, steam room, swimming pool, all lavishly decorated with frescos and polished stone. It was also, to his surprise, empty. He and the slaves undressed, and he allowed Xanthos and Pyrrhus to help him first to the hot plunge, then to the cold, and then to the steam room. He was lying on the bench between the two slaves, allowing the heat to soak the aches out of his muscles, when he heard the sound of voices just outside the door. He grabbed his crutch and sat up, steeling himself.

The first man through the door was Tarius Rufus.

They recognized one another at once. Rufus looked less intimidating naked than he had in consular purple: a heavy, hairy body, with a pronounced paunch. He was still wearing all his rings, though, and Hermogenes braced himself against the bench and held the crutch in front of himself like a shield. Rufus, however, stared for a long moment in shock and evident horror, then whirled and shrieked to the man behind him, "Oh, Jupiter, the *Egyptian's* here!"

The man behind shoved forward to see; he was, as Hermogenes had expected, Tarius Macedo, looking thin and hard as a dagger—more formidable than when clothed, in contrast to his patron. He stared wildly and exclaimed, "It's not possible! He's still at the moneylender's!"

"Don't be stupid!" bellowed the consul. "It's *him*. Gods and goddesses, what do we do now? I can't kill Titus, but you know what'll happen if we try to sell!"

"I'll strangle Gunthar!" muttered Macedo, and strode rapidly into the steam room.

Pollio's two slaves were both on their feet, and Pyrrhus

stepped quickly in front of Hermogenes. Macedo halted, glaring. Hermogenes had noticed that both the slaves who'd accompanied him were young, strong, and athletic looking. He'd assumed that they'd been chosen for their decorative appearance, but he suddenly doubted it.

"Ah, my dear Hermogenes!" exclaimed Pollio, waddling into the room behind his guests—a grotesque figure, with his swollen feet and hands and shriveled torso. He had another two sturdy slaves behind him. "I hope you are enjoying the steam bath? Lucius, I believe you've met my other guest, Marcus Aelius Hermogenes? He was injured the other day by robbers in the Subura, and was very fortunate to escape with his life."

Rufus had turned nearly purple and seemed unable to speak. Pollio waddled over and sat down on the bench beside Hermogenes. "I didn't know you had so many bruises," he remarked. He squeezed his guest's shoulder, gazing at the black blotches that marked his torso with avid admiration. "What a pity they didn't catch your attackers!"

Hermogenes set the foot of the crutch on the floor and pushed himself to his feet. He felt no more able to speak than Rufus, so he inclined his head politely to his host and limped toward the door. His two guards followed him, keeping between him and the visitors. Rufus, however, did not move away from the door, and Hermogenes was forced to stop.

"What are you doing here?" the consul demanded in choked voice. He spoke in Greek, though everything else had been in Latin. Hermogenes suddenly suspected that the other man didn't realize that he spoke Latin. All their dealings had been in Greek. That "I can't kill Titus!" had been something he wasn't expected to understand.

"I came here to ask Publius Vedius Pollio if he wished to buy a debt," Hermogenes told him evenly, in Greek. "He has yet to decide whether he wants to do so. I neither know nor care about anything else that may be involved."

"You foul, greedy, moneylending parasite!" roared the consul.

Hermogenes stood where he was, trembling with a rage he had not expected. "I practice a useful trade honestly," he said fiercely. "You are the one who abused your power as governor of Cyprus to force an honest businessman to lend you more than he could afford, and who defaulted when you could have repaid him easily. When I asked you for what you unquestionably owe, you tried to have me killed. Foul, greedy parasite? That's a very good description of *you*, Consul."

Rufus swung at him. The slaves had been braced for it, however: Xanthos blocked the blow with his forearm, while Pyrrhus grabbed Hermogenes round the waist and half dragged, and half carried him out, shoving Rufus aside. Pollio laughed and clapped his hands.

Back in the changing room, Pyrrhus deposited the guest in the chair, which was still standing where they'd left it on arrival, and began hauling their clothing and sandals from the storage niches. Xanthos came out from the steam room, his forearm bruised red and a ring scrape along his bare shoulder. From behind him came the sound of Pollio's voice, high and gleeful, and an angry reply. Xanthos glanced back and spat, then looked at Hermogenes in the chair and Pyrrhus with his armful of clothing. Hermogenes could see him wonder how to move everything at once.

"Give me the clothes," he said. "We can get dressed outside."

Xanthos said nothing, merely nodded, and Pyrrhus piled the clothing into his lap. They fled the bathhouse and hurried out into the long colonnade which led back to the main part of the house. A passing gardener looked at them curiously: two stark naked slaves carrying a naked visitor up the hill in a chair piled with clothes. Xanthos and Pyrrhus went about twenty paces, then seemed to decide that it was far enough, and set the chair down.

"Thank you," Hermogenes told Xanthos, handing the slave his tunic. "And I am sorry. I knew he is prone to violence, and I shouldn't have said anything."

Xanthos looked surprised. "The master said we were to keep you safe," he replied. He examined the scrape on his shoulder, rubbed the blood off with his hand, then pulled on the tunic.

"If you can stand up, sir," Pyrrhus said respectfully, "I'll help you with your clothes."

Hermogenes stood up, balancing with one knee against the seat of the chair, and let the slave help him. He was still belting his tunic when Cantabra came down the colonnade at a run, her face flushed and her tunic hitched up above her knees. She stopped abruptly when she saw him, and dropped the folds of cloth. Pyrrhus began donning his own clothing hurriedly, his embarrassment at being seen naked by a strange woman the first normal human feeling he'd shown.

"Where have you been?" Hermogenes asked his bodyguard angrily.

"I heard that your enemy is here," she replied breathlessly.

"Yes. I just met him." The rage shook him again. Pollio had sprung him on Rufus like the worst sort of practical joke: open the steam room door, and whoops! here's the man you tried to kill, somewhat battered, as you see, but still alive to cause you trouble!

He suddenly wondered if his own death was likely to figure in any bargain Pollio made with Rufus: Do as I ask, and I will get the documents from the Alexandrian and hand him over to you.

"What is the matter?" asked Cantabra quickly.

He shook his head glumly: nothing he could discuss in front of Pyrrhus and Xanthos. "My foot hurts," he said instead. "We should go back to my rooms." He sat down in the chair again.

Back in the room, he sat silent, trying to puzzle it out.

Pollio was trying to blackmail Rufus into killing someone called Titus: that much was clear. Who, though, was Titus?

There were far too many possibilities; the Roman male population only had about half a dozen first names among them. Obviously Rufus's Titus wasn't Titus Fiducius Crispus, the first who'd leaped to his own mind. Pollio wouldn't need any help to kill a minor businessman. It had to be a rich and powerful Titus, someone Pollio couldn't get to without the consul's help.

It wasn't the emperor, whose first name had been Gaius

when he was young, and was now officially Imperator. It had never made any sense that Pollio would want to harm the emperor, anyway. He owed everything to the fact that he had been useful to Augustus during his rise. A new emperor would lack the old one's tolerance of a creature who had served him well. Still, it was a relief. Anyone suspected of involvement in treason could be tortured, and the estate of anyone convicted of the offense was confiscated.

So who was Titus? The emperor's deputy and designated successor was a Marcus—Agrippa. Pollio's superior and rival in the imperial circle had been a Gaius—Maecenas—and he was now out of favor anyway, unless rumor lied. Who else was there? And what benefit did Pollio expect from his death?

He suspected that this plan, whatever it was, aimed at restoring Pollio to the imperial favor he had enjoyed before the incident of the crystal cups. Now that he thought about that story, it seemed less straightforward than it had when he first heard it. The emperor had known Pollio for years: he must have heard about the lampreys long before he came to dinner that night. That smashing of crystal suddenly seemed to hold a calculated message: *I no longer need you, and I will no longer tolerate you.* Pollio was a man from the humblest of backgrounds—the son of a freed slave!—who'd risen to power and enormous wealth through his service to Augustus. Without the emperor's friendship, what was he? He must find his fall from favor frightening as well as humiliating. He must long to get back into the charmed circle, to do something to show the emperor that he was still a necessary man.

Kill Titus. He did not know enough about court politics. Nobody did, apart from the players themselves. All the
world ever heard was rumors, and the official proclamations
in which there was never any trace of ambition or jealousy,
greed or hatred or pride.

He was not sure, anyway, that he really cared who Titus
was or how the struggle between Rufus and Pollio turned
out. If he could be certain that the consul would be forced
to pay his debt in some form, and that he himself would get
some benefit from it, he would take his money and go
home. He found that he no longer believed, though, that
anyone was going to allow him to do that.

Was he himself *important* enough for his life be part of
the price for "killing Titus"? Would Rufus really insist on
getting him, as well as the documents? The consul was a
violent man, arrogant and easily moved to hatred, but he
must hate many people, and he couldn't go around killing
all of them.

With a sinking of the heart he decided that yes, he
probably *was* important enough. His appearance in Rome,
and his stubborn insistence on his rights, had caused the
consul's current crisis, and his very existence was an accusation. Rufus would want him permanently silenced. And
Pollio, he was quite certain, wouldn't hesitate to oblige if it
got him what he wanted.

They still needed the documents and his letter. He
shivered. If this suspicion hadn't occurred to him, he would
have fetched them from the record office and the priest the
moment Pollio agreed to buy the debt.

Of course, he didn't *know* that Pollio planned to give

him to Rufus. The idea was mere suspicion. Perhaps the consul would even resist the blackmail, and the whole matter would come to court. He didn't expect it, though—and he knew that he was not going to risk giving those documents to Pollio. The more he saw of the man, the less he trusted him. He needed to make plans to escape. He needed to speak to Cantabra—privately.

He looked up, and saw the barbarian woman sitting quietly on the floor in a corner of the room, frowning over one of her much-mended sandals. Pyrrhus and Nestor were perched on stools in the other corner, playing in silence a game that involved trying to match each other's gestures. Xanthos had gone back to whatever other duties he had been given.

"Cantabra," he said, and forced a smile as she looked up. "You told me that at the gladiatorial school they know a kind of massage which is good for muscle injuries. May I try it? I think I knocked my foot against something during that unwelcome meeting, and now my whole leg hurts." Understand me, he pleaded silently with his eyes; don't suspect me of wanting to seduce you, and take offense.

She put the sandal down and gave him a hard blue stare. "If you like," she said. "I need some oil." She glanced at the two slaves. "Lamp oil will do, if it's clean."

"Pyrrhus will fetch some massage oil," Nestor told her. Pyrrhus at once stood up and went off to do so.

Cantabra shrugged, but went over to the sleeping cubicle, and drew back the curtain. "You should lie down," she told her employer. "Let me see the leg."

He got up quickly, hobbled into the cubicle, and lay down on the bed on his back. She knelt down on the floor beside him and ran a hand fastidiously down his right leg below the knee. "The muscles are in knots," she told him. "Turn over on your stomach."

He did so. Pyrrhus came back with a flask of oil, and Cantabra poured some on her hands and set to work kneading the back of Hermogenes' calf. Her fingers were very strong, and the muscles *were* sore. He made a noise of protest.

"It will help," she told him severely, then glanced up at the two slaves, both watching from the doorway.

Hermogenes dismissed them with a wave. "Go back to your amusement."

They went back into the dressing room, drawing the curtain. Cantabra paused to put more oil on her hands, and as she did so, lowered her mouth to his ear and whispered, "They are still listening."

He closed his eyes a moment in relief.

"I used to do this to my fellows in the hall," Cantabra went on, in a normal tone of voice, "to some of them, that is. It is good for muscle strains. You should eat ashes, too."

"Eat ashes?"

"The ashes of beef bone. It is good for injuries. The barley broth the doctor is giving you is good, too, but I don't think he should have given you so strong a purgative." She moved her head near his so he could whisper to her.

"I want to get out of here as soon as possible," he whispered, and said, in a normal tone, "It was certainly very powerful."

Her face didn't change. "I have found a place to cross the garden wall," she whispered back. "Also, I have stolen and concealed a rope." In the normal tone: "It was more powerful than it needed to be."

He closed his eyes again, so deeply relieved that he feared he might break down. So that was what she'd been doing that morning! It was more than he had hoped for, much more. He had given no instructions, but she had anticipated, considered the possibilities, acted. He supposed that was the difference between a free employee and a slave. It might well be the difference between death and escape. "Thank you," he whispered.

Cantabra smiled widely. "That was only a small infection," she said dismissively. "In the school we would not do anything about one like that, except keep it clean." Whispering again: "I do not know what we do about the slaves. I do not think I can overcome both of them silently, and if there is any sound, there are many, many others who will hear it, and come."

He whispered, "I'd prefer it if we could avoid hurting them," and added, "Gladiators are much tougher than businessmen—Let me think."

"You are not so soft," Cantabra told him, and pinched a muscle in his calf. He yelped. "Your legs have muscles like a runner."

"It's true I used win races at school," he told her. "Until Demodokos's son Aristarchos grew taller than me, that is. Then he won them all. Now all the exercise I get is playing ball games with my slaves and trudging about the city to business meetings—and now I can't even do that."

"Will your foot bear you?" whispered Cantabra.

"It must," he replied grimly.

There was a brief silence, during which they both realized that the massage would have to go on a bit longer if it were to look natural, and that they had said as much as they wanted to risk in the hearing of the eavesdroppers.

"What happened when you met Tarius Rufus?" Cantabra asked.

He began to tell her, at first just to reassure the listeners, then, as the account progressed, because the ridiculousness of it struck him, and it satisfied him to reduce his own terror and rage to a scene from a farce. When he reached the point where Pyrrhus had picked him up and carried him bodily from the room, Cantabra laughed. She had a loud, hooting, thoroughly uncivilized laugh, and it made him grin.

"All of you naked?" she asked.

"All of us," he confirmed, "though Rufus wore all his rings—which, I assure you, are a deadly weapon. They marked poor Xanthos. Anyway, Pyrrhus snatched all the clothes from the shelves like a thief in the public baths, and we ran out into the colonnade, to the amazement of the gardeners—and there you found us."

Cantabra, grinning, slapped his leg. "The story is done, and so is the massage."

He sat up, caught her oily hands, pressed them, and said loudly, "Thank you. Thank you very much. I feel much better now."

She grinned back at him conspiratorially.

Pollio's doctor came in a little later. He examined the cut and the ankle—again without undoing the splints—and expressed his satisfaction. He cleaned and anointed the wound again, and recommended rest, plenty of fluids, and a diet restricted to barley broth for the next day. Hermogenes thanked him politely, then said tentatively, "That purgative you gave me was very strong."

"Yes," agreed the doctor with satisfaction. "I brew them that way. It worked well, didn't it?"

"Indeed," Hermogenes agreed. "Very well, and I'm grateful. My guts are still upset, though, and I don't know whether I *will* be able to rest as you recommend. To tell the truth, I've been having trouble sleeping anyway, what with this crisis in my affairs. I was wondering if you could give me something to dry up my guts and perhaps help me sleep."

The doctor had no objections to this. He rummaged in his leather bag of supplies and brought out a small redware flask with a stopper. "Have you ever had opium before?" he asked.

"No," said Hermogenes, who'd taken it several times for an enteritic fever.

"A very useful drug, and, I think, exactly what you want. It dries and tightens the bowels and promotes sleep. Here, I'll leave you a dose, and when you're ready to go to bed, just mix it with some of your barley broth and drink it down."

"Make it a good dose," Hermogenes told him. "I haven't slept well for months."

The doctor smiled and poured a good dose into a cup. Hermogenes covered it with a cloth. Now he had to think of a way to make sure the slaves drank it.

The doctor left. The steward Socrates arrived. He nodded to Pyrrhus and Nestor, smiled at Cantabra, who was

Gillian Bradshaw

sitting on the floor in the corner again looking bored, and
inclined his head respectfully to Hermogenes. "Sir," he said
politely, "my master invites you to eat dinner with him."

"That is very kind of him," Hermogenes replied, forcing
himself to smoothness, "but the doctor has just advised me
to eat nothing but barley broth for another day."

That actually threw the steward—for a moment. "I will
see that the cook knows that," he said, recovering. "I think
that really my master wishes to discuss business with you."

"In that case, I am delighted to accept his invitation."

Xanthos appeared back at the room about an hour later
to help Pyrrhus carry him to the dinner. As the two young
men carried his chair along the corridor with Cantabra
stalking silently behind, he asked the young man how his
arm was.

Xanthos gave him a surprised smile. "Still sore, sir,
thank you. That fellow hits hard."

"He gave me this," Hermogenes informed him, touching the stitches on his cheek.

"Then I'm glad he only hit my arm!"

"Hush!" said Pyrrhus, in a tone half-frightened and
half-scandalized. Xanthos glanced around nervously and
hushed.

They weren't allowed to talk to guests, Hermogenes
suddenly understood, even if the guests invited it. Slaves in
this household were expected to be obedient domestic con-
veniences. Normal human conversation from them was a
fault which could be reported to the stewards, who, on the
master's orders, would punish it. He discovered that he
hated Pollio just as much as he hated Rufus.

"I'm sorry," he told the two young men sincerely. "I don't mean to get you into trouble. I'll stop." They both gave him looks of surprise and doubt.

Pollio's dining hall was, like the rest of his house, huge and lavish. The high domed ceiling was blue, with constellations picked out on it in gold, and the floor was decorated with a superb mosaic of sea creatures and fish. Pollio reclined in it alone on a gilded couch, nibbling something off a dish on a small gold table set up in front of him. When the slaves brought his guest in, he patted the cushions next to him. "Come and join me," he said.

There didn't seem to be any other choice: the other couches had been moved back against the wall. Hermogenes levered himself out of the chair and reluctantly lay down next to his host. Xanthos and Pyrrhus carried the chair out, and Cantabra, after a moment's hesitation, moved over to stand silently next to the wall, where, he noticed, a number of slaves stood waiting for their master's orders. A beautiful young girl came over to him with a cup of green glass, bowed, and handed it to him.

It was barley broth, but it was steaming and it smelled of spices. Pollio giggled. "I gathered you're allowed nothing else," he said. "I told my cooks to try to make it interesting for you."

"That was very considerate," Hermogenes replied, and sipped the drink. It had been flavored with nutmeg and pepper and sweetened with honey: hardly what the doctor had in mind. "This is delicious."

Pollio helped himself to some of his own first course—eggs stuffed with forcemeat. "I can't stand the stuff myself," he said. "The doctor says he's cured the infection, though, and that your ankle is beginning to knit, so we won't argue with him, eh?" He patted his guest's arm affectionately. "Tell me, are you sleeping with your gladiatrix?"

"No," Hermogenes replied, without heat. "I hired her as a bodyguard."

"I thought you'd have better taste than that ugly red-haired heifer. What do you like, then, eh? Boys, girls, women, young men? Dark or fair, heavy or slim? Tell me, and tonight I'll send you whatever you want. I have a couple of hundred people here, and most of 'em are young and pretty. I only keep the older ones if they're useful." He put his hand on his guest's arm again. The swollen fingers were hot.

"The doctor also recommended that I rest, Lord Vedius Pollio."

"Killjoys, doctors. If a man obeyed them, he'd have no pleasures left. Go on, what do you prefer?"

"Women who want me."

Pollio laughed. "Any of my women'll do for you, then. If they don't want a guest, they know better than to let him see it."

"Lord, I am tired and bruised, my ankle is broken, and I am still recovering from your doctor's very potent purgative. I do not want a woman tonight."

"Oh, that purgative, I'd forgotten! That's a fierce decoction, isn't it? Well, a pity, then. Tomorrow night, perhaps." Pollio took his hand away and used it to stuff another egg into his mouth. "Right now I suppose you want to know what I decided about the debt?"

"Yes," he said truthfully. "I would."

"I'm afraid I've decided to buy it, rather than help you collect it. You did annoy Lucius this afternoon; Hercules, you did!" Pollio laughed again, his rheumy eyes glinting with malicious pleasure. "I think helping you collect after that would be more trouble than it's worth. But I will give you your two-thirds, plus the interest. I'll have the contract drawn up tomorrow morning. When we've signed, you can go collect the documents. You notice that I don't ask for them beforehand."

Hermogenes was silent a moment, checking through his options and trying to find a way to discover what he wanted to know without giving away his suspicion. "I will be extremely glad to have the matter resolved," he said at last, trying to sound merely relieved. "Extremely glad. When should I tell my bodyguard to fetch a sedan chair for me?"

"I will lend you my own litter, and instruct the bearers to take you wherever you want to go."

"I would prefer to hire a chair, lord."

"I insist."

"Lord Vedius Pollio, Rufus's men may recognize your litter. I do not trust him. He might attack me in the street if he thought he could get the documents that way."

"He isn't that stupid—and my people will protect you. I *insist*."

That emphasis. No, he would not be allowed to collect the documents by himself. He still would not be permitted to slip away.

"If you insist, lord, I must accept," Hermogenes said, with an inclination of the head.

"Oh, very smooth!" Pollio clapped his hands, and two of the slaves darted forward to collect his plate and his guest's empty cup. "You might almost have the talent to be someone."

"I believe I am someone. Marcus Aelius Hermogenes."

"No." Pollio smiled at him, picking a scrap of force-meat from one of his pointed teeth with the nail of his little finger. "No, if you were someone, Rufus would written to you promising to pay the debt the moment it came into your hands. He would have known, you see, that he could not ignore you the way he did Nikomachos. But you were just a small man, playing at moneymaking with a handful of syndicates and staying well clear of politics. Nobody to worry about." He put his hand, finger still wet from his mouth, back on his guest's arm. "You still think that money is for buying *things,* don't you? You haven't tried buying power."

"That would make me happy, would it?" Hermogenes asked dryly.

Pollio blinked at him, nonplussed, as though he had countered a remark about shipping with one about philosophy.

"I think I know my limitations, lord," Hermogenes told him. "I prefer to be the nobody I am." *Particularly,* he thought, *if being "someone" means you end up foul and sick and universally despised, reclining on a gold couch in a huge hall alone—apart from slaves who don't dare show what they really feel.*

The two servitors hurried forward again, one with a covered dish for Pollio, the other with a gold cup. The cup contained barley broth heated with salt and parsley and fish sauce. The dish contained lampreys.

"My favorite!" said Pollio, with a pointed-toothed smile.

He knows everyone's heard. Hermogenes thought, forcing himself to sip the broth unconcernedly. Another joke, like the steam room. "Too rich for me," he said calmly, "and I fear that fish sauce doesn't really go with barley broth, though your cook is to be complimented for the attempt."

Pollio laughed and patted him on the arm again.

Throughout the lampreys, Pollio talked about Alexandria, sometimes questioning his guest, sometimes telling anecdotes of his own. He had been there after the conquest of Egypt, and had acquired various items of plunder, some of which he had profitably disposed of, some of which he had kept. He kept touching his guest, usually on the arm or shoulder, occasionally on the thigh. Hermogenes endured it with composure. Pollio liked both young men and girls—that was clear from the way he looked at his slaves—but he himself was not so young, and he was certain that the caresses were intended principally to worry and disturb him. That, too, seemed to be something Pollio liked.

The lampreys were cleared away, and the servitors brought Pollio a dish of stuffed dormice, and Hermogenes a crystal cup full of chilled barley broth sweetened, thickened with barley grounds, and scented with cloves. They also brought Caecuban wine.

"Have just one cup, and damn the doctor!" his host urged him.

Hermogenes accepted the one cup, and sipped it alternately with the barley broth, although they didn't mix well.

Pollio downed his own cup quickly, called for another, then sat up a little and patted his guest on the thigh. "I had an idea earlier how we might entertain ourselves this evening, eh? Your gladiatrix is quite a formidable fighter for a woman, and last time she was here she nearly came to blows with one of my men, who was a gladiator in the same school. He's itching to get back at her. What do you say we have them fight?"

Hermogenes stared at him, finally unable to keep his composure. "No!" he said angrily.

"Come! You're as joyless as my doctor. Don't you like fights?"

"I hate fights, and I have never liked the games."

Pollio rolled his eyes. "What, you're a *philosopher*? You're going to tell me that the games inflame all the baser passions, and suffocate the nobler ones; that the deaths of men and women should not be treated as mere entertainment?"

"If you know that, there is no point in me saying it."

"The trouble with Plato's Republic, dear simpleton, is that it's a place which never did exist and never could. Men *have* baser passions, and they *will* indulge them, regardless of what philosophers may think of it. That's the reason philosophers will never rule. I named all my household stewards after philosophers, and like their counterparts in the world, they take orders from power." He clapped his hands and ordered, "Fetch Ajax."

A slave ran off to do so. Hermogenes sat very still, struggling to reason despite the white-hot blaze of indignation. Little as he knew of the games, he did know that female gladiators usually fought each other, not men. This was a blatant attempt to get rid of his bodyguard and make things easier for the men who would seize him. It was also, he decided, looking at Pollio's avid face, something his host genuinely wanted. The foul old man considered Cantabra grotesque and amusing, and he would find it entertaining to see her injured or killed.

He sat up and swung his feet off the couch. Cantabra was still standing motionless by the wall, as she had done for the whole meal. They had been speaking in Latin, however, and she had heard and understood: that was immediately clear from the grim set of her face and from her hot eyes. Hermogenes bent and picked up his crutch.

"What are you doing?" demanded Pollio sharply.

Hermogenes stood, then bowed his head. "I am sorry, Lord Vedius Pollio. I am suddenly feeling most unwell. I think I should not have drunk the wine; the doctor did warn me to avoid it. That purgative . . . please excuse me, but I simply *must* use the latrine."

Pollio glared at him. "Go, then. But leave the woman. She's happy enough to fight; she had to be restrained from it when she was last here!"

"I work for Lord Harmogenes," Cantabra announced suddenly. "He says he does not want me to fight. I cannot disobey him."

Hermogenes nodded to her once, gestured for her to come, and began to hobble forward. He had taken only one hopping step, however, when the slave Pollio had sent out came back, leading two men in red tunics. One was carrying weapons and pieces of armor; the other was already fully armed as the type of gladiator called a retiarius, with a harpoon, a net on a cord, and leather and metal bands at his ankles, waist, and left shoulder. The fight must have been arranged beforehand, and everything was in hand for it to proceed, regardless of objections and evasions.

The two guards looked around for Cantabra; when they saw her, the retiarius leered. He was a tall, slim young man in his early twenties, heavily scarred on the arms, good-looking in a dark, sullen sort of way. Cantabra stared at him impassively, then caught up her long tail of hair and twisted it about the front of her head. She began to tuck the end back into the leather band that held it. Somehow the gesture made it utterly clear to everyone that she would fight.

"Sit down," Pollio ordered Hermogenes, and settled himself more comfortably on the couch.

"Lord Vedius Pollio," Hermogenes replied, "I fear that I must play the part of your doctor, and advise you that your pleasures are likely to do you harm."

The old man frowned at him.

"This is not an arena," Hermogenes told him. "It is a private house. These people are no longer gladiators. They are a free man and a free woman. In the arena, if one of them should kill the other, it would be lawful. Here it would be murder—particularly when there are witnesses to the fact that the woman does not wish to fight."

He looked away from his host, and addressed his next words to the two guardsmen—the ex-gladiator and the other, who he suspected was the commander of Pollio's bodyguards. "Murder is a crime for which a man who is not a citizen—as I presume you are not—would be punished by a cruel death, or by being sent to the mines. You should bear that in mind, because if one of Lord Pollio's enemies should learn of it, and decide to take advantage of it, I do not think he would sacrifice anything to protect you." He turned back to Pollio. "Lord, you *know* that you have enemies, and you *know* that the protection you once had is something you do not presently enjoy. Are you going to give your enemies this gift—a legally valid charge of incitement to murder—for them to use against you in any way they please?"

"Who would tell them?" Pollio asked, very softly. "You?"

Hermogenes spread his hands. "Lord Pollio, do you think that swaggering bully with the net won't boast of this to all his friends in the barracks? Do you think they won't laugh about it in the taverns? Do you think that Rufus isn't watching you—now, of all times? He would *love* to find a charge to use against you. I repeat, I am playing the part of a doctor. Can you really believe that this entertainment you propose is good for your health?"

Pollio stared at him for a long moment, picking his teeth. Then he waved a hand to his bodyguards. "Go back to your barracks," he ordered.

The retiarius, Ajax, looked keenly disappointed. The other man merely shrugged. The two left as silently as they had come.

"You should be careful, Alexandrian," Pollio told him, still very softly. "You people always consider yourselves the most cunning and intelligent in all the world—but you often seem to forget that we defeated you."

"I do not forget," Hermogenes told him. "Lord, I truly am not well, and tomorrow we have much to do. If you excuse me, I would like to go to my room now and rest."

H E ENDED UP WALKING BACK TO HIS room, since Pollio didn't send for the chair and he was too proud to ask for it. It was several corridors, and there was one short flight of steps. His armpit and left leg were both hurting by the time he reached that, and he stood gritting his teeth and wondering if he dared use his right foot. Cantabra came up from behind him, took the crutch out of his right hand and put it in his left, and pulled his right arm over her shoulder. He managed the steps.

"Thank you," he told her at the top.

She looked at him sideways. "Thank you for refusing to make me fight."

He set his teeth again, this time against the rage. "He wanted you out of the way, do you realize that?" he said in a vehement whisper. "He wanted you dead, to make it easier for his people tomorrow."

"You said he was not going to kill you," she pointed out, frowning.

"I was wrong. I think he means to give me to Rufus. As part of the bargain."

Her frown deepened. "How do you know that?"

He hesitated. "I don't. But I think it is what he will do. It's the kind of man he is."

She nodded. "An evil man." She tugged at his arm to start him moving again. Her shoulder was bony and hard under his sore armpit, but the curve of her breast was soft against his side. He felt a spasm of tenderness toward her, a tingle of improbable desire.

"I was never going to make you fight," he told her warmly. "That oily bully would have killed you!"

She gave him one of her hard blue looks. "I might have won. Ajax was a retiarius. I have beaten retiarii. I think maybe I should have fought him, and let Lord Pollio have his show."

He felt obscurely slighted. "I thought women didn't normally fight men."

"Normally, no. But sometimes, if they're good, and if the organizers think it will please the crowd. I was a secutor or a dimachaeri; I could fight retiarii. It's not the same as going against a Thracian or a myrmillo."

He remembered the savage efficiency with which she'd killed his attackers in the Subura. Perhaps she *could* have won. "But then what?" he asked aloud. "Even if you did kill or disable that idiot, you might have been injured—and why should you fight to amuse that . . . that *disease*? I could never have let you fight!"

"I did not want to fight," she said, very serious. "I hated the school and the arena, and I would never go back to them. I refused to reenlist; even when I was hungry on the streets, I preferred to starve. I was glad when you refused, and again when you made him give way. But it made me afraid, too." They had reached the rooms, and she stopped, just outside the door. "You fought Pollio in your way so that I wouldn't have to fight Ajax in mine," she whispered. "He had not expected that, and certainly he had not expected you to get the better of him. He will think about you differently now, not as a weapon but as an opponent. That is not good."

She was probably right, he realized. If he succeeded in getting away, he would be viewed not just as a lost tool but as a potential threat—a dangerously perceptive man who had probably understood things Pollio didn't want known. Pollio would want to kill him just as much as Rufus did. "Oh, Isis!" he groaned, and took his arm from around Cantabra's shoulders to rub it wearily through his hair.

She opened the door for him and helped him through.

Nestor, who was on his own, was surprised to see the guest arrive back without Pyrrhus and the chair. He dithered miserably, clearly unsure whether to go and fetch his partner or stay to keep watch over the guest. Hermogenes took pity on him, and told Cantabra to pass the message to Pyrrhus, if she could.

"And perhaps you could see if the kitchens have any more of that special barley broth," he suggested. "The first kind, with the nutmeg, not the one with fish sauce. Tell the cook it was delicious."

She looked startled, but nodded and went off.

She returned not long afterward. With her came Pyrrhus, carrying a steaming jug and a cup on a tray. "The cook sends this," said the young man.

"My thanks to him and to you!" Hermogenes exclaimed, smiling. He had had time to regain his composure now, and he knew exactly what he meant to do. "But that's far more than I need. I only wanted a little to mix with the medicine the doctor left for me. Would the rest of you like to share what's left? It's very good, and it should be drunk while it's hot."

The slaves were uneasy about it: they undoubtedly felt there was something wrong with sharing a guest's drink. On the other hand, they were, he was certain, very seldom offered delicacies, and the broth smelled delicious. "Thank you, sir," quavered Nestor, blinking. "That's very kind."

Hermogenes sent Pyrrhus into the study to fetch a cup he'd used earlier that day. It was then a simple matter to wait until Nestor had gone to help his partner search for it, and to divide the dose of opium between the cup which went with the room's water jug and the cup which had come with the tray. "It may be in the sleeping cubicle," he called to Pyrrhus, and began to pour out the spiced barley broth to conceal what he'd done.

Pyrrhus and Nestor came back with the fourth cup, which had of course been in the sleeping cubicle all along. He filled that too, emptying the jug, and handed it to Cantabra. Her eyes were puzzled. He realized she didn't know what the drug did: he and the doctor had spoken in Greek. She probably thought it was another purgative. He picked up his own cup—the one which both the slaves knew had held the drug—and raised it to the others. "Good health!" he said, smiling. "I hope this gives me the sound sleep the doctor promised." Cantabra's expression cleared.

"Good health, sir!" the two slaves echoed, and drank the broth with guilty pleasure.

He made all the usual preparations for going to bed, then lay down in his cubicle in the dark, staring up at the ceiling. Tarius Rufus wanted to obtain the documents and kill him. If he escaped, Vedius Pollio would simply want to kill him. Where could he go now? Titus Fiducius's house wouldn't be safe, but he didn't have much coin. Perhaps he could go back to the house, collect his letters of credit, and take them to a bank and an inn.

And then what? Write off the debt, and try to sail back to Alexandria in secret?

He remembered his daughter, waiting for him to come home. Probably she was *not* getting on well with Aunt Eukleia, whom he had brought back from Cyprus only that spring. Eukleia was querulous and irritable with grief, and she felt strongly that her grand-niece had been allowed to run wild far too long, and should definitely be taken in hand at once. Probably she was right, but he so adored his wild little acrobat that it hurt him to think of her prim and subdued and ladylike. What would become of her, without him? There was money set aside for her dowry, but how would she live until then? What would she do, what would she *feel,* if he never came home?

There were the slaves, too. If he didn't come home, Eukleia would have to sell most of them, and move to a smaller house. They had been part of a household for years—for their whole lives, in many cases—and it would be a total degradation, a change from being a member of a family to being property. How could he inflict it on them?

But how could he accept letting another man cheat him, beat and abuse him, and try to kill him, with impunity? Some hard knot of pride and self-respect inside him would be severed forever: he would not be the man he had always believed himself to be. He would not be "someone" at all but what Pollio had called him, nobody. He would rather be dead.

Besides, would going home be enough to secure his safety anymore? Wouldn't Rufus or Pollio send men after him? Pollio at least had many connections in Egypt, and he was not the man to let a potentially dangerous opponent slip away. No. He could not risk bringing the trouble back home. He had to see this through to whatever end he could force on it.

What, then? Sell the debt to Gaius Maecenas, who loathed Rufus and probably didn't like Pollio, either? Or try to find "Titus"? Was any powerful Roman going to be better than Rufus and Pollio?

This all assumed, he reminded himself, that he succeeded in slipping out of Pollio's house that night, which was by no means certain.

He thought of the way Nestor had smacked his lips after drinking the drugged broth, and the real gratitude in the old man's eyes for the treat. He remembered Pyrrhus dragging him out of the steam room and depositing him in the chair. He hoped they would not be punished for letting him escape. If he did escape.

After what seemed eons worrying, he got up and limped into the dressing room. Nestor and Pyrrhus were barely discernible heaps in front of the door. They did not stir when he went through into the study and lit the lamp.

Cantabra sat up. "It is still too early," she whispered reprovingly. "We should wait another hour."

He grunted, went to the desk, and rummaged about for papyrus and pens. Cantabra got up and came over. "What are you doing?"

"I don't want Nestor and Pyrrhus to get into too much trouble," he whispered back. "It wasn't their fault."

He found ink, sat down, and wrote: *Do not blame the slaves. I drugged them with opium I obtained from the doctor through a lie. I began to suspect that you mean to sell me to Rufus.*

"What does it say?" whispered the barbarian irritably.

"Just that I drugged them," he whispered back. He put away the pens and ink and moved the sheet of papyrus to the center of the desk.

She shook her head. "You are a strange man."

"You've said that before."

"Because it is true." She looked down into his upturned face. In the lamplight her hair was the color of embers, and her exotic pale eyes seemed dark. "I never knew any Greeks before. Are you like other Greeks?"

"I don't know. Are you like other Cantabrians?"

"No," she replied at once. "Before the arenas I was. Now I am not."

He looked away. "Yes. The arenas would change any-one."

She grunted, then suddenly said, "Tonight at the dinner. You said you hated the games, and Vedius Pollio replied as though he knew all the things you would say about them. Do many other Greeks say things like that—that 'the deaths of men and women should not be entertainment'?"

"That is something that our philosophers say, and I agree with them. But I fear that most other Greeks like the games almost as much as the Romans do. There is an amphitheater in Alexandria, and whenever they give games there, the mob rejoices."

"Still. I like it that your pil-o-sop-ers say that. What does that word mean, pilosoper?"

"'Lover of wisdom.'"

"Huh. The lovers of wisdom hate the games. I like that." She smiled.

He smiled back. "You have a good memory for what we said."

"I always listen if an enemy is talking. Sometimes I learn things that let me prepare for what he will do."

"You are a clever woman—and very good at your work. This afternoon when you told me you had been looking for a way to escape before I'd even thought about it . . . I was very, very glad."

She touched his cheek with the backs of her fingers. "I told you you would be glad that you decided to hire me."

He caught the hand in both his and pressed it. "So you did. And so I am."

She froze, her eyes widening, then snatched the hand

away. She rubbed it against her tunic as though he'd dirtied it. He felt a surprisingly sharp stab of hurt and indignation.

"Maybe it is late enough to go," she whispered. "Do you want to take the splints off, or leave them on?"

He swallowed his feelings. She had told him flatly that love wasn't included in her hire, and given what she must have suffered since she was enslaved, he couldn't blame her. She had almost certainly been raped by soldiers before being sent to the arenas, and probably abused by her keepers afterward. The real surprise was that he'd started to think of her as a desirable woman at all.

"Let me untie them and see what feels best," he said matter-of-factly.

The ankle was no longer swollen, though it still felt sore. He unwrapped it and cautiously tried his weight on it; it hurt, but bearably. He tried it with no splints, then with both, and settled for one, on the inside behind the joint. Cantabra helped him retie the bindings, and then he went back to his cubicle and collected his sandals, cloak, and belt. He checked his purse: it contained only six denarii and a few coppers. He would *have* to get some more coin. He glanced round the cubicle again, then picked up the crutch from its place against the wall. In the last resort, it was the only weapon he had.

The two slaves had not stirred even when he went through the dressing room with the lamp. Nestor's breath whistled a little in his sleep, but Pyrrhus's was soft and even as a child's.

Cantabra was looking at the two men. "How did you persuade the doctor to give you the right drug?" she asked him.

"I told him I had symptoms they normally prescribe it for. I assumed they wanted me incapacitated anyway."

"Huh! You are as cunning as that evil man said. Blow out the lamp now: we must let our eyes get used to the dark."

He blew out the lamp and set it down, and they stood together in the darkness, listening to Nestor's whistling breath.

"Now," said Cantabra at last, and moved soundlessly to the door.

It would not open wide enough to let them slip out: Pyrrhus was in the way. Eventually, seeing this, Cantabra took hold of his mattress and dragged it aside. The young man sat up abruptly and gazed at them, his eyes shining liquid even in the dimness. Everything seemed to freeze: Hermogenes was certain that even his heart stopped beating. Cantabra put her hand down the front of her tunic and pulled out a knife.

Pyrrhus muttered indistinctly and lay down again. His soft, childlike breathing resumed as though it had never stopped.

After a long minute, Cantabra prodded the young man's shoulder with a cautious knuckle. He did not stir.

"Probably he was never really awake at all," Hermogenes told her, his voice unsteady. "Opium does that."

The bodyguard shook her head and slid the knife back into its place. She must have a sheath for it stitched into her breast band, he thought, and wondered when she'd acquired that. The shopping trip before she carried his message to Pollio's house, probably: the knife looked like the one she'd taken off Rufus's man. She opened the door, stepped carefully around the sleeping slave out into the corridor, and Hermogenes followed her, closing the door behind them. Cantabra strode off, a shadow in the blackness, and he limped after her as quickly and quietly as he could.

They met no one in the corridor or the colonnade. Cantabra turned right at the bathhouse wing and led him along a path under the trees. The night was dark, with a half moon occasionally showing as a pale blur behind low cloud. Water gleamed on his right, and he wondered again about the lampreys.

When they neared the bottom of the garden, Cantabra made him wait in the shadows under a bush while she went to retrieve her rope and check that the wall was clear. Hermogenes sat quietly rubbing his sore foot for what seemed to be hours. At last, however, the barbarian woman reappeared, the rope in her hands. It was dark with dirt and smelled of compost: presumably she had buried it.

She put her mouth against his ear and breathed, "The place to climb the wall is there," pointing with a hand held low near the ground. He looked where she indicated, and saw that the ground rose slightly, making the climb less. "There is a tree to tie the rope to, there. But there are spikes on top of the wall, and there is a drop on the other side. You will have to be careful."

"*I* will?" he murmured back. "What about you?"

"I am going to distract the watchman."

"There's a watchman? Where?" His voice had risen, and she made an angry hushing gesture.

"Over at the far end of the wall," she told him, gesturing

into the darkness. "At the foot of that tree. He is half-asleep, but he would notice you climbing the wall. I am going to go up the slope from him and make small noises, like an animal caught in the bushes or a slave trying to hide. When he comes to investigate, I will slip away silently and follow you over the wall. I will go now. Count to two hundred, then go, tie the rope to the tree, and go over as quickly as you can."

"Will you be able to 'slip away silently'?" he asked with dread.

"Yes," she replied at once, and slid off into the night.

He counted to two hundred, then stood and walked down to the place his bodyguard had indicated. He made himself move quietly and carefully, despite the desperate desire to hurry: the last thing he needed was to turn the ankle again by running in the dark. He looped the rope about the tree, tied it, then approached the wall. Despite the rise in the ground it was higher than his head, and, as Cantabra had warned, the top was guarded with spikes of sharpened wood. They were angled outward, however, to catch thieves trying to climb in, and he thought they would not cause too much trouble to someone trying to climb out. He tossed the end of the rope over the wall, took off his cloak and threw it over the spikes, then worked the end of his crutch into the ground, got his left foot onto the handle, and scrambled up onto the top of the wall. A trapped pine-cone fell, rattling against the brick, and he thought for a moment he would be sick. He caught hold of the rope and slid off on the other side; dangled a moment above a half-seen roadway, then lowered himself quickly, careful to land on his left leg.

He pressed back against the wall, trying to control the harsh gasping of his breath, which seemed as loud as a shout in the stillness. He realized that he'd left his crutch on the other side of the wall. He reached up and caught the trailing edge of his cloak, but did not pull it down: Cantabra might want it.

She might want to pull herself up the rope, too. At the thought he caught a loop around his forearm, got both hands on it, and prepared to brace himself.

He stood waiting, his back against the rough brick. The only sound was the occasional hush of wind in the pines of Pollio's garden. As the minutes wore on he told himself that it was *good* that everything was so silent. The thing to worry about would be shouts of alarm.

A footstep rustled on the other side of the wall and he braced himself. There was no pull on the rope, however, merely a dark shape appearing on top of the wall. It dipped, then reappeared, and then Cantabra slid down the rope, and he had to jump aside so that she didn't land on top of him.

She handed him his crutch, her teeth gleaming in the darkness. "That was useful," she remarked. "Thank you." She caught up the end of the rope and threw it back over the wall. It would, he knew, become almost invisible as soon as it was on the ground, and no one was likely to notice it until morning. He tugged at the trailing edge of his cloak, then caught it as it fell on top of him. Cantabra was already moving away down the road, so he followed with the cloak bundled in his arms together with the crutch.

They walked down the Esquiline through an unbroken silence. Hermogenes found himself listening almost desperately for cries and the sound of people running behind them, but there was nothing. They might have been the only human beings awake and about in all the city.

When they approached the main road, the silence ebbed. Torches half a block away shone from an oxcart that was rumbling in to the city markets, and in an insula across the road a baby was crying. Hermogenes stopped on the corner, stunned at the ordinariness of it all. They had escaped; they really had *escaped*!

He looked vaguely at the bundle in his arms, then set down the crutch and put on the cloak, draping it neatly over his left shoulder and under his right arm, the way he would wear it for a casual occasion. He tugged the ends straight and picked up the crutch again.

Cantabra had stopped as well, and was waiting patiently, a tall thin shadow in the darkness.

"We need to go to my friend's house," he told her. "It should be safe if we go now. I hope that Rufus called off his watch after meeting me at Pollio's house, and probably Pollio won't set one up until tomorrow, after he knows that we've gone."

She nodded. "We will stay there? Or will we just collect money and leave again?"

"We will collect money and leave."

She nodded again, in a satisfied way. "Can you walk that far?"

He looked down at his bandaged ankle. "I think so. It might be better, though, if I didn't try. Perhaps we could ride on a cart."

They caught up with the oxcart ahead of them without

difficulty. It was carrying vegetables to market, along with baskets of eggs and a few live chickens. The driver and his two assistants were suspicious at first—strangers on the edge of the Subura were potentially dangerous—but apparently decided that a woman and a man with a crutch and a bandaged foot were unlikely to be dangerous. It was agreed that they could ride on the tail of the cart for small change. They rumbled and jolted slowly down the Via Labicana and into the Julian Forum, where the cart stopped and the two passengers got off.

It was about midnight, but there were plenty of people about—carters, mostly, making deliveries, with some early market vendors setting up stalls. The two fugitives picked their way through them and onto the Sacra Via.

It was still a long walk to the Via Tusculana, and Hermogenes' foot was aching badly by the time they drew near the house. He did not protest when Cantabra told him to wait in a shadowed alley mouth while she went ahead to check that there was indeed no watch on the house. He leaned against the wall of an insula, propped his foot up on the crutch, and stared up at the clouded sky. In a nearby apartment a couple were having a drunken argument. A child woke, and began to cry. Another cart rumbled past along the main road, taking a load of timber to supply the workshops of Rome.

Cantabra came back and told him the way was clear, and he nodded and limped the last block with the aid of the crutch.

There were no torches in the dolphin holders tonight, and he had a momentary nightmare as he faced the iron-studded door: what if there was nothing behind the door but rubble and the dead?

He told himself that that sort of blatant destruction of a well-known businessman would be too dangerously arrogant even for Rufus, and knocked on the door.

There was no answer. He considered knocking more loudly, then decided that he did not want to advertise his visit to the whole street, and went over to knock on the window of the lodge instead. When there was still no response he shoved the end of his crutch up behind the shutters and wriggled it about.

After about half a minute, somebody grabbed it, and then the window opened and the masklike face of Kyon looked out. At once the mask creased. "Sir!" cried Kyon breathlessly. "You're back!"

"Yes. Let us in, please! Quietly!"

Kyon ran to fling open the door, and Hermogenes limped through and stopped in the entranceway, trying to put his thoughts in order. A dim form came to the door of the lodge, and then Tertia's voice, soft with relief, said, "Oh, sir, you're back!"

Kyon's family must share the lodge with him at night. "Yes," he agreed again. "But I dare not stay long. Kyon, will you tell Titus that I am here?"

Kyon shot off into the house, so quickly that he even forgot to close the door. Cantabra shut it for him, and bolted it firmly.

Another shape came to the door of the lodge, and Hyakinthos exclaimed delightedly, "Sir! We were afraid." Erotion's voice could be heard from behind him, demanding to know if it was the nice Greek. "Yes!" Hyakinthos snarled at her impatiently, then went on, "Rufus's barbarians went away this afternoon, and we were afraid it meant he'd caught you!"

"No," Hermogenes said. "My foot hurts. I need to sit down."

He blundered through into the atrium and slumped onto the bench. Tertia darted past into the dining room and returned with a lamp.

There was a sound of voices from further inside the house, and then Titus Fiducius Crispus came running in, dressed only in a hastily snatched cloak. With him, however, came Menestor, tousled with sleep and dressed in nothing at all. Hermogenes sat up straight, gaping in shock. For the first time he registered that Hyakinthos had been sleeping with his family instead of his master. Menestor dropped to his knees beside him and seized his hand, his face radiant with relief and joy.

"My *dear* Hermogenes—" Titus began warmly.

"What is *this*!" Hermogenes roared furiously, waving an arm at his unclothed secretary.

Titus's face fell. "He s-said you w-wouldn't m-mind."

"I asked you to *look after* him! I told you I wanted to *free* him! How could you possibly think that meant you could just *take* him the minute I left the house?"

"Sir!" protested Menestor, understanding the emotion, if not the Latin words, "Sir, no, please, we didn't *mean* it!" He was almost in tears.

His master looked at him in confusion, and Menestor looked back directly and reached out to touch his chest nervously. "Oh, please, sir, please understand! I didn't . . . I didn't know what to do when you didn't come back. When the guards disappeared this afternoon, we thought . . . I was afraid . . . Titus Fiducius was very kind to me. He said he was sure you'd come back, but he swore he'd do everything he possibly could to find you. He sent a letter to Pollio's house, and he said that if he didn't get a response, he'd even write to Rufus. I was grateful and I was so anxious and I . . . and it's true, I told him you wouldn't mind. I'm *sorry,* sir!"

Hermogenes stared at him in disbelief, and Menestor dropped his eyes and said bitterly, "It's not as though you ever wanted me yourself."

He had absolutely no idea what to say, and he simply stared at the slave in shock.

"What has happened?" Cantabra asked sharply, in Latin.

"He . . . nothing," Hermogenes managed at last. "Nothing. I . . . thought Titus had forced himself on my secretary, but I misunderstood." He made himself look at Titus, who was twisting the edge of his cloak in both hands like a nervous little girl.

"I am sorry I shouted," he made himself say. "I misunderstood."

"That's q-quite . . ." stammered Titus. "That's . . . I do understand, I would've . . . that is, I understand."

"I need to tell you what has happened," he went on, trying to gather his wits again.

"Do you want to come into the dining room and have some wine?" offered Titus.

They went into the dining room. More people were

coming in from the back of the house—Stentor, Gallus, three or four of the other slaves, all relieved to see their master's guest back in one piece for a change. Someone ran to fetch wine.

"Menestor," Hermogenes ordered, "go get some clothes on."

Menestor looked down at himself as though only just realizing that he'd run out of the bedroom naked. He blushed and left in a hurry.

"I truly, truly didn't mean to," said Titus humbly. "It just . . . happened."

Hermogenes sighed and rubbed at his face. "Yes. Well, I need to explain what has happened to me. Will you listen?"

Titus sat down on one of his red-upholstered couches and clasped his hands together attentively.

Hermogenes made the explanation rapidly—Pollio's blackmail of Rufus, the meeting that afternoon in the bath-house, his suspicion that his own life formed part of the bargain; his escape. "I don't dare stay here," he finished. "Even if I could justify putting your household in danger— which I cannot!—it would not be safe for me to stay in the first place they'll look for me. I must go somewhere else. I need to get my letters of credit, though—and I think I should draw up some kind of document giving Menestor his freedom."

"I, um, had one drawn up this morning," Titus said hesitantly. "Because you'd *said* you wanted to free him, and I thought, if I had one drawn up—"

"Thank you," Hermogenes interrupted. "I will sign it."

Menestor came back in, clothed.

"But I thought," Titus went on, looking sick with apprehension, "I thought maybe you would sell him to me, and then *I* could free him. Oh, please, please, my dear friend, let me do that!"

"Why?" Hermogenes demanded bluntly.

Titus went red. "Because then he'd be Fiducius Menestor instead of Aelius Menestor, and my freedman, not yours."

Hermogenes stared at him a moment, then turned to his slave. "Menestor," he said, in Greek, "Titus asks me to sell you to him, so that when you are free you will bear his name, not mine. What do you want?"

Menestor reddened and looked at the floor. "I don't know."

"You must make up your mind quickly," Hermogenes told him sharply. "I have to leave again very soon, and I want your freedom established before I go. I should not have left before without settling the matter."

Menestor's head jerked up. "Where are you going?"

"I don't know yet. I will have to hide, for a few days at least. Understand this: going home is no longer an option. I think now they would send people after me. I still hope that I can find a way out, but I am by no means confident of it." It was the first time he'd admitted it, and he was surprised at how steady his voice was.

"Take me with you!" exclaimed Menestor, gazing at him desperately. "Please, sir! I won't ask you to give up and I won't complain. I don't even want my freedom. I just want to be with you. I can't stand it, staying here, not knowing where you are or what's happening to you. Please, sir!"

Hermogenes shook his head in bewilderment. He'd always been supposed an observant man. How had he failed to notice *this*? "Menestor, you may think yourself in love with me—"

"*Think?*" cried Menestor in anguish. "Oh, gods, I've been in love with you for *years*!"

Hermogenes held up his hand. "Child, you are old enough to know better! I am *never* going to love you, and if you come with me, you will be no help but a hindrance. I know you are loyal and intelligent, but *you don't speak Latin.* I would have to provide for you, and explain you, and interpret for you, and in the end, perhaps, watch you die for me—pointlessly. No: I will not take you with me. Accept your freedom and stay here, for now, at least. I will give you money for your fare back to Alexandria before I leave to-night, so that if I don't survive, and if you still wish it, you can go home. Discuss it, if you like, with Titus Fiducius. I am going to fetch the things I need."

He limped off toward the Nile Rooms.

Cantabra followed him. "What was all that?" she asked.

He snorted. He felt, despite the desperation of his situation, a sense of profound shock. He thought of Menestor sharing a room and a bath with him, Menestor helping him dress in the morning, Menestor tenderly washing the blood off his shoulder. The awareness of what Menestor must have been feeling through all that filled him with a mixture of pity and revulsion. He remembered the longing in the young man's voice in response to his own question as to whether Menestor would be willing to sleep with his master in exchange for his freedom. It hadn't been, as he'd thought then, a longing for freedom, but for something that Men-estor had already known he would never obtain. "The boy thinks he is love with me," he told the barbarian in disgust.

There was a silence. They reached the Nile Rooms, and he fumbled in the darkness for the lamplighter. "I heard Greeks were like that," Cantabra said.

"What does being Greek have to do with it?" he asked in bewilderment. "Don't Cantabrians ever sleep with boys?"

"No," she replied at once. "If they did we would kill them."

"Zeus!" he said, shocked again. He found the lamp-lighter, lit it, then lit the lamps on the lighthouse stand. The tawdry Egyptian decor formed around them, full of mysteri-ous shadows.

"I don't think it is particularly Greek," he said, going to the trunk. "Most of us like women, and there are plenty of Romans who like boys. My friend Titus, for one, and Vedius Pollio, for another."

"I saw how he kept touching you."

"I think that was only to provoke me."

"It was disgusting."

He looked at her in surprise. She stood in the doorway, her arms crossed and her face grim. He shrugged. "Yes. Agreed. Should I have allowed myself to be provoked, when it was what he wanted?"

She uncrossed her arms and came forward to kneel next to the trunk beside him. "*You* don't sleep with boys, do you?" she asked anxiously.

He felt like hitting someone—her, Titus, Menestor. Pollio, he thought yearningly, or Rufus. "No," he snapped. "I do not, and at the moment I feel that I never want Menestor near me again. Satisfied?"

She looked away.

"The poor young man is seventeen, honest, intelligent, and wretched. I am his master, and he loves me. I brought him here, to this city where he cannot speak the language, took him into dangers he could not cope with for a cause in which he did not believe, then left him in this house with a fat Roman who had fallen in love with him. He looked for comfort, and now feels he betrayed me. He will have the choice between going home on his own to a ruined house, or staying here with Titus Fiducius. He has been utterly devoted to me, and I have treated him *shamefully*—and now I don't want him near me. Would your people consider that proper conduct?"

"I am sorry," she said in a whisper. "I had no business saying anything."

He grunted and unlocked the trunk.

The strongbox contained only another twenty denarii in coin. He put that in his purse, then collected the letters of credit. He rolled them up in a clean tunic. His good cloak was sitting folded on the edge of the desk: he put the tunic on top of it, then rolled up the whole bundle and secured it with a spare belt. He was about to stand up when he noticed the pen case with Cantabra's money in the corner of the trunk. He fished it out and handed it to her in silence, then closed and locked the trunk. He blew out the lamps and left the room.

Back in the dining room, Titus and Menestor were standing together next to a table on which lay some sheets of papyrus. Titus seemed to be pleading with Menestor, who was shaking his head. They both stopped when Hermogenes limped in.

"Have you made up your mind?" Hermogenes asked the slave.

"Yes, sir," replied Menestor in a low voice. "I want *you* to free me."

Hermogenes nodded. "Very well. Menestor, I am sorry. You have deserved better of me than you've received. I wish we could do this properly, with the ceremony it deserves, and not in this harsh haste, but I *must* leave at once. Is this the document?"

"Oh, please!" gasped Titus, coming over. "Please, won't you sell him to me? I'd give you any sum you ask, and I swear I'd free him myself later. Please?"

Hermogenes paused, staring in surprise. Titus blinked back, his round face pale, his jowls trembling, a man in the grip of an overpowering emotion. For once a "lovely boy" had accepted his advances willingly, and he was altogether smitten.

"I'm sorry," Hermogenes told his friend, in Latin, so that Menestor would not understand, "I swore I would give him his freedom, and you know that he is cruelly distressed. How can you ask me to refuse him this, since he wants it?"

"B-but I *love* him!" stammered Titus. "And if he isn't my slave, and isn't my freedman—well, he's going to leave me, isn't he? Nobody ever loves me. You don't know how lucky you are, to have people love you the way they do."

It was, Hermogenes reminded himself, the middle of

the night—and from the smell on his breath, Titus had been drinking some of the wine his slaves had brought. He sighed in exasperation and put his hand on the other man's shoulder. "Titus, he slept with you of his own free will and choice, because you were kind to him. If you continue your kindness, perhaps he *will* love you. He has a generous and affectionate nature, as do you."

"He won't," sobbed Titus, and wiped his nose with the back of his hand. "Nobody ever does."

"I have no *time* for this!" Hermogenes exclaimed impatiently. "How can you expect anyone to love you if you never give them the freedom to choose you? You can't refuse them that, and then complain!" He picked up the document from the table. It was a bill of sale. He picked up the one underneath it: the manumission. He read it through, saw that it was in order, found pen, ink, and wax, and signed and sealed it.

"Will you witness it?" he asked Titus, offering him pen and document.

Titus wiped his nose again, took the pen, and signed his own name as witness.

Hermogenes handed the manumission document to Menestor, then tipped out his purse. "I'm sorry, this is all I have with me," he said, giving it to the young man. "It should pay your way to Alexandria if you travel on deck, or if you find work on the ship. You could inquire if any captains or pursers need a secretary. I will try to arrange to have the full fare sent to you when I can get coin, but I do not know whether I will be able to. Titus." He turned to the businessman.

Titus was looking stunned and subdued.

"I fear I may have put you in danger," Hermogenes told him. "I think you should take whatever steps you can to protect yourself and your household. Report as much of this as you think reasonable to whoever is in charge of such things at Rome—the prefect of the city, would it be? You do not need to accuse the consul of anything: it would probably be sufficient to say that a guest of yours had a disagreement with him, and that some of his men have been hanging about your house in a threatening manner. Imply that what you fear is barbarian guardsmen out of control, not malice from their employer. Mention that I've quarreled with Pollio as well. Tell your friends, too. Complain about me for having stirred up trouble and left you to face the consequences. Make sure that Rufus and Pollio both *know* that you have told the authorities that you are worried: it makes it much less likely that they will do anything to you. Make sure, too, that they know that I am not here, and that you do not know where I am. I hope that will be enough."

"What will you do?" asked Titus anxiously.

"I still need to decide. Oh, one more thing, though. Cantabra has served me loyally, with intelligence and courage. I would not be here without her help. If I am killed, please will you see to it that she finds another, more fortunate employer? I am certain that anyone to whom you recommeded her would come to thank you for it."

"You really do expect to die," said Titus, staring at him.

Hermogenes smiled tightly. "I *hope* to escape, but it is best to be prepared for the worst. Will you do as I ask?"

"Yes," whispered Titus. He seized Hermogenes' hand

and began to wring it. "Oh, gods and goddesses! My dear friend . . ."

"Please!" said Hermogenes, detaching himself. "I need to keep my head clear. I am very sorry for all the trouble I am causing, to you and to all your household. Menestor," he switched back to Greek, "I am sorry. I wish you joy of your freedom. Farewell!" He picked up the roll of his cloak, gathered up his crutch, and limped quickly to the door.

The whole household followed him into the entrance hall, talking and exclaiming. Menestor tried to catch hold of him; he shrugged the boy off, advised the others to be quiet, for their safety and his own, and managed to unbolt the door and step out into the night. Cantabra followed him silently.

He walked back down the Via Tusculana to the alley where he'd waited before, then stopped. The silence of the empty streets was infinitely welcome after the harried meeting.

He had behaved badly, he acknowledged silently. He had treated both Menestor and his friend Titus with a casual impatience that would have offended him deeply if he had met it in someone else. They had each given him more than he had any right to ask, and he had not even thanked them.

But it had been so hard, with this desperate need to gather all he was into an attempt to outface death, to spare anything for the requirements of those who claimed him. He let out a long breath and looked up at the overcast sky. He wondered what time it was. Dawn came early at this time of year, and he needed to be safely hidden when it did.

He remembered watching the day dawn in the garden of his own house in Alexandria, the morning that he left. Now it seemed like a scene from a painting, perfect and unreal: a cat staring into the small pond, fish shifting in its shadows, and the sky a delicate shade of rose. He remembered it in tiny, perfect detail: the vine trellis, the date palms, the whitewashed kitchen wall, the shadowed colonnade, and the smell of cardamom bread baking. He wondered if he would ever see it again.

Myrrhine had come out and begged him to take her with him, and he had comforted her and told her that he would only be away for a month or two; that it was summer now, and there would be no storms to sink his ship. *I will be home again soon,* he'd assured her. At the time he had believed it. He felt now as though he stood on the verge of a voyage to somewhere much, much further than Rome, looking back at her longingly, afraid to go, but unable to remain. He shivered.

"Where do we go now?" Cantabra asked him.

He shivered again, then shook himself, trying to clear his mind and bring his attention back to the present. "An inn," he replied. "Somewhere where we can rest, and where they will not find us."

"I know a good place," she said at once. "It is over the other side of the forum, though. Can you walk that far?"

"I will have to."

The carts had left the forum by the time they reached it, setting out in the small hours so as to be out of the city by dawn. A few goods were still being arranged for the morning, but most of the great plaza had fallen still. A few beggars and visiting carters slept in the porticoes of the temples, and stray dogs snapped up dropped scraps.

By that time the sore foot was hurting badly, and Hermogenes walked with the crutch under his left arm and Cantabra's shoulder under his right. He could feel the tension in her—the quick, wary glances at every alley mouth, the continual alertness to those shapes sleeping in the porticoes. It was not a good time of night to be about.

Near the bottom of the forum she drew him aside suddenly into an alleyway, then into the doorway of a building. They stood there for a couple of minutes, pressed against the door in the darkness. He could feel the warmth of her body, the curve of her hip against his own, and the unlikely desire tingled again. He began to speak, and she stilled him with an impatient finger across his lips.

They stood silent for another minute or two, and then she relaxed. She helped him out of the doorway and the alley and back into the forum.

"What was it?" he whispered.

"I thought someone was following us," she replied. "Either they were not, or they lost interest."

They skirted the Tabularium to the right and made their way along a narrow roadway which Cantabra said was called the Clivus Argentarius, then turned left, toward the river. Presently Cantabra turned right again, into a dirty alley, and knocked on the door of an insula.

There was no response, and she knocked again, more loudly. Hermogenes handed her the crutch and braced himself against the wall. She began to beat on the door with the handle.

A window opened, and a woman's voice called angrily, "Go rot, whoever you are! It's the middle of the night!"

"It's Cantabra!" the barbarian called back. "And it's nearly dawn."

There was a silence, and then the woman at the window said, in a milder tone, "So you're back? What d'you want?"

"Rooms for myself and my employer," Cantabra replied, stepping back from the door to look up at the window, though it was far too dark to make out much.

"Your *employer*, is it?" scoffed the woman at the window. "And what is it he employs you to do? You've seen reason at last, have you?"

"I am his *bodyguard*!" Cantabra replied fiercely. "Do you want to let us in or not?"

"Bodyguard? You're not going to tell me you want *two* rooms!"

"I am. A pair of rooms together. Two beds."

"Heh! Who would've thought it? Payment in advance till the Kalends?"

"Fine!"

The window shut. Cantabra handed the crutch back to Hermogenes.

"What is this place?" he asked her in a low voice.

"It's a lodging house," she informed him. "It belongs to a widow who lives on the ground floor and rents out the other apartments. I stayed here for a while when I was first discharged from the school. She was kind to me." The door opened, and she went in. He followed her, wincing at each step.

The narrow entranceway was pitch-black and stank of

urine. He could not make out the woman who stood holding the door.

"So you really did get work as a bodyguard," the woman said wonderingly to Cantabra.

"I did," she agreed. "This is my employer."

"Herophilos, son of Hermesianax," Hermogenes put in smoothly. "I apologize for the suddeness of our arrival. I have had a falling-out with my business partner."

There was a startled silence, and then the landlady asked dubiously, "A Greek?"

"Is that a problem?" he asked.

"No, no!" she exclaimed. "It just seems odd to find a *Greek* hiring Cantabra. She's not much for culture. I'll show you the rooms."

The rooms were on the fourth floor of the insula. He struggled up them with the aid of Cantabra and the crutch. The landlady must have realized that something was the matter as soon as he started, but she said nothing. When the long agonizing climb finally ended she opened a doorway and showed them into an indistinguishable darkness, then crossed to a window and opened the shutters. The night illumined the dimness just enough for him to make out a tiny box of a room with a couch under the window and a curtained doorway to one side.

"Two rooms," said the landlady triumphantly. "This one, and that one." Apparently "that one" was through the curtain. "No cooking fires allowed, and you can fetch your own water or have it fetched for an as extra a day. Cost you six denarii till the Kalends."

"What is the date today?" Hermogenes asked.

The landlady harrumphed. "At dawn it'll be the twenty-fifth. But I'm charging for tonight, even if it is nearly dawn. Payment in advance."

"I cannot see you to pay you," he pointed out. "Payment in advance, but in daylight."

"Fair enough," she conceded. "You speak good Latin."

"So I have been told."

"Herapolis, you said your name was?"

"*Herophilos.*"

"Never could pronounce Greek names. I'll see you in daylight, Herapilus."

She went out. He hobbled over to the couch, collapsed onto it, and hauled his sore foot up onto his lap. The ankle had swollen so much that the bandages were biting into the flesh, and he began to loosen them. Something hopped against his thigh. The bed had fleas.

He sat still for a moment, then laughed: it was that or burst into tears. "Oh, Zeus, oh, Lady Isis!" he exclaimed. "What would my father say if he saw me now?"

Cantabra came over silently and squatted beside him. "I am sorry. I thought we should stay away from the inns where rich men go, and Gellia calls me a friend, so I thought this place would be good."

"I am sure you are right. Gellia? That is the name of that . . . person?"

"Gellia Bibula. She was kind to me when I was first discharged." A shrug, more sensed than seen in the darkness. "When I took a room here I had a little money—they give you prize money when you win. It ran out, though, after a couple of months. She shared food with me then, and tried to find small jobs for me, and never pressed me about the rent."

"Apart, that is, from urging you to prostitute yourself to obtain it?"

A hesitation. "She told me I would never get work as a guard, and there wasn't anything else I knew to do in Rome. There are men who will pay to sleep with a woman gladiator. She thought that was the way I could best get money to live on."

"But you wouldn't."

"No." There was pride in her voice. "I have never willingly slept with any man but my husband, and those who took me against my will had to tie me up or beat me senseless first. So in the spring, I sold my cloak, and paid her the rent, and went off to sleep in temple porches and make what living I could."

It was what he'd been beginning to suspect. "You're a very brave and honorable woman," he said quietly.

She touched his ankle. "That is swollen again."

"It will go down, if I rest it. My girl, I am going to try to get a few hours' rest before making war on all those stairs to go to the bank. Which of us has which room?"

"You have this room. There is no bed in the other. I saw these rooms when I was here before."

"No bed? Then where will you sleep?"

"My people don't use beds. I will sleep on the floor."

"Probably wise," he sighed. "There will be fewer fleas. Sleep well, then."

"Sleep well."

The curtain rustled as she went through into the adjoining room. Hermogenes lay down on the lumpy, flea-infested mattress and arranged his cloak over himself as a blanket, then lay staring into the darkness. His ankle throbbed. He was suddenly possessed by a nightmarish sensation that the bed was horrendously tall, and that he hung suspended above an unimaginable gulf, into which he would tumble at the first incautious movement.

He forced himself to drop one hand off the mattress, and brushed the dirty floorboards with the backs of his fingers. *A bed in a room in a Roman insula,* he told himself. *That's all it is.* He forced himself to close his eyes.

He remembered Pollio picking his teeth at the end of their meal together, watching him with those rheumy, calculating eyes. *You should be careful, Alexandrian. . . .* He saw the circular mouth of a lamprey, the ring of needle-sharp teeth and the wet black tunnel of its gullet.

He remembered Rufus erupting from his chair on their first meeting, and the impact of that ringed fist against his face. Scylla and Charybdis, he thought, with a kind of horror: the sucking whirlpool and the violent monster, and somehow a ship had to steer a course between them, if it was to survive. Not even Odysseus's ship had managed that unscathed:

> —screaming
> in deadly pain they stretched out their hands to me:
> of all the sights my eyes beheld in all my toil
> upon the salty water, that one was the worst.

How was a banker supposed to succeed where a hero had failed?

No, no, no, he told himself wearily. Rufus and Pollio are not mythological monsters any more than I am a hero. They are men, and all men make mistakes. Rufus made one when he named somebody called Titus, and Pollio when he gave me the opportunity to escape. There is, still, a chance.

Again he touched the floor: he was not falling. He had escaped, he was in safe in bed in a place where his enemies couldn't find him, and he was not falling. In the morning he would wake, and decide what to do. He would be careful, he would be wise, he would not fall. It might even be enough.

H E WOKE WITH A START TO FIND HIMSELF lying on a shabby couch in a small and dirty room. His ankle ached, his head ached, the stitches on his cheek pulled, his mouth felt furry, and his skin itched and felt too tight all over. There were fleabites, too.

He sat up, ran his hands through his hair, then reached over to open the window shutters. From the light it was early afternoon. He groaned. The banks would be shut by now.

Cantabra appeared, pulling aside the curtain to the adjacent room. She was holding a leatherworker's needle, threaded. "You slept a long time," she pointed out. "How is your foot?"

He picked it up and had a look at it. "Better," he

observed. The swelling had gone down, anyway. "Cantabra, you should have woken me. The banks will be shut."

She gave him a look he couldn't interpret. "Why must you go to a bank?"

"To get coin," he said impatiently. "Your friend Gellia wants six denarii in advance, and I gave Menestor all I had with me."

"I paid Gellia. You can repay me later."

"Oh!" he said, taken aback. After a moment he added, "Thank you." He rubbed at his face again. "I think I will pay her the extra to fetch water."

Cantabra pointed at a large amphora in the corner. "I fetched it."

"Oh!" he said, again. He hobbled over to the amphora. There was no cup and no basin. He tipped the container and drank directly from its mouth, then poured water into his hands and splashed it repeatedly over his face. The excess trickled down his neck and made a damp patch on the bare boards of the floor. He wiped his hands against his thighs, since there was no towel. He glanced around.

"There's no chamber pot," he said unhappily.

"There's a tub downstairs," Cantabra informed him, "but I think men mostly piss out the window."

"Herakles!" he exclaimed in disgust. He thought of dragging his sore ankle down all those stairs and back up again, winced, and went to the window. It opened onto a narrow stinking alleyway, and nobody was watching. He pissed out of it quickly, then sat down on the couch, feeling coarse, common, and contemptible.

Cantabra was grinning at him. "It's very well for you," he told her with dignity. "*You* weren't brought up to be a gentleman."

She laughed. "Do you want food? I bought rolls."

They were small narrow rolls, flavored with celery seed, moist inside and very good. Halfway through the first of them he remembered that he was supposed to spend another day eating only barley broth, and nearly choked. Cantabra gave him a questioning look from her seat on the floor.

"I remembered I am supposed be convalescing on barley broth," he told her. "Isis! Was that dinner only last night?"

She nodded and put the rest of her own roll in her mouth. "You do not need more broth," she told him, chewing. "You need good food, to make your wits strong."

"Is that a tactful way of telling me I must decide what to do?" He glanced at the window. "I should not have slept so long. The longer I delay, the more precautions my enemies will think of, and the harder it will be to achieve anything."

"You needed to rest," she told him reprovingly. "If you cannot think clearly, we are dead."

"I am probably dead anyway," he told her. He didn't *feel* nearly dead, though: with the food inside him and the escape behind him he felt alert and powerful. He warned himself severely not to trust that feeling, dusted off his hands, and picked up another roll. "Cantabra—you heard what I said to Titus? You can go to him if I am killed. He *will* help you now."

She made a face. "I do not think you will be killed. You are much cleverer than Pollio or Rufus."

He gave a rueful snort. "I am flattered. But even if it were true, cleverness and cunning don't win wars, as Pollio reminded me. Power does. Still, I thank you, and I will try to justify your good opinion." He had a bite of the roll.

"So!" she said, resting her elbows on her knees. "You have ideas?"

"I believe I have two options. The first is to go to Gaius Maecenas. He might be willing to buy the debt simply in order to spite Rufus, and he is probably still powerful enough to protect us. The risks of that course are, first, that I have no reason to trust him, nor he to trust me; second, that he is reportedly out of favor and may be unwilling to risk acting against Rufus; third—and this is the one that troubles me most—that Pollio will *expect* me to go to him. I hinted I might, and I could see that he hated the idea. Gaius Maecenas is precisely the sort of man Pollio would worry about most—a financial rival who has likewise fallen from the imperial favor, who could understand Pollio's plots and might be interested in taking advantage of them. If I were Pollio I would take precautions against my obtaining any help from that quarter."

"What sort of precautions?" Cantabra asked, frowning.

He shrugged. "The most basic one would be to have his house watched in case I try to go there. A more subtle one would be to send Maecenas a letter full of lies about me."

Her frown deepened. "What, that you were an assassin?"

"That I was an assassin, that I was a spy, that my offer was a ruse to involve Maecenas in some kind of disgrace. I don't know enough of court politics to guess or to guard myself. Pollio and Maecenas were members of the same circle and both in finance. I believe they did dislike one another, but there are probably people against whom they were allies, and Pollio could credibly represent himself as being willing to help Maecenas against one of them." He finished his roll.

"Then you should not go to Maecenas," said Cantabra. "What is the second option?"

"Someone called Titus." He shrugged. "He is the man Pollio wants Rufus to kill, so one presumes he would be grateful to learn of the plot. He has the advantage over Maecenas in that I am fairly confident that neither Rufus nor Pollio know I heard his name, and won't expect me to turn to him. Rufus mentioned the name in the bathhouse, but I don't think he realized that I understood him—he was speaking Latin, and all our dealings had been in Greek— and I don't think Pollio heard, because at that stage he was still in the changing room. He undoubtedly heard Rufus shouting, but bathhouses echo, and I doubt very much that he made out the words. The problem is that I don't know who Titus is. Somebody who was on first-name terms with Rufus, somebody powerful whom Pollio couldn't reach on his own, and somebody from whose death Pollio expects to benefit: that's all I can say."

"Statilius Taurus?" suggested Cantabra.

For a moment it was simply a name vaguely familiar from public affairs, impossible to place. Then he remembered: one of the emperor's great marshals, the man who'd commanded the land forces at Actium, second only to Marcus Agrippa. There was more, though, more recently . . . he suddenly recalled the Rubrius brothers mentioning that name. Statilius Taurus, they'd complained, hadn't given any games that summer, even though he liked games and was prefect of the city.

Prefect of the city. The man in charge of Rome in the absence of the emperor and his deputy; the man in command of all the troops stationed in the capital; the man responsible for the maintainance of order. Suppose the prefect of the city were assassinated, and rioting broke out; suppose that at that dangerous juncture Vedius Pollio stepped forward, and selflessly spent his wealth to quell the disturbances. Wouldn't Pollio expect to be received back into the imperial favor as a reward?

It was possible—but there were too many suppositions in that piece of reasoning, and it seemed an unnecessarily tortuous plot. If Pollio wanted to quell a riot, he could presumably send out agents to start one, and then quell it at his leisure, without need of assassinations at all. Or did he have some reason to be certain that he needed to get rid of Statilius Taurus first?

"It might be," he said cautiously. "Statilius Taurus is a Titus, is he?"

Cantabra nodded. "He is a cruel man," she said in a low voice. "He loves blood and killing. But he is honest. He keeps his word and he honors courage."

He remembered abruptly where *else* he had heard that name recently: the school of Taurus, where Cantabra had suffered as a gladiator. No wonder he was the first powerful Titus who had had occurred to her.

"It might be," he said again. "I don't know how to check it, though. I can't go to him with an accusation against a man who is probably his friend unless I'm more confident than I am now—and I don't even know how many other possibilities there are among the friends of the emperor. I cannot just go into a barbershop and ask 'How many very important Romans are named Titus?'"

"Why not?" asked Cantabra. "Men talk about stupid things in barber shops."

He snorted. "Admitted—but Rufus and Pollio will have men out looking for me. They'll have people asking in barbershops about a Latin-speaking Greek with a bruised face, a cut on his cheek, and a bad ankle. At the moment I am fairly unmistakable, and that sort of question would be remembered. If Pollio learned that I was asking it, my last chance would be gone." He fingered the stitches on his cheek, trying to think it through. "It would probably be better to go to Maecenas. Even if Pollio does write him a letter, he may not have written it yet."

It would certainly have been safe to approach Maecenas first thing that morning. It would have taken Pollio a couple of hours to work out that Hermogenes was not at the house on the Via Tusculana. If he had not slept late, if he'd got up at dawn and gone directly to the house of Maecenas . . .

. . . He would almost certainly have been refused admittance. A very battered and bedraggled Greek, accompanied only by a barbarian female ex-gladiator, could not turn up on the doorstep of one of the wealthiest and most distinguished men in Rome without an appointment and expect to be received.

Besides, he admitted, if he had woken up earlier, he

wouldn't have gone to Maecenas; he would have gone to the bank. He needed coin, and he didn't know how long it would be safe for him to get it. The number of banks in Rome which would accept a letter of credit from a bank in Egypt could be counted on the fingers of one hand—and all of them had connections with the East, which meant, with Pollio. If he didn't hurry, going to one might shortly prove as dangerous as going to Maecenas. Only he couldn't hurry, because he'd slept late, and now the banks were shut.

Cantabra was giving him a level blue look. "You should not go to Maecenas," she said firmly.

He raised his eyebrows. "Which of us hired which?"

"You should not go!" she insisted. "If your opponent is stronger than you, you must not make the move he antici-pates. I learned that in the arenas. You must do something he does not anticipate: that is the only way to get the better of him. Besides, if you go to Taurus, the worst that can hap-pen is that he does not listen to you. You would still be able to try Maecenas. But if Pollio has written to Maecenas, and you go to him, you would not be able to get away again. Pol-lio will tell him something that would make Maecenas give you back to him, and Pollio would not let you escape again. No. We should first try to find out whether Titus is Statilius Taurus. You will think of a way to do that that does not need questions in barbershops."

It sounded like an order, and he snorted in disgust. She said "Huh!" back at him, then got up, went into her own cubicle, then came back with a thick leather belt he did not remember her wearing. She sat down, laid the belt across her lap, and took her needle out of the breast of her tunic, where she'd set it for safekeeping. She arranged some coins against the inside of the belt and began stitching a leather lining across them.

"Keeping your money safe?" he asked curiously. "When did you buy that?"

"This morning," she said, and continued stitching. "I can fit eighty coins in here. I will have to hide the rest. It is not good to leave money about in this insula. Gellia does not steal, but some of the others in this building are whores and thieves, and the doors do not lock."

"There are such things as banks."

She shook her head. "Too Greek."

"What's wrong with Greek?" he asked, smiling.

She looked up and smiled back. "Nothing. But I am Cantabrian, and not used to it." She began sewing again.

He watched her bowed head, with the fiery hair sleek to the scalp and swinging in its long tail behind. Her strong scarred hands forced the needle firmly through the leather. "Do you think you could learn Greek?" he asked, after a silence.

She looked up again, surprised. "Why?"

He shrugged. "If I survive, I would like you to come back to Alexandria with me."

The surprise darkened into suspicion. "Why?" she asked again.

He shrugged once more. "You have saved my life twice, if we count last night. I like you and trust you. I could give you a position where you were safe, comfortable, and respected, and it would benefit both of us if you took it.

You're a much better bodyguard than poor Phormion. You try to anticipate: he never did."

She gave him long blue stare. There was pleasure in it, he thought, but also suspicion, and perhaps apprehension. He thought she was about to speak, but there was a knock on the door.

Cantabra set down the belt at once, her eyes hardening. "Who is it?" she called.

"It's me!" came a voice Hermogenes recognized from the previous night as Gellia's. "I just want to check that everything's all right." The door opened before either of them could respond.

Gellia proved to be a thin, angular woman of about forty. She wore a Roman matron's stole over a dirty gown; her black hair was held up by copper pins, and her cheeks were rouged. Her bright black eyes at once fixed on Hermogenes with avid curiosity.

"Oh, Juno!" she exclaimed. "You poor man! Cantabra did say you'd been attacked by robbers. Terrible, what the streets are like these days! Are the rooms good enough for you, Herapilus?"

Hermogenes smiled brightly. "It is good of you to come and ask. I hope you will be able to do something about the fleas."

The curiosity froze into misgiving. "Fleas?"

"This couch is infested. Also, whose responsibility is the upkeep of these rooms? They are filthy."

"The tenants are supposed to look after their own rooms," Gellia told him nervously.

"And there are no arrangements to clean them between tenants?"

Clearly, there were: she was supposed to have done them. Gellia now looked as though she regretted visiting. "But you don't want them done now, while you're in them!" she protested.

"I plan to go out shortly to a bathhouse. You could do them then."

She grimaced. "You *did* arrive unexpectedly."

"I admit it!" he said, waving a concessionary hand. "I know there was no time to prepare the rooms last night. But I would be grateful if you would clean them today. Also, the couch should be beaten thoroughly before the floor is swept and washed. Also, there is no sheet. Also, would it be possible to borrow or rent a table and a lamp?"

"The sort of people who normally stay here don't want tables and lamps," Gellia told him resentfully.

He spread his hands. "I am sure that I am an unusual tenant for you. As my bodyguard probably informed you, I have had a quarrel with a Roman business partner, and the result is as you see. I had not included funds for an inn in my budget, let alone for being robbed. So I am grateful for this place, but I hope you will understand it if I seem to you demanding. Perhaps you could consider this as experience in catering for a better class of tenant, and in future rent out some of your rooms at a higher cost?"

The landlady clicked her tongue. "What *is* your business, sir?"

"I am a shipping agent," he said, without hesitation.

"With the corporation of Myrtilos and Firmus. You have heard of them?"

"No," she said, becoming interested again. "What do they ship?"

"Grain." This was evidently disappointing, but he went on, "Egyptian grain. The emperor, of course, has been supplying this great city increasingly from Egypt, but, to tell the truth, getting the shipments here is a labor for Herakles. That harbor at Ostia is a joke. It won't take a ship larger than about thirty tons."

"Isn't that big?"

"Tiny!" he said with contempt. "Oh, it would do for luxury goods, but for *grain*? It's not economic to ship grain in lots that small—and when the ships arrive at the port, there isn't even a good-sized crane to unload them. It has to be done by porters, which puts the cost up again." He had begun speaking simply to lull into boredom any suspicion she might have conceived, but he was beginning to get an idea. "Our corporation and a couple of like-minded ones have been petitioning the emperor to improve the harbor at Ostia. It needs dredging and a breakwater as well as cranes, and that means important public works. We collected some money to pay one of the emperor's friends to put the matter to him, and we found a Roman go-between who said he would find the right man to give it to, but I suspect that this Roman, the business partner I mentioned, has kept all the money himself. That is what we quarreled about."

"No!" exclaimed Gellia, with delight. "And when you confronted him, he turned you out of the house in the middle of the night?"

"I walked out after a loud quarrel," Hermogenes informed her ruefully. "Ai, Zeus, we both lost our tempers. But it occurs to me now that perhaps you could help me."

"Me?" asked the landlady in surprise.

He nodded. "You see, my Roman partner says he gave the money to a friend of the emperor, but I do not know the name of that friend, except that my partner referred to him as Titus—to impress me, I suppose, that he was on such good terms with a great man. Now that I have quarreled with my partner, I want to see if this Titus knows anything about our petition or the money he is supposed to have received. I am not a Roman, though, and I don't know who among the emperor's friends might bear that name. You seem to be a knowledgeable woman of the city, and I am sure that if you do not know yourself, you know someone who would. I would give a denarius for a list of names."

Gellia smiled widely, showing a blackened tooth. "And what then? You'll go around them all asking whether they've received any money from you?"

"No, no, no!" he told her, smiling. "Probably there are not too many of them, and I will be able to rule most of them out at once. Fortunately Titus is not so common a name as, say, Gaius. When I have narrowed it down to two or three, I can make very careful inquiries among their associates or their slaves before I contact them. Then, if my partner *has* cheated us, I can report it to Myrtilos and Firmus."

"You're right about the name not being too common," the woman said thoughtfully. "The only important Titus I can think of at the moment is General Statilius Taurus. Could it be him?"

"It might be," Hermogenes replied without blinking. "He is prefect of the city, so he would have an interest in the grain supply. But I would like to be certain that there are no other possibilities before I start asking questions. I would not want to do anything that might offend such an important man."

"I see your point. Well. Well, you want to give me that denarius? I know one or two old men who know the names of everybody who's been anybody since Julius Caesar became a god, but they'll only talk if I give them wine." Her eyes sparkled eagerly, and he was sure that she wanted the wine for herself.

Cantabra silently picked up one of the coins she'd been stitching into her belt and handed it to the landlady. Gellia took it with pleasure and slid it swiftly into her purse.

"If you could ask them *quietly* . . ." Hermogenes said apologetically. "I don't want my partner to find out what I'm doing."

"Oh, he won't!" Gellia told him happily. "Leave it with me." She bustled out eagerly.

Hermogenes watched her go, then sighed. "I do not think my room will be cleaned this afternoon."

"No," agreed Cantabra. She was grinning. "She will take that money, buy a large amphora of cheap wine, and invite her friends round. By this evening she will be very drunk. But that was clever. She and her friends will know about every Titus who holds office. I knew you would think of something."

He stretched. "I owe you seven denarii."

"Thirteen," she corrected him. "The seven I have given Gellia, plus three days' wages."

"Lend me some change to pay for a bath and a barber, and I will call it twenty."

She frowned at him. "You should not go to a barber. You've said they will be asking about you in such places. Probably you should not go out at all."

He raised his eyebrows. "I want a bath and a shave. I didn't have a shave yesterday, and I am covered in fleabites. Even if they do ask in barbershops, and even if they ask at the *right* barbershop within the next day or so, they still will learn nothing more than that I was there. Please. Lend me the money, or I'll have to pawn the pin off my tunic."

She scowled ferociously, but went off, fetched her pen case, and tipped out some coppers. "I have never understood it," she muttered, handing them to him. "All this washing! Every day, baths, baths, baths! And what is *wrong* with a beard?"

She made him wait while she finished sewing her belt, then accompanied him on the expedition, carrying his letters of credit and her pen case full of the rest of her coin rolled up in his good cloak, so as not to leave them unattended in the lodging house. The nearest bathhouse was only a couple of blocks away in the Campus Martius, new and very grand. It did not admit women in the afternoons—they were supposed to come in the mornings—so Cantabra sat down in the portico outside it, the rolled-up cloak on her lap. He worried that the men coming out would think her a prostitute waiting for custom, but when he suggested that she wait at the nearest public fountain instead, she simply scowled at him. The thought of her waiting made him take his bath in a hurry—that thought, and the fact that he had to leave his clothes unguarded in the changing room. He tried to remember when he had last gone to a bathhouse without at least one slave in attendance, and decided that it might have happened a few times when he was at school, but certainly hadn't happened since. It felt very odd. It felt, in fact, like being a truant schoolboy again.

He used the latrines at the bathhouse, had a shave at one of the barbershops in the portico, and they set out back to the lodging house. Cantabra still had an air of disapproval. Highly improper in a hired attendant, he thought irritably, and wondered about the offer he had made her earlier. Would he have made it if she'd been a man?

Yes, he decided. If a male ex-gladiator had come to his rescue in the Subura, asked for a job afterward, then proven his loyalty and ability in the escape from Pollio's house, he would have offered him a permanent job and taken him back to Alexandria if he were willing to come. The fact remained, however, that Cantabra was *not* a male, and that his feelings toward her were increasingly different to what they would have been if she were. He found himself watching her out of the corner of his eye, liking the way her hips moved with each long step, liking the proud way she held her head, and the bright color of her hair. He wondered if mere proximity really was enough to make a man begin to want a woman.

He remembered the attacker curled up on the cobbles in the Subura, and remembered what she'd revealed the previous night—that men had had to tie her up or beat her senseless before they raped her; that she had been willing to starve rather than prostitute herself. He remembered the way she'd wiped off her hand after he pressed it, as though he'd dirtied it. It did not seem likely, he admitted to himself, that he would get what he was beginning to want. This being the case, was it wise or kind to invite her to Alexandria, a strange city where she knew no one and could not speak the language, and where she would inevitably discover that her employer wanted to take her to bed? She would probably see it as both a betrayal and a threat.

He would worry about her, though, if she stayed in Rome. What sort of job could she get, even with the help of Titus Crispus? If she found a place bodyguarding another rich man, she was likely to run into lust in authority sooner or later, if not from the man himself then from a subordinate of his or fellow guard. Bodyguard to a rich society lady might be a better possibility, but how would Cantabra, with her fierce, forthright manner, fit into the household of a noble Roman matron? There would probably be some disaster. He sighed.

Cantabra scowled at him. "What?"

"I am trying to think what sort of job I could get you if you decide not to come to Alexandria," he replied honestly.

"You should think about your own future," she advised him severely. They were almost at the lodging house, and she paused to scan the street. The sound of loud voices could be heard from nearby—from Gellia's insula, he realized. The landlady had, indeed, invited all her friends round to share his bounty.

"I know my own future," he objected. "Either I lose, and die within the next few days—or I win, and go home, where I have a house and a daughter and a business to look after. It's your future that worries me."

"Why should you worry about me?" she demanded, glaring at him. "I am as good as most men, better than many. I survived two years in the arena. You are not my master or my keeper: it is my job to protect *you!*" She stalked on to the alley and beat on Gellia's door.

He limped after her, feeling, once again, slighted and indignant. He glared at the barbarian, who ignored him and beat on the door again, then again. At last it opened.

"Oh, there you are!" Gellia exclaimed happily, giving them a glazed smile. "Do you want to come have some wine? I told my friends what you wanted, and we've come up with a list of names. Not very long at all, you were right!" She punched Hermogenes on the arm.

He was not ready for this news. He realized that he did not want to know the name, not yet. Once he knew the name, he would have to act, and if he'd got it wrong there would be no more hope. He did not believe that if he went to Taurus with an accusation against a friend the prefect would simply allow him to walk free again. Far more likely that the man would hand him over to Rufus. Then there would be nothing left but death in one shape or another.

He smiled insincerely. "If it truly is not a long list, perhaps you could just tell it to me now." He was shaken, and still angry at the woman beside him: the last thing he wanted was to join the drunken gathering he could hear talking loudly at the back of the house;

"Well," said Gellia, pulling herself up, "the only friend of the emperor anybody knows of with the first name Titus is Statilius Taurus, like I thought. There's an ex-consul called Titus Peducaeus, though, and a Titus Cornelius Messala who's a senator and a member of the Arval Brethren, and a couple of rich businessmen called Titus-something-Balbus and Titus Salvidienus—"

"The man I want is not a businessman," Hermogenes interrupted. "Do you know anything about the second two you named—the ex-consul Peducaeus or the senator?"

"Oh, you'll have to ask the others!" Gellia exclaimed genially. "Come on, come have some wine with us." She cackled. "You paid for it, after all!"

He glanced uneasily at Cantabra, then forced a smile and followed Gellia into the ground-floor apartment.

It was immediately apparent that this was where Gellia herself lived. It was a comfortable, well-furnished apartment, though not much cleaner than the rest of the building. He was ushered into a central dining room with a floor paved in plain tiles; there was a curtain to the right that probably concealed a sleeping cubicle, and a kitchen just visible through an open door. Gellia's friends consisted of three women and a pair of old men. One woman and one old man reclined side by side on the couch, and the others perched on stools or cushions around the room. There was a mixing bowl half full of wine in the center of the floor, and everyone had a cup.

"This is the Greek I was telling you about!" Gellia told her drinking companions cheerfully. "The one who thinks his partner cheated him, Herapilus son of somebody I can't pronounce. He's a real gentleman, and he's only here because he hired my friend Cantabra after she helped him when he was being robbed."

The drinking party obligingly cheered for him, and the couple on the couch made space for him to lie down. Cantabra, her face expressionless, sat down on the floor by the door, the rolled-up cloak still in her lap.

It took a little while to get the drinking party to talk about Romans called Titus: they were far more interested to hear about the robbery, and eager to recount their own stories on the same subject. Eventually, however, he managed to turn the conversation and learn that Titus Peducaeus had been consul many years before ("oh, it was before the war of Actium!") and had not been active in public affairs since. The senator Titus Cornelius Messalla, in contrast, was young, not yet thirty and still ineligible for the consulship. Nervous and unhappy, he chased up futher Tituses—the two businessmen, a couple of praetors, a minor military figure, and even, in desperation, a Marcus Titius—but there was no real competition to the dark and bloodily reputed prefect of the city.

"Well, it sounds like you want General Statilius Taurus, then!" exclaimed Gellia triumphantly.

He forced a smile. "So it does. I shall begin my inquiries in the morning. Thank you."

"Let's have another drink to celebrate!" cried Gellia.

The wine, however, was all gone. Gellia asked Cantabra

to fetch more, and gave her a couple of sestertii to pay for it. One of the old men suggested that she buy some food as well. There was a collection among the guests to pay the cookshop and the wineshop, and the old man whose suggestion it had been went along to help carry things.

"A dinner party!" cried the other old man enthusiastically. "Now all we need is some music!" He gazed at Hermogenes with an expression of slightly nervous hope. "I heard once that Greeks all learn to play music when they're in school."

Hermogenes shrugged. "I can play a little on the kithara."

"My Sentia has a kithara," the old man said at once, nodding at the middle-aged woman at his side. "Maybe she could fetch it."

Sentia, a plump shapeless woman in a shapeless brown tunic, giggled, said she wasn't sure it still had all its strings, and went off to fetch it.

She arrived back at about the same time Cantabra returned with the other old man, the wine, and food consisting of a pot of lamb and bean ragout and a basket of bread. The food was dished out, the cups were filled and the party got under way.

The kithara had two broken strings, but Sentia had found spares. Hermogenes restrung the instrument and tuned it between bites of bread and ragout. When he played a scale, the Romans all fell silent, their drink-flushed faces suddenly quiet and eager. He felt his mild contempt for them dissolve: they were not the drunkards he'd been considering them, but working people, middle-aged and older, struggling to make a living in a harsh and dangerous city.

They had been enjoying a rare and unexpected party, and the chance to hear some music made it a real occasion. They did not hear much music in their lives.

He played the first song that came into his head, an ever-popular drinking catch:

> "Boy, bring me wine by the bowlful,
> so I can drink without pausing for breath!"

The third string of the kithara slipped and played slightly flat by the end, and he knew that his voice was merely an indifferent tenor, but the Romans applauded loudly when he finished, and asked him what the Greek words meant. When he'd explained, everyone laughed and had more wine. The old man informed him proudly that Sentia could sing cantica most beautifully. Before long Hermogenes found himself playing a makeshift accompaniment as Sentia launched into a canticum, which, it seemed, was the term for an aria from a Latin mime. Rather to his surprise, the shapeless woman revealed herself to possess a beautiful voice, a clear sweet soprano which managed the difficult cadences of the music without straining. Her husband watched her proudly, nodding at intervals, his eyes alight with love.

After that, they took turns singing, until the wine was all gone and it was growing dark. Then Gellia's friends reluctantly said good night, all of them thanking their hostess for the wine and Hermogenes for the music. It had been, he thought as he struggled up the stairs, quite a good party. He had certainly enjoyed it more than he'd enjoyed the dinner Titus Crispus had given him, and it had kept his mind off Statilius Taurus, for which he was grateful.

Cantabra went into the room ahead of him, very silent. The dusk through the open shutters showed that the room had, as expected, not been cleaned. Hermogenes went to the window, gazed out and down into the narrow smelly alleyway, and realized that he'd forgotten to use the tub downstairs.

"Titus Statilius Taurus," he said out loud, and pissed out the window. When he'd finished he turned to say something to Cantabra, and found that she wasn't there.

He went to the curtained alcove at the side and found her sitting on the floor under the window, hugging her knees. He hadn't known that she not only had no bed but no mattress either. When he appeared in the doorway she picked her head up and looked at him, her face shadowed in the half-light from the window behind her.

"Is something the matter?" he asked hesitantly.

"You are such a very strange man," she replied. Her voice was thick.

"You keep saying that," he told her. "Have I done something which hurt or offended you?"

She caught her tail of hair with one hand and twisted it around her fingers. "No. I am sad because of the music. Leave me alone."

He came over very quietly and dropped to one knee beside her. "Why?" he asked softly. "Most of it was happy music."

"Just that it . . . that it made me . . . to remember being

at home. We took turns singing sometimes in the evening there. Just it made me sad." She let go of her hair and added abruptly, "You didn't need to play for them. They'd already told you what you wanted to know. You didn't need to treat them like friends."

"You sound like my father!" he exclaimed, in unhappy surprise.

She wiped at her eyes. "What?"

"My father was always telling me things like that."

"Oh. Yes. Because you were brought up to be a gentleman." She peered at his face through the gathering dark. "To be a rich man and a master, who gives orders and expects to be obeyed. Instead, you are always liking people, and trying to make them like you. Even me. That is not the way a gentleman behaves, is it? What is Alexandria like?"

The abrupt change of subject made him blink. "A lot like Rome, I suppose," he said, after a moment. "It, too, is a very big city, and parts of it are dangerous. That is why I had a bodyguard to begin with. I suppose in some ways Alexandria is even worse than Rome—there are riots sometimes, between the Jews and the Greeks, or Romans and Egyptians, and I think that does not happen here. The city is more beautiful than Rome, though. It didn't just grow, one little street on top of another: it was founded to be great, and laid out with wide avenues. The Canopic Way is wide enough for four carriages to drive abreast of one another, and it is lined with porticos and public buildings for almost its entire length. There is nothing like that here in Rome."

"And you, you have a house there."

"Not on the Canopic Way. In the harbor district, not too far from the Heptastadion—that is the causeway that divides the two harbors, and goes out to the Pharos, the lighthouse that is one of the wonders of the world. It's a good big house, about the size of my friend Titus's. There would be space for you, if you wanted to come."

"If you are not killed," she said grimly, and rubbed at her eyes again.

"I thought you said that would not happen," he replied after a moment.

She caught at her hair again. "You are going to try to see Statilius Taurus tomorrow, yes?"

"I will write him a letter asking for an appointment."

"I have been thinking," she said slowly. "What if he does not believe what you tell him, and sends you to his friend Tarius Rufus?"

So she'd seen that now. "That is a danger. I can only hope that he does not."

She made no reply, only sat staring at the floor in front of her feet.

"The other choice is to go to Maecenas."

"No. That way you would be sent back to Pollio."

"If you can think of a better course," he said impatiently, "please tell me!"

"You should have abandoned the fight before it came so far!"

"I couldn't do that."

"Men!" she exclaimed, in fierce disgust. "It is always *honor* with you, and *freedom,* and other fine, brave, empty *words*! You never care for your families, for the people who will suffer when you are gone!"

"That's not true! And you are a fine one to complain. If bare *life* is so important that we ought to preserve it at the cost of honor and freedom, why didn't *you* do what Gellia urged, and prostitute yourself?"

"I would have done it, for my babies," she said in a tight voice. "I would have. But when the soldiers came and threw me on the ground, my son tried to fight them, to protect me, and they killed him. He was seven. They ran him through with a spear, and he screamed, and tried to pull it out, and kicked at the ground, and then he died. And then my little girl cried and cried, so they killed her, too, because she would not be quiet. She was only three, and they killed her with swords; her little head was broken, and there was blood and brain all over the blades, all over her beautiful hair that I used to comb. After that I didn't care. It didn't matter what happened to me, after that; I fought them. They said, 'Since she is so fond of fighting, send her to the arenas.'"

"Oh, Lady Isis!" He touched her shoulder in the darkness. "Ai, talaina!"

She began to cry, and knocked his hand away. "This is *your* fault!" she said bitterly. "Playing *music*, and making me think of it again. Leave me alone!"

He knelt next to her in the darkness, looking at her unhappily. She hugged herself, rocking back and forth a little and swallowing the sobs now. "Go away!" she ordered him.

He got up, then stared at her a moment longer where she sat huddled on the bare floor. He took off his cloak and draped it over her shoulders. "You'll sleep more comfortably with that," he told her. "I'll use my other one."

He had to feel around the couch for the bundle that was his good cloak and his letters of credit: it was now almost completely dark. Eventually, however, he draped the Scythopolitan linen over himself and lay down on the flea-infested bed. He imagined the soldiers raping Cantabra and murdering her children, and opened his eyes wide, staring up into the darkness. He felt suddenly that the power of Rome was a vast cloud of choking smoke, a gas which had erupted from this dark city and covered the whole earth. How did *he* expect to get free of it?

Taurus owned the gladiatorial school which had owned Cantabra. She hadn't made any comment on the fact that the current plan involved saving his life, but she must have noticed. He wondered how she felt about that.

Probably they would not succeed. Statilius Taurus sounded no better a man than Tarius Rufus or Vedius Pollio. Either he would refuse to listen to the warning of a despised Egyptian, or he would hear the warning but abandon the man who delivered it. There wasn't really much hope. Perhaps he'd do better to try Maecenas, after all: the diplomat at least had the reputation of being a gentleman.

Cantabra did have a point, though, with her gladiatorial advice against making the move a stronger opponent would anticipate. She had some knowledge of Taurus, too, and she seemed to think he constituted an acceptable risk: honest and honorable, she'd called him, if bloodthirsty. He would have to trust that. Probably, though, they would not succeed.

He thought of Myrrhine. Menestor had thought to write his family, and probably such a letter would be a comfort to them if he never came back. He ought to write to Myrrhine. He ought to explain that he loved her, and that he hadn't decided to risk his life because he didn't care about what happened to her but because he couldn't endure feeling that she was the daughter of a slave.

He wondered how much he'd *decided* to do any of this, anyway. Certainly he had known that he was taking a risk, but almost until the moment he'd left Pollio's house he had believed that he would win in the end. He wondered if he would have made the same choice, given what he knew now.

He remembered Myrrhine as a baby in his arms; remembered her toddling to the door shrieking "Daddy! Daddy!" when he came home; remembered her sobbing against his chest at her mother's funeral; remembered her clinging to him as he said good-bye. He wished he had a lamp, and a table, and ink and papyrus to write to her at once.

He slept badly, waking before dawn and lying on the couch for a long time, scratching at the fleabites and waiting for the morning. At last the darkness became a little less black, and there came the sounds of people getting up in the neighboring apartments. Voices sounded in the street outside as the households of the neighborhood went to fetch water and start the day. He rose, washed his face and hands with water from the amphora, then sat down to examine the bindings on his foot, still working mostly by touch. The ankle was finally beginning to feel usable again, and he unwrapped it, took off the last splint and began wrapping the joint with the linen bandage alone, looping it across his instep so it wouldn't slip.

Cantabra came in, shadowy in the gray predawn. She watched him a moment in silence, then said quietly, "I am sorry. Last night I said things to you that a hired attendant should never say to her employer."

"You have suffered terribly," he replied, tactfully watching the bandage instead of her. "I can understand how it must grieve you that while you finally have a chance to escape to a better life, that chance depends upon a man who may already have thrown it away." He tied the bandage.

"I do not want you to die," she said, in a low voice, almost frightened. "Yesterday, when you insisted that you would go out, for no reason, just to have a bath—I felt so angry with you. It has been a long time since I cared that much about a man's life. I want you to live, and I want to go to Alexandria with you and get away from this terrible city. Thank you for asking me."

He felt suddenly and shockingly happy. "Well, then," he said, smiling at her. "I will do my best to stay alive, and take you there."

She seemed to relax at that. She smiled back at him, her teeth white in the dimness. "If you agree to do your best to stay alive . . . may I say another thing? You should not go to your bank. You say that Pollio will have men out asking for news of you in barbershops; won't he have sent them to the banks? I don't know much about banks, but it seems to me that the letters you have can't work at all of them, so he would not have many to watch."

He hesitated. "You are right about that," he admitted,

"but I need coin. I think probably he has not done anything about them yet, and that it will still be safe if I go early this morning."

"'Probably'!" she protested. "I don't like 'probably.' I have coin, more than enough for the next few days. You do not need to take the risk!"

"I gave you that coin for saving my life," he told her unhappily. "I hate to borrow it back."

"Huh! You are a moneylender; you should not mind borrowing."

"Most of my money is in ships, not loans," he said, and sighed. "But—well, I admit, I don't like 'probably' either, and if you do honestly urge this, I accept, and thank you for it."

"Good!" she exclaimed, and smiled again. "Good. I have been thinking, too, about what we should do, how we should approach Taurus. If you write him a letter, then it will go through his office and his secretaries, and there will be delays, and perhaps your enemies will find out. What you must do is see him when he goes to visit the school. He goes there most mornings. I can get the Savage to introduce you."

"The Savage?" he asked, with misgiving.

"Gaius Naevius Saevus," she explained: the cognomen, saevus, or savage, was unheard-of, and he wondered if it was a true nickname. "The lanista in charge of the gladiatorial school. He knows me, and I will ask him to introduce you to Taurus."

"What is a lanista?"

"A man in charge of a gladiatorial school!" she said impatiently. "The Savage is hard and merciless, but he likes

me because I helped him get his job. He will introduce you
to Taurus, and you will find a clever way to convince Taurus
that you are telling the truth about Rufus. Then we will be
safe."

"I hope you are right," he told her, and considered her
proposal. She was right that it would be better to contact
Taurus quickly and quietly through an introduction, rather
than by sending him a letter which someone might report.
He just wished he didn't have to contact the man at all. He
wondered again how she felt about trying to save the life of
someone she had every reason to hate.

That she urged this must mean she had good reason.
"Very well," he said, and sighed again.

"Good," she said again, and nodded in satisfaction. "We
should go soon. Taurus usually visits early."

He stared at her in dismay. A part of himself gave a
silent cry of *No, please, not yet!* "I want to write a letter to
my daughter first," he managed at last.

She blinked at that. "Perhaps we can buy some things
for you to write with on the way," she suggested. "Then you
can write it and . . . how do you send a letter so far?"

"Titus Fiducius used a courier service," he told her.
"Otherwise, one finds a ship that's going there."

"We will buy you some things to write with on the way
to the school," she repeated. "Then you will write the letter,
and give it to me, and I will give it to your friend."

He swallowed, and surrendered with a nod. "Very well.
We'll go now." He looked her up and down, and added, "You
should wear the cloak I lent you last night."

She was surprised. "It is hot. I do not need a cloak."

"You should, nonetheless, wear one. It looks more respectable. If I had gone to the bank, the first thing I would have bought with the money would have been a good plain cloak for you—*and* a new tunic, *and* a new pair of sandals."

She scowled. "That would have been expensive."

"Worth it, I assure you. If my hired attendant is dressed like a domestic slave, what does that say about me? Come! We are going to visit this school where you were a slave. Do you want them to know how you have struggled since you were discharged?"

She thought a moment, then grinned. "I wish I had the new tunic."

She went into her room and came out a moment later with the cloak, still crumpled from being slept on, once again hung around her shoulders like a shawl. He shook his head, and came over to take it away from her. "That isn't how you wear it!"

"I know how to wear a cloak!" she told him indignantly. "We do have them in Cantabria."

"I bet you *pin* them. This is a himation, and it is meant to be draped." He shook out the cloak, then gave it back and stood facing her. "Put it at your back, the way you had it before, only with the left corner even with your left shoulder, and the rest hanging off your right side. Now take that left corner straight across your shoulder, and tuck it in well under your left arm. Use your arm to hold it there, against your side. Now . . ." He caught the right corner of the cloak, drew the top edge up it so that it covered her head like a hood, held it out a moment to her right to adjust the length, then drew it over her right shoulder and tossed it back over the left. "See? It is weighted so that it drapes."

She blinked at him from under the hood, her bright hair hidden, the heavy folds of linen suddenly transforming her into a Greek. The urge to lean forward and kiss her was so strong that he almost obeyed it; only the memory of her antagonist curled up on the cobblestones stopped him.

"I can't move my arms!" she protested, flailing her right elbow against the folds.

"You can pull it up on the left now, to free your hand," he told her. "And work your right arm until the folds make a sling, then slip your hand out the top."

"Huh!" she said, working at it. The hood fell back, and she stopped, frowning at him suspiciously. "*You* put it *under* your right arm."

"*Men* can wear it that way on informal occasions," he told her. "Women wear it the way you have it."

She worked her right arm vigorously until it was completely free of the folds. The draperies, disturbed, sagged crookedly. He considered pulling them straight again, then gave up. She was not a Greek, would not become one however much he draped her cloak for her. He should be glad that at least the cloak looked better draped askew than it had as a shawl. He took up his own cloak, shook it thoroughly to get rid of the fleas, draped it as neatly as he could, and they set out.

About three blocks into the Campus Martius they found a booth belonging to a scribe who wrote letters and drew up documents for the illiterate. They stopped, and after convincing the scribe that he could write his own letters, but was willing to pay the full charge for just the papyrus and ink, Hermogenes was supplied and allowed to sit down in the booth. He gazed at the blank page for a long moment, aware of Cantabra standing over him impatiently, and of the way the light was brightening in the street outside. The long letters of explanation and defense which he had composed in the course of the night now seemed shrill, deluded, pointless. He sharpened the pen, dipped it in the ink, and wrote hurriedly:

MARCUS AELIUS HERMOGENES GREETS HIS BELOVED DAUGHTER, AELIA MYRRHINE.

My darling, things have not gone as I planned. My attempt to collect the debt from Rufus has brought me into opposition to two very powerful men who have schemes I knew nothing about, but to whom I have now become a threat. I do not know whether I will be able to survive. If I die, please believe always that I loved you, and that I never intended to abandon you. The money for your dowry should be safe: choose a man who will make you happy. My dearest, I am so sorry I will not see you grow up. I pray that the gods favor you in all things, and grant you health and a long life.

He could think of nothing to add. He rolled the letter up, wrote the address on the back, and borrowed cord and wax from the scribe to seal it.

"Is it done?" Cantabra asked.

He nodded. Slowly and reluctantly he handed her the letter, and she tucked it under her cloak into the pen case, which also held her money and his letters of credit. He thanked the scribe, and they set off.

THE GLADIATORIAL SCHOOL WAS A VERY large building. Constructed solidly of brick, its sheer, windowless walls frowned four-square down on the streets of a small city block. Cantabra led him along two sides of the square to reach the single entrance.

The door was plated with iron, and the barbarian woman stood staring at it for a long minute. Her face was expressionless, but something about her stance proclaimed her loathing of the place. He remembered how she had said that she had been willing to starve rather than return here, and he wanted to tell her that she didn't need to, that he would go instead to Maecenas. The words were on his tongue when she knocked.

The doorkeeper opened the window of his lodge almost

at once, and gazed out suspiciously, his face reduced to a red blur and some eyes behind a grill. "What d'you want?" he demanded.

"I want to see the Savage, Pimp," Cantabra told him.

The eyes blinked, and the red blur split with a grin. "Cantabra! You coming back to us?"

"No," she replied flatly. "I just want to see the Savage."

"He'll want to see *you*," said the doorkeeper with a confident leer, and closed his window.

"His name isn't *really* Pimp, is it?" Hermogenes asked in an appalled whisper.

She shrugged. "It's what everybody calls him."

The door opened, and Pimp, a large, fat, red-faced man with a wooden leg, stood aside with an elaborate bow. When Cantabra had gone through, however, he flung out an arm to bar Hermogenes. "What's he?" he demanded of the barbarian.

"My employer," she replied. "He wants to speak to the Savage. He's why I've come."

The doorkeeper regarded Hermogenes with unfriendly eyes. The man's face was deformed from old breaks in the bone, marked with scars, and the whites of the eye were red, covered with a tracery of small blood vessels damaged by a lifetime of fighting. "What d'*you* want with the Savage?" he asked suspiciously.

"Are you his secretary?" Hermogenes asked mildly. "Should I have applied to you for an appointment?"

The doorkeeper frowned, sensing mockery, but unable to grasp where it lay. "You're Greek!" he said accusingly.

"This is true," he replied politely. "Does it mean I'm not allowed in?"

"Here, what'd you hire Cantabra for, Greek? She don't even let nobody fuck her!"

"I hired her as a bodyguard after she saved me from some robbers in the Subura. May I pass, please? Or should Cantabra go to the Savage and explain that you will not let me in?"

The doorkeeper stood aside quickly, and Hermogenes limped past him. Cantabra at once set off along a narrow, tunnellike passageway into the heart of the school.

That heart appeared to be an exercise yard enclosed by the brick framework of the building and spread with sand. About twenty men were jogging about it in armor while another ten or so sparred with one another in the center, using wooden swords. Fifteen more, guards supplied with clubs and whips, lounged in the sun against the far wall. The joggers at first merely eyed the visitors curiously, without pausing. Then suddenly one of the men stopped, staring, and shouted, "It's Cantabra!"

At that they all stopped, though some of them seemed merely confused, and the men sparring in the center of the yard turned to stare. A stout unarmored man, who appeared to have been supervising the sparring, hurried over, grinning widely. He wore a dirty tunic and was carrying a heavy whip.

"Why, Cantabra, darling!" he purred. "You've come back to us!" His eyes raked her Alexandrian cloak, and his lip curled. "What are you doing got up like a Greek whore?" He lifted one of the sagging folds of her cloak with the end of his whip.

She tugged it away again, frowning. "I've come back

because my new employer needs to talk to Taurus, Savage," she said evenly.

The Savage looked at the new employer: Hermogenes could see him taking in the expensive Greek cloak, the bruises, the bandaged foot. He bore the inspection for a couple of breaths, then said smoothly, "Greetings. I am Marcus Aelius Hermogenes of Alexandria. What my bodyguard says is true: I urgently need to speak to Titus Statilius Taurus, prefect of the city. Cantabra assures me that you would be able to introduce us, if you are Gaius Naevius Saevus, and I do beg that you do so."

The Savage's eyes narrowed, becoming dark slits in his slablike face. "What do you want to speak to Taurus about, Greek?"

"A matter of great importance to him," Hermogenes replied. "I am not able to discuss it further. My bodyguard knows of it, and believes it to be something which the prefect would wish to know."

The Savage turned back to Cantabra. "What are you doing with *him*?" he demanded. He sounded both angry and disgusted.

She shrugged. "He was being robbed; I helped him; he hired me. What he says is true, Savage. He accidentally came across a plot the old bull will want to know about. He didn't want to come here, but I told him he should. I thought it would be safer this way than if he went through the city offices."

The man called the Savage regarded her a long minute, eyes still narrowed, tapping his whip against his calf. Then he glanced around at the runners and the fighters, all of whom had paused to watch. He flicked the whip at the two men nearest him, crack! crack! and they retreated hastily, rubbing a knee and a neck. "Get back to it!" snarled the Savage, and flicked the whip at a third man who had already begun running again and just happened to be passing.

"The old bull should be arriving any minute," the Savage told Cantabra. Something about the way he said it made the word *taurus*, bull, a nickname rather than a formal cognomen. "I'll tell him you want to see him. It'd better be something he wants to hear, bitch." He studied her a moment longer, than bared his teeth in what was probably meant to be a smile. "So you're not reenlisting?"

"No," she said flatly. "I told you I would sooner starve."

"You said you'd sooner starve than be fucked, too," replied the Savage. "But . . ." He used the whip to indicate Hermogenes.

"Roman," said Hermogenes coolly, "I can afford the very best courtesans. I do not need to sleep with my bodyguards."

The Savage gave him the slit-eyed look again. He reached out with the end of his whip again, and touched the Scythopolitan linen cloak.

The familiarity was, Hermogenes recognized irritably, an implicit threat: *I am a big, tough, strong man and I could beat you bloody if I wanted to.* He responded with a look of disdain and an implicit threat of his own. "You may well admire it," he remarked, easing the cloak away from the whip. "I imagine it would cost more than a year's worth of the wages your sort get." *I am wealthy and powerful, and I could buy more trouble than you could possible survive.*

The Savage understood perfectly. His face darkened. "Rich bastard!" he muttered. He looked back at Cantabra. "The old bull better want to hear him, bitch, that's all I can say. Go wait over there, out of the way—unless you're sparring?"

"No," she replied, and strode over to the place near the gatehouse he had indicated.

There was nowhere to sit, so they leaned against the brick wall and watched the runners jog past and the men in the center cut and thrust, encouraged occasionally by the Savage's whip. After a little while, the men in the center were sent to join the runners, and ten runners replaced them.

"There are no women," Hermogenes remarked, after a silence.

"This is only the first shift," she replied. "The First Hall, the best fighters. They get to exercise early, when it's cool. All the women are in the Fourth Hall. We exercised later."

"Is that why Taurus normally comes early?"

She nodded. "He likes to spar with one of the best gladiators to start his day. They get special thin wands for it, and he gets a wooden sword to fix things so that he can win. He gets armor, too, and they don't. He likes them to try hard, though, and if they beat him he gives them money."

He snorted and glanced round the bare courtyard again. "Four Halls?" he asked. "Where are all the others?"

She waved a hand at the blank walls. "Locked in their cells. They never let out more than one hall at a time. You stay in your cell unless it's your turn to exercise or eat."

He looked at the dirty brick walls. "No windows," he said in a low voice.

She nodded. "That was hard. I hated that."

Two years, he thought, locked up in the dark, let out only to exercise in this bare yard; taken, once a month or so, to the arena to kill or be killed. He couldn't imagine it. He shook his head.

"They don't allow real weapons in the school," she said abruptly. "They're afraid the gladiators would kill themselves, even if they didn't attack their trainers."

One of the fighters in the center took a blow to the face and stopped, hand clapped over his bleeding nose. His opponent stood back; the Savage immediately rounded on the pair, and began striking both men with his whip, shouting at them until they began cutting at each other again. The man with the nosebleed was half-blinded, and his opponent drove him back, and back again. The Savage got behind the casualty and began whipping him, shouting for him to attack. He did, and his opponent caught him in the belly, then tripped him. "Hit him!" yelled the Savage, "Get the bastard!" and the opponent obediently rained down blow after blow.

"How did you help that brute get his job?" Hermogenes asked in disgust.

She snorted and crossed her arms. "When I first arrived at the school, the man in charge was called Papinius Macer. He and the Pimp used to take money from citizens to allow them in. Some people want to fuck a gladiator." She glanced at him warily. "Some women, even rich ones, want that. And men who like young men, and some who like women. It doesn't matter what you look like, it's the smell of blood they want. Anyway, I wouldn't. I said I'd rip the balls off any man that tried, and they didn't want that happening to a citizen, so they couldn't make me. At first it didn't matter because Macer just gave them somebody else, but after I'd fought a couple of times, he started getting requests. He offered me half the money, but I still wouldn't. So he would beat me and put me in the punishment cell every time I said no. The old bull—that is, General Taurus—came by once and asked what I'd done, and Macer just said I'd been disobedient. And then he had me chained and thrown in the punishment cell before a fight, for three days. He only let me out for the dinner the night before. He wasn't supposed to do that: you're not supposed to be sent out to fight unless you're fit for it, because it's bad for the reputation of the school if you get killed easily. Everybody thought I was going to die, because I was tired and stiff, and he'd fixed me up against a retiarius, a man. Only I won. The old bull saw the fight, and he went and checked the record, and then he had me brought in and asked me, in front of Macer, why I'd been in the punishment cell immediately before I was supposed to fight. I told him."

She grinned fiercely. "So then the old bull said to Macer, 'What are you, a lanista or a pimp? If she's willing to fight, it's no concern of yours whether she fucks!' and sacked him. He brought in the Savage to run the school instead, out of a smaller school down South. After that nobody tried to make me fuck anyone."

He was silent, once again confronted with a thing he couldn't begin to imagine.

"The Pimp's still here, though," she said regretfully.

There was a stir at the doorway beside them, and then a band of six guardsmen trooped through—not barbarians, and not toughs in livery, but Roman soldiers in strip armor and red-crested helmets. Despite the ban on real weapons, they all carried spears and wore short swords: ordinary rules didn't apply to the praetorian guard. They halted, three on each side of the gate, and stood to attention as a man in the long red cloak of a general strolled through. Another two guardsmen followed him.

Titus Statilius Taurus was older than his friend Tarius Rufus—perhaps sixty—but tall and powerful where Rufus was thick and flabby. He had a dark face with heavy brows, a large nose, and deep lines at the corners of his mouth. He paused at the edge of the yard, studying the fighters. The Savage at once stopped his supervision and came over to him. The two men talked briefly, and then both turned to look at Cantabra and Hermogenes. The Savage beckoned them over.

Hermogenes came warily. Cantabra was slightly ahead of him, and when she stopped, she saluted Taurus with the outflung arm he had seen her employ for the purpose once before. He smiled in reply, his teeth very white in his dark face.

"Cantabra," he said, in a deep strong voice. "With a rich employer. I'm glad of it. What is it you want?"

"That you listen to my employer, lord," she replied earnestly. "He has news which you should hear."

The dark, deep-set eyes turned to Hermogenes, who drew a deep breath, straightened his shoulders, and committed himself. "Lord Statilius Taurus, good health. I am Marcus Aelius Hermogenes, a businessman from Alexandria, and, as my bodyguard has said, I have come across some information which concerns you closely and which I thought it best to put before you . . . privately." He glanced significantly at the Savage.

Taurus regarded him for a long moment in silence, his face forbidding. "Marcus Aelius Hermogenes," he repeated at last. "I have heard your name frequently in the last few days. In fact, last night I issued an order for your arrest."

Hermogenes stood frozen. He was aware, without looking away, of how Taurus's guardsmen had come alert and were watching him. "On what charge?" he asked quietly.

"On no charge," Taurus conceded. "Simply for questioning. Some days ago my friend Lucius Rufus informed me that he was having a house on the Via Tusculana watched because he had had some kind of trouble with a guest of the man who owned it. Yesterday the owner of the house turned up complaining of harrassment, which he says is the result of quarrels between you and Rufus, and you and Publius Vedius Pollio. Pollio had his people search the house, and the owner complained about that, too."

"He had his men search a private house?" Hermogenes asked, shocked. "Was anyone hurt?"

"Not to my knowledge," replied Taurus, his face unyielding. "Pollio also has men searching the city for you. They claim that you were his guest, but stole a valuable statuette and absconded during the night. He has not brought charges against you before any magistrate, but I believed it prudent to question you."

"Lord, I am here and ready to answer questions." He was appalled, but he was also aware of an old niggling worry settling. Rufus's intimidating barbarians had not been as stupid a move as they'd seemed: the consul had cleared them with his friend the prefect of the city before posting them. "I assure you, I am not a thief, and this story that I am was invented to give Pollio a pretext for searching for me. The matter at stake is far more important than a statuette. I would prefer to discuss it in a less public place."

Taurus grunted. He glanced round at the Savage, then snapped his fingers. "Come, then," he ordered, and walked directly across the exercise yard to a doorway on the other side, forcing the fighters and the runners to halt abruptly or hurry aside to let him pass. Hermogenes and Cantabra followed, enclosed by Taurus's eight guardsmen. The Savage, at the end of the procession, stopped to haul one of his own guardsmen away from his place in the sun and set him to supervise the yard.

The doorway led into what appeared to be the offices of the gladiatorial school: there was a large front room with a desk and a bench, a number of large chests, and two more doors, one at either end. A set of wooden swords of various types hung on a rack along one wall; the wall to the right, more ominously, held iron shackles of various sizes and weights suspended on pegs. Taurus went directly to the desk and sat down in the chair, turning it to face into the room. He snapped his fingers, gestured for four of his guards to stand watch outside, and waited while the rest arranged themselves on either side of the room. The Savage shut the door.

"Now," Taurus commanded, "search them."

Cantabra stiffened. "Lord!" she protested, and took a step forward. Taurus merely nodded, and two of the guardsmen seized her and pulled her off to one side of the room.

Hermogenes stood stiffly while the other two guardsmen turned their attention to him. They pulled off his good cloak, tossing it onto the bench, unfastened and examined his belt, checked his empty purse. They found the trunk key on the cord around his neck, and set it down on the desk. They ran their hands down him, checking for the sheath of a concealed knife, and ordered him to take off his sandals. They untied the bandage on his ankle and shook it out. Then, empty-handed, they stood holding him by the arms and watching as their fellows finished searching Cantabra.

One man was examining the stitching on her belt; the pen case was already lying on the desk in front of Taurus. The other man, grinning, was feeling her breasts. He raised his eyebrows. "Take off the tunic!" he ordered. "I think you've got a knife there."

The barbarian woman spat, shoved his hand off with an elbow. "I have a knife," she admitted. "To defend myself, not to attack anyone, still less to kill the bull."

"It is an offense to carry a concealed weapon on the streets of Rome," said Taurus levelly. "Give it to my men."

She drew it out and reluctantly handed it over. "Now take off the tunic," the general commanded.

Her head came up angrily, but she took off the tunic. Her body was thin and hard between the plain breastband and the cloth about her loins, and marked with scars. The sheath of the knife stood out, stitched into the breastband.

It was evident that the knife she'd just handed over was the only one she'd had.

Taurus grunted and picked up the pen case. He opened it, drew out the letters, tipped the money onto the desk, then slid it back in. He began to examine the letters of credit.

"You have seen that I am unarmed," Hermogenes told him angrily. "And that my bodyguard has only the sort of weapon which, if illegal, can hardly be uncommon among those of her profession. I came here to speak to you about a matter which ought to concern you. I understood that you wanted to ask me questions."

Taurus looked up at him with grim satisfaction. "And so I do." He glanced at the guardsmen and ordered, "Take the man, strip him, and chain him to the pillar. Shackle the woman and put her in the cell until we've finished with him."

"No!" screamed Cantabra, and flung herself forward.

The two men beside her had hold of her and wrestled her to the floor before she'd gone two steps. Hermogenes noticed the Savage shaking his head as he took a set of manacles from a peg, and then his own guards had marched him through the door to the right.

This was evidently the place where the slaves of the gladiatorial school were punished for any offense against its rules. Three whips hung in prominent positions along the long outer wall, one of leather, one of knotted cord, one, with four lashes, of both; beneath them stood birch rods bound together in a stack. In the center of the room stood a thick pillar of stained wood, fitted with iron manacles on an adjustable chain, so that it would secure for flogging a victim of any height. Hermogenes stood helpless with outrage while the guards stripped him. Cantabra was cursing and screaming behind him. Hermogenes's guards shoved him against the pillar and drew his arms around it, crossing his wrists above his head. The iron manacles locked with a snick, and one of them turned a wheel to tighten the chain.

He stood with his stitched cheek pressed against the wood of the pillar, the sweat cold on his bare skin as it dried, shaking with rage. "I am a *Roman citizen!*" he announced loudly.

No one replied. Somewhere behind him, Cantabra was still cursing, muffled now. He could not see her—could not see anyone, with his face against the pillar.

Footsteps sounded, deliberate and unhurried, from the direction of the office.

"I am a Roman citizen," he said again. "This proceeding is not legal."

"I am prefect of the city," Taurus's deep voice replied. "I am entitled to hold extraordinary hearings . . . which I declare this to be."

"You are *not* entitled to flog freeborn citizens without trial!" Hermogenes answered fiercely. "I came here to *save your life,* Roman! This is my reward, is it?"

Taurus's face appeared in his field of view, still with that expression of grim satisfaction. "Publius Vedius Pollio. When did he hire you?"

"He did not," Hermogenes replied flatly. "You said yourself he has accused me of theft and is searching the city for me: would he do that if I were his hireling?"

Taurus shook his head. "Perhaps you've fallen out with

him. Perhaps you did steal something from him: it wouldn't be the first time greed has got the better of one of his creatures. Pollio hired you. I think you have been helping him to blackmail a friend of mine."

Hermogenes gave a choking laugh. "Your friend Rufus has *sold* you to Pollio, O wise prefect of the city. He has agreed to kill you, in exchange for the cancellation of some debts and my life."

The dark eyes held his own. There was a sense of something massive behind them, something that was shifting, like a great weight under the delicate manipulation of a cunning machine. "Debts," Taurus repeated softly. "What debts?"

The wood of the pillar stank of old blood. Hermogenes leaned his head back and looked up at the chain wrapped around its top. From outside in the yard came the weary beating of footsteps, the clatter and thump of wooden weapons, the shouting of a guard: "Hit him! *Hit* him!" For a moment he could feel nothing but contempt for the man beside him, who owned this place.

"Rufus spent a hundred million sestertii," he stated with cold disgust, "all the capital he possessed, on land in Picenum—then discovered that if he was to make a profit from the land, he needed to pay for improvements to it. He borrowed the money from Pollio, using the land as security. The interest on the loan is either nearly as much as the profit from the land, or slightly more. If he sells, his indebtedness will come out, and the price of his assets will crash. He was managing to keep Pollio at bay, however, until I chanced to arrive. Many years ago in Cyprus Rufus borrowed money from my uncle which he never repaid; I inherited the debt last autumn, and arrived in Rome determined to press my claim. I am a Roman citizen, able to use the courts; I have documents proving my right, and though Rufus tried to intimidate me, he failed. He found himself unable to escape my claim, and to pay me, he would have to sell. Pollio has offered to buy out my debt and, so I believe, hand me over to him, if he will take your life. He has agreed."

A hand grabbed his chin and wrenched his head around again. "So you say," rumbled Taurus.

He tried to speak, and could not: the hand was crushing his jaw. Taurus saw it, and let go. Hermogenes rested his cheek against the pillar again, looking into his captor's eyes. "I am sick of you Romans!" he whispered. "Pollio said that Rufus, more than most of you, has always the sense that we Greeks are sneering at you as barbarians behind your backs. Let me sneer at you to your face, then. Look at you! You have no respect for justice, for law, for contract and the obligations of civilization—you, prefect of the city, and Rufus, a consul, are both of you happy to flout every law the Senate and People ever decreed the moment it conflicts with your own self-interest. You are and ever will be *savages*. Your great contribution to culture is out there in the yard hitting each other with swords; your arts are oppression and the shedding of blood. May the gods destroy you all."

Taurus hit him. It was a calculated blow, a hand jabbed edgewise under the arm to catch the nerve, and it hurt horribly. He caught his breath with a gasp, trying to support himself against the pillar. His arm was numb. A second blow caught him under the ribs, knocking the breath out of his lungs. He hung in the chains, struggling to get air.

"You forget yourself, Greek," said Taurus.

Hermogenes pulled himself upright by the chains, still panting. "No: you forget yourself, Roman," he managed. "Or is it *legal* for prefects of the city to beat citizens during 'extraordinary' hearings?"

Taurus raised his hand again—then lowered it and turned away.

There was a silence. Hermogenes leaned against the pillar, breathing hard. All he could see now was the wall, and the whips hanging there. He nursed his anger, letting it burn hot and high and keep away the fear. Three times he had gone to an important Roman, asking for things he had a right to ask for; three times he had been insulted and abused.

"There is a letter here which your bodyguard was carrying," came Taurus's voice from somewhere to his left.

He tilted his head back and managed to turn it and get his other cheek against the pillar. Taurus was standing a few feet away, the letter to Myrrhine in his hand, opened.

"That is a private letter," he told the general bitterly. "You had no right to see it."

Taurus wagged it back and forth. "Why did your bodyguard have it?"

"She was to pass it on in the event of my death, and our lodgings aren't safe. I knew the risk I was taking, coming to you: I never imagined you would welcome news of a friend's treachery. You have no reason to prevent my bodyguard from sending that letter. Since you have read it, you have *seen* that it is a private letter, and of no interest to you at all—unless you intend to amuse yourself by mocking it and me. If you do, may you die childless and alone."

"'My attempt to collect the debt from Rufus,'" Taurus read out, the Greek words strange and sonorous in that place of Roman punishment, "'has brought me into opposition to two very powerful men who have schemes I knew nothing about, but to whom I have now become a threat.' *Two* powerful men, Greek? Rufus and who else?"

"Pollio," Hermogenes answered impatiently. "I already told you that, if you recollect. He wants to kill me because he fears I have guessed enough of his plans to betray them—to you. A pointless and stupid fear, isn't it? Here I am, trying to do exactly what he fears, and there are you, preparing to flog me to prevent it. Pollio could have sent me to you himself, and spared himself trouble."

"All I want from you is the truth, Greek."

Hermogenes spat. "You could have had the *truth* for the asking, Roman. I came here to tell it to you, and I said as much. No: you want me to lie. You want me to say that your friend is blameless, and that I am not an innocent businessman caught up in the schemes of powerful Romans but a wicked conspirator and blackmailer myself. Torture me long enough and I probably *will* say it. Perhaps I will say it now, and spare myself the torture. Then you can give me to Rufus, and he will kill me—and, in due course, kill you."

"Tell me about this debt you came to collect from Rufus, 'innocent businessman.'"

"And if I say something you dislike, will you use the

whip yourself, or will you allow the Savage to change my story?"

Taurus stared at him for a long moment, his jaw working. Then he raised a hand. "Unchain him," he ordered.

There was a moment of hesitation, and then the guards came over, loosened the chain, and unfastened the manacles. Hermogenes drew his arms down slowly and stepped away from the pillar. His right arm was still numb from the general's blow, but it had started to prickle with pain. He flexed the fingers, staring at them as they moved, then glanced around for his clothes. Taurus gave a nod, and one of the guards handed him his tunic. He put it on, belted it clumsily with his numbed hand. "My bodyguard," he said, without looking round.

Someone went behind him to the far wall: he turned to watch them, and saw that the "punishment cell" adjoined the room—a narrow cellar, too small to stand in upright, windowless and with a single door. The Savage unlocked the door and went in. After a little, he came out again, carrying the iron shackles. Behind him came Cantabra, still naked apart from her underclothes. She looked at him anxiously.

He indicated the door to the office and started for it himself. The guards stirred, but Taurus raised a hand, and they subsided.

Back in the office, Hermogenes moved his good cloak to one side of the bench, then sat down to put on his sandals. Taurus had followed him out of the punishment room, and watched him put them on. At the other side of the room, Cantabra was hurriedly pulling on her tunic.

"So," said Taurus. "Now will you talk?"

Hermogenes turned to face him. "Am I under arrest, Lord Prefect? And if so, who has charged me, and with what crime, or who has called me as a witness? For one or the other must be true, if I am under arrest and this is a legal hearing."

Taurus frowned.

"If this is a legal hearing," Hermogenes went on, "where is the prosecutor? For I think that, however 'extraordinary' it may be, the judge who hears the case is not allowed to play that role himself. And where is the counsel for the defense—and, for that matter, what *is* the case that is being heard? I should like to know that, if I am under arrest."

"You are not under arrest," Taurus conceded.

"Then I will go." Hermogenes marched to the desk and picked up the pen case. The letters of credit were underneath it, and he rolled them up and stuffed them in.

"No!" Taurus exclaimed impatiently. "You said you came here to tell me about this!"

"So I did," Hermogenes replied, rounding on him again. "But if it escaped your notice that you responded by having me stripped and chained to a flogging post, I assure you, it did not escape mine. And now I find myself strangely unwilling to help you, and—I do not know why!—suspicious of your goodwill and your good faith. So I think I will simply go away again and see if I can't find a way out of my difficulties which does not involve relying upon a Roman. Kindly return to me the letter I wrote to my daughter."

"You are very angry," observed Taurus. "Consider that you are accusing a man I have for many years regarded as a protégé and friend, and that I have cause to believe you are his enemy and the agent of a man I despise."

"I considered it before," Hermogenes replied. "I expected suspicion; I feared that you would not believe me. I did not expect violence and the threat of torture as the *first recourse*—the *first* recourse, before you had even questioned me! Zeus! Can you really expect me to trust you now?"

Taurus looked at him for a long moment, then said slowly, "I am ready to listen to you, Greek. You can talk, or you can satisfy your indignation by walking out."

Hermogenes stood still, trying to get control of his breathing, which kept threatening to turn into pants of rage and pain. Then he shuddered, set down the pen case, pressed his hands to his face, and swore.

"Tell me about this debt you came to collect from my friend Lucius Rufus," ordered Taurus, sitting down at the desk again.

He told him briefly, keeping back the whereabouts of the documents and the token that provided access to them. He recounted his meeting with Pollio, the way he had been detained, the encounter with Rufus in the bathhouse, Pollio's decision to buy the debt, and his own suspicion and escape. Taurus listened in forbidding silence, occasionally glancing at Cantabra, and seeming to find confirmation of the story in her expression.

When he had finished, the Roman sat staring moodily at the desk for a long time. Hermogenes stood before him cradling his arm, which now ached and felt hot.

"Even if you are telling the truth," Taurus said at last, looking up, "you do not know that Rufus has agreed."

"Pollio told me he would buy the debt," Hermogenes pointed out. "If Rufus had refused he would have told me that he would protect me while I summoned the consul for nonpayment."

"Which you would have done," said Taurus, with a flash of anger.

"Do you recommend a general cancellation of debts?" Hermogenes asked acidly. "If you do, is your friend the emperor aware of it? In Egypt there are laws, approved by the Romans, which call that recommendation treason. Or is your opinion merely that friends of the emperor have the right to take money from whomever they please without repayment? I had the impression that the emperor would not like that view any more than the other, since he has proclaimed the restoration of the Republic—and the Senate would like the notion even less."

Taurus glowered, then made a gesture of concession. "Rufus should have repaid your uncle. I suspect even he realizes that now."

"He does not," Hermogenes said flatly, glaring at the Roman. "He considers he was fully entitled to take money from a Greek, and he blames his troubles upon my insolent refusal to accept that—as do you."

"Because you are indeed a very insolent and troublesome man!" replied Taurus, leaning forward to fix him with a lowering glare. "Understand: I could charge you with treason. You prayed for the destruction of Rome. I have witnesses to that. You saw fit to rebuke me for striking you for it, but I could legitimately have you *killed*."

"Your witnesses would also have to testify that I cursed

Romans during a proceeding which was clearly illegal," Hermogenes said coolly. "I do not think you are likely to call them. As for my opinion of Rome and Romans—I am a Roman citizen, and until I came to this city, I was proud of it. I have never advocated or practiced any sedition. I have never called for the cancellation of debts, or pretended that the laws pronounced by the Senate and People don't apply to me and my friends."

"Enough!" shouted Taurus, and slapped the desk.

There was a silence. Hermogenes noticed that his ankle was hurting again. He remembered that the guards had taken away the bandage for it, and glanced around to see what they'd done with it. The long strip of linen was crumpled up under the bench. He went over, picked it up, sat down, took off his sandal, and began wrapping the foot again—slowly, because his right arm hurt.

"You said," Taurus resumed at last, "that Pollio feared you had guessed enough of his plans to betray them. What *have* you guessed of them?"

Hermogenes shrugged. The bandage was creased, and he tried to straighten it. "I think he plans to create some sort of public disorder. Riots, or a fire. Something which would allow him to step forward with money and help, and be restored to the emperor's friendship on a wave of popular acclaim. From the way you speak of him, you are his enemy, and presumably he believes that if he tried such a trick while you were alive, you would instantly suspect him and take steps to find him out—which, as prefect of the city, you would be well placed to do. Rufus, on the other hand, as consul would be in a position to help him."

Taurus grunted. After another silence he said, "I do not take your bare word for any of this, Greek."

"I never imagined that you would." Hermogenes tied the bandage and pulled his sandal on again. "You will have to investigate it, obviously, and perhaps devise some test of your friend's intentions." He straightened, facing the prefect again. "You will find that it is as I say."

Taurus grunted again. "When does your letter go to Scipio?"

"The first of July."

"Four days," the prefect commented with distaste. "That is not very long. Scipio is an arrogant bungler with more ancestors than wits; he must at all costs be kept out of a delicate business like this one. You must collect that letter."

"No." He met the prefect's indignant eyes. "However, if I had reason, and if I was certain that no one was spying on me, I could arrange a postponement."

Taurus's jaw worked again. "And suppose I said that if you want my help you must give me the letter—and the documents?"

"I would refuse," Hermogenes answered at once. "You have given me no reason to trust you. Even as it is, I think it very unlikely that you will help me."

"Even though by your reckoning you have *saved my life*?"

"I think you hold the same opinion as your friend: that a debt to a Greek is a debt that can be ignored."

The Roman's face darkened. "You are mistaken."

Hermogenes shrugged. "When you *prove* your good

faith, Roman, I will be very happy to admit that I misjudged you, and I will gladly acknowledge you to be an honorable man. Until then, I reserve judgment. Am I free to go?"

"No. Not yet."

"Am I a prisoner, then?"

"No!" said the prefect impatiently. "You are a man who is required to wait quietly while I try to think what to do."

Hermogenes leaned back against the wall and put his bad foot up on the bench. He noticed Cantabra standing silently on the other side of the room, the cloak he'd loaned her once more draped like a shawl. Her face was very pale, making the scar on her cheek stand out sharply, and she looked enormously shaken. He moved up along the bench and indicated the place beside him. She hesitated, then shook her head.

After another long silence, Taurus said slowly, "You suggested that I devise a test of my friend's intentions. I think the best test would be to offer him you."

He took his foot off the bench and straightened slowly. He was surprised at how calm he felt. "This is how an honorable Roman repays debts, is it?" he asked.

Taurus raised a hand forbiddingly. "I said *'offer,'* Greek. I did not say 'give.' He knows that the affair of the house on the Via Tusculana has brought you to my attention. I could tell him that I had apprehended you for questioning, and that you had on you some documents relating to a debt owed by him. If he thought himself secure, he might inform on Pollio."

"He would want me dead and the documents destroyed

before he felt 'secure,'" Hermogenes stated in disgust. "And even then, he would never admit that he had agreed to kill you."

"I could arrange that Pollio also knew that I had you." Taurus began to smile. "You said neither of them knew that you'd heard my name. I could let Rufus know that Pollio wanted you. He would talk if he feared that I'd let Pollio get hold of you again. Even if everything you say is true, I don't believe he *wants* to kill me." His eyes began to glint. "Perhaps I could *also* offer you to Pollio, and see what he has to say for himself. Yes." He slapped the desk and stood up. "I will need you to cooperate with this, Greek. They will have to *see* that I have you, and fear what you might say or what use might be made of you."

"I have told you, I will *not* give you the documents!" Hermogenes declared angrily.

"Then don't!" snapped Taurus. "All this requires of you is that you present yourself at my house on the day I appoint, and play the role of prisoner in front of Rufus and Pollio."

"Prisoner," repeated Hermogenes warily. "Why would I be a prisoner?"

"Because you are a suspicious person who has been causing trouble in the city," replied the general. "Because Pollio has accused you of theft, but not brought charges. Because I questioned you, and was not satisfied with your account of yourself. Ha! That would worry them both. They would both start talking."

"Start *lying!*" Hermogenes objected.

"They would say enough truth that I would know where they're guilty," Taurus declared confidently, baring his teeth. "And Lucius cannot lie to me. I raised him from the ranks and promoted him, and we have fought side by side. If you're unwilling to do this, Greek, I will conclude that *you're* the one who's lying."

Hermogenes was silent a moment. The notion of taking on the role of prisoner filled him with dismay: it seemed only too likely that it wouldn't be a role at all. On the other hand, if Taurus wanted to take him prisoner, he was quite capable of doing so on the spot. He had turned to this man. That now seemed a mistake, but it was too late to correct it. He had to see it through. "I am willing to do it," he said in a low voice. "When do you want it done?"

The prefect regarded him a moment, then nodded. "Three days' time. That will give me time to make some other investigations into the matter. But . . . yes, I think I will want to have you arrested the day before. Publicly, and somewhere that Pollio's spies would see it. That would be the best way for him to learn that I have you."

"At my bank, then," Hermogenes suggested resignedly, "or attempting to visit Gaius Maecenas. Pollio will have men watching every bank where I could conceivably use an Alexandrian letter of credit within two days, if he doesn't have them there already, and he probably had watchers posted outside Maecenas's house yesterday."

"At your bank," Taurus decreed. "I would prefer to leave Maecenas out of this. An intervention by him would complicate matters and make them more difficult to settle."

"Very well, then. At the Bank of Gabinius, at the third hour, the day after tomorrow. I do ask that you have plenty of people in place in good time. I think Pollio would prefer to recapture me, if he could, but he will certainly have given his men orders to kill me rather than let me fall into your hands."

Taurus smiled. "You're a cunning fox, aren't you, Greek? Not one to be caught in a trap. What is your price?"

"I am not a slave," he declared proudly.

Taurus made another gesture of concession. "What do you expect to gain from this, if it turns out that you are telling the truth, and that you've saved my life?"

"I want to go home safely," Hermogenes replied at once, "and I want Rufus to pay his debt."

"If you are telling the truth, both things will happen in the natural working of events. What do you want from *me*?"

"Nothing."

Taurus leaned back in his seat. "You like money. That's clear from the risks you've taken to get it."

"This has never been about the money, Roman. This has been about whether Roman officials can rob, cheat, and murder with impunity."

There was a silence. "You are a strange man," said Taurus.

Hermogenes laughed: he couldn't help it. "So I have been told."

"Do you have a safe hiding place until the day after tomorrow?"

"I believe so," he replied cautiously.

Taurus snorted. "Your bodyguard was carrying money," he remarked. "You had none—only letters of credit allowing you up to . . . ten thousand sestertii, if I recall correctly?. . . which you cannot use while you believe the banks are a trap. Was your bodyguard keeping your funds as well as your letters, or do you need money?"

"Not from you," Hermogenes replied proudly.

Taurus regarded him a moment impassively. "You will borrow from your bodyguard?"

"If I survive I will repay her," he answered. "If you give me to Rufus, I hope you will repay her yourself—if you are, as you claim and she believes, a man of honor."

"You are one of the most arrogant and self-righteous men I have ever met!" exclaimed Taurus, his face darkening. "I will not give you to Rufus: you have my word on it. If you really have saved my life, I will reward you."

Hermogenes got to his feet. "I want nothing from you, Statilius Taurus—only that you honor the law of Rome, and see that it gives me my rights. If you do that, I will be more than content. Am I free to go?"

Taurus, still dark with indignation, grunted and gestured at the door. "The Bank of Gabinius," he said warningly. "The day after tomorrow, at the third hour."

"I will be there." Hermogenes picked up his cloak, tossed it around himself quickly, then went to the desk and picked up the pen case. "The letter to my daughter!" he reminded the prefect.

Taurus, looking thunderous, glanced round, found it, and gave it to him. Hermogenes slipped it into the pen case, which he handed to Cantabra, and limped proudly out of the room.

There was a different group of men jogging and sparring in the exercise yard. They, too, paused with surprised exclamations of "Cantabra!" until the Savage, who had followed the visitors from the office, flicked his whip at the nearest and ordered them to get on with it.

The lanista followed them all the way to the gate. While the Pimp was unlocking the bolt to let them out, the Savage said to Cantabra, "This is a real prizewinning employer you've got yourself, girl. Do they chain him up at the full moon?"

The barbarian rounded on him. "If you're so wise, Naevius Saevus, why don't you have ten thousand in a bank? And if you're so brave, let's chain you to the post and hear what *you* say!"

"That wasn't brave," said the Savage, shaking his head. "That was stupid." He gave Hermogenes a last slit-eyed look, then moved aside to let them go.

Hermogenes walked blindly away from the gladiatorial school, paying no attention to where he was going. He stopped only when he reached the Tiber. It ran between steep embankments, low in this summer season, with grass growing on the mud banks, and it stank of sewage. The day had grown overcast and muggy, and the river swarmed with gnats and blowflies. A low wall separated it from the street.

He leaned against that wall, then sat down on it and bent over, cradling the arm Taurus had injured. What had just happened was like a huge, unwieldy bundle which he had somehow managed to carry through the crisis itself, but which now seemed far too heavy to pick up again. The rage that had supported him was gone, and the fear that had waited behind it shook him.

"Are you hurt?" Cantabra asked anxiously.

"He hit me under the arm," he told her. "When I cursed Romans."

She caught the arm and began chafing it. "I could hear . . . most of it. But I couldn't see."

"I shouldn't have cursed Romans," he admitted. "It was, as the Savage said, stupid."

She looked up earnestly into his face. "He believed you. You've almost won."

He considered that. She didn't, of course, mean that the Savage believed what he'd said about Romans but that Taurus believed what he'd said about Rufus. "I think probably he knew enough to recognize that it was true," he said slowly. "He probably already knew that his friend had problems with money, and he knows Pollio and was expecting him to try something. Yes. He believed that I was telling the truth about Rufus the moment I accused him." He tried to laugh. "And Myrrhine's letter convinced him that I wasn't acting as Pollio's agent. He still had no right to look at it, though."

Cantabra gently brushed his hair out of his face.

"As to whether I've almost won . . . oh, Zeus! I *don't* like it that I've agreed to let him make me a prisoner; I don't like that at all. You know him better than I do. Can I trust him?"

"He is honest," she told him. "If he promises, he will keep the promise. And he promised that he would not give you to Rufus, and that he would reward you for saving his life."

He spat. "I want *nothing* from that maker of gladiators. His money has blood on it. I only hope that he doesn't let Pollio get me, or give me to Rufus."

"I am so sorry," she said humbly. "I know you only went there because I insisted, and . . . and . . ." Her hand tightened on his sore arm, the grip painfully strong, and suddenly she was almost in tears. "Och, oh, when he ordered them to chain you to the post, I thought I would lose my mind."

"Cantabra!" he exclaimed, astonished and touched.

She wiped at her eyes. "And they put me in the punishment cell again," she said in a choked voice. "I thought that was one place I would never have to endure again, but they put me in, and I thought I would have to listen while they whipped you, and *I* was the one who made you come. I thought I would lose my mind." She let go of his arm. "And then you *won*, you forced him to back down, and they let us out! Do you *know* how wonderful you are?"

"Me?" he asked in amazement.

She gave him a radiant, tremulous smile, and kissed him. He was so surprised that he was unable to move, and he sat frozen in amazement at the wet warmth of her mouth and the strong suppleness of the body pressed against his.

"I am sorry," she said, pulling away hastily. Her face had gone red. "I shouldn't have done that. I know you think I am an ugly red-haired heifer. But I—"

"I don't think that!" he protested. "That wasn't me! That was Pollio!"

She frowned. "You don't think that?"

"I . . ." He faltered, aware of a gulf opening up on either side of him. He tried to find a way carefully across the middle of it. "I . . . if I said I found you desirable, would you be offended and . . . how was it you put it? Rip my balls off?"

"Of course not," she said impatiently. "I would never do anything to a man just for what he *said*."

"Ah. Good. Well, I do. Definitely. Very much so. However, I . . . you made it very plain that I could not expect anything, and I accepted that. The offer to take you to Alexandria was not . . . was . . . that is, I am not going to try to force you or blackmail you or buy you, please believe that, and I would have made the same offer to a man who had done for me what you have. It was, and is, an honest offer."

She was still frowning. "You *want* me?"

He shrugged helplessly. "Yes. If that displeases you, you can safely forget it, because nothing will ever come of it."

"But you're rich! You can hire the most beautiful courtesans—you told the Savage so, and he believed you: it made him angry."

"I *said* it to make him angry, but it was perfectly true. I can hire courtesans, and I have. I don't see why that should mean I'm incapable of wanting you."

"I'm not beautiful."

He hesitated, then answered honestly, "I don't think you're beautiful. I *like* the way you look, though. I like your hair, and that look on your face when you're thinking hard, and the way you smile and the way you walk and the way you laugh. I *like* you—and that does seem to mean that I also want you, perhaps simply because I am a man, but it does not mean that I expect you to be my whore. It does not mean anything more than you want it to mean." He looked away from those steady blue eyes and added, trying to make it sound like a joke, "I do not want to have my balls ripped off."

She touched the side of his face, and when he looked back, kissed him again. Something inside him seemed to turn like a key in a lock, and he felt himself shaken to the core by the sudden opening of a thousand possibilities.

It was not, he knew, going to be simple. This was not a woman with whom to conduct a casual dalliance: this was a woman who was strong, courageous, and passionate, and who had suffered abominably. An affair with her would require the commitment of important assets, the calling in of other debts, the investment of the capital of himself— and he wanted to do it. That was the shocking thing: he wanted it very much. That tingle of desire hadn't been simply a matter of proximity, after all. He regarded the strength and the certainty of his own feelings with astonishment.

"I thought you thought I was just an ugly barbarian," she told him, looking into his face. "I was sure you found me repulsive."

"No," he said thickly. "Not at all." He reached out to put an arm around her.

She froze, as she had when he pressed her hand, then seized his arm and pushed it back at him. He sat still, staring in confusion, and she lowered her eyes but not the hand that held him off. "Please," she said shakily. "Please understand. I . . . I am not trying to . . . to tease you, but when you touched me . . . when a man touches me like that, I want to hit him. But I don't really want to hit *you*, I just . . . ach, I am being so *stupid!*" She let go his hand and turned away.

"I do understand," he told her, withdrawing his arm. "You suffered things no one should have to endure, and you made yourself strong enough to endure them and fight back. Of course you cannot stop fighting all in an instant." She looked back at him, and he felt once more that sense of being shaken to the heart. Just from her *eyes,* he thought incredulously; just from the look in her eyes!

"You are very wise," she whispered. "I . . . I like you so much. Yesterday I went into your room to wake you, and when I saw you sleeping, I . . . realized. Then I reminded myself that you didn't want me, and I was angry, with you and with me. I was awake all night, telling myself how I was being stupid, that you were doing everything I'd hoped for—hiring me, and trusting me, and treating me honorably, and it was stupid to want anything more. Now you say that you do want me, and part of me is very glad, but part of me is frightened. When I look at you, it seems good, but when you touch me, I feel angry and confused. Don't touch me, please!"

"I won't," he said impulsively. "I will never touch you without your permission, and nothing will happen except what you want. I want to be one person who has never hurt you. *Never.* If I ever do, I want you to tell me, and make me stop."

She looked at him very doubtfully, then laid her palm against the side of his face and simply looked at him for a long, aching moment. Then she kissed him again.

He fought the very strong desire to put his arms around

her. He put them behind his back instead and clutched his hands together to keep them still. It was, he told himself, an utterly ridiculous situation—and what on earth and heaven did he think was going to happen now? Would she *sleep* with him without letting him touch her? Was he going to sack her as his bodyguard, and keep her as his mistress? Bring her into his household and keep her . . . where? Set her up in another house in Alexandria? Have her learn another trade, employ her, let her find other employment of her own?

He didn't really care. His heart was pounding and his battered body seemed to have been transformed, flooded with an elixir of life and joy. *One step at a time,* he told himself. *Survive the next few days, and then you can decide what to do next.*

THEY WANDERED BACK TO THE LODGING house, pausing along the way to buy and eat bread and a salad from a corner cookshop. When they arrived it was nearly noon.

"Oh, there you are!" exclaimed Gellia happily, letting them in. "Oh, Herapilus, sir, what a beautiful cloak! I don't like to *think* what that must've cost. What's the dye?"

"*Dyes,*" Hermogenes corrected her. "Iron alum and saffron." He was feeling very cheerful, and he added, "You are *supposed* to think what it cost. That is the point of it: to impress people with how much it cost, so that they hope the fool who wasted the money on it will part with a little more."

Gellia giggled. "How did your inquiries go?"

"Not so well at first, but they improved. I have an appointment for the day after tomorrow. Gellia, I am sorry to trouble you about this again, but have you cleaned the rooms?"

Her face fell. "Well . . ." she said, and coughed. "To tell the truth, sir, after the party last night I didn't get up very early, and I've only got back from shopping just now. And now you're back, you won't want me fussing around . . ."

"Give me the cleaning things, and I will do it," said Cantabra.

"Will you?" cried Gellia in relief, and bustled off to fetch them.

"You should not have said that," Hermogenes told her disapprovingly. "It is her job."

Cantabra shrugged. "She hates cleaning, and she does it very badly. I don't mind. When I stayed here before, when I was first discharged, I used to sweep the floor and wipe down the shutters twice a day, just because I was so glad to have a place of my own to look after, instead of a place where I was kept."

He started to touch her hand in sympathy, but recollected himself in time. "No wonder Gellia liked you," he said instead, and she smiled.

Gellia came back with a broom, a dustpan, and a bucket of tepid water with a handful of fine ash in it to serve as soap. Cantabra took these up the stairs and energetically set about cleaning the room. She beat the flea-infested bed mattress with the broom handle, swept the floor under it, then tipped the sweepings into the alleyway. She turned the mattress over and commenced beating it again. He was suddenly and uncomfortably reminded of the gladiators that morning, the victorious man raining blows down on his half-blind and fallen opponent. He shivered. He remembered that Cantabra had said she'd fought thirty times in the arena. At least some of those fights must have ended in a death. He wondered whether his new sense of life and joy might not be misplaced.

Cantabra stopped beating the mattress and began to sweep again. He moved out of her way, then wondered if he ought to help. After all, this was as much not-his-job as not-hers: there weren't any slaves. There was only one broom, though. That was lucky: if his father had been alive to see his son and heir wield a broom, the shock would certainly have killed him. "Should I do something with the water?" he asked.

She paused, leaning on the broom and grinning. "Have you ever cleaned a room in your life?"

"No," he admitted. "But I've seen it done."

She laughed her hooting, uncivilized laugh. "I'll do it. You can sit down: the bed should be better now."

He sat down. Cantabra continued to sweep vigorously—the floor, the walls, the corners of the ceiling. He leaned on the windowsill and looked out. The overcast sky was becoming dark.

"Does it rain in Rome in the summer?" he asked hopefully.

"Sometimes." She came over to have a look for herself. "I think there will be a storm," she declared, with some satisfaction. "You will not be able to go out to the bathhouse."

He stared in surprise. "Why not?"

"You'd get wet."

"One expects to, in the bath."

"You'd get your *clothes* wet," she told him impatiently. "Then you'd have a wet cloak to sleep under. Nobody goes out in the rain if they can help it!"

"I like rain," he told her. "If there's a storm, does that mean there will be thunder and lightning?"

She stared at him. "Don't you have storms in Alexandria?"

"Not often," he admitted.

She stared harder. "Huh!" She piled the sweepings into the dustpan, threw them out the window, then paused and frowned at him again. "Do you have *rain*?"

"Sometimes. Not often. I've seen storms enough, though, in Cyprus." He remembered Uncle Nikomachos laughing at him over his childish enthusiasm for thunder and lightning. He found that he longed for there to be a storm now, to clear the muggy air and the stinking streets, to relieve the rage against the Romans that even Cantabra couldn't still.

"Not much rain!" said Cantabra wonderingly. "What do you do for water, then?"

"The river. Egypt lives by the Nile."

"No wonder you think it's sacred!" She took the bucket of water and knelt to begin wiping down the framework of the bed. She shook her head in amazement. "A city where it doesn't rain!" Then she snorted and added, "No wonder you think you can go walking in the rain! Probably you think it's *fun*!"

He felt irritated by this assumption that it wasn't. "Does it rain much in Cantabria?"

"All the time!" She rinsed out the rag, then leaned back on her heels, and said wistfully, "Everything there is green, even in the summer. Not like here."

"I thought Iberia was supposed to be dry."

"Huh! *Iberia* probably is. I've never been there." She got up and began to wipe down the window shutters.

"I thought Cantabria was part of Iberia."

"No. Iberia is to the south of the mountains. To the north are the Galicians, the Asturians, and the Cantabrians. We are all Celts. The Iberians are a different people. Their language is different, and their customs, and their gods."

"I didn't realize there were Celts in Ibe—I didn't realize you were a Celt." It explained the red hair, he supposed, and the bold, warlike nature.

She turned from the window and gave him a look very far from warlike, a look of tender affection. "You don't know anything about barbarians at all, do you? You think the *Romans* are barbarians. I wish my uncle were alive, and I could tell him that."

It was absurd, he told himself, that he should feel this swelling of the heart just because she *looked* at him. "I wish he were."

Then for the first time he wondered if she had anyone left in Cantabria—a widowed aunt or mother, perhaps; a sister, or orphaned nieces and nephews—people who would rejoice at her return, who would give her a home and family again. "Do you have anyone alive there?" he asked her recklessly.

Her face closed forbiddingly. "Why?"

"If you wanted to go back there to see them, I would pay your fare."

She gave him another of those heart-stopping looks, then shook her head. "I can't go back there. Not after two years in the arenas of Rome. They would . . . they would not welcome me." Then she added, in a very small voice, "Thank you for offering."

"I am so sorry," he said helplessly.

"You mustn't go out to the bathhouse," she told him, suddenly very earnest again. "Today *or* tomorrow. Pollio has men searching for you. You must stay hidden."

He rolled his eyes. "Cantabra, Rome is a very great city. Finding one man in it is like trying to find one particular mouse in a wheat field. I'm sure Pollio can hire searchers by the hundred, but even so he can't post people in every bathhouse! I *know* I was worried about the barbershops, but that was because one man could make inquiries in a dozen barbershops in an hour. With a hundred people asking, it would be possible to check enough of them that you *might* get news, if you were lucky. *Posting* people somewhere to catch someone is different."

"But he's been searching for you so hard that Taurus had heard of it," she said anxiously. "He's called you a thief to give himself an excuse. He broke the law to search your friend's house. He could already have learned that you were at the Baths of Agrippa yesterday—and that means he could've posted people there today. He must want you back very badly. Without you he can't make Rufus do what he wants, and he knows now that you are very clever: he must be afraid of how much you might have guessed. Please, you must not go out. Just stay here quietly until the day after tomorrow."

The day after tomorrow, when he had to allow Taurus's men to arrest him in front of Pollio's. He groaned, and resolved not to think of it.

She had a point about the Baths of Agrippa, he supposed, but there were other bathhouses in the region. The fleabites itched, and besides, it seemed shameful to hide in the apartment like a robber, when he was a free man, and innocent.

"Please!" she said, and put her hand on his wrist. "Please, be careful! It's only for two days!"

He groaned again, but surrendered. "Very well! I suppose I can manage without a bath for two days."

She smiled, and he felt ridiculously pleased with himself, because he had pleased her. He regarded that feeling with astonishment, and advised himself to stop behaving like a lovesick youth.

The storm began about an hour later: an ominous rumble of thunder, and then suddenly, rain. It smashed down in torrents, darkening the light and rattling against the roof tiles. Hermogenes threw open the window shutters and leaned out: the drops instantly plastered his hair to his head. He watched them splash high and white off a lower roof nearby. He craned his neck, trying to see the lightning, but the street was too narrow, and the window faced the wrong way. Water ran into his mouth and eyes and trickled down the back of his neck.

"You're getting wet," Cantabra pointed out disapprovingly.

"And I'm going to get wetter!" he exclaimed. He took off his cloak and started down the stairs.

She followed him, alarmed. "Where are you going?"

"I just want to *see* it," he told her. "I like thunderstorms. Look, I left my cloak behind, so it will be dry to sleep under."

The narrow alleyway stank worse than ever as the accumulated filth of many hot summer days was flushed away by the torrent. Hermogenes picked his way around it as well as he could, then paused on the corner. Lightning cracked overhead, and he laughed and tilted his face up to the rain.

"You're mad!" said Cantabra, behind him.

"I just like thunderstorms," he corrected her. "You can't pretend that Pollio's men are going to find me in *this*! Where shall we go? Where's the best place to watch it?"

She rolled her eyes, but led him a block and a half down to the river. Every street was a stream in flood, and the thunderclaps were deafening. They passed a few people huddled in doorways, but nobody else was about in the rain.

At the Tiber bank there was a huge theater, with an open space around it, and beyond it the rain was turning the surface of the river white. The force of the downpour was already beginning to ebb, however, and the storm was moving off, flickering lightnings up to the north and grumbling sullenly. Hermogenes stood by the riverbank and watched it go.

When the first break appeared in the clouds southward, Cantabra touched his arm. "Can we go back now?" she asked.

She couldn't have been any wetter if she'd just climbed

out of the Tiber. Her tunic was plastered to her skin so closely that he could see the outline of the sheath for her knife, and her hair was dark and dripping. He sighed. "I suppose so."

They started back. "Sorry," he said. "I just like thunderstorms."

She stopped, stared at him for a moment, then burst out laughing. She caught his arm, holding him. Water from her hair was trickling along her sword scar, and her blue eyes glinted. "You are a strange, strange man," she told him. "If someone had told me you existed before I met you, I would not have believed him."

"I'm not *that* strange," he objected indignantly.

"Yes, you are!" she said firmly. "Come back and get dry."

The rain had stopped by the time they reached Gellia's insula, but the landlady was still slow to answer the door. When at last she opened it and saw them, she exclaimed in dismay. "Oh, you poor things, you got caught in the rain! I didn't even know you'd gone out again. And it was a *terrible* downpour, look at it, the streets are still running!"

"He likes thunderstorms," Cantabra informed her, and led the way up the stairs.

When they were back in the rooms, Cantabra shut the door firmly, then turned to him, still with that glint in her eyes. She flung her strong arms around his neck and kissed him fiercely. Her body, wet and cold and smelling of rain, pressed against his until he felt like clay taking an imprint. He had to put his hands behind his back again.

"I am going to take that wet tunic off you," she told him,

smiling into his face. It was odd, looking *up* into a woman's eyes, but he found that he had no objection to it, when the eyes in question had that light in them.

"You are?" he asked hopefully. "And what will I do?"

"Exactly what I tell you."

"Ah. Well then. Whatever you say."

A little while later, stark naked on the floor with Cantabra on top of him, he started laughing. "Woman, you're *killing* me!" he protested. "Please can't I touch you?"

"No!" she told him. "Lie there and hold on to the bed."

He held on to the legs of the bedframe with both hands. "Oh, please!"

"No!"

"I'm going to die!"

"No, you aren't."

"Mercy! *Mercy!*"

"Ha!" she exclaimed. "You surrender, do you?"

"Yes! Yes! I surrender unconditionally!"

"Then I will take your sword."

When she'd finished taking it, she sighed, and folded herself down beside him and on top of him, long-limbed and graceful. Her hair, still wet from the storm, spread out in tangles across his chest. She began tracing the stitches in the half-healed cut on his face, her eyes gentle and heavy and deep with love.

"Can I touch you now?" he whispered. "Just on the face?"

"Mmm."

He thought that was agreement, so he brushed back her hair and traced the line of her eyebrows, her crooked nose, her lips, her scar. "I was wrong," he told her. "You *are* beautiful."

She kissed him.

"I didn't expect this," he went on. "Not so soon. I thought, maybe by the time we reach Alexandria . . ."

"I didn't expect it, either," she admitted, smiling. "But I didn't expect you to run out into the rain. Why something so stupid made me want you so much, I do not know. Har-mo-genes."

He hesitated on the brink of one reply, and then asked quietly, "Your name isn't really Cantabra, is it?"

Something seemed to change in her, some deep-caught grief breaking into a smile of profound happiness. "No," she admitted, kissing him again. "It's Maerica."

"Maerica. I like that."

She kissed the cut on his face, then lowered her head against his chest. "You are a magician. Restoring a name is magic . . . You can put your arm around me."

He did. It felt very good.

"It was at Taurus's school that they started calling me Cantabra. 'The fierce Cantabrians: even their women are deadly!' They used to say that when they announced my fights, and I hated it. But afterward . . . it was what I was, 'the fierce Cantabra.' Maerica was gone. I thought she was dead—but then I met you."

He kissed the top of her head. "I love you." He hadn't meant to say it, but it was true.

She picked her head up and looked at him very hard, then relaxed into his arms. "I love you, too. You must not die. You must never die. If you die, I will have to be Cantabra again."

"I will try very hard not to die. Maerica."

They lay wrapped quietly in each other's limbs. Water drying on bare skin made them cold; he reached across the floor, found his discarded cloak, and draped them both in Scythopolitan linen. Outside the window there was sun on the streets, and the sounds of Rome were beginning again. He thought, idly, that he would never have run out into the rain that way if he'd had slaves around to make him behave like a master. He was glad that he was here alone with only her. In that moment it seemed possible to spend the rest of his life alone with only her, enclosed in this one room and her arms and perfectly content.

"What will I do in Alexandria?" she asked, breaking the spell. "Will I still be your bodyguard?"

"You will be anything you want to be," he told her contentedly. "There is time and there is money, as much as you need. There is no need to make any decisions now."

"Huh. Will your daughter like me?"

He thought about what Myrrhine would make of the arrival of an exotic barbarian ex-gladiator in the household, then began laughing. Cantabra—*Maerica!*—sat up in alarm.

"It's all right!" he told her at once. "You are *not* to teach my daughter sword fighting. Promise me you won't teach her sword fighting, no matter how much she begs you to. Oh, Lady Isis, what have I done?"

"She will beg me to?" Maerica asked in anxious confusion.

"She will admire you unspeakably," he replied confidently. "Oh, by the immortal gods! The two of you will conspire together, I foresee it—and even *one* of you is too many for me. I won't have a chance. Promise me you won't teach her sword fighting!"

"I promise," she replied, still unsure of it. "How old is she? What is she like?"

"She is ten. She is little and thin, with long black hair and big eyes. She wants to be an acrobat."

"An acrobat? Surely a rich girl—"

"Shh! No, of course she can't be an acrobat. I have told her that, but . . . well, she practices anyway, and I don't stop her, though I know I should. I admit it, when she asks me to watch, I applaud. My aunt was horrified when she found out." He frowned. "I fear that my aunt will be even more horrified when I introduce her to you. Well, we will simply have to solve that problem when we meet it."

She lay down and put her arms around him again. "I want to meet your daughter. What is her name?"

He realized that he'd never even *named* her to Maerica. He had a blissful sense of time stretching away before them both, full of all the things they would learn about one another. "Myrrhine. You will like each other. I am sure of it."

"Mur-ree-ney," she repeated softly. "Mur-ree-ney. Harmo-genes. I like the way Greek sounds."

"You will have to learn it."

"What was your wife's name?"

"Eudaimonis. It means 'Lucky,' though she wasn't, poor sweet girl."

"No?"

"She died so young, in so much pain . . ." He remembered her lying in the bed they'd shared, her face white, gaunt with agony, her eyes dark and astonished. He remembered her small hand burning with fever in his own, and her labored breathing, and the terrible smell.

"You loved her," said Maerica. She was watching his face closely.

"Yes," he agreed. After a moment he went on, "It was an arranged marriage, of course. I don't know how things are among Cantabrians—maybe you fall in love and carry one another off?"

She snorted. "Mostly our parents arrange our marriages for us." She hesitated. "My uncle arranged mine."

"He sounds an important man, your uncle."

"No. Just in our village." She snorted again. "There were five families in our village, and my uncle was the headman. My father died in a war against the Astures, so I belonged to my uncle's household. When I was sixteen, he arranged for me to marry Deivorix, who was the son of the headman in the next village."

When she said no more, he went on, "Well, my father and Eudaimonis's father arranged our marriage—they were business partners; I still have dealings with him. I was twenty; she was fifteen. I wasn't very happy about it, because I had another girl and my father sent her away, but I knew it wasn't Eudaimonis's fault. I felt very sorry for her from the moment I met her—she was so small and frightened. On our wedding night she curled up in the bed and cried. She missed her mother and her little sister and she was afraid I would hurt her."

"What did you do?"

"Patted her on the back and told her she could visit her family as often as she liked. I didn't sleep with her then. She was so frightened. We sort of . . . danced around the act . . . for the better part of a month." He smiled, remembering the growing pleasure and desire, the way the bedroom had slowly filled with erotic excitement: will we tonight? tomorrow? "She made me feel wise and strong," he admitted. "I wanted to protect her. Five years is such a huge gap at that age."

She snorted. "Deivorix didn't fuck me on our wedding night, either, but that was because he was drunk. I sat in our new hut waiting for him, but the men's feast went on and on, and when he finally came in, he was sick all over the floor and passed out. I had to clean up. It wasn't his fault, though. He was my age, and he'd never had mead before, and he was nervous, too. Next morning he was terribly ashamed. I poured water over his head, and he told me I was entitled to. That made me like him."

"What was he like?"

She shrugged. "Tall. Thin. He had beautiful hair, the color of wheat separated from the chaff. It was long, and in the evenings I would comb it and kill any lice. Our men always grow their hair long. In battle they wind it about their heads."

"I've seen you do that."

"Yes. Because I am a warrior. Deivorix was a warrior. Well, between the wars he was a shepherd and a hunter, but when war came, he was a brave warrior. He boasted a lot, and he drank too much whenever he could, and he lost his temper easily, but that is what warriors are supposed to be like. Young men are such fools." She was silent a moment, and then said slowly, "He never even tried to be clever. He would have thought it was dishonorable somehow, to fight with words and your wits instead of your sword. If Taurus had chained *him* to a post, he would have cursed him and died bravely. None of our people ever fought with his mind. That is one reason why we lost the war."

"We lost our war, too," he murmured. He tried to imagine Deivorix, the tall, brave young warrior with wheat-colored hair, the last man Maerica had slept with willingly. He wondered uneasily how he compared.

"Did you fight? You are old enough to have fought."

"I was old enough, but no, I did not fight. Ai, Zeus! the truth is, the queen never trusted the Alexandrians, and she certainly wasn't going to allow us arms. We'd fought against her in the past, and she was probably right to think we would have fought against her again if someone had turned up promising to throw out the Romans. We knew she would *never* do that. So we played very little part in the war in which we were conquered. All the troops who fought at Actium, on both sides, were Roman. Only the fleet was Egyptian, and even it had Roman officers. I know, I know: the Romans say that it was a war against the queen of Egypt—but that is because it sounds better to call it that than to admit that it was a war between two Roman nobles over which of them got to rule the world." He sighed. "The fact is, Egypt was conquered in all but name long before Actium. The queen's father bought his throne by bribing the Roman Senate, and he borrowed the money from a Roman financier, then put that same rapacious moneylender in charge of the taxes of Egypt. The queen was no better—always a Roman general in her bed and Roman thieves in her offices. When the emperor arrived, most people felt we'd be better off as a Roman province: then at least we could use the empire's laws to get redress when we were robbed. And in many ways, they were right."

"But you regret that you never fought."

It was not a question. "Yes," he admitted. "I do." After a minute he added, "My father had me taught Latin from when I was very young. That's very unusual, but my father was an unusual man. He wanted me to understand how our rulers saw us. The trouble is, I did. I heard the way they talk about us when they think we don't understand. These degenerate half-Greeks, they say, these Alexandrian cowards: led by a woman and a rabble of eunuchs, no wonder they didn't fight even for their own country."

She stroked his hair. "So now you are fighting to make them see you differently?"

He laughed. "I suppose I am. How did we get onto this?"

"My husband."

"Oh. Yes."

She ignored his lack of enthusiasm for the subject and continued her cautious probing. "You said your wife died five years ago. But you have not remarried."

"No. I made arrangements with a couple of courtesans. Not both at the same time, of course—one after the other. I . . . don't really want to marry again. Poor little Eudaimonis, she suffered so much at the end it still hurts when I think of it. Childbed fever, after a stillborn son. Everyone kept telling her she must give me a son, she must give me a son, even though I said I was perfectly happy with my daughter. She wanted that boy so badly, but he killed her. I sat with her, and gave her opium as I could, and watched her die. My mother died the same way, when I was nine, and I had to watch that, too. I don't think I could bear to do it again. Courtesans use contraceptives."

"What if *I* have a child?" she asked, in a very small voice.

He hadn't even considered that—but of course it was entirely possible. More than that: it was very likely. And he knew, without any word spoken, that she *wanted* a child. Nothing could replace the ones the soldiers had murdered, of course—but if she had a child she would become fully herself again: Maerica, a woman who could love and be loved, and not a gladiator anymore.

It was perfectly respectable for a gentleman who'd lost a wife to take a concubine, but bastards were another matter—particularly when the gentleman had legitimate children, and in-laws who might be insulted. Contraceptives were in order, and, if they failed, abortion—and, if that failed, exposure of the unwanted infant in a public place, to die or to be raised in another man's house as a slave. He could not require that of this woman. He recognized it between one shocked breath and another: he could not and would not require it. He had promised that he would never hurt her.

"You will have to try very hard not to die," he made himself say.

She hugged him so hard he winced. "I won't die," she whispered into his ear. "I am strong, and I will give you a strong son. *You* must not die, either."

He felt another delicious stirring in the groin. "If I promise not to die," he said, beginning to smile again, "will you let me touch you?"

The rest of the afternoon and evening passed in a daze of erotic intoxication. Maerica got up at one point, put on her wet tunic, and went to buy some supper. Then they sat on the floor together feeding one another morsels of leek and sausage and talking about Rome and Alexandria. He started trying to teach her Greek.

Morning brought a visitor. They'd risen—late—and Maerica was preparing to go out to buy food and fetch water when there was a knock on the door. She opened it warily and found Gellia.

"Sorry to disturb you two," the landlady said with a leer, "but Calvus wanted a word with your 'employer'—heh!—if you can spare him for a minute."

Maerica went red: the color stained even the back of her neck and her ears, which were all Hermogenes could see of her face. They hadn't taken into account how flimsy the apartments were. Probably the whole building had heard his shrieks for mercy.

Embarrassed, and eager to show solidarity with his embarrassed lover, he hurried forward. Standing nervously on the landing behind Gellia was the old man from the party, Sentia's music-loving husband.

"Ah!" said the old man, with relief. "There you are, sir."

Hermogenes smiled politely. "Greetings, Calvus." He was glad Gellia had mentioned the name: if he'd ever heard it, he'd forgotten it. "You want to speak to me?"

Calvus nodded and edged past Gellia into the apartment, still with that nervous air. Hermogenes suspected an appeal for money, and braced himself to refuse.

Maerica surveyed the old man a moment, saw no threat, and picked up the amphora to resume her errand. She scowled when Gellia, avid for gossip, followed her off down the stairs.

"What I come about," said Calvus, as soon as the door shut, "is—I don't know how to say this, sir. That partner you mentioned, the one you think cheated you—I think he's looking for you."

Hermogenes blinked, off-balance.

"See, they were talking about it at the barbershop wheres I get myself seen to," Calvus went on, into the silence. "How the word's out from Vedius Pollio that a Greek called Hermogenes stole something from him, an' I know you said your name's Herapilus, but they said a short man with a cut on his face and a bad foot. There's an offer of a denarius for news."

"Did you collect it?" Hermogenes asked sharply.

The old man shook his head. "I remembered what Gellia tol' us, that you suspected your partner was keeping money you give him as a present for this Titus you was asking about, and that he turned you out of his house in the middle of the night when you asked him about it. I thought to myself, maybe he wasn' tellin' us the whole story, maybe he did mean that villain Pollio. I always heard how that scoundrel has lots to do with money matters in the East.

And it seemed to me that if it was you Pollio wanted, it wasn't nothing to do with anything stolen; no, it'd be because he knew you were going to show him up to Statilius Taurus, and he wanted to kill you before you could. So I didn't say anything, and I warned my friends not to say anything neither. But I thought probably you'd like to know."

"Yes," Hermogenes said grimly. "Thank you very much." He regarded the old man a moment with respect, then added, "I'd like to give you the denarius you lost by your silence. My bodyguard has the money, but if you'll wait until she gets back—"

"That's all right, sir," Calvus interrupted with a smile. "I couldn't take it from you, not after you were robbed on the street, and turned out of the house by that scoundrel, and falsely accused an' all. Anyway, you got my Sentia singing cantica again. She hasn't done that since our boy died, and to hear her sing again is worth more to me than a *hundred* denarii. I just thought you should know. Will you be all right?"

"Yes," Hermogenes replied, humbled. "Thank you. I have an appointment to speak to Statilius Taurus tomorrow, which should settle the matter."

"Ah, he'll do right by you!" Calvus declared, with satisfaction. "They all say he's a man of honor, and he never liked that Pollio. You should never have gone to such a rogue in the first place—but I suppose that bein' a foreigner and all, you couldn't know that. You just lie low then, till tomorrow, and you'll be fine."

He shook hands with dignified formality and took his leave.

When Maerica returned with the water and a loaf of bread, he told her the old man's news.

"Huh!" she exclaimed in disgust, banging the water down in the corner. "I *told* you!"

"So you did," he admitted. "You were right."

It didn't seem to appease her. She hunkered down on the floor, ripped a chunk off the loaf as though it were a mortal enemy, then sat scowling at it.

"What is the matter?" he asked in surprise.

"Gellia!" she spat. She set her chunk of bread down, gazed up at him in anguish, and cried, "People *heard* us yesterday! Gellia *congratulated* me: she thinks I set out to *catch* you!"

He didn't know what to say. "You know you didn't," he managed at last, "and I know you didn't, so what does it matter what Gellia thinks?"

"Because she won't be the only one!" snarled Maerica. "A man like you—a rich man who's lost a wife—*lots* of people must've tried to catch you. And I'm an ugly barbarian—"

"Not ugly!"

"—an ugly barbarian who was sleeping in temple porches and living on scraps when you hired me! I was a gladiator, which means I'm no better than a whore, as far as the law's concerned. I'm infamous—you know what that means?"

He did, vaguely. As a term in Roman law, *infamy* meant a diminishment of legal status. An infamous person could not normally appear as a witness in court, and was unable to marry, inherit, or undertake most sorts of legal contract. He'd been aware that prostitutes were infamous, but not that the status also applied to gladiators, though it wasn't really surprising.

"We can try to get your status changed," he said after a silence. "After all, you're not a gladiator anymore."

"Then what am I?" she demanded miserably. "You said I can be anything I want, but it's not true. I can't be a respectable woman again. Nobody's going to believe that I didn't set out to catch you the moment you crossed my path, and they'll think it's a terrible shame I succeeded. Even your courtesans will turn up their noses, and say, 'How could he love her, after us?' All your friends will be horrified. Your aunt will be furious, and your wife's family. They'll all think I'm a disgraceful old whore!"

He remembered how desperately she had resisted that trade, and understood some of the anguish. He came over and sat down beside her. He considered putting an arm around her, then reconsidered.

"I will tell my friends you're nothing of the sort," he promised. "If they are my friends they'll believe me, and if they're not, I'm well rid of them."

"Huh! *None* of them will believe you, but the ones who are your true friends will tell you you so, and the ones who aren't will be polite to your face and laugh at you behind your back. Everyone who cares for you will tell you to send me away. They'll be especially horrified if you let your daughter be friends with me."

"What am I to say?" he asked impatiently. "It will not be easy, and I'm sorry, but I can live with their opinion if you can. Eventually they will see that they were wrong."

"Maybe you'll decide they're right," she whispered.

"I will not," he said flatly. "Maerica, please." He held out his hands to her. She did not take them, though she looked into his face.

"What would your father say if he saw you now?" she asked bitterly.

It stung. He lowered his hands.

"He was an important man, wasn't he? He made you what you are, a gentleman and a businessman and a Latin-speaker; you always listened to him, didn't you? And he would be as horrified by me as your aunt, wouldn't he?"

He let out his breath unsteadily. "He's *dead*," he pointed out.

"If he were alive, he'd make you send me away."

"I wouldn't have obeyed him." Even as he said it, he realized with a shock that it was true. He could not remember ever having defied his father, but he would have, over this. "Please. It won't be as bad as you think. I am a respectable businessman, not a silly youth, and you are a sober woman, not some extravagant dancing girl or scandalous actress. People may raise their eyebrows at my choice, but if I say I want to keep you as a concubine, they—"

She looked shocked. "Keep me as a what?"

"A concubine."

"No! I won't accept that!"

He hesitated, puzzled by the ferocity of that cry—then remembered that most of her Latin had been learned in a gladiatorial school. "Do you know what the word means?" he asked gently.

She frowned suspiciously. "It's a kind of whore, isn't it?"

"No," he said firmly. "It's a kind of wife. Men of my rank not infrequently fall in love with women who for some reason they cannot marry. Maybe he's Alexandrian and she's Egyptian, or he's a Roman citizen, and she isn't, so there's a legal bar, or maybe it's just that she's a slave and he's rich and of good family—for some reason, he can't marry her. If they settle together anyway, she is called a concubine. It is a far more respectable title than 'whore' or even 'mistress.' Only a wife's name is more honorable."

"Oh," she said, and looked at his face searchingly.

"I'm not lying," he told her. "You're not a citizen, so concubinage is the best I can offer you. There are things we can do to improve your status, though. We can apply to get you the status of a free resident of Alexandria, and we can get you title to some property. Maybe you could try running a business. You are a clever woman, and so strong that even the school of Taurus couldn't crush you. However bad this is, it has to be better than the arenas. Don't surrender to the opinions of fools!"

She bit her lip. "This word 'concubine'—do you really mean that you would *marry* me, if the laws allowed it?"

He was silent a moment, shocked by himself, by the certainty of his own feelings. Then he said simply, "Yes."

She looked as shocked as he felt. "I . . . didn't expect that."

"You were talking about having children!"

"Yes, but . . . I don't know what I was expecting. Not that."

"You keep telling me what a strange man I am, but do you think there's another woman like you in all the world?

The whole weight of the Roman Empire fell on you, and you not only survived but preserved your soul in integrity. Don't you see how extraordinary you are? That cruel Taurus—he thinks he owned you, that you were his slave, property at his school. He was wrong: he never even knew your name. You never sold yourself, never yielded your consent to any of the degradations they forced on you, never broke. But what all the power of Rome could not force from you, you gave to me. Do you think I don't know that that is a jewel beyond price, and treasure it?"

To his astonishment and horror she burst into tears. He exclaimed helplessly and incautiously put an arm around her shoulders. For once there was no recoil, and she flung herself into his arms, sobbing loudly. He kissed her and murmured endearments in Greek, and slowly she calmed down.

"I'm sorry," she managed at last. "Oh, dear heart. I never thought anyone would *love* me again."

"I already told you I love you!"

She shrugged, warm in his arms. "Yes, but that was in bed."

"Am I supposed to feel less loving when I'm in bed with you?"

She looked into his eyes a moment, then kissed him. "No, you're supposed to feel less loving once you get up."

"Well, as it happens, I don't. My dear life, in all truth, people won't despise you as much as you fear they will. We *can* make you a place in Alexandria. We will simply have to work at it."

"You said I should *run a business?*" she asked disbelievingly.

He thought about that. "Yes," he concluded. "It will be important for you to have some property in your own name, first because a woman who owns property is immediately much more respectable than a woman who doesn't, and second because I do not want you to be dependent on my heirs if anything should happen to me."

"But—*run a business*?"

He shrugged. "I could buy you a farm, if you prefer. The trouble with that, though, is that I don't know anything about farming. I could help you with a business."

"I don't know anything about *business*! In Cantabria we barely even used *money*!"

"Well—what about leatherworking? You seem to know something about that, and not many Egyptians do."

"I can mend my shoes, but nobody would pay me to mend theirs!"

"I was never for a moment suggesting that you should set up as a cobbler! No—can you tell whether a hide is cured well or badly, and whether it will be useful for shoes or stitching or something finer?"

"Yes, but—"

"So, there you are! You know more about it than most people in Alexandria. Leather isn't made much in Egypt, and what is made tends to be inferior stuff. I know, because most of the ship captains I deal with refuse to use Egyptian leather on their vessels. One man I know swears by Iberian; another prefers Numidian. Somebody who knew about leather, who could pick the best hides and sell them on to the most appropriate users, who could deal with the captains—somebody like that could make a lot of money. I could set you up in it, get you a good scribe, introduce you to people. You could make it a success."

She was silent a moment. Then she laughed weakly. "Och, oh, what you mean is that someone like *you* could make lots of money!"

He held her more tightly. "No. *I* don't know enough about leather." He was beginning, however, to warm to the idea he'd thrown out at random, and he went on, "With your knowledge of leather, though, and my business contacts, this really could be a very profitable venture."

She looked at his face earnestly. "Do your laws *allow* women to run their own businesses?"

He sighed. "It's customary for a woman to have a male guardian to represent her in law. There are plenty of women, though, who run their own affairs and just get a brother or a patron to sign for them. We'll have to get legal recognition for me to sign for you—or, if you prefer, you can employ somebody else."

She was silent.

"You don't have to do it if you don't want to," he told her, though he found that he was liking the idea more and more. "You could pick a different business. Or a farm, if you prefer."

"And you don't think your friends will be even more disgusted to see you giving so much away to . . . to me?"

He shrugged. "If you were a *man* who had saved my life, and I set you up in business or bought you a farm as a reward, everybody would simply accept it. Yes, they'd say it was generous, but they'd also believe it was appropriate. Because you're a woman, they will raise their eyebrows—at first, anyway. But I don't think it will be as bad as you fear—

and if we can make a success of a partnership, everyone will say how very wise I was to take up with you. Money, I fear, is the chief god of the Alexandrians."

She was silent, playing with his face.

"Do you really not even *use* money in Cantabria?"

She laid a finger on his lips. "You talk too much, and you question everything."

"Of course: I'm Greek."

"I don't want you to talk now."

He began to smile: the crisis was over. "What do you want me to do instead?"

The rest of the day passed in the same intoxicated haze that had engulfed the previous afternoon. At dusk they moved the mattress from the bed onto the floor, as a compromise between floor and bed, and fell asleep in each other's arms.

He woke at dawn, instantly aware of where he was and who was beside him, but aware, too, of what was to happen that day, as though it were a toothache. Maerica was already awake, lying motionless with her head inches from his own, watching him with wide quiet eyes. When their eyes met, she whispered, "I dreamed of the mountains last night."

He stretched. "Is that a good omen or a bad one?"

She shrugged. "I don't know. It is a long time since I dreamed about home, that is all. I think I know why I dreamed it now, though."

"And?"

"You are like the mountain I dreamed about."

He laughed. "It take it this is a *small* mountain."

She smiled, but shook her head. "It was near home, and we called it the Vulture, because of its shape. The lower slopes are good pasture. They are open, and covered with flowers. There are pure streams, many of them, all good sweet water, and the grass is thick and rich. It is a very beautiful place. Everyone would take sheep and cattle up there in the summer, and it would feed and support them."

"And this reminded you of me? I am flattered."

"I am not finished. That was only the lower slopes. The heart of the mountain is a pinnacle of rock, sheer and strong and too steep even for goats. Only the kings of the air, the great birds go there—the vultures we called griffons, for their size, and the breakers of bones, the lammergeiers and the eagles. In my dream, though, I had wings, and I flew up the cliff face, and I turned on the air and saw how all those pleasant pastures were held up by the stone, and when I woke I knew that really I had been dreaming about you. Because people meet you, and they think you are kind and gentle, such a pleasant man, and they don't see that underneath it there is stone. I don't mean that you pretend, because you *like* to be pleasant to people, and maybe the Vulture *liked* to support our flocks—but it was a mountain, not fields that could be worked with a plough." She laid her palm against his chest. "If you love me, I think it is because I am the only woman who has gone above the slopes, and met you on the steep places, there, in your heart, where there was only stone and snow and silence."

He found that he was holding his breath, and he let it out slowly, then made himself breathe again. "That's very poetic," he managed. Inside he cowered at the frightened sense that, whether or not he was like a mountain, she had certainly reached some part of himself which no one before her had ever touched, and which was very much harder and colder than the self with which he was familiar. It was the part of himself which had insisted on the attempt to humble a Roman consul, even if it cost not just his own life but the ruin of everyone he loved. Stone and snow, yes, and the sheer cliffs of his pride. It felt—strange—to have someone else there. It felt as though she had suddenly acted out some secret dream which he had never divulged to anyone, both achingly sweet and frighteningly private.

She dropped her gaze and lowered her head against his shoulder. "I'm frightened," she whispered. "Everything is too good. That means something terrible will happen."

"Don't say that," he whispered back, stroking her hair. "Or I won't have the nerve to go through with it."

"We don't have any choice," she said miserably, then, more resolutely: "Taurus is honest. He promised to reward you."

"If you believe him, I will trust *you*," he told her.

They made love one more time, urgently, then got up. Hermogenes washed as well as he could with cold water from the amphora, and changed into his carefully preserved clean tunic. He put on his cloak, taking time to get the drape exact. When he'd finished with it, he helped Maerica with hers. She put the pen case with the letters of credit in her belt, and they set off.

It was still only the second hour of a bright, sunny day, and the streets were busy. They walked slowly up the Clivus Argentarius—Hermogenes found with relief that he barely limped at all—and past the Tabularium into the forum. They checked the time there on the public sundial in front of the Senate building, and paused to buy some sesame rolls for breakfast. He showed Maerica the milestone Hyakinthos had shown him a lifetime before, with the distances to the great cities of the empire—Alexandria and Antioch, Carthage and Cyrene. She named a handful of Iberian cities, but he could find only one of them: Tarraco. "The port," she said, nodding. "The ship which took me to Rome sailed from there." She touched the inscribed name, then touched the lettering for Alexandria and smiled.

The morning seemed to have stuck on the second hour, so they sat down on the steps of the Basilica Aemilia to eat their sesame rolls and watch the crowds. Hermogenes considered looking for a shipping agent who could take charge of Myrrhine's letter, then decided against it: with luck, that letter would never be sent.

They watched the crowds for a little while longer. Then a great party in togas arrived for a law case at the basilica, and they rose and got out of the way. When they recrossed the forum to the sundial in front of the Senate House, the shadow of its gnomon pointed exactly at the boundary between the second and third hours. They both looked at it, then at one another.

"It's time," Hermogenes declared. He straightened his cloak and set off.

The Bank of Gabinius was on the Vicus Tuscus, south of the forum at the foot of the Palatine. Hermogenes had made a note of its location while on the tour of the city with Hyakinthos, because his letters of credit were addressed to its managers: it had long been established in Egypt. They walked past the side of the Temple of Castor and emerged on the narrow shopping street, paused to check directions, then walked on.

They were still a hundred paces from the bank when Pollio's men stepped out of a cookshop behind them.

Hermogenes' first warning was when Maerica abruptly halted and spun round; what she had heard or sensed, he did not know. By that stage, however, the three men were only a dozen paces away—three tall, lean figures in the dark red tunics favored by Pollio's guards, without their swords, but carrying long knives gleaming in their hands. One of them was the retiarius Ajax, who had been so very eager to fight. The crowds around them were already starting to shy away in alarm from the swift, menacing advance.

Maerica seized the back of her own cloak and dragged it loose in a whirl of white linen, meanwhile thrusting Hermogenes behind her with a jab of the elbow. "Run!" she ordered him.

For a bare instant he hesitated, unwilling to leave her. Reason reminded him sharply that it was him they were after: if he ran he would, at the least, draw some of them off, and at best, find Taurus's men and help. He turned on his heel and ran. He had gone only a few strides, however, when something struck his legs and he fell, sprawling heavily onto the paving stones. Behind him people were yelling, and ahead of him someone had started to scream. His legs were tangled in something, and as he kicked to free them he found that the something was a net—a small round net, weighted in the corners: the retius that gave the retiarii their name. He finally shook it loose and got a knee under himself, but someone ran up from behind him and grabbed a handful of cloak and his arm. He kicked wildly at the man's legs, missed, and then the other was leaning over him and holding a knife at his throat. It was the gladiator, Ajax.

"Get up!" Ajax ordered in a low voice.

The retiarius was still holding his left arm, twisted in his cloak behind his back, and he jerked on it to emphasize the order. Hermogenes got up slowly, glancing around frantically for some source of help. He saw only shoppers and shopkeepers moving desperately away. Ajax hauled on his arm to turn him around—then stopped.

Maerica was fighting the other two, an unarmed woman against two men with knives, and she held them at bay with nothing more than a cloak. She had wrapped the heavy linen three or four times around her right arm and she let the rest of it trail, whirling and flaring in her opponents' faces as she dodged and turned, parrying their lunges with her frail protection of cloth.

One of her opponents glanced impatiently away from her and saw that his comrade had secured their quarry. He gave a yell of relief.

It was a mistake. Maerica had not admitted any distraction, and as soon as her opponent's attention faltered, she attacked. The linen cloak flew over the knife-man's head, and her foot came up in her favorite kick. The man screamed and slashed blindly; Maerica kicked him again, and he shrieked and crumpled. She left him to fall and threw herself into a roll across the paving stones, dodging the other assailant's lunge. He ran after her, and she kicked again, hooking his leg out from under him while she was still flat on her back. He twisted as he fell, stabbing at her.

Hermogenes felt the knife slip a little from his own throat and seized his chance. He made a grab for the gladiator's wrist, trying, at the same time to get a foot around his ankle and trip him—a wrestling throw, half remembered from school. It didn't work against a trained opponent: Ajax swore and sidestepped, but his knife hand had been wrenched aside. He began twisting his captive's imprisoned left arm. Hermogenes bent over double, trying to escape the pain, but kept hold of the other's wrist, struggling madly to keep the knife away from his throat. Ajax began shaking him by the twisted arm. Hermogenes craned his neck and managed to bite the other's knife hand. Ajax swore and threw him forward violently; he tried to catch himself as he fell, but the gladiator was instantly on top of him again, kneeling on his back and buffeting him about the head, cursing him.

The blows stopped suddenly in a whirl of white linen, and Ajax flung himself off and into a roll. Hermogenes got his right elbow underneath himself—the left one didn't seem to be working—and tried to sit up. The white linen cloak was half on top of him, half trailing in the gutter, and Maerica was standing over him, a knife in her left hand. Its blade was red, and she had her right arm pressed against her side. The right side of her tunic was covered with blood.

"Cantabra," said Ajax, getting to his feet. "I knew we'd end up fighting."

"Go away," she ordered. She was out of breath and her voice was rough with pain.

"Can't," he said, grinning. "The boss wants your boyfriend. He's worth more alive, but I suppose now I'll have to kill him." He edged round to the right, trying to get on her injured side.

"Whatever Pollio is paying," Hermogenes panted, "I'll double, if you go away."

No one paid any attention. Ajax continued to edge to the right, and Maerica turned, keeping her face toward him. Hermogenes picked up the discarded cloak and looked about for something to use as a weapon.

Ajax attacked in a sudden, flowing dash, not to the right but to the left, strength to strength, knife hand whipping up and across, free hand splayed. There was a slithering squeal of knife on knife; Maerica grunted in pain. The retiarius flowed backward again—until Hermogenes whipped the cloak around his legs, and he tripped.

Maerica moved while the other was still falling, stepping forward with that savage deliberation she had used in the Subura. She did not bend over or use her knife: instead she kicked, not at the groin, for once, but at the ribs. Ajax gasped as the breath was knocked out of him. He rolled away, but Maerica went after him, faster now, kicking again, and again, and again, keeping him on the defensive and giving him no chance to regain his feet. He rolled into the side of a building and tried to get to his knees, and she aimed a high, smashing kick at his head. He fell, and she slammed a heel down into his face. He jerked, screaming, his back arching with pain, both hands flying instinctively to his eyes. She paused a moment, then dropped to her knees beside him and cut his throat.

Hermogenes staggered to his feet and stumbled over to her. She looked up at him, her face white under the fiery hair, her eyes scarcely human. Her right elbow was still pressed against her side, and the patch of blood had dyed half her tunic red. "Maerica!" he whispered, dropping to his knees beside her. "You're hurt, you're hurt!"

The inhuman look went out of her eyes. She let go of the knife, turned away from her opponent's body, and folded forward into his arms.

"My darling girl!" he said, not sure now even what language he was speaking. "You're hurt . . . let me see. . . ." He pulled her over onto a clear space of pavement, pulled off his Scythopolitan linen cloak and put it under her head, and moved her right arm, trying to see the wound. There was too much blood. He looked around desperately, saw the knife she'd used to kill Ajax, and went to pick it up.

"Are you Marcus Aelius Hermogenes?" asked a new voice. He looked up dazedly and saw a party of soldiers in strip armor standing squarely in the road that led to the bank.

"Yes. My concubine is hurt," he said, and went back to her. She seemed now to be only half-conscious, but her eyes fastened on him. "I have to stop the bleeding. Help me."

"You're under arrest," said the soldier.

He ignored the man. He needed bandages. There was the other cloak. He went to fetch it—and found one of the soldiers grabbing his arm.

"You must come with us," said the soldier, frowning as he took away the knife.

"My concubine is hurt," he said incredulously. "She's bleeding badly. She needs help."

The soldier gave her a contemptuous glance. "We don't have any orders about the whore."

Hermogenes hit him.

It was a bad mistake, and he cursed himself for it afterward. The soldier hit him back, and so did the soldier's friends. They kicked his feet out from under him, forced him down onto the pavement, and tied his hands behind his back. Then they hauled him back to his feet and told him to march. He screamed at them to see to Maerica, and they slapped him. He tried to break free, and something struck the side of his head, hard. Everything went dark.

HE CAME HALFWAY BACK TO HIS SENSES to find himself being carried down a street. His head hurt abominably and he felt very sick. He retched feebly, and his captors unceremoniously dumped him onto the pavement and stood around him while he vomited into the gutter. His arms were still bound, and his left shoulder ached fiercely, so that the spasms were agony. When he'd finished, they hauled him to his feet and forced him onward, holding him by the arms and half dragging him to a stumbling walk. He felt too faint and ill even to notice where he was. They went up some steps into a building and stopped; he promptly lay down and curled up. He was aware of people talking angrily above his head, but he could not summon the concentration to understand them. At one point someone asked him if he was Marcus Aelius Hermogenes, the Alexandrian, and he said yes.

After a little while, two men hauled him back to his feet and dragged him along a corridor and down a staircase. It was dark, cool after the sunny June day outside. Someone unlocked a door, and the men who had hold of him pulled him through and put him down on the floor. He lay there, watching dazedly as they went out again and locked the door behind them.

At once the room became even darker. The floor was cold. He suddenly remembered Maerica lying on the Vicus Tuscus, her tunic red with blood, her dazed, half-conscious eyes focusing on him. He tried to get up, but this caused a wave of so much pain and dizziness that he had to lie still again. He felt cautiously at his head where it hurt, and discovered a wet and sticky lump on his skull just above his right ear. He realized that at some point someone must have untied his hands, and he felt pleased with himself for understanding so much. Moving very carefully, he looked around himself. He was alone in a small, dimly lit room, lying on a rough stone floor. The only light came through a barred window in the room's single door, and it was faint and gray.

He tried to get up again, more cautiously this time, and made it to his feet. He staggered to the door and beat on it feebly. Nothing happened. He searched for a handle: there wasn't one. He tried to shout, but the effort hurt his head, and he clung to the edge of the window, feeling sick and giddy.

He was in a prison, he realized: he'd been arrested and

taken to a prison. Where was Maerica? Had they just left her lying in the street?

He began to curse them, then cursed himself. How *stupid*, how criminally *stupid*, to have hit a Roman soldier! He should have offered the guardsmen *money*, immortal gods! If he'd said, "A hundred denarii to the man who helps her!" they would've fallen over themselves to see to her wound, but no, he hadn't had the presence of mind, he'd struck out with his fists, and they'd clubbed him and left her lying in the street to bleed to death.

He thought of her dying alone on the streets of Rome. He slid down the door and began to weep. The grief began like a tiny hole in his soul, then suddenly swelled so that he felt he couldn't endure it, and he howled with it, despite the pain in his head.

The light from the window in the door suddenly dimmed, and a voice demanded, "What's the matter with you?"

He struggled to swallow another howl of anguish. He could not afford to be stupid again. He didn't know how long it had taken for them to bring him here, or how long it took a woman to bleed to death: it might be that he could still correct his mistake. "Please," he gasped, getting up on his knees again. "My concubine was hurt, and she needs help, urgently. I am a rich man, I will pay a hundred denarii to anyone who goes to help her."

There was a silence, and then the voice at the door asked, "What concubine?"

"Her name's Maerica. She was with me when I was arrested. I'm sorry I hit the soldier, I only wanted to help her. She's hurt, she was bleeding, and they left her lying there. I have money; I will pay anyone who helps her. Please. It's urgent."

"Nothing to do with me," said the voice.

"No, please!" Hermogenes pushed himself back onto his feet and found himself looking out the barred window at a stubbled, hawk-nosed face in a helmet. "Please, if you *send* someone to help her, I will pay you, too! I am a rich man, I can afford it. They left her on the Vicus Tuscus, near the Bank of Gabinius. She was hurt, I only wanted to bandage her wound, otherwise I would have come when they asked me, and I wouldn't have hit anyone!"

"You're saying the praetorian guards wounded your concubine?" demanded the jailer indignantly.

"No, no, no!" he protested, struggling to keep control of himself and not make another criminal mistake. "Not the praetorians. It was Pollio's men. We were attacked by Pollio's men before the guard arrived. Please, won't you send someone to help her? She is a good and noble woman, she doesn't deserve to die like that! I will pay anything you like!"

"I don't know anything about this," said the guard warily.

"Please. I'm not asking that you leave your post, only that you report the matter to your superior. Urgently. Statilius Taurus *knows* my concubine, he wouldn't want her to bleed to death. He promised to reward me for saving his life—"

"I don't know anything about this!"

"Yes, yes, I *know*! But we had an arrangement which went wrong, and he would be very displeased to know that she was hurt, and nobody helped her. Please, *please*, just ask your superior! Tell him I am willing to pay a great deal of money if it keeps my concubine alive. Surely it's not against the rules for you to speak to your superior, and ask him to send a doctor to the Vicus Tuscus?"

"You say you have money?"

He leaned against the door, breathing hard. "I can get it. I have letters of credit to the bank—had them, my concubine had them. Has them. I have a friend in Rome, too, Titus Fiducius Crispus, a wealthy businessman: he would lend me money if I asked it. I can get money. I am a rich man."

"Well," said the guard, after a moment's thought, "I'll ask."

He went away. Hermogenes slumped down to the floor. His head hurt, and his left shoulder hurt, and his right knee, and he felt sick. He thought of Maerica lying on the paving stones, of the dazed way her blue eyes had fixed upon him. *Oh, my darling,* he thought wretchedly, *I am so sorry I wasn't wiser!*

He woke, shivering, and realized that he'd slept. He needed to use the latrine. He pulled himself to his knees and thumped on the door, then called a few times weakly. Presently there was a sound of footsteps, and he dragged himself to his feet and found another helmeted face in the window. It was a different face from last time.

"What's the matter?" demanded the guard.

"I need the latrine," he faltered.

"Bucket in the corner," said the guard, and turned away.

"Wait! Please!"

The face turned back, scowling.

"I asked the man who was here earlier to send someone

to help my concubine," he declared breathlessly. "I promised him money. He said he would ask. Do you . . . do you know what happened?"

"No," replied the guard shortly, and turned away again.

"No, wait! Please! I would pay you, too. . . ."

But the man's footsteps retreated. He pressed his face against the bars of the window and saw the armored back retreating along a walkway of dark tufa stone that ringed a well covered by a grating. The guard turned right and disappeared.

He inspected his cell—rough brick, a tiny box—and found a dank and noisome corner containing an encrusted bucket, which he used as instructed. Then he curled up on the floor in the opposite corner, shivering. Maerica's face appeared again to his imagination, and he pressed his hands against his eyes. After a few minutes' struggle with the grief and the guilt, he gave up and began to weep.

After another long dark time, and with his head aching worse than ever, he went back to the dirty corner and vomited air and bile from an empty stomach. Then he returned to the clean corner and prayed to Isis and Serapis, and to Apollo and Asklepios, gods of healing, to help the woman he loved.

After another interminable silence a light appeared in the window of the door, making him realize that it had become completely dark. He sat up with a start, then winced at the pain in his head. The lock clicked, and the door opened. A guard came in with a jug and a loaf of bread on a tray; another man stood in the doorway behind him, holding up a lantern. The light showed the cell clearly for

the first time: a bare cubicle with stained walls and a dirty
tufa-stone floor. The first guard set the tray down on the
floor and prepared to leave.

"Wait!" Hermogenes gasped. "Please, I've been asking
about my concubine, who was injured—"

The guards went out, and the door closed. Hermogenes
staggered up and over to the door as they locked it. "Please!"
he begged. "She was hurt. Statilius Taurus knows her, he
would want you to help. I have money, I can pay—"

"You have money in *there*?" asked the man with the
lantern. He was different again from the two Hermogenes
had seen earlier.

"No, but I have property, I have money in banks, I have
friends here in Rome. I can pay for help."

"He isn't Roman," said the man who'd carried the tray.
He sounded surprised.

"You get all sorts in here," replied the man with the
lantern. "Foreign kings, even."

The man who'd held the tray peered through the bars at
Hermogenes. "That one don't look like a king."

"Don't know who he is," replied the lantern bearer
unconcernedly.

"Please," said Hermogenes, clutching the ragged edges
of his self-control. "I am an Alexandrian businessman. All
I want is to know what happened to my concubine. I asked
one of your comrades to send help to her, but I don't know
whether he did. I promised him money. I would be glad to
pay it, if he would come back and tell me what happened,
and I would pay you, too, for news. I am very worried
about her."

"We don't know anything about it, Greekling," said the lantern bearer, though with regret. "We only came on shift an hour ago. If you talked to someone this morning, he was in a different unit. Nothing to do with us. Ask the magistrate at your hearing."

He hit the door. "What am I charged with?" he demanded. "When is this 'hearing'? Where am I?"

"Don't you even know?" asked the man who'd carried the tray.

"You're in the Mamertine Prison, Greek," said the lantern bearer. "Where they keep the enemies of the state." He jerked a thumb over his shoulder at the well in the floor. "Down there is the Tullianum, where they *kill* the enemies of the state. Maybe you'll see it, maybe you won't. As to the rest, we don't know. Our unit is responsible for providing guards here overnight until the end of the month, and that's all we know about it. We're not responsible for what the law does with you: we just make sure you don't leave before it does it."

"Please!" he began again, but the two men laughed and went away.

He stood in the dark, clinging to the edge of the window, watching the lantern retreat. It winked out suddenly, and he remembered that they'd dragged him down stairs to bring him here—at least, he thought he remembered stairs. The Tullianum. He'd heard that name before— "He starved to death in the Tullianum," and "They were strangled in the Tullianum"—but he wasn't sure where it was. Somewhere central, he thought. That had to be good news: it meant that he wasn't too far from the Vicus Tuscus, and if the first guard had sent someone quickly, that someone might have been in time. Unless Maerica had bled to death already. He wondered how badly she'd been hurt, and flinched at the memory of blood.

He turned back to his corner, then remembered the tray the guards had brought, and felt for it in the darkness. He nearly knocked the jug over, but caught it in time. It contained water, and he brought it back to the corner with him. His stomach was still queasy, and he did not want the bread, but he was very thirsty.

He wondered how big the Mamertine Prison was, and whether there were presently any other prisoners in it or whether he was alone. He wondered if there was anyone dying down in the Tullianum. The water he had drunk suddenly churned in his stomach.

He went back to the door and called softly, but there was no reply. Everything was black, and he couldn't even make out the grating over the top of the dark well. Probably he was alone in the prison. The guards had gone upstairs after bringing him the tray, and he hadn't heard them visit any other cells, though he might have been too dazed to take it in; that blow to the head had affected him badly. He supposed that it was a good sign that he could appreciate that—if any signs were good anymore.

Even if there was some poor wretch dying in the Tullianum, there was nothing he could do for him. He hadn't even been able to help Maerica. Maybe he wouldn't have been able to save her even if he'd behaved sensibly and bribed the guardsmen at once.

He remembered her saying "Something terrible will

happen," and his complacent assumption that if it did, it would happen to *him*, and he began to weep again. Even if he couldn't have saved her, he should never have left her to die alone.

There was another long dark interval. The image of some miserable enemy of Rome dying in the blackness nearby refused to leave his mind. It began to seem as though he could see the man, lying naked in the filth of the prison's heart—and then there were several men, their bodies marked by torture, their faces plain to see despite the darkness, swollen from the garotte that had killed them. They clustered around him, whispering among themselves and staring at him. "Is he one of us?" they asked each other, in voices like the twittering of bats. "Is he one of us?" He tried to answer them, but he could not speak, and then he saw that he didn't know the answer to the question himself. More of them came, and more, until he thought that he was looking at all those whom Rome had slaughtered in her rise to power. Then Maerica was standing over him, pale as bleached linen, her tunic soaked with blood.

He woke trembling and choking. She was not there. He had dreamed. He used the latrine bucket, then huddled up in his corner and managed to sleep again. He woke once more and finished the water in the jug. The gray light was coming through the window in the door again, so he supposed that it was day.

At last came another sound of footsteps. He glimpsed a face peering through the window at him, and then the door was unlocked and another pair of guards tramped in. They were complete strangers, both in armor, one with the sideways crest to his helmet that meant he was a centurion. The ordinary guardsman was carrying a spear; the centurion had a set of heavy iron manacles.

"Get up!" ordered the centurion.

He braced himself against the wall and got up. "Please—" he began.

"Turn around!"

He turned to face the wall, and the centurion chained his hands behind his back. "Please," he tried again. "My concubine was injured just before I was arrested. I have been trying to—"

"Quiet!" snarled the centurion. "Now, we're taking you to see the prefect of the city, and we expect you to behave. Give us any trouble and you'll regret it, do you understand?"

"I understand." At least they would take him to see Taurus.

"Good. No talking. You keep your mouth shut unless the prefect asks you to speak. Got that?"

"Yes."

"Good." The centurion seized his arm and marched him out of the cell.

There were only a few cells in the Mamertine, arranged to face into the middle of a rough trapezoid of brick, with the well of the Tullianum in the center. Hermogenes glanced into it as he was marched past: it looked as though there was a sizable room down there, but it was pitch-black, and he couldn't see if it contained a victim. It stank of filth and pain.

Just beyond it, there was an entranceway and a short

flight of steps. The man with the spear went up it first, then Hermogenes, then the centurion. They emerged through a doorway, and Hermogenes found himself blinking and half blinded by daylight. The air was blissfully warm. The two praetorians marched their prisoner down a corridor to a larger room where four more guards stood waiting.

"Jupiter, he's a mess!" exclaimed one of them, looking Hermogenes up and down in disgust. "Should we clean him up first?"

"No time," said the centurion. "The general wants him now."

He expected that they would march him out into the street and across the city, but instead he found himself escorted along another corridor and up a flight of stairs, then across a grand marble landing and into a room.

There were frescoes, glass in the windows, a carpet on the floor. Titus Statilius Taurus was sitting in a high-backed chair under the window at the far end of the room, wearing his scarlet cloak and a gilded breastplate worked in relief with the she-wolf of Rome. On a couch to his right sat Lucius Tarius Rufus, dressed in consular purple, with his freedman Macedo beside him in crimson. The guards escorted Hermogenes into the center of the room and stopped with a stamp of attention.

"Jupiter!" exclaimed Taurus, as the guard had, looking the prisoner up and down. "Centurion, why is the prisoner in this state?"

"He was involved in the incident on the Vicus Tuscus before his arrest, sir," replied the centurion smartly, "and he resisted the arrest."

"I—" Hermogenes began.

"No," said Taurus quietly, and the centurion, who'd been about to hit the prisoner, lowered his hand at once. The general leaned forward slightly in his chair, his dark eyes implacable. "Understand me," he said in Greek. "You will keep silent unless I give you leave to speak, or you will be gagged."

Hermogenes stood silent a moment, shaking with rage and despair. "Your men left my concubine lying in the street to bleed to death," he said at last, in the same language. "A woman you *knew*, whose courage you approved, who believed you to be honorable!"

Taurus gestured to the guards. There was a brief exchange of glances and some fumbling, and then one of them came forward with a piece of cloth which he shoved into the prisoner's mouth. It tasted of ash and oil: armor polish. Another man came up with a cord and secured the gag before he could spit it out.

"Get him a seat," ordered Taurus. "He looks like he's about to fall over."

Two of the men fetched a small bench from beside the wall, put it behind the prisoner, and pushed him down on it. Hermogenes sat there, shackled, gagged, battered and filthy, his mouth burning with the taste of ashes. In silence, he cursed Rome.

"So," said Taurus, turning to his friend Rufus and speaking Latin again, "this is the man who has been causing you so much trouble?"

"Yes," said the consul, smiling widely. "Yes. I can't thank you enough."

"My secretary has the documents I mentioned. He says they are genuine."

The consul's smile faded slightly and was joined by a look of embarrassment. "Well . . ."

"Explain to me what this man has done to deserve the arrest I ordered."

"He threatened me," declared Rufus, his face darkening. "He tried to blackmail me."

"With what?" Taurus asked evenly.

Rufus glanced uneasily at the guards. Taurus flicked a hand at them. "Centurion, stay here. The rest of you go outside."

The guards trooped out, leaving only the centurion to stand silently by the door.

"He threatened to summon me for debt," said Rufus, angrily now. "Me, a victor of Actium, to be summoned from the curial chair by an *Egyptian*! And he said he would send a letter to that overbred idiot Cornelius Scipio if I did anything about it!"

"Did 'anything'?" asked Taurus. "What do you mean?"

There was a moment of silence. "I could not submit to taking orders from an Alexandrian moneylender!" Rufus declared vehemently.

Taurus grunted, regarding his friend levelly. Rufus couldn't meet the gaze, and shifted uneasily in his seat. "It would disgrace the consulship!" he protested.

Taurus grunted again. "Pollio was looking for him. Do you know why?"

"Yes. The fellow tried to sell the debt to Pollio when he

realized it was going to be hard to collect. And you know Pollio: he'd do anything to disgrace us."

"I know he'd do anything to disgrace *me*," Taurus answered coldly. "I never noticed that he particularly disliked *you*. How much is this debt?"

Rufus cast an uneasy look at his freedman.

"Four hundred thousand sestertii, Lord Statilius Taurus," Macedo supplied in a tone of deep respect. "Plus some interest."

"Four hundred thousand sestertii," repeated Taurus. "Not a great sum to a man of your resources, Lucius, surely? Why didn't you just pay it? The documents are genuine: the man has title."

"Why should I pay an *Egyptian*?" Rufus demanded proudly.

"Because you are a *Roman*," declared Taurus, "and more than that, you are a Roman *consul*, entitled to carry the emblems of the Roman state, the symbols of its power to enforce its laws. If you break those laws, you dishonor more than yourself, Lucius: you dishonor Rome."

Rufus looked down, angry but also ashamed. Macedo glared at Taurus indignantly.

"I looked into this Alexandrian," Taurus resumed, unhurriedly. "The archives say that at the conquest of Egypt his family were listed as friendly toward the emperor—or, at least, as hostile to the monarchy, a position they had held as far back as the reign of the last queen's father. His father gave financial support to Aelius Gallus for the expedition against Arabia, and was rewarded for it with the citizenship.

My own man of business informs me that he is much sought after as an investor by the shipping syndicates of Alexandria, since his reputation both for honesty and fair dealing, and for shrewdness and discernment in committing his money, do much to ensure the success of an enterprise. This debt he was attempting to claim from you is one he inherited from an uncle, a prominent man of business in Cyprus, whose ruin last year was much lamented on the island. The son of my friend Quirinius, who was proconsul there at the time, went so far as to say that it has done harm to the reputation of Rome, since it was clearly caused by your default. Lucius, I ask you again: why didn't you pay your debt?"

"I *meant* to!" Rufus protested resentfully. "I did repay some of it. But then I had better uses for my money, and then . . . you know that my lands have not been profitable, Titus; you know that it has been a terrible strain for me to afford the purple."

"And because of *that* I have had an innocent man arrested and thrown into the Mamertine—a prison which should only hold the enemies of the state?" Taurus demanded.

Rufus fidgeted and grimaced. Macedo said softly, "The Egyptian is a man who would injure your friend, Lord Statilius Taurus, and who would bring shame on the consulship of Rome. He *is* an enemy of the state."

"I was speaking to my *friend*, freedman," Taurus replied coldly. "Not to you. Lucius, if I give you this man, what will you do with him?"

There was an uncomfortable silence.

"I see," said Taurus. "You should know, Lucius, that Pollio is aware of his arrest, and has also asked me for him. In fact, Pollio claims that the man is a common thief who stole a valuable statue from his house, and that he needs to question him to determine what he did with it."

"Pollio just wants to disgrace me," said Rufus at once. "Probably the Egyptian is a thief, but the reason Pollio was looking for him was so that he could use him to injure me. He is the very last man who should be given charge of him."

Taurus looked at him darkly, then turned to the centurion. "Tell the men to admit Publius Vedius Pollio."

The centurion saluted and went out.

"No!" protested Rufus in horror.

"No?" repeated Taurus, turning back to him. "You say that probably this Greek *did* steal from Pollio, but you would deny Pollio the right even to question him about the theft? This, after you as good as admit that you intend to *kill* the man for no greater crime than that of being your creditor? You are going to have to do better than that if you want my help, Lucius."

"You can't—" began Rufus, sweating, then stopped himself. He looked anxiously at his freedman.

"Lord," said Macedo, "surely you cannot want to see a Roman consul summoned for debt by an Egyptian money-lender?"

"Of course I don't want to see anything so disgraceful!" replied Taurus forcefully. "If the Roman consul *paid* his debt, it would not happen! You have land, Lucius, that is worth a very great deal more than four hundred thousand sestertii: what is to prevent you from selling some of it?"

"I . . ." Rufus faltered—and then the guards admitted Pollio.

The old man was wearing a toga, its snowy folds loosely draped over a tunic that appeared to be made of gold. He waddled forward between the centurion and another soldier, his pointed teeth revealed in a smile. "Lucius!" he exclaimed, nodding at Rufus, and "Titus! Thank you for catching my thief. Hercules, doesn't he look a villain! Why have you had him gagged?"

"Because he would not be silent," replied Taurus. "I will listen to no slanders—not until I have had a chance to learn the truth."

Rufus was beginning to look sick, but Pollio merely smiled. Taurus snapped his fingers and gestured for the guards to pull out another chair from the side of the room.

Pollio settled into it gratefully and folded his hands on his stomach. "So, did you find my statue?" he asked.

"What statue is this?" asked Taurus, with a look of distaste.

"The one the fellow stole, of course. A gold-and-ivory statuette of Hermes, which he took from my dining room while a guest in my house, the rogue. I have had people searching all over the city for it and for him."

"You brought no charges to any court," said Taurus levelly. "Had you done so, I could have ordered my men to do your searching."

Pollio shrugged. "I didn't want to trouble you, Titus. I know you've never had much time for me."

"It is the duty of the prefect of the city to be troubled on such matters. Your people searched a private house, over the protests of the owner, one Titus Fiducius Crispus. He has complained of your conduct—which he was entitled to do, for it was completely illegal."

"We did no harm to the house or its inhabitants," replied Pollio easily. "I knew the thief had been staying there, and I had to be sure he wasn't there still."

"You think that is an adequate explanation? You sent a force of twenty of your bandits, who threatened to set fire to the place if they were not allowed in, and who terrified the household by their search. The owner of the house, a respectable businessman, insists that your people were not searching for a statue at all but for a man—that man there. I will tell you, Pollio, that my friend Lucius agrees that this alleged theft was only a pretext. He has accused you of wanting to use the Alexandrian to disgrace him. I want a fuller account from you before I give you the man."

Pollio was quiet a moment, then smiled viciously. "Has Lucius also explained *why* the Alexandrian is in a position to disgrace him?"

"Not adequately," said Taurus. "However, let us continue with you before we turn to him. You found neither man nor statue in the house of Fiducius Crispus, so—still without bringing any charges before a magistrate!—you sent men out into the city. Yesterday three of them were involved in an assault on the prisoner in the Vicus Tuscus. There were several dozen witnesses, all of whom testify that your people came out of hiding and attacked the prisoner and his bodyguard with knives."

"Those were not my men," Pollio replied at once. "I dismissed them from my bodyguard some time ago. What they wanted with the prisoner, I do not know. Perhaps they were after the statue for themselves. It is an extremely valuable piece."

"You received the survivor into your house yesterday," Taurus said coldly, "when my men presented him to the guards at your gate. The same men received the bodies, and I have witnesses who can place one of the dead men, a former gladiator, as a member of your household only days ago."

"Lies," said Pollio with a shrug, and smiled.

"*Two* incidents," insisted Taurus, "two *crimes* allegedly committed in pursuit of this statue, without any charges being brought or any evidence being offered that the piece ever existed or that the Alexandrian ever saw it. I am sure that if I have my men search the prisoner's lodgings, they will find no statue. If you had *your* men search, of course, things would be different—but they have done enough illegal searching. Someone could bring charges against you over this—and I remind you, Pollio, that *I* am entitled to judge the case."

Pollio stopped smiling. "So is Lucius Rufus," he said venomously.

Taurus looked at Rufus. "Lucius. He seems to think you might give him a more lenient judgment than I would. Why is that?"

Rufus's face was red and swollen. He said nothing.

"I would like to hear why this Alexandrian is in a position to disgrace my friend Lucius," Taurus declared, turning back to Pollio. "And I would like to know why you wanted him so badly."

The rich man hesitated a moment, then sneered. "Your friend Lucius owes him a large sum of money, and tried to have him murdered in preference to paying it. I thought I could use that to convince him to speak to the emperor for me. That's all."

"Really. Lucius?"

Rufus nodded, not looking at him. "Yes. He offered to pay the debt for me. Titus, I know you hate him, but—"

"So you are claiming that Pollio himself did *not* lend you any money?"

Rufus's head jerked up. He cast a frightened look at his freedman.

Pollio laughed. "Did the Alexandrian tell you that?"

"Answer my question, *Lucius.*"

"I . . . I . . . I . . ."

"Lucius!" barked Taurus in a voice that shook the windows. "Did you borrow money from Pollio?"

"Yes," admitted Rufus, in a whisper.

There was a long silence. Then Pollio laughed and slapped his thigh. "Well, so you found out! Four million, at five percent, isn't that easy to hide. And he can't pay it back, can you, Lucius? So you can see why the Alexandrian was so—"

"I've paid the interest!" snarled Rufus. "I could've gone on paying it, even with the consulship, if that filthy *Egyptian* hadn't—"

"What was the bargain, Lucius?" Taurus interrupted, his deep voice cracking across the room as it must have done across the battlefield. "The lamprey had his teeth in

---

you *deep,* and if you try to tell me that he agreed to let go for nothing more than a promise to *speak* for him, I won't believe you. He would *never* let you off so easily."

Pollio's forced glee had vanished as quickly as it arrived. "What lies has the Alexandrian been telling you?"

"Perhaps you should hear them yourself," Taurus replied. "Centurion! Let the prisoner speak."

The centurion stepped forward. At the same instant, Macedo leaped off the couch, whipping a tiny dagger from a concealed pocket on his tunic, and lunged toward Hermogenes.

The centurion yelled and began to draw his sword, but Taurus was even faster. He seized both arms of the chair and swung himself out, legs first, catching the freedman in midlunge. The two men crashed to the floor together at Hermogenes' feet; he watched numbly as Macedo rolled away and tried to get up.

Taurus was already on his knees, his eyes alight with joy and hatred. He clasped his hands together and brought them smashing upward into the point of the other man's jaw. Macedo's head flew backwards and he fell back onto the floor, his neck twisted. Taurus got to his feet and kicked the freedman in the stomach, once, then again. Macedo didn't move, and Hermogenes realized that his neck was broken. The freedman's eyes stared upward with an expression of amazement, and the knife was still clenched in his fist.

Taurus spat on the body, then turned to Rufus, who sat frozen, all the color finally drained from his face. "Why did your freedman try to kill my prisoner, Lucius?" he demanded. "Could it be that, clever fellow that he was, he finally realized that the Alexandrian speaks fluent Latin, and was in a position to *understand* a certain incautious remark you made when you saw him in Vedius Pollio's bathhouse?"

"What remark?" asked Pollio. His face had gone red in mottled blotches across the skin, and he was pressing both hands against his chest.

"*'I can't kill Titus,'*" Taurus said, grinning savagely, "*'but you know what will happen if we try to sell.'*"

Rufus covered his face. "I'm sorry!" he cried. "I wouldn't have *done* it, Titus, I wouldn't have actually *done* it! I only agreed to buy a little time!"

Pollio folded over, gulping for air and pressing his hands against his chest.

"Scum!" Taurus spat at the old man. "Filthy lecherous little thief! You hated me ever since I put a stop to that business of yours in Bithynia. I knew you'd kill me if you ever got the chance—but *you*, Lucius! If there were two men I trusted more than you, there weren't three."

"I wouldn't have *done* it!" wailed Rufus.

"Oh, you wouldn't have done it—just in the same way that you *would* have repaid your debt. But if you can find better things to spend your money on than keeping your pledged word, why should I believe that you wouldn't have found better things to do with your fortune than sacrifice it for friendship? Do you know what the Alexandrian replied when I asked him what reward he wanted for saving my life? He asked that I honor the laws of Rome." He kicked Macedo's body again. "A *Roman consul*, Lucius, and you have less respect for the laws of our glorious city than he does. Centurion! Free the prisoner. He is the only innocent man here."

The centurion came over, sheathing his sword. He struggled a moment with the knot on the gag, then gave up and cut the cord with his dagger. Then he unlocked the manacles.

Hermogenes reached up and took the gag out of his mouth with trembling hands. He looked down at Macedo's body at his feet, then across at Pollio, still panting and gulping on the couch, his face now gray; then at Rufus, now sobbing bitterly, his face buried in his hands. He wished suddenly that he were in his own house in the harbor district, playing with his daughter—that he had written off the debt back in Alexandria, and never come to Rome.

"I had a concubine," he said numbly, as though none of the rest had happened. "She was wounded when Pollio's men attacked me on the Vicus Tuscus. I do not know what happened to her."

"If you mean Cantabra," said Taurus, "she is in the military hospital at the Colina Gate."

For a moment the words had no meaning at all, and he felt nothing. Then emotion began to seize him, shaking his body and bringing tears to his eyes while he still had no conscious awareness of any feeling at all. "She's alive?" he asked faintly.

"Yes." Taurus turned away, frowning down at Lucius Tarius Rufus.

Hermogenes got slowly and unsteadily to his feet. "Am I free to go to her?" he whispered.

Taurus glanced back at him. The dark eyes narrowed for a moment, and then he said, "You may go to the hospital. Stay there until I give you permission to leave it, and tell the doctors they have orders to see to you as well as her. I will speak to you again later today. Centurion, find him a litter or a sedan chair, and give him an escort."

The centurion saluted. Hermogenes limped slowly to the door, then turned back. "Lord Statilius Taurus," he said, and the general glanced round at him again.

"I admit that I misjudged you," he said levelly, "and I am glad to acknowledge that you are an honorable man."

The general's lip curled in distaste, and he waved a hand to send his prisoner out.

The centurion led Hermogenes back across the landing and down the stairs. He followed the man dazedly. Part of his mind wondered whether Pollio would die of his gasping fit, and what Taurus would do about Rufus, but most of his awareness was taken up with the news that Maerica was alive. Like stars at sunrise, all other concerns faded next to the enormous need to be sure that that news was true.

In the large room where they'd brought him from the prison, several other guardsmen were waiting. The centurion detailed one of them to arrange the transport and the escort to the hospital, then turned to go back upstairs. In the doorway he turned back again. "Treat him gently," he ordered his men. "He saved the general's life."

They treated him, in fact, with enormous respect after that, though he was far too stunned to take any of it in.

Someone found him a chair to sit down in; someone else offered him wine; someone else went off, and came back presently with the news that the litter was waiting for him. He let them help him up, out of the building, and down some stairs. He was, he realized numbly, at the northeast corner of the forum, only a few blocks from the place where he'd been attacked.

The litter was a small one, with four bearers. They all stared at him in horror, and he wondered what state he was in, that it shocked people so much. He sat down in the conveyance, drew the curtains, and examined himself. His tunic was covered in filth from the street and the prison, and liberally stained with blood. He had quite a bad cut on his right knee which he had no recollection of getting, through presumably it had happened when he fell during the attack. His elbows were grazed, too, and he was covered in dirt and bruises. There was dried blood crusted in his hair. No wonder the litter bearers were unhappy about having him in their litter: they'd probably have to wash it after he got out. Yes, undoubtedly he was a villainous-looking spectacle, the sort of person he would have avoided in a marketplace.

But it didn't matter. Maerica was *alive!*

The journey across Rome passed in a daze; it seemed that he'd barely got into the litter before the bearers were setting it down, and a soldier drew the curtains to inform him that they had arrived.

The military hospital was an old-fashioned house near the edge of the city, a two-story building built around a central courtyard with a garden. It was not attached to any camp: the three cohorts of the praetorian guard stationed in Rome did not live in barracks but were billeted among the citizens. The soldier in charge of the escort seemed familiar with the place, though: he showed Hermogenes to the door and held a murmured conversation with the guard there. They both looked up sharply.

"You said you're looking for your *concubine*?" asked the escort.

"Yes," replied Hermogenes, who was propping himself up against the wall.

"There is a woman we took yesterday on the orders of the lord prefect," said the doorkeeper, "but we were told she was a bodyguard."

"That too. Where is she?"

They both stared at him. "She's *Cantabra*!" said the escort. "She was a *gladiator*. I seen her fight. You said she was your *concubine*!"

The doorkeeper sniggered. "No wonder he's in that state."

"No, no!" said the escort hastily. "He got the injuries from Vedius Pollio's men, and the general gave orders that he's to see a doctor."

Hermogenes glared at them both. "Will you tell me where she is?"

The doorkeeper gave a snort of amusement. "Injuries ward. South wing. You sure you're up for another bout?"

"Get the doctor for him," ordered the escort irritably. Then he hurried after Hermogenes, who was already blundering off through the gateway and toward the left, southern side of the courtyard.

The ward was a long, wide corridor, with large windows which opened onto the courtyard, all of which were shuttered against the heat of the noon sun. At one end were three or four praetorians, recovering from accidents or injuries; at the far end, only a single occupied couch. Hermogenes hurried along the ward toward it, through the shocked and curious stares, then stopped, his heart beating hard.

It was her. She was lying with her back to the room, but he recognized the line of her hip in the worn slave's tunic, let alone the hair spread out across the pillow, dark in this shuttered afternoon light. She wasn't moving; she didn't even seem to be breathing, and for a horrible moment he was certain that he had come too late. Then she felt his eyes on her and glanced round.

Her face lit, and she tried to turn toward him, then winced. He ran forward, hesitated helplessly with his arms out while she tried to sit up, then went round the couch to face her. He dropped to his good knee beside the bed, started to throw his arms around her, then hesitated again, afraid to hurt or offend her. She shook her head impatiently, took his arms and arranged them around herself, putting one round her shoulder, the other further down her body, clear of the lump of bandages under her right arm. Then she put her own arms around him, very carefully because of all the blood and bruises, and kissed him.

"Och, look at you!" she said when they had to stop to breathe. She ran her fingers gently across the blood in his hair, flinching from the lump. "My poor love, what happened?"

"I was so afraid you were dead," he told her breathlessly, holding her tightly in the bandage-free area. "I was so stupid, I didn't even try to bribe them, and they left you there. . . . Are you all right?" He wanted to cry, or shout, but mostly he wanted to hold her, to feel the shape she made in his arms, bony and awkward and indisputably alive.

"Stab wound in the right side," she said matter-of-factly. "The second man, that was. He was falling, though, so he struck shallow and crooked, broke a rib but didn't reach the vitals. He cut a vein and it bled a lot, but the doctor here stitched it." She stroked his hair again. "That is a terrible lump. Who did that?"

"One of the praetorians." He rested his head against her chest. The scent of myrrh from the bandages was almost overpowering, but underneath it could could smell the scent that was just her. "I resisted arrest—that is, I tried to stay to look after you, and I was stupid, I hit one of them instead of offering him money. Oh, my life and soul!"

"Sshhhh," she whispered, her eyes shining with joy, stroking his hair. "My love, what has happened? I have been worrying and worrying ever since I woke. Nobody here knows anything: all they will say is that they have orders from Taurus to care for me."

"I think it's over," he told her, not moving his head. "I think we won."

STATILIUS TAURUS ARRIVED AT THE HOSPI-
tal late that afternoon.

By that time Hermogenes had been seen by the hospital doctor, and had also managed to wash in the hospital
bathhouse. He was sitting on a cushion on the floor beside
Maerica's bed, bandaged at head and knee, dressed in a
borrowed military tunic, holding his lover's hand and gazing
contentedly into her face. She was now lying so that she
faced the door, so she saw Taurus before he did: she stiffened, and he turned to look.

The prefect of the city processed slowly down the ward
toward them, flanked by his usual troop of guardsmen. He
was still wearing the gilded breastplate and long scarlet
cloak he had had at the meeting that morning. He halted a

couple of paces away and looked down at them, his dark face impassive.

"Lord Prefect," said Hermogenes. There was no hope for it: he had to make the enormous effort involved in getting to his feet. He caught hold of the bed and pulled himself slowly upright.

Taurus grunted. "Marcus Aelius Hermogenes." He enunciated the full Roman name as though it had an unpleasant taste, then glanced at Maerica. "And your *concubine*. I confess I am surprised by that."

"It is not for money, lord," Maerica announced proudly.

To Hermogenes' surprise, Taurus smiled at that—a rather sour smile, but a smile. "I never imagined it was. I am pleased for you, girl. Let me say, too, that I am sorry you were injured. I had given orders that my men were to be at the Bank of Gabinius before the third hour, but they interpreted that to mean they should go there at the second hour and sit around in the back room playing dice and waiting for you to arrive. They have been disciplined."

"They left Maerica lying bleeding in the street," said Hermogenes, with quiet anger.

Taurus gave him a disapproving look. "They did not. After you were arrested, four of them brought you to the prison, and four stayed behind. They treated the injured, collected the bodies, and questioned the witnesses as to what had happened. If you had not resisted arrest, you would have been aware of that."

"I would not have resisted arrest if they'd shown any sign of being willing to help her!" Hermogenes objected, more loudly and just as angrily.

"Did you expect them to arrest you *politely*?" Taurus replied sarcastically. "That would have made Pollio's people suspicious. No: they'd been told that you were wanted for questioning concerning a plot against the state, and they treated you accordingly."

Hermogenes glared at him. "Did you *tell* them that Pollio was looking for me, and was likely to have people at the bank?"

Taurus frowned, but nodded.

"And they went and sat in a back room? They told the staff at the bank what they were doing—and then just sat there? They didn't even station someone outside to keep watch?" It was perfectly obvious now what had gone wrong. Pollio's people had almost certainly been tipped off by a contact within the bank. An ambush on a crowded street in broad daylight had been a risky and extreme move, but obviously better, from Pollio's point of view, than allowing such a potentially dangerous witness to fall into the hands of his enemy Taurus.

"I agree that they should have been very much more careful," snapped Taurus.

"More careful?" He snorted. "That is putting it very mildly, Lord Prefect. It doesn't strike me as sensible to club a man who's wanted for questioning, either. A blow like that might silence him. I think you should be asking yourself whether they were in Pollio's pay."

"They were criminally negligent," said Taurus, scowling. "I do not think, however, they they were dishonest— merely slovenly, lax, and stupid. As I said, they have been disciplined."

"Oh, but they certainly *were* dishonest," Hermogenes informed him. "Maerica had a pen case with my letters of credit and nearly fifty denarii in coin. When I asked about it, the hospital succeeded in locating the pen case, but the coin has all gone. I suspect that the only reason the letters are still there is because your men can't read Greek. My best cloak, which I left with her, has also disappeared—and *that* cost over three hundred drachmae in Alexandria: the value must be half again as much in denarii at Rome."

Taurus sighed. "I will order inquiries, and if they cannot find the cloak, they will repay you its cost. For now, there are things I need to discuss with you. We will use the doctor's office. Come."

Hermogenes stared at him for a long moment. That was all? The soldiers had neglected their duty, injured a crucial witness, stolen money and a valuable cloak from a woman as she lay wounded and unconscious in the street—and this was all Taurus was going to do about it? Say that they had been "disciplined" and that he would "order inquiries"?

The praetorian guard, he thought bitterly, were of course purebred Romans and Taurus's own men, and Taurus—still!—could not bear to condemn them in front of a barbarian and a Greek. Rage and grief at this new injustice, heaped upon so many, many others, tightened his throat so that he could not speak, and he simply glared at the prefect, unable to move.

Maerica pressed his hand. He glanced down at her, saw the love and concern on her face, and the tightness in his throat relaxed. She was alive: compared to that, what did the rest matter? He should be pleased that the soldiers were being held to account at all. That, for a barbarian and a Greek, was something of a victory. He returned the pressure of her hand and followed Taurus out of the ward.

The doctor's office, or consulting room, was at the southeast corner of the hospital, just beyond the injuries ward. The doctor, a nervous young Campanian who had trained in Alexandria, was in the office, but removed himself hurriedly when informed that the general wanted it. Taurus also dismissed his guards. He sat down in the doctor's chair, frowning.

Hermogenes sat on the examining couch. "Excuse me that I don't stand," he said. "Thanks to the 'carelessness' of your men, I find it difficult at the moment."

Taurus grunted. "The first thing I must tell you is that Lucius Rufus has agreed to pay his debt."

Hermogenes looked at him a moment, wondering why he felt no triumph. "When?"

"As soon as he has determined the best method of freeing the sum. Within the next few days. I trust that you will collect your letter to Cornelius Scipio tomorrow?"

"I will postpone its delivery, if I am confident that I can do so without being spied upon as I do so," Hermogenes said coldly. "I will not *collect* it until Rufus has paid. The last time he promised to pay me, it was a trick to lure me into a trap where I could be tortured and killed, so I hope you will understand my reluctance to trust him now."

"This time he will pay you," said Taurus, though without heat. "I have told him to send the draft to you at the house of your friend Fiducius Crispus. I hope that will be satisfactory?"

He hadn't thought about it. The prospect of returning to the house on the Via Tusculana, of being again a master among slaves, seemed unbearably strange, almost like a return to childhood. He felt a sudden aversion to it, and at the same time a panicky awareness of some deep rift in himself. "I have caused my poor friend a great deal of trouble," he said slowly. "I do not know whether I should go back there, or whether he would welcome me if I did."

"The trouble is over," Taurus replied. His tone left no room for doubt. "I am sure your friend will welcome you with relief. He has sent me a letter about the matter proclaiming your innocence, protesting at your treatment, and offering to take charge of you if you were found injured."

"Oh!" exclaimed Hermogenes, in surprise. Despite Titus Fiducius's resolute support, he still hadn't expected this of him. He felt a moment's guilt at his own assumption that the other was too cowardly to protest to consuls and prefects. "Very well, then," he muttered, ashamed. "I will stay with my friend Titus Fiducius, and Rufus can send the money there."

Taurus nodded in satisfaction, then sat scowling at him darkly. Hermogenes returned a look of inquiry.

"There is to be no discussion of this affair," Taurus ordered fiercely. "Gossip about this kind of conduct by a man like Tarius Rufus—a consul, and a friend of the emperor—would be damaging to the majesty of the state. I have settled the matter, and I do not want it discussed."

Hermogenes stared at him in disbelief. "Lord Prefect, Pollio termed me a thief in every barbershop in the city. My friend has had his house watched by Rufus and searched by

Pollio—things which, you may be sure, have been noticed and discussed by all *his* friends with all of *their* friends. How can you possibly expect that the whole affair can now be covered over in silence? If I tell people that I am forbidden to discuss it, all that will happen is that they will draw their own conclusions."

"Very well: discuss it *in confidence,* and only with those who can't manage without an explanation!" snapped Taurus. "I do not want this to be the gossip of barbershops."

"Unlike my career as a thief?"

Taurus raised a hand forbiddingly. "An unsubstantiated accusation from a man such as Vedius Pollio will not harm your reputation. I will have it posted in the prefectures that he never brought the charge before the law and submitted no evidence that any crime had taken place. If anyone does go to him with news of your whereabouts, his likely reception will both convince him of your innocence and discourage any of his friends from trying the same."

Hermogenes glared at him.

"I am certain that you are well able to find some form of the truth that will keep your associates quiet," Taurus said, meeting the glare with a flat, implacable gaze. "You must do so."

Hermogenes sighed, then bowed his head in acquiescence. "May I ask *how* you have settled the matter, Lord Prefect?"

"Very polite all of a sudden, aren't you?" said the Roman, with distaste. "Pollio has agreed to write off Lucius's debt to him, in exchange for my taking no further action on the matter." His lip curled in distaste. "He is ill. I hoped this morning might prove the end of him, but unfortunately he recovered and went home. Still, I think he is unlikely to last too much longer: he is much decayed since the last time I saw him. The emperor would undoubtedly prefer to allow him to die quietly of natural causes, without further scandal."

"And so you asked him to cancel Rufus's debt?" Hermogenes asked angrily. "All *four million* of it? It sounds to me, Lord Prefect, as though you are still trying to save Tarius Rufus."

Taurus shrugged defensively. "Lucius has served the state well, and led our troops to victory many times. He holds the consulship by the emperors's appointment. He was my friend for many years." There was real pain in his voice as he said the last phrase. After a moment of silence he went on, "He has been . . . unlike himself . . . ever since that business with his son."

"What business?" asked Hermogenes warily.

Taurus gave him a look of affront, then said harshly, "His son and heir plotted his murder, some years back—or so Lucius believes. He heard the evidence privately at a family council, and then sent the young man away, exiled until his father's death. Obviously something like that preys upon a man, undermines his confidence in his friends . . . and then there was that freedman of his, Macedo, giving him bad advice. I never liked the creature: he always believed his patron had the right to do anything he pleased, and told him so. I'm glad I broke the ugly parasite's neck!" His voice had become a snarl.

Hermogenes kept his face carefully blank.

Taurus settled in his chair again, like a ruffled eagle. "You disagree, do you?"

"I think Macedo told Rufus what Rufus wanted to hear," Hermogenes replied. "And when the man attacked me this morning, he must have known that he'd die for it. He must have believed that if I were silenced, Rufus would be safe. He sacrificed his life for his patron. One has to admire his loyalty." He shrugged. "But I have to admit that I am grateful to you for stopping him."

Taurus snorted in amusement. "Sometimes, Greek, I almost think I could like you." They looked at one another for a moment, and then the general went on angrily, "Then I remember that you cursed Rome."

"Sometimes I almost think I could like you, too, Roman, if you weren't so bloodthirsty," replied Hermogenes. "I never meant that curse. I have Roman friends, whom I have no desire at all to see destroyed by the gods. I think even you will admit that I had every reason to feel very angry."

Taurus gave another snort. "Then you should work to control your tongue. Well, I accept that you are honest. I have let both Pollio and Lucius know that they are not to interfere with you in any way, and I've told Lucius to give you your money. Now, name what reward you want from me."

"I told you before, I want nothing from you."

"You're a very proud man, aren't you?"

"Yes," agreed Hermogenes evenly. "I came to Rome to claim what the laws of Rome grant me as my *right*. If you 'reward' me, then what I have obtained isn't a right at all but a favor dished out by a master of the state to a slave who has done him a service. It diminishes it and me."

Taurus smiled sourly. "A very proud man," he repeated, but this time it was with approval. "I will tell you one more thing. When that woman Cantabra was a slave in my school, I asked her to sleep with me. She has a certain kind of magnificence, don't you find? And great courage, which I admire. I'd watched her win a fight despite having spent the previous three days in a punishment cell—win it through sheer refusal to be beaten—and I wanted her."

Hermogenes sat very still, remembering the way Maerica had left out that detail when she told the story, and remembering also how she had insisted that Taurus was honest and honorable. "I am grateful," he said slowly, "as I know she was, that you respected her refusal and accepted it."

Taurus snorted appreciation. "You do know her, don't you? Yes, of course she refused me: she hates Romans even more than you do. What was the name you used for her?"

"Maerica. It is her real name. I do not hate Romans, Lord Prefect. I've just told you that. As for the empire, it rules the world, and there's no future in opposing it. I simply want it to be an empire where all citizens have rights, and not just those who are Italian-born and powerful."

"You want a Roman empire run by Greeks for their own benefit, you mean," said Taurus softly. "That was what Marcus Antonius would have made of our republic, him and your Queen Cleopatra. That was what we fought against at Actium, and we shouted with joy when we got the victory."

There was real feeling in the words—and a real threat implicit. "I was never a supporter of Cleopatra," Hermogenes said carefully. "As your own researches proved."

"When we occupied Egypt, our informants readily

assumed that anyone who'd opposed the monarchy was the emperor's friend," Taurus replied. "But at Alexandria, as I recall, those who opposed the monarchy mostly did so because they believed it to be subservient to Rome. They supported anyone who promised to throw *all* the Romans out."

"No one promises that anymore," Hermogenes told him flatly. "The battles have all been fought, and Rome won. Lord Prefect, I am not a political man. This past month has been the only occasion when I involved myself in affairs of state, and, I assure you, I will be *extremely* glad to get back to shipping syndicates."

At that, Taurus laughed. "And introduce your gladiator to them. It still seems an odd pairing—a wild Cantabrian warrior woman and an Alexandrian businessman—but I wish you good fortune in it." He got to his feet. "I trust you will see to that letter tomorrow morning. I will tell the hospital to provide a litter to take you and your concubine to your friend's house now. Good health!"

✦

When the general had gone, Hermogenes sat down by Maerica again and took her hand.

"Well?" she demanded.

He kissed a scar on her thumb. "He says he's told Rufus and Pollio both to leave me alone, and that Rufus will send me the money at Titus Crispus's house within the next few days."

A slow grin spread across her face. She caught his chin with her free hand and pulled his head over to kiss him. "Victory," she whispered.

He grimaced. "He's also told Pollio that he'll take no action against him if he writes off the whole of the debt Rufus owes to *him*, and Pollio's agreed. *Four million sestertii!* Let off that, it's no wonder Rufus can suddenly afford to pay *me*. And Taurus wants to keep the whole business quiet, to protect Rufus. He's prepared to blame most of Rufus's troubles on the freedman."

"Oh." She was quiet a moment. "Rufus was his friend," she said at last. "They may have had debts of their own. The main thing is, you won. You have what you wanted. A Roman consul has been forced to humble himself and obey the laws. And that evil man Pollio is punished, too. His plan has failed, he remains out of favor, and he has lost money as well."

He grimaced again. "Perhaps. But it doesn't feel like victory. It feels more like—what do they call it in the arenas, when a fight has no clear winner?"

"We say the fighters are 'dismissed standing,'" said Maerica. "Dear heart, believe me, this is not a dismissal, it is a win. Just because the losers are spared instead of killed doesn't mean you are any less a victor."

He began to believe it. He grunted, though, still not entirely satisfied, still without any feeling of triumph. "Taurus said one other thing," he told her. "He said that when you were his slave he asked you to sleep with him." He linked her fingers with his own and looked up into her face. "Why didn't you tell me that?"

Her eyes had gone hard. "He told you he'd had me?"

He shook his head. "I think he wanted to see if I would conclude that, but he was not surprised when I didn't. He never pretended you did anything but refuse. I don't know, though, why you didn't tell me that he was willing to *honor* your refusal. After all, you were his slave. Most men would be indignant at being refused by their own slave. Many would have made you suffer for it. It would've reassured me to know that he was willing to respect it."

"I was afraid you'd believe that I'd agreed," she said in a small voice. "That I was his castoff."

He shook his head and kissed her thumb again, smiling. "Even if you had agreed . . . you were a slave. He could have destroyed you—and he could have brought you out safely from the arena, given you your freedom. Who wouldn't choose life and freedom over slavery and death?"

"I could never sleep with him," she declared fiercely. "He commanded the Roman forces at the beginning of the war that destroyed us. I told him I would fight for him, but I could never love him. He understood."

"I see."

"And . . . why I didn't tell you . . . I was afraid that if you knew, and if you believed me, you might think I wanted to protect him," she went on, quietly, but also more confidently now. "If you thought I was protecting him, you wouldn't pay attention to what I said. You would have gone to Maecenas. It was what you wanted to do, and I was afraid that if you did it, Pollio would get you. It was the move he anticipated."

"And *did* you want to protect him?"

She shrugged. "Mostly I wanted to protect *you*. But yes. I did."

He thought of the enmity to Rome she had shown so

clearly right from the start: *I knew you were not Roman, and I knew your enemies were.* He thought of his dream in the Mamertine Prison. "Why?" he asked quietly.

She was silent, then said slowly, "When Statilius Taurus commanded the enemy, he was fierce and brutal, but so were many of our own people. He was also brave and honorable, and we respected him. He was replaced, though. First we fought against the emperor and Marcus Agrippa, and then, when they had defeated us, the peace was given to the charge of a man called Publius Carisius. A butcher, a man who loved only gold. It was only then that we understood that the Romans were not like us at all, that to many of them honor matters not at all.

"There are worse men than Statilius Taurus. He believes in the right of Romans to rule the world, but he also believes in duty and discipline and fairness. If he had been left in command, and Carisius had stayed in Rome . . ." She trailed off, then resumed. "For such a long time, I hated all Romans. But that was in my own country, when I met only enemies. Once I was here in Rome, even in the arenas, I met some who were kind to me, some whom I respected, some whom I liked. And Rome rules the world. What will become of the world, if we allow those Romans who are honorable to be murdered by those who are like Rufus and Pollio?"

"The empire isn't going to fall," he suggested, "so our only option is to support those parts of it that make it something we can endure?"

"Yes," she agreed, relaxing. "That is how it is."

He thought of all that she had suffered, and was moved

by a respect bordering on awe that she could say that—that she could move beyond the suffering and hatred and plan for a better future. He kissed her. "We are agreed, then."

The doctor bustled up, looking indignant. "They tell me that the general has given orders that you're both to have a litter over to some place on the Via Tusculana this evening," he said accusingly.

"Yes," agreed Hermogenes. "Is that a problem?"

"Yes!" declared the young man, drawing himself up. "Your, um, concubine took a serious wound, and has lost a great deal of blood. I have stitched the cut, but it has barely begun to knit. I would strongly advise against moving her for another two days at the very least."

"Thank you," Hermogenes replied at once. "We will take no risks with my concubine's life, and she will not leave here until you say it is safe for her to travel."

"Huh!" said Maerica in contempt, while the doctor blinked in surprise at the ease of his victory.

"I myself," Hermogenes went on, "have several important errands to run tomorrow. Would the hospital be able to find me a sedan chair in the morning?"

Maerica pressed his hand.

"Certainly!" agreed the doctor. "You mean to stay with her tonight, then? Very wise: your own head injury needs watching. I will tell the orderlies to make up a bed for you at this end of the ward. Um. Though I *do* think it's good that you stay here a little longer, we don't actually have any orders about it, so can I ask if you can, um . . ."

"One of my errands will be to the bank," Hermogenes told him. "I am happy to pay."

In the morning he reclaimed his own tunic, which an orderly had washed, collected his letters of credit, and limped out to the sedan chair. The bearers—two burly local men who'd been hauled off the street by the praetorian guard, and who obviously expected that they would receive no payment for their work—greeted him with scowls, and carried him into the city in sullen silence. It turned out to be a couple of miles.

He went to the bank first. When he announced himself to the clerk at the counting table, the man dropped his pen and stared in horror.

"Do not concern yourself," he said sourly. "The praetorians arrested me the day before yesterday, and neither they nor Publius Vedius Pollio is interested in me today."

The clerk stammered, blinked, and went off to consult his superior. The superior appeared wreathed in smiles, and kept Hermogenes waiting for a long time while—he was quite certain—someone ran down to the prefecture to *check* that nobody was still interested. Eventually, however, the letters of credit were accepted, and he withdrew spending money to the amount of fifty denarii, which was as much as he could fit in his purse. He advised the bank that he would want more in a few days.

It felt wonderful to have money in his purse again. It was the power to reward, to induce, to provide, and he hadn't realized how much he'd missed it. Even though he knew very well that he still looked a disreputable wreck, it made him feel rich and respectable again, and he paid the hospital's chair bearers and tipped them generously as soon as he came out. The men at once became all smiles, and when he dismissed them, protested that they were happy to carry him about for the rest of the day. He refused them politely, with thanks. It still seemed better to ensure that no official could question them and know where he went next.

The basement of the Temple of Mercury was locked, but an inquiry at the main temple produced the young priest, who greeted Hermogenes with relief, mingled with anxiety about the accusation of theft, and horror at all the bandages and bruises. Hermogenes assured him that there was no cause for concern—indeed, he *had* had a quarrel with the notorious Vedius Pollio, but the prefect of the city had intervened, and now the matter was resolved. So was the disagreement with Tarius Rufus, and he hoped to be able to call his business in Rome successfully complete within a few days.

"So you want to take back that letter?" asked the priest, with relief.

"I am almost entirely certain that I will want to take it back," he replied, "but . . . I don't know, I have a certain superstitious fear that if I do so before the business is safely into harbor, something will go wrong. Could I leave it with you for just ten more days?"

The priest was not entirely happy with this, but he agreed. Hermogenes soothed him with a gift of money to buy incense, and accompanied him down to the basement to offer it, together with a prayer of thanks.

He'd made the suggestion largely to pacify the religious young man, but in the shrine itself he found his heart suddenly swelling with gratitude—not so much to the goddess in her curtained-off alcove as to Fate, or the world, or the mysterious god of the philosophers—and yet Isis seemed as good a focus for the emotion as anything. Against all the odds, he had survived the fight. More than that, he'd won. The triumph he hadn't felt the day before suddenly ran into his heart like water into a dry irrigation ditch at the flooding of the Nile. He'd survived; he'd won; he'd found a woman whom he loved! "'I broke down the government of tyrants,'" sang the priest, raising his voice fervently in the familiar chant of Isis.

> "I made an end to murders.
> I made the Right stronger than gold and silver.
> I ordained that the Truth should be thought good."

Hermogenes found that he could not sing. He choked on the words, struggling with himself, then sat down and wept.

The priest finished the hymn and smiled at his congregation of one. "Great is the goddess," he said warmly.

"Great is Isis," Hermogenes agreed weakly.

After that, there was nothing else to do but head back up the Via Tusculana to the house of Titus Fiducius Crispus. Hermogenes walked the last few blocks slowly. It was late in the morning now, and the day was hot. His head ached, and his knee, even his ankle was becoming sore again. As he approached the house, he increasingly felt that he wanted to turn around, go off to some inn or bathhouse, and rest for a while before going back to the hospital.

He stopped outside the door, trying to reason with himself. He had behaved badly on his last visit, true. He had

brought all sorts of trouble down on the household, true—
twenty of Pollio's thugs, from what the prefect had said,
with threats of fire and violence, on top of all the upheaval
from Rufus and his barbarians. There was every reason to
believe, though, that the household would welcome him
with relief, that Titus would exclaim "My *dear* Hermogenes!"
and clasp his hand, that Menestor would be overjoyed. . . .

Dealing with Menestor would be awkward, true. That
wasn't the reason, though, that he was standing here in the
street in the hot sun staring at the door, unwilling to knock.
No: for a handful of days he had been *free,* unconstrained
by dignity, nobody's master, and he had liked it. Despite the
danger and the hardship, despite even the *fleas,* he had
liked it.

More than that, he had changed. He remembered
Maerica's dream of the mountain. He felt now that all his
life he had been pretending that there was no pinnacle of
rock in his heart, that the pleasant slopes were all there was
to him—that he was, as Titus had put it, Philemon's faultless son, who respected his father and always managed his
business wisely and never got into any trouble. He knew
differently now. He doubted whether the sheer cliffs he had
discovered inside himself were creditable, but he could no
longer pretend that they weren't there, and to take that
knowledge back into his old life—it would be hard.

What, then? Go off on his own with Maerica, *be*
nobody's master, a wild, undignified . . . financier?

He had to smile at the thought. The only trade he knew
was the one he'd been brought up with, and he liked it. He
liked what money could do—the way it allowed things to

happen: timber cut, ships built, towns raised on the edges of desert, cities thriving on an exchange of coin. He liked the thrill of making judgments—*this* risk is worth taking; *that* one is not—liked the sharp edge of dealing with the people. No, he had a business to go back to.

And a house, and a daughter. He would just have to accept becoming dignified and pleasant again. He knocked on the door.

Kyon opened the window in the lodge, yelled, and shut it again. A moment later the bolt slid back, and the door-keeper rushed out into the street. "Oh, *sir!*" he cried, grabbing Hermogenes' hand. "Sir! You're safe!"

"Yes," Hermogenes told him with a smile. "And I think it is over now, Kyon. I know I said that before, but I think this time it's true. May I come in?"

It happened very much as he'd imagined it: Titus did indeed exclaim "My *dear* Hermogenes!" and Menestor wept for joy. He smiled, thanked them, apologized, accepted a cup of watered wine and one of the red-upholstered couches. He provided a simplified explanation of what had happened, and passed on Taurus's strictures about gossip. He spoke in Greek, so as to avoid spreading the information around the household.

"And you think this time he'll pay and that will be the end of it?" Titus asked anxiously.

Hermogenes remembered Rufus weeping into his hands. "Yes," he agreed. "I think this time he'll pay—though I count on nothing until I get the money."

"Well, I thank all the gods!" the Roman exclaimed, with feeling. "This business has been . . . oh, I would say it's been *dreadful,* but then *some* of it has been the most wonderful thing that ever happened to me." He beamed at Menestor, who looked down modestly.

Then he frowned, "And when you've got the money, you'll go back to Alexandria?"

"As soon as Maerica's well enough to travel."

Titus cast another anxious look at Menestor, but the boy was frowning at Hermogenes. "Maerica?" he repeated. She had not featured much in the explanation, which had dealt almost exclusively with the Romans.

"Cantabra," Hermogenes informed him. "It's her real name. One thing I didn't mention was that some of Pollio's men tried to kill me, and she was wounded defending me. She's in the military hospital at the Colina Gate now, and I'm going back there to stay with her tonight, but I'll bring her here as soon as the doctor says it's safe for her to come."

"I'm, um, glad she's served you so well," Titus said politely. "Um—what about when you leave for Alexandria? About the woman, I mean."

"She'll come with me," Hermogenes said firmly. "As my concubine."

Menestor flushed red and gave him a wounded look. Titus just looked horrified. "*That* creature?" he asked. "That creature and *you*? But she's . . . she's . . ."

"Titus, I beg you, do *not* say it!"

Titus stopped, blinking.

"Please do not criticize her," Hermogenes told him, "or try to tell me that she is only after my money. It isn't true, and if you say it I will become angry—and I don't want to become angry with you, not after all your generosity, and the courage and resolution with which you've supported me. I am deeply in love with this woman, Titus, quite apart from the fact that she has saved my life three times. When I thought she was dead, I felt as though my soul was running out of me. Please, not a word against her!"

Titus opened his mouth, closed it, then spread his hands helplessly. "Well, then," he said. "Well, then."

Menestor got up and left the room.

Titus watched him leave, then turned back to Hermogenes, suddenly hopeful. "Maybe he'll want to stay here now!" he exclaimed breathlessly.

"It's possible," Hermogenes agreed, not knowing whether to be amused or dismayed.

"Oh, I pray he does! He is such a *wonderful* young man—sensitive, intelligent, honest, *beautiful* . . . oh, gods, how I love him! I don't understand how you can *not* love him. He *adores* you."

Hermogenes shrugged. "Titus, when you were growing up, people must have tried to interest you in girls. You've complained that they still press you to find a wife. You've never married, despite all they could say, because you don't like women. Well, I'm afraid I don't like boys—not that way, anyway."

"Poor Menestor," said Titus, but he did not look sorry. He cleared his throat. "If . . . if Menestor *does* decide that he doesn't want to return to Alexandria, you'll need a valet, won't you?"

"I suppose I could manage without," Hermogenes replied warily.

"No, no, you couldn't do that, a gentleman of your quality! What I'm trying to say is, my last boy . . . well, it's difficult for him here now, and he seems to admire you, so if you wanted him . . ."

"You're offering to sell me Hyakinthos?"

"*Give* him to you, if you want him."

He looked at Titus's anxious face, and again felt torn between amusement and contempt. It was clear enough that Titus was the one who found it difficult to have his previous lover underfoot—and perhaps he felt that if Hyakinthos went, it became even less likely that Menestor would.

Then he suddenly wondered if he wasn't being unfair again. Perhaps this eagerness to send Hyakinthos away was meant primarily as a message for Menestor: *I want no one but you.* Perhaps it was meant for Hyakinthos: *I am sorry I hurt you; I will give you to the master you prefer.* Perhaps it was even meant for Hermogenes himself: *I am going to try now to notice when my people are unhappy, and do something about it.*

"I would be ashamed to allow you to give him to me, after all your generosity," he said. "But I might well buy him from you. He's a good boy, and it would be useful to have a slave who can speak Latin. Let me speak to him about it first. It's a long way to Alexandria, and I don't want to take him if it's going to make him desperately unhappy."

"No, of course not," said Titus hastily.

There was a moment of uncertain silence, and then Titus said, "I was very surprised to see you turn up without even a cloak."

"My good one was stolen by the praetorian guards," Hermogenes replied.

"No!"

"Yes. I mentioned it to Taurus—"

"You did *what*?" exclaimed Titus, aghast.

"They're his men. If they're stealing, he ought to know about it. However, I'm not sure I really even want that cloak back. Every time I've worn it of late somebody's hit me or threatened me or tried to kill me. Maybe it's superstition, maybe it's just bad memories, but I don't think I'd want to wear the thing again even if I did get it back. I'll buy a new one." He shrugged, smiling. "After all, I should have half a million sestertii to spend, and Nikomachos's debts won't take more than a third of it, now that his creditors have eaten his estate and had a few bites of mine."

"Oh, my dear friend!" exclaimed Titus, laughing. "Don't tell that to the syndicates, or you'll be *mobbed*!"

"We will have to consider some investments together before I go," Hermogenes said, smiling. "We haven't done any business with each other this trip, and I would like to have more dealings with you, if you can still endure me."

Titus went pink. "I . . . would like to have more deal-ings with you. I've always admired you so much. Your father as well, of course, but . . . I always felt he planned how to create an effect, while you hardly even seem to notice it. When you were in school, you must have been the boy who wins all the prizes, the one who's effortlessly good at every-thing. When you come into a room, suddenly everyone's paying attention; when you're in a syndicate, you're the one everyone listens to. I've never been . . . that is, at school I was the fat boy everyone made fun of, and now I'm a silly fat man, and everyone thinks I'm a fool. . . ."

"I don't," said Hermogenes, touched. "You've always been a shrewd businessman and a sensible one. You do yourself an injustice, Titus."

Titus smiled. "I told Stentor what you said," he confided. "That my household really wants to please me, but I don't let them know how to do it. He agreed with you. He was very enthusiastic, in fact."

"He is devoted to you," Hermogenes told him.

Titus nodded. "Maybe you're right," he murmured. "Maybe people would choose to like me more often, if I gave them the choice." He looked at Hermogenes, more confidently now. "Did I hear you say you plan to go back to this military hospital tonight?"

"Yes. The doctor there advised me that my concubine should not be moved until tomorrow at the earliest, and I don't like to leave her there alone."

"But then you'll come here?"

"If I'm welcome. I am only too aware of all the trouble I've caused you."

"Oh, you're very welcome. Do you want to collect anything from your room before you go?" Titus frowned. "I'm afraid Pollio's men smashed the lock on your trunk and threw all your things all over the room, but I had the slaves put everything back."

"Thank you," Hermogenes told him. "Yes, I would like to collect some things. Could I perhaps borrow your sedan chair as well?"

The Nile Rooms were not much different from the way

he remembered them. Pollio's men appeared to have smashed one or two of the knickknacks, but the ugly Pharos lampstand was—unfortunately—still intact. The trunk stood in the same place by the wall, the broken lock and some scars on the leather the only trace of the assault on it. Tertia and Erotion were in the sleeping cubicle, making up the bed.

"Welcome back, sir," said Tertia, coming into the day-room to greet him with a shy smile. "We're all so pleased to see you safe."

"He's hurt his head," Erotion said anxiously, holding her mother's skirts.

"And my knee," Hermogenes informed her, showing her the bandage. "I fell over. It will get better, though. Tertia, I'm sorry you've had this work now for nothing. I don't plan to stay here tonight. Maerica—that is, Cantabra—is in a military hospital near the Colina Gate, and I'm going back to stay with her until she's well enough to come here. I hope that will be tomorrow, but I intend to listen to her doctors."

The slave woman looked at him doubtfully, and he added, "She was wounded defending me. I am very much in love with her, and she will be coming to Alexandria as my concubine."

"Oh!" said Tertia, now thoroughly taken aback. "Oh!" After a minute she added, even more doubtfully, "I am sure she is very lucky, sir, and I hope you will be happy."

"What's a concubine?" asked Erotion.

"Hush!" said her mother disapprovingly. "Um, sir—will she sleep in here?"

"Yes," Hermogenes replied at once. "She prefers a mattress on the floor to a bed, though. Apparently Cantabrians never use beds."

"Then she can have Menestor's," said Tertia—then blushed.

"I take it Menestor has continued to sleep in your master's room?" Hermogenes asked resignedly.

"Yes, sir." There was resignation in her voice as well.

Hermogenes hesitated. "Your master made a proposal to me concerning your son."

Tertia guessed at once what that proposal had been. Her face quivered, caught between emotions he could not identify. She licked her lips. "Did you . . . that is . . ."

"I told him I wanted to discuss it with Hyakinthos first. Alexandria is a very long way from here. I certainly do not want to take him there against his will, and I would value your opinion on the matter. Do you and his father think it would be the best thing for him?"

"That's kind of you, sir. I . . . I do think it would be the best thing for him, yes. In this house now . . . well, his father's just sick, thinks the boy's wasted the best chance he'll ever get, and the master's kind, but still it's awkward. I'm sure you would be a very good master to him, and he thinks very highly of you."

"What are you talking about?" demanded Erotion.

"Hush, darling. Later," said Tertia. "Shall I send Hyakinthos here to discuss it with you, sir?"

"Please." As she started out, he added impulsively, "Your master and I were also talking about doing more business together. If that happens, it would probably mean that I'll visit Rome again."

She understood the message—*You will see your son again, fairly regularly*—and smiled widely. "That's good to hear, sir. Thank you."

She went out, and he gave his appalled consideration to what he'd just told her. Come to Rome *again*? Return to this terrible city?

The practicalities said yes. The current of Alexandria's business had increasingly flowed toward the Tiber, and in a few more years it would be hard for a businessman of any stature to *avoid* the occasional trip to Rome. And—of course—it was true that he had an edge over most Alexandrians, due to his command of Latin. It would not be businesslike to waste such an advantage. And if he *did* make some substantial investments in Italy, as he'd half promised Titus, obviously he would need to come back to adjust them from time to time.

He gave a snort of disgust, went to the trunk, and opened it. Everything was stacked neatly inside. He picked out another clean tunic, then selected a comb, and considered whether to take his sole remaining cloak or just give up on an outer garment. The remaining cloak wasn't even a himation but a chlamys, a short cloak for riding and traveling, more the sort of garment for a dashing youth than for a sober businessman. He'd only packed it in case he found himself doing any riding.

He pulled it out and put it in the pile to bring along. He realized that he had no idea what had happened to the linen cloak he'd lent Maerica: he hadn't even asked about it. Well, let it go: it had been knife slashed anyway. He resolved to buy her a new cloak—blue, like her eyes. And a

tunic to match, and some jewelry and some expensive sandals, so that when she came off the ship in Alexandria everyone would see at once that she was an important woman,
and there would be none of this *"That* creature!" and "I'm
sure *she's* very lucky" nonsense. He grinned at the prospect.

Hyakinthos came in, eager and grinning. "Greetings,
sir!" he exclaimed, eyeing the bandages with interest. "I'm
very glad you're back safely. My mother said you wanted to
talk to me."

"That's right." Hermogenes sat down at the desk. "Your
master considers that I will need a valet on the voyage back
to Alexandria, and he has offered to give or sell you to me. I
did not want to accept without knowing how you would feel
about it."

The boy's eyes widened and he stared for a long minute.
Then he said breathlessly, "I'd like it very much, sir."

Hermogenes raised his hand warningly. "It's a long way
to Alexandria. Probably I will come back to visit Rome
occasionally, but still, it would mean saying good-bye to
your family."

"I'd like it, sir," Hyakinthos insisted. "I want to get away
from here. I'd *love* to see Alexandria. And sail on a ship,
and . . . and you do business all the way to Cyprus and the
Red Sea as well, don't you? I'd get a chance to see the
world!" His eyes were beginning to glow. "They were saying
in the kitchen just now that you've taken that gladiator
woman Cantabra as your concubine: maybe she could
teach me sword fighting!"

Hermogenes had no idea what to say to this. "She's
been hurt," he murmured.

Hyakinthos nodded vigorously. "Yes, they were saying that, too—that she saved your life, only nobody was sure whether it was Pollio's thugs or Rufus's barbarians who were trying to kill you, but she's in a military hospital, and you're going back there tonight to stay with her. She'll get better, though, won't she?"

"The doctor thinks so," he replied cautiously.

"Good. I like her. She's like one of those Amazons, in the stories. The others are saying they think it's terrible, a gentleman like you and a barbarian, but I wasn't surprised at all. I mean, a man like you isn't going to take some silly *girly* woman, he needs somebody *heroic*."

Hermogenes stared at him.

"I would like it if you took me, sir," Hyakinthos continued excitedly. "I really would. If Cantabra taught me sword fighting, maybe next time you get into a fight with some important people, I could defend you, and—"

"Next time'?" repeated Hermogenes in horror. "Let me assure you, I have no intention of getting into *another* fight with the rulers of the world. Once was enough."

"Well, then," said Hyakinthos, dismissing this breezily. "With pirates, then, on the Red Sea—"

"Child, I don't *sail* ships. I just invest in them. I think you may have misjudged me. I am a businessman, not some kind of hero. I was considering taking you as a *valet,* not as a . . . a . . . whatever it is you seem to expect to become!"

Hyakinthos looked bitterly disappointed. "Does that mean you won't take me?"

Hermogenes stared at the boy a moment longer, than laughed. "No, it means that you must not expect any *hero-*

ics. If you do, you will be bored and disappointed. I *am* a businessman, not very different from your present master."

"That isn't true, sir," Hyakinthos said, quietly but with bitter force. "You're *completely* different from him."

"In certain tastes I suppose I am. You can ask Maerica to teach you sword fighting, but whether she obliges you is up to her: she may feel she wants to put that behind her."

"So you'll take me to Alexandria?" asked Hyakinthos eagerly.

"Since you wish it, I will arrange it with Titus Fiducius. If you change your mind—"

"I won't!"

"*If you do*, tell me at once. One thing, though."

"Yes, sir?" Hyakinthos was grinning again.

"I don't normally change the names of my slaves, but . . . your name has certain implications which are not appropriate, and I wonder if—."

"I *hate* my name!" the boy cried passionately, grin vanishing. "The master gave it to me six months ago, when he . . . you know, decided he wanted to fuck me. Before that I was called Tertius, after my mother." He grimaced. "I don't really like that name, either, though. It's dull. I think I'd like to be called Achilles!"

Hermogenes shook his head. "That's inviting people to make fun of you."

The boy looked crestfallen.

"I will call you Tertius for now," Hermogenes suggested. "If you think of something you like better which is also *sensible*, we'll switch to that."

"Yes, sir. Is there anything I can do for you now, sir?"

"No—or rather, yes: tell Stentor that I'm ready to start back to the hospital, if he could arrange the chair."

Tertius went out; a moment later there was a whoop of joy from the colonnade. Hermogenes shook his head, wondering quite what he was letting himself in for.

He picked up the chlamys and swung it over his shoulders; unlike a himation, it fastened with a pin. He bundled his clean clothes together, then went back to the trunk and took out the writing supplies. He had never sent the last letter to Myrrhine, and now he felt confident enough to send another letter in its place.

He arrived back at the hospital in the middle of the afternoon. Maerica was asleep, but woke when he sat down beside her.

"Well?" she asked.

"I postponed the letter for another ten days. I saw my friend Titus, and arranged that we'll go there tomorrow, if the doctor permits. I got some money."

"You didn't see Gellia? She must be worried."

"Tomorrow," he said firmly. "I will go to see her tomorrow, and give her some money to pay for another party with her friends."

She smiled. "You're wearing a cloak with a pin!" She fingered the pin, which was bronze with a cameo medallion. "I thought you said Greeks didn't wear that sort of cloak."

"I never said that. *I* normally wear a himation, but some Greeks wear a cloak of this sort. Dashing young men, mostly."

"It suits you."

He kissed her. "Careful. I may end up thinking myself heroic. Do you remember that boy Hyakinthos, one of Titus's slaves?"

"Tertia's son."

"Him. His real name is, in fact, Tertius, though I think he may decide to change it to something more military. Titus Fiducius has offered to give or sell him to me, as a valet, since Menestor is now free and probably staying in Rome. The boy is delighted with the idea, and wants you to teach him sword fighting so that he can kill pirates on the Red Sea, which he seems to feel is something I might call upon him to do. I tried to tell him otherwise, but I'm not sure I convinced him."

She laughed hootingly, one hand pressed to her side. "Young men are fools!"

"I won't dispute it. Well, he thinks *you* are very heroic, and wholeheartedly approves of you, so I think he will do very well, once he gets over his disappointment with me."

She grinned. "He will not be disappointed."

"Ah, woman, I have to go back to being a quiet well-behaved dignified businessman again. Maybe you will be disappointed, too."

She shook her head. "No."

"I love you," he told her. It seemed more natural, and more inevitable, with every repetition.

She gave him a radiant smile.

"My own dear heart. I am waiting to see what you look like without the bruises."

"I think you'll find an improvement." He set down his

bundle and took out the writing things. "I'm going to write another letter to Myrrhine."

"Telling her about me?"

"Telling her about you, yes, and that I'm safe and well."

"So you're beginning to believe that you won."

He nodded. "I went to the Temple of Isis and . . . well, I started to believe it." Another thought struck him. "What gods do you worship?"

She shrugged. "We worshiped gods up on the mountains. We worshipped Bandua and Neton, who were goddess and god of war, and Endovellicus, lord of the Underworld, and Lug, the radiant one. None of them helped us. At the school, most of the gladiators said prayers to Fortune, and to Nemesis, and to Mercury, guide of souls. They didn't help, either. I was surprised when you found that priest of Isis for the funeral. At the gladiatorial school I heard that the worship of Isis was banned at Rome."

"Apparently it is, but she has worshipers anyway."

"Maybe I'll worship her, then."

"You could do worse." He paused, then whispered again the words of the hymn.

> "I broke down the government of tyrants,
> I made the Right stronger than gold and silver.
> I ordained that the Truth should be thought good."

"Huh!" said Maerica, impressed. "That is Isis?"

"Yes." He shook his head ruefully. "It was when the priest sang that that I began to believe I'd won."

He took out the pen, moistened the ink, and wrote carefully,

MARCUS AELIUS HERMOGENES GREETS HIS DAR-
LING DAUGHTER, AELIA MYRRHINE.

My sweetest girl, I think my business in Rome is almost finished, and I will start for home early next month and arrive back in August, if the winds are favorable. It has been very, very hard, much worse than I ever expected. Rufus sent men who attacked us, and poor Phormion was killed. At one point I feared I would be killed as well, but Fate, the gods, and my friends protected me, and now everything is almost settled, and I expect to receive the money in a few days.

One very important thing that has happened is that I have met a woman called Maerica who has become my concubine. She is a barbarian woman, a Cantabrian, from the mountains beyond Iberia. She is brave and clever and honorable, and she saved my life. I am sure that you will like her.

"What have you written?" asked Maerica, frowning at the Greek words.

He interpreted.

"Huh!" Maerica shook her head. "You should never say 'I am sure you will like her.' It will make her suspect that she won't."

"Well, too late, I've said it," he replied.

"Will she be able to read that herself? Or will somebody else in the household read it to her?"

"She can read."

"Huh! A clever girl, then. Write down what I say to her now."

He nodded and dipped the pen in the ink.

"Tell her, 'Maerica says that she loves your father above her life, and that for his sake she would love you whatever you were like.'"

He swallowed and wrote,

> Maerica is with me as I write this, and she says to tell you, first, that she loves me very much, and for my sake would love you whatever you were like.

"Now say, 'But she also believes already that she will like you, because your father talks about you, and says that you are clever, and want to be an acrobat, and she thinks you sound like a girl she will like very much.'"

> She says she also believes already that she will like you for your own sake, because when I talk about you I tell her that you're clever and that you want to be an acrobat, and she thinks you sound like the kind of girl she likes very much. *Please don't mention the bit about the acrobatics to Aunt Eukleia!* I fear there may be some trouble with her over this anyway, even without adding that . . .

"Why have you drawn a line under that bit?" Maerica asked suspiciously.

"I told her not to mention to my aunt the fact that you approve of her acrobatics," he answered guiltily.

Maerica grinned. "Good. She's sure to like me now."

AUTHOR'S NOTE

A S USUAL, I HAVE TWO REASONS TO WRITE an epilogue. The first is friendly: to fill in historic details which lie outside the narrative. The second is defensive: to protect myself against the charge of having got it wrong when I say something contrary to popular belief.

The Roman monetary system in the early empire was as follows: there were four quadd rans to an as, four asses to a sestertius, four sestertii to a denarius, and twenty-five denarii to an aureus. Large amounts were usually given in sestertii.

Timekeeping was based on the division of the day and the night each into twelve hours; since the day was reckoned from dawn to dusk, this meant that daylight hours were longer in summer than in winter. In Rome at midsummer, an "hour" lasted roughly one and a quarter hours, and the first hour began at approximately 4:30 A.M.

The quotation on p. 278 is from *The Odyssey,* XII, 256–59; that on p. 436 is from the Cyme version of the *Hymn to Isis.*

This book is set fairly exactly in Rome during the summer of 16 B.C. It is probably a sad comment on the period— or perhaps just on human nature—that the villains are historical figures, while the heroes are inventions. Lucius Tarius Rufus, Publius Vedius Pollio, and Titus Statilius Taurus all existed and held the ranks I assign them; Rufus did ruin himself by investing in land, and the story about Pollio's lampreys was certainly current in antiquity. There is no evidence that Pollio loaned money to Rufus, however, or that he and Taurus were particular enemies. This *is* a work of fiction, after all.

Publius Vedius Pollio died in 15 B.C., leaving all his property to the emperor Augustus in the hope that this would preserve his memory. Augustus did not fulfill that hope: he not only razed Pollio's house on the Esquiline but he built a shopping mall on the site—the Portico Livia, named after his own wife. Titus Statilius Taurus probably died not too long afterward, though he left descendants—a granddaughter, Statilia Messallina, was the third wife of Nero. Lucius Tarius Rufus may have survived to be curator aquarum in A.D. 23–4 (though this has been questioned and it does seem inherently unlikely for a man who was old enough to hold command at Actium in 31 B.C.).

My defensive comments this time are:

1) Female gladiators are not a feminist invention. There are plenty of references to them in ancient literature, and some representations in art. It's clear they were never as common as male gladiators, but they were by no means unheard of.

2) Yes, there *were* Celts in Spain. The northern part of the Iberian Peninsula was, and still is, a different world from the South.

3) The Romans *did* ban the "Egyptian cult" in the city of Rome: contrary to the belief that they tolerated everyone except Christians, they fairly regularly took steps to suppress cults they viewed as undesirable, though usually just in a local and sporadic fashion.

4) Hermogenes' comments on Cleopatra and the war of Actium are an attempt to imagine the opinions of an Alexandrian of the period, but they are not factually inaccurate.

5) Augustus did indeed describe his foundation of the empire as the restoration of the republic. (Politicians!)

6) Please remember that this book is set in 16 B.C. Most accounts of the city describe it as it was a century later.

For those who would like to know more about the principate of Augustus, the best primary sources are Dio Cassius, Suetonius, and the beginning of Tacitus's *Annals*. Readers familiar with the history of Rome in the early empire have probably already recognized the influence of two classic secondary sources of Roman historiography: Jerome Carcopino's *Daily Life in Ancient Rome* and Ronald

Syme's *Roman Revolution*. Readers unfamiliar with these works, but interested in learning more, might like to have a look at them. (Carcopino is eminently readable; Syme is aphoristic and brilliant, but extremely heavy going.)

ABOUT THE AUTHOR

GILLIAN BRADSHAW'S HISTORICAL NOVEL *The Sand-Reckoner* won the 2001 Alex Award. She is the daughter of an Associated Press reporter and a confidential secretary to the British embassy. Rather than join the Diplomatic Service after getting her master's in classics from Cambridge, Gillian married a physicist, had four children, and began writing historicals (not necessarily in that order). She currently lives in Coventry with her husband, children, garden, and dog. When she's not writing, she cooks and reads, goes for hikes in the countryside, travels around the world with her family, and sings in a choral society.